MAN
Whisperer

Dear Reader:

What is seduction? What is charm? What is beauty? How do you define such things? From now on, whenever someone asks you to respond, your answers will be simple. Allegra Adams! Allegra Adams! Allegra Adams! A world-class seductress who leaves men flustered and fulfilled in her wake, in *Man Whisperer* Allegra shows us all how to really have men falling at your feet globally. How to bring every fantasy—whether realistic or far-fetched—to life, simply by knowing how to control men without them realizing they are being controlled.

Throughout history, there have been women who are remembered as the greatest seductresses of their time: Cleopatra, Helen of Troy and even Eve. Now comes the story of Allegra Adams, the modern-day siren/courageous beauty who will not take no for an answer when it comes to love, and everything else that her heart desires. She is brilliant, tempting, and charming. So get ready for a whirlwind tale of what romance should *really* be about.

As always, thanks for the support shown to the Strebor Books International family. We appreciate the love. For more information on our titles, please visit www.zanestore.com; and you can find me on my personal website: www.eroticanoir.com. You can also join my online social network at www.planetzane.org.

Blessings,

Zane

Zane
Publisher
Strebor Books
www.simonsays.com/streborbooks

ZANE PRESENTS

MAN
Whisperer

ALLEGRA ADAMS

SBI

STREBOR BOOKS

NEW YORK LONDON TORONTO SYDNEY

Strebor Books
P.O. Box 6505
Largo, MD 20792
http://www.streborbooks.com

ISBN 978-1-59309-311-2
ISBN 978-1-4391-9856-8 (ebook)
LCCN 2011926868

First Strebor Books trade paperback edition June 2011

Cover design: www.mariondesigns.com
Cover photograph: © Keith Saunders/Marion Designs

10   9   8   7   6   5   4   3   2   1

Manufactured in the United States of America

For information regarding special discounts for bulk purchases,
please contact Simon & Schuster Special Sales at 1-866-506-1949
or business@simonandschuster.com

The Simon & Schuster Speakers Bureau can bring authors to your live event.
For more information or to book an event, contact the Simon & Schuster Speakers
Bureau at 1-866-248-3049 or visit our website at www.simonspeakers.com.

Dedicated to Safe Sex, Warm Hearts and Passionate Love

Thank you to my brilliant Sara Camilli
and Steve Camilli for his insightful, fresh eyes.

If they truly knew their power, we would be doomed.

— UNKNOWN

1

"My toes curl when I'm aroused; especially when I forget to wear panties," Allegra whispered into the ear of the muscular TAM Airlines captain as their bodies purposely brushed, then lingered, igniting a magnetic force field between them in the galley of the Boeing 767-300ER. The bushy eyebrows of the striking, chisel-jawed, Afro-Brazilian stud arched in anticipation of their erotic dalliance, as his throbbing penis swelled behind his navy blue, starched pants.

During pre-boarding for first-class, his proud strut captivated every woman in the international concourse of Rio de Janeiro Galeão International Airport, causing them to rubberneck as he passed. Ignoring the swoon of his female admirers, the captain, pulling his black monogrammed flight case, tipped the brim of his cap, finger-waved and winked at an occupied Allegra. Though Teofilo Branco, the Governor of Rio de Janeiro, held her soft waist, resting his head on her shoulder, Allegra returned the captain's brazen gaze over the rim of her Giorgio Armani tinted sunglasses. Amused by the captain's bravado at ignoring the presence of the clutching Governor Teofilo, Allegra clucked her tongue against the inside of her cheek. The pilot was familiar to Allegra, and together they harbored unfinished business. During her last layover in Argentina, the two had flirted in the sky lounge before jetting off to their respective international destinations.

Flanked by his embarrassed bodyguards, Teofilo, unable to face the inevitable, murmured, "*Perco-o já. O meu coração quebra!* (I already miss you! My heart is breaking.)"

The airport terminal intercom system pierced the din of travelers swarming the terminal corridor. "Good evening, passengers. This is the first-class boarding announcement for TAM Airlines flight 782 to New York City's JFK airport. We now invite our first-class passengers to begin boarding at this time. Please have your boarding pass and passport ready. General boarding will begin in approximately ten minutes. *Obrigada!*" The blonde TAM gate agent repeated the announcement in Portuguese.

Allegra gently separated herself from Teofilo's reluctant grasp. "I must go, Teofilo, my sweet." Teofilo dove his angular face toward Allegra's full, red lips, hoping for one last kiss. Instead, Teofilo received her cheek. His mouth frowned in disappointment. Teofilo should have known by now that Allegra required her permission to be granted before any sexual overture.

"*Peço desculpas. Perdi a minha cabeça. Por favor perdoe-me, Allegra!* (I apologize. I lost my head. Please forgive me, Allegra!)" Teofilo pleaded when Allegra backed away from him.

"*Ciao, querido.*(Goodbye, darling.) Keep me posted on your hearings. Everything will work out for you," Allegra whispered, stroking his cheek with her index finger.

"I will phone you to make sure that you arrived safely, okay?" Teofilo said, hoping to acquire a few extra seconds of time with Allegra.

"That's okay. I'll text you when we can Skype, Teo," Allegra promised, before swaying toward the gate entrance, her shoulder-length, auburn twists bouncing along with her red, Jimmy Choo stilettos, sounding like Latin *claves* against a marble dance floor. Eager paparazzi frantically snapped photographs of the parting couple, destined to be splashed on the morning cover of *O Globo*, Brazil's flagship newspaper.

The red-eye flight reached a cruising altitude of thirty-five thousand feet from Rio de Janeiro Galeão Airport, flying east of the mysterious Amazon River and out to the Atlantic Ocean into the purple and gray night sky. After dinner service, the dimly lit first-class cabin held snoozing passengers sated and satisfied from the delicious *feijoada carioca ca riocan*, *bombocado* and *mousse de maracuja* and *caipirinhas* (stew of pork and black beans over rice; Brazilian coconut dessert, fruit mousse and Brazil's national cocktail: cachaça sugar and lime.*)*

Slowly sipping Merlot, letting the fleshiness of the grape flavor swish inside her mouth, stimulating her senses, Allegra closed her eyes and reminisced about her Brazilian adventures over the past two weeks. Something about Brazil kept Allegra's juices flowing, from the intoxicating beaches to the beautiful bodies and the open expressions of love between men and women. There was something about this country, located in the southern hemisphere, a nine-hour flight from New York City, that had captivated Allegra five years ago, when she was there attending the wedding of a family friend. To her, Brazil was everything the rest of the world was not—wild, enchanting and mesmerizing. Brazilian culture was layered and complex due to its racial diversity, history, landscape and music. The people of Brazil placed first importance on family and the relationship between a man and a woman.

Aside from Teofilo, there were other worldly men who aggressively pursued Allegra. This woman from Harlem had unearthed passions within themselves that they had never known. These domineering, charismatic men ruled nations, industries and of course, other women who were unlike Allegra. Women who were assertive in their careers but who became passive birds with these men and after a short time, uninteresting, causing the men to move on in search of a bona-fide challenge; an anointing of their souls.

Tearful goodbyes, persistent invitations for Allegra to return, requests to visit her in Harlem to establish domestic partnerships, or marriage proposals always followed her departure. From anywhere. Her lovers desired, sometimes demanded, to be at her beck and call, which Allegra thought was endearing. But no matter what Allegra gave, her lovers were insatiable, inconsolable and eager to forget the life they had to return to after her departure; that is, unless she permitted otherwise.

Teofilo failed to meet with the Canadian Prime Minister, who had specifically traveled to Rio de Janeiro to formalize an agreement to export oil to Montreal. **"The Governor is missing! Victim of A Kidnapping?!"** the newspaper headlines read.

Disappearing from the Palácio das Laranjeiras, the official residence of the governor of the state of Rio de Janeiro, the paparazzi were alerted by a political rival that Teofilo was having his sensory perceptions drained by Allegra's plump lips alongside the tranquil reflecting pool in the lush presidential suite of the Iberostar Bahia hotel. Teofilo was so delightfully incapacitated, his competence to continue to serve as governor was daily called into question by influential political media commentators. Members of Teofilo's cabinet gossiped about just who was this mesmerizing African-American woman who had the governor embarrassingly distracted and missing, causing a delay in critical legislation and the cancellation of meetings with various heads of state. Other cabinet members strategized to remove Teofilo, so they could take over his office. Oblivious to the scandal, Allegra eventually convinced Teofilo that he had to face his constituents, but she asked him to please leave her out of the controversy.

"Teo, let's not kid ourselves. I'm not the first scandal you've been embroiled in, and I won't be the last. You're a man who loves drama. Long after your people forget about this so-called episode with me, I'll be back in Harlem, where my life is," Allegra repeatedly explained to him, to no avail.

Two days before her departure, Teofilo followed her wisdom and announced that he would face the Brazilian people. "*As senhoras e cavalheiros, membros de imprensa* (Ladies and Gentlemen, members of the press), I deeply apologize for disappointing the citizens of Rio de Janeiro by my sudden absence. No apology can condone my actions, but sincerely, I have no regrets for what I have done. You see, *meus amigos*, since my wife and I separated three years ago, I have become unhappy, frustrated and lonely. This may surprise those of you who saw me so elated, so joyful when we won the 2016 Olympics Games or when I debated with Presidente da Cruz over different issues. However, inside, though I buried myself in the affairs of restoring our economy, I was a very lonely man. I never thought that I would feel the passion of a woman's love and embrace again until I recently met my *amor belo* (beautiful love). Please do not think that I have not been honored to serve you, but I am only a man. With God's will and your support, I will continue to serve you, *meus amigos maravilhosos*. But now I have been blessed to be able to love again and for the first time in a very long time, I feel free and alive."

Teofilo's eyes sparkled as he beamed at Allegra, who crossed her arms uncomfortably, and cowered behind his lanky deputy and adoring aides, standing on the side of the noisy press briefing room. In their attempt to appear supportive, Teo's aides clapped their hands like hungry seals whenever he paused. Onlookers rubbernecked to stare at Allegra, the woman whom the Governor of Rio de Janeiro adored. Some reporters rolled their eyes and snickered behind their notepads.

I didn't sign up for this. I had no idea that Teofilo was going to put me on Front Street like that. We fucked at some memorable places. So what? That's all that it was. Next thing you know, he's going to say something crazy like I'm going to be the next First Lady of Janeiro or some shit, Allegra thought. The Rio de Janeiro press corps salivated, eager to take a bite out of Teofilo's political flesh. Reporters frantically scribbled on notepads; shouted their accusations, and demanded to be recognized by Governor Teofilo Branco. Elevated television monitors on walls around the press room aired the live broadcast throughout Brazil, interrupting regularly scheduled programming further south, near the border of Argentina.

"The people deserve responsible leadership! Governor, resign now! Resign, Governor," hurled a short, dark-haired television journalist, standing on his chair in the rear of the room. A stern-looking captain posturing behind Teofilo gestured to a First Sergeant, who promptly removed the man, kicking and screaming, from the crowded room, causing a hush to sweep over the press corps, as they did not want to be ejected next.

Though seething inside at the insolence of reporters' questions, Teofilo remained composed, ignoring the commotion, and continued—"and it may be too early, but after my legal personal affairs are in order, and if God will bless me, I pray that my beautiful Allegra might become the next First Lady of Rio—" Teofilo announced, extending his arm, motioning for Allegra to join him at the podium. Cameras flashed and the hordes of reporters and Teofilo's supporters and naysayers turned toward Allegra, who waved her hand as if his public declaration of love was an irritating mosquito. Three aggressive reporters surrounded Allegra, who faked a smile, and then ducked out of the side security entrance to make her escape.

On subsequent days, Allegra refused Teofilo's telephone calls and visits to her hotel. His secret security force was stationed in the hotel and ordered by Teofilo to shadow her activities, in an attempt to encourage her to see him before Allegra departed Brazil. "Teo, I'm not going to be able to see you before I leave tomorrow. My symposium at the Steven Biko Institute and consultations thereafter will run until late. So why don't we say our goodbyes now," Allegra advised him, when he encountered her inside an antique shop in the neighborhood of Santa Teresa.

Though Allegra had future aspirations, she loved the life she was now living. A former international chief purser for American Airlines, Allegra had switched careers, deciding to pursue her long held desire to earn a master's degree. Now an anthropology doctoral candidate and senior teaching fellow at New York University, Allegra was invited to present the keynote address "The DNA Psychology of African People" at the annual African Diaspora Conference in Rio de Janeiro, Brazil. Attendees consisted of bearded intellectuals from the Caribbean, groups of university psychologists, reparations activists from Canada, black professors and social workers from Detroit and a Liberian New Deal Movement delegation, all adorned in variations of cultural attire ranging from dashikis, to *kente* ties, tie-dyed kaftans, *aso-oke* kufis and headscarves.

Teofilo hosted the conference coordinators and speakers at a VIP reception in his plush, private villa on the island of Praia do Forte. Accessible only by yacht, the burnt-orange colored estate sat on a bluff overlooking the desolate Manguinhos Beach surrounded by acres of organic vegetable gardens and tropical fruit trees. Nude statues by Auguste Rodin bordered the impressive estate's cobblestone grand entrance.

Flaunting her cinnamon brown complexion with pouty lips, shoulder-length twists, ample breasts and buttocks, Allegra walked with the sway of a hula dancer and the sensual authority of Isis. Arriving after the other VIPs, Allegra made her own grand, yet demure, entrance. A male attendant greeted her at the sixteen-foot iron door. "*Boa noite, Senorita.*" Allegra smiled in return and was immediately enamored with the decor of the inviting foyer: floor-to-ceiling windows, textured suede wallpaper, twenty-four-foot-high cathedral ceilings with a Swarovski Spectra chandelier radiating sparkles of light throughout the expanse. The stone and cherry staircase with forged, black iron panels lay in the distance leading upstairs to a brightly lit extension of the mansion.

"*Senhorita*, I take you to the others," said the attendant, in broken English, beckoning Allegra to follow him. Allegra did a circular turn as she made mental notes of decorating ideas to complement her Harlem brownstone. *That cherry staircase would be the shit in my house*, she thought, swaying behind the attendant down a long corridor of mahogany floors toward loud voices and gales of laughter. Allegra sauntered into the living room as Teofilo raised his champagne flute to make a toast. "*Meus amigos, bem-vindo a minha casa goza!* (My friends, welcome to my home!)" he said, in a baritone voice, with his palm flattened over his heart. He stood six foot five with a glistening blue-black complexion, brilliantly white teeth, a large Roman nose and broad chest. His tailored, white shirt was unbuttoned to reveal curly black chest hairs that matched his facial hair. Teofilo's booming laugh rose and fell over the other spirited conversations in the crowded estate.

"*Obrigado!*" the guests replied, some with heads angled, directing their curiosity toward Allegra, the self-assured woman gone solo. Assorted women did a who-does-she-think-she-is eyeball roll at Allegra, whose ample brown breasts sat like ripe melons on top of her low-cut, tangerine-colored blouse. A fitted, electric white pencil skirt framed her hips in a curvaceous silhouette, while strappy, open-toed, four-inch heels accentuated her supple, manicured toes. Female guests claimed their territory by gripping the forearm of their male companions, praying that Allegra, an obviously dangerous woman, would not notice them. The men grinned slyly, like eager pups, at the alluring woman who stood alone in their midst without companion, inhibitions, or purse. She radiated freedom, not needing anything or anyone to validate her presence. Allegra's face held a spirit from mythical times; Egyptian one moment, Grecian the next. Like a queen, her presence caused conversations to stall while curious bodies moved aside to clear a path for her passage. Allegra was a defiantly free woman who lived without the shackles of societal constraints. Men saw what they craved and needed in her. She was a snow-covered volcano. Allegra stood motionless, and allowed them to drink in her energy, and either love or loathe her. She became joined with their dreams. Allegra properly returned every nod, every glare, wink or lust-filled stare to its sender.

An erotic *coup d'état* had taken place. This was Teofilo's estate, but Allegra's domain.

"Welcome, *Senhorita!*" Teofilo bellowed, a throng of female admirers surrounding him as he stepped toward Allegra with his raised champagne flute. Allegra, glancing around, returned his greeting with warm eyes, and murmured a soft, "Hello. Lovely estate."

"*Muito Obrigado*! This estate is one of many that I own. My villa in Salvador is slightly larger and is where I raise show horses, just as my fat—"

Instead of listening to Teofilo boast about his estate holdings, Allegra moistened her bottom lip, dismissed him in mid-sentence, and whirled to stroll throughout the living room, admiring the striking and priceless works of Brazilian art.

"*Bela* (beautiful)," Teofilo whispered, gulping the remainder of his liquid courage, while silently watching Allegra's derrière saunter away.

In her absence, Teofilo's female admirers immediately flocked back to his side, with hopes of being chosen to perform any number of erotic pleasures and erase the memory of this female intruder. Allegra ultimately found her way through the triple glass panel door and onto the cobblestone terrace overlooking the haunting beach where powerful waves crashed on the slate rocks below.

"How do you know this Americana?" asked the angular blonde wearing a gold halter dress.

"Hmmm?" Teofilo replied absentmindedly, continuing to stare at Allegra's wake.

"Who is she?" the blonde repeated, not realizing she was being ignored.

"Please, Bianca. I'd like a refill," Teofilo replied, handing his flute to the blonde without looking at her.

The air on the terrace was hypnotically healing, with the ocean waves below sounding a robust symphony. Allegra had needed this temporary solace long before her chaotic arrival in Brazil. Her class "Traditional Indigenous Sexuality Patterns" had the highest enrollment of any class at New York University. Up until two hours before her flight, Allegra had had to prepare next semester's curriculum, hire an assistant, grade term papers, make progress on her dissertation, and supervise the renovation of her brownstone. Allegra had always vowed to live by two rules: One—never go shopping without a grocery list and two—never travel horny. To do either can leave a woman vulnerable to food she doesn't need and dick she really doesn't want.

2

Allegra believes that every woman must have a committee of men, on call, to serve her needs each day of the week, whatever those needs might be, so the men in her life never sense desperation or urgency for their company, but see only that she follows her whims, and chooses to be with them. A new committee member to Allegra's circle was a familiar voice in urban talk radio.

Thunder Poole, news director and host, the voice of WBBC-FM for nearly a decade, Allegra had heard his radio program on occasion and was attracted to the bass tone of his voice; accepting, measured, confident. Even while interviewing the most corrupt of politicians, Thunder never revealed that he knew where the official's skeletons were buried, until it was necessary. During last November's heated City Council campaign, Thunder interviewed the unscrupulous challenger to a popular incumbent for her Brooklyn council seat.

"Maya Jean is being controlled by rich, white, real estate developers in this city. Elect her and the people who are in dire need of affordable housing will be forced out of the city. You think it's hard to find affordable housing now? Vote for Maya Jean and see what happens."

"Is that right?" Thunder answered, already knowing the truth.

"Absolutely! She supports giving real estate developers big tax subsidies, so that they can price out more low-income people of color."

"Hold on, Brother! Hold on! None of that is true, and you know it."

"Well, according to my, um…" the challenger ventured, shifting nervously in his chair.

"Councilmember Jean has consistently opposed the gentrification of downtown Brooklyn. In fact, last spring she introduced a bill in City Council opposing eminent domain. Meanwhile, my research indicates that your five top donors are rich, white real estate firms! Now why would you come here, my brother, and deliberately attempt to mislead my listeners and me? Disrespect this radio station and this microphone? Tell you what, why don't you let the brothers and sisters know what your payback will be for the generosity of their vote, Brother? And I want specifics," Thunder scolded, turning the challenger into a bumbling fool in front of five million listeners.

Allegra was impressed with the way Thunder publicly destroyed the delusional credibility of this corrupt candidate, and how he stood up for Maya Jean, a beloved Brooklyn community servant. During the exchange, Thunder never raised his voice, but maintained control of the interview and handily gave notice that he was not going to tolerate any candidate intentionally duping his listeners with rehearsed talking points. During his 'Open Hour' segment, his loyal followers, mostly adoring women and longtime radio revolutionaries, expressed their admiration, with "You're sounding sooooo good, Thunder! I have the radio right here in my bed!" and "Keep speaking truth to power, Brother Thunder! The Boogie Down Bronx has you on loud and strong, Big Thunder. Make no mistake. This black woman always got your back!" and "We're streaming you live in the ATL."

Still, as mesmerized as his flock of women were, Allegra surmised that he was just another radio vigilante, a man who used his powerful microphone, rallied the comatose and disappeared back to his life in an upscale New York City suburb. "Radio vigilantes always talkin' shit, raising hell, causing confusion and then no one sees them again until the next crisis," Allegra often quipped to her friend-girl, Luisa, when they would talk politics, while on the treadmill at NYU's faculty gym.

Allegra's groundbreaking research on sexuality and DNA landed her appearances on CNN, the three major networks, quotes in *Cosmo* and *Essence* and a television agent pestering to become her media representative. When the WBBC-FM producer phoned to book her, Allegra was intrigued to see if the voice matched the man. Traditionally, most male broadcasters have perfect faces for radio, and the less their adoring public saw of them, the better.

Thunder was definitely attractive, but in an ugly-manly sort of way. He stood at an even six-foot-three inches tall, with a thick football player body and a strong jawline. The shadow of his beard had not decided whether or not it was going to grow in. His pillow soft lips and chocolate brown skin were sexy as hell, and Thunder was the perfect muscle to protect you in an alley fight. His wide, open face and tired, greenish eyes reflected a weariness of late-night studio work and marathon broadcasts. Tastefully attired in a black silk, tailored shirt, exposing a strong Adam's apple, Thunder wore a stylish gold chain and black trousers, which hung perfectly to accentuate his broad hips.

Sitting in the corner, observing the activity in the studio, was a regal, impeccably dressed, elderly gentleman, wearing a black pin-striped shirt, with a bow tie and herringbone vest, black trousers and classic black patent leather shoes. He twirled a satin-lined black fedora, while appreciating the presence of Allegra.

"Pops, this is Allegra Adams. Sister, Pops. Legally known as Thunder Poole I, my granddaddy; the man who raised me."

"Pleasure to meet you, Sugah," Pops replied, tipping his fedora with his customary name for all women whom he found attractive.

Remembering her manners, Allegra rose, crossing the studio, shaking Pops' hands. The men in the studio froze their activities as their eyes trailed Allegra's movements until she returned to her chair at the polished console.

"Pops was the founding member and drummer of the Rhythm Quartet, a jazz group that did their thing back in the fifties," Thunder boasted proudly as two attractive women with plunging necklines entered, carrying a platter of Chinese take-out food, a pitcher of iced tea, plates and plastic forks. Each woman poured the sweet and sour chicken, calamari salad and shrimp fried rice and broccoli on the paper plates. Serving Thunder first, the shorter of the two women, with a distinctive black mole on the right side of her thin lip and a shoulder-length weave with bangs, placed his food on his console, the aromatic ginger and garlic flavor filling the studio.

"We're *still* doing our thing, Thunder; except when Melvin's arthritis is flaring up," Pops asserted, still keeping his eyes on Allegra over the rim of his wire-framed glasses.

"Before he died, my father revered his jazz collection; Sarah Vaughn, Dizzy, and he had a protective seal around all of your albums. Nice meeting you, Mr. Poole," Allegra replied. "He's smiling from heaven that his daughter met his jazz idol."

"I been telling Thunder here that he needs to play some Lena Horne if he's serious about increasing the ratings," Pops quipped.

"Don't get him started," Thunder said. While Thunder appreciated the exchange between Pops and Allegra, he spoke to shift her attention back to him. The short woman serving his food remained close to Thunder, leaning her hip into his right shoulder.

"You want ice in your glass, Thunder?" she whispered close to his ear, luring him from fascination with Allegra.

"Huh?" Thunder answered, his eyes darting from Allegra to his food. "No ice. And what's up with the plastic fork? You know I don't get down with no plastic!"

"Sorry, Thunder," the woman said apologetically, snatching the plastic fork and running out of the studio, followed by her companion.

"Can you scoot a little closer...to the microphone, Sister Adams?" Thunder asked with a rich, urban accent as he reached across the console to push the microphone closer to her pale peachy-beige lips from his throne on his black leather, swivel-back chair. Allegra's allure was not lost on Thunder and Luther, his chubby, cork-barrel eyeglass-wearing engineer. Both men were distracted by Allegra's sensual manner as she signed the talent release form with delicate, manicured fingers.

"How long will this segment be?" Allegra whispered. Chuckling and speaking louder than normal, the rest of the WBBC-FM crew dug deep in their arsenal to draft Allegra into their obvious flirtation. "The segment will be about twenty minutes; but I anticipate a lot of listener telephone calls, so do you think you could stay for the hour? That is, I don't wanna make your man angry or nothin'..." Thunder chuckled at his own corniness and feeble attempt to elicit information about Allegra's personal life.

"Let's just keep it at twenty minutes, please?" Allegra answered lightly, sliding the release form across the console toward Thunder. The crew raised their eyebrows, scratched their temples and brainstormed another strategy to get the attention of this woman. The two women reentered, carrying steel forks that they distributed to the crew. The shorter woman carefully placed Thunder's fork, wrapped in a napkin, before him.

"Then in that case, I won't take any listener telephone calls. Maybe I'll include a couple of tweets and Facebook messages, but other than that, I wanna keep you to myself." Thunder flirted brazenly with Allegra's blank stare, while ignoring the woman with the fork, who lingered for a few moments until she realized that Thunder was paying her no heed.

"Very well," Allegra replied.

"You from New York, sister?" Thunder asked quietly.

"Clinton Hill section of Brooklyn and now Harlem; so, yes," Allegra replied.

"We're looking at broadcasting from New York University in the spring. Doing a town hall meeting and what not."

"Hmm, that's nice."

"Is that something you could help set up?"

"No, you should go through the normal channels. Contact the facilities department. They should be able to direct you," Allegra replied, absentmindedly.

In defeat, Thunder thought, waited, and exhaled. Chatting up a woman had never been this difficult for him. By now, Thunder would have gotten a woman's telephone digits and her panties. The studio on-air light sign shone on the wall above the engineer. The imaging for the program sounded with a female voice, "You're listening to WBBC-FM and the voice of the community, the Night Rider, Thunder Poole."

"And we're back. This is Thunder Poole, the Night Rider. And in studio is our very lovely and special guest, Ms. Allegra Adams of New York University. Thank you again, Sister, for being on the show."

"Thank you for having me."

"Now in the last segment you were just about to share with the listeners about your research and the conclusions you've reached."

"Yes. I was explaining that my research concludes that DNA reveals more than paternity and a proclivity toward certain ill-nesses. DNA is the foundation of one's sexuality, whether or not it's…" Allegra paused to moistened her lips and reconsider her thoughts, before continuing." DNA is the foundation of one's sexuality and your sexuality is in your DNA. It defines your behavior, your urges, your preferences and most importantly, your soul's sensual desires."

Thunder and his engineer leaned toward Allegra, mesmerized by her seductive persona as she described to his five million listeners, the mystery of sexual DNA. "The more I hear black people protest against racism or succumb to life's rollercoaster, the more I hear their sexual souls scream for nourishment, healing, or at the very least, recognition. And until that occurs, the yearning that each of us has will continue to seek, I dare say, demand, satisfaction. The lack of sexual healing is the fundamental cause of war in the world. We all need sexual healing, don't you agree, Mr. Poole?"

Allegra's round, brown eyes and soft whisper hypnotized Thunder, so that he could not wrap his brain around a question to attempt to challenge her. He could only mutter, "Uh huh."

Allegra continued with her thesis, just as she had done while teaching her students. Her intent was serious, intellectual, but her naked charisma spoke another enticing language.

Thunder and his drooling engineer swallowed, their nostrils flared, subtly. "Um, wow, Sister," Thunder said, rubbing the side of his nose and chuckling to hid his nervousness. "That's um, pretty deep. So how does one do that?"

"Do what?"

"Um, how do I…? I mean, how does one nourish one's sexual soul?"

The producer hid his face behind his closed fist to stifle a snort. Thunder glared at the producer, who quickly gathered himself and resumed answering listener telephone calls, and then placing them on hold. Allegra uncrossed her legs and sat with her knees slightly apart as she reached down to rub her calf, revealing her cleavage.

"My book *Unleash Your Primal Scream* will be out this fall. I trust you'll have me...you'll have me back to discuss it," Allegra continued.

"Oh, absolutely! You're welcome to come; come back on the show any time you want, sister. Any time at all," Thunder giddily replied, departing from his normal laid back, on-air persona. "So, um, I want to thank my lovely studio guest, Dr...."

"Allegra Adams."

"Sorry?"

"My doctorate has not yet been granted."

"Excuse me. *Sister Allegra Adams.* Thank you for joining us this evening."

"Thank you for having me."

"Okay, brothers and sisters, this is Thunder Poole, your Night Rider. Until next time, family, keep your loved ones safe and your enemies close. Sleep tight. WBBC-FM New York."

The on-air light on the studio wall became dark. Thunder exhaled, leaned back in his chair and stared at Allegra, who rose to leave, gathering her purse and research. Thunder leapt to his feet, adjusting his pants, and lurched around the console to assist Allegra with her already empty chair. "I-I I'll—lemme, lemme walk you out...out to the elevator...get you a cab, to your car. I can drive you; which way you headed?"

"Thunder, your food is gonna get cold," one of the women advised, her words falling on deaf ears.

"I can drive her!" the producer volunteered.

Thunder swiftly raised his hand, silencing his producer into silence. After ten years of working with Thunder, he should have known that the Night Rider always had first dibs on all of the gorgeous females who daily visited the radio station. Thunder, in an instant, had claimed his territory, and anyone who violated his authority risked the threat of professional death.

"Pleasure meeting you, Allegra," Pops called as she left the studio.

"You as well, Mr. Poole," Allegra said, turning to shake his hand before the studio door closed behind her. In her absence, the men dissolved into a juvenile fraternity, slapping five, bumping their fists, and shaking their heads. "Man, oh, man, where did you meet that sister?" the crew asked simultaneously.

"Humph, Humph, Humph! You don't see many women built like her today. Now that's a woman, Son. Reminds me of Lena and Dorothy Dandridge all mixed up in there together. Humph!" Pops reminisced.

"With all due respect, Pops, that sista is more Jennifer, with those…" The producer jumped to his feet, zigzagging his hands to form the shape of a woman's body.

Thunder killed further comparisons of Allegra with any female celebrity, past or present, with a grunt of his voice.

Allegra's hired black Town Car merged into northbound traffic on Greenwich Street. Reaching Allegra on her BlackBerry, her friend, Luisa, exclaimed in her Boricua accent, "You were great, Allegra!"

"Thanks, Girl! It would have been interesting to chat with his listeners though. The lights on the switchboard were completely lit, his Facebook page was blowing up, and he received so many tweets, he had to turn off his BlackBerry. He wanted to extend the length of the interview, but I believe less is more. So Thunder decided not to cut the chat and open the telephone lines for whatever reason…said doing so would take too much time away from the focus of his interview. Humph, whatever."

"So, what does he look like?"

"He's alright. Mannish in the face with starter locs. Nothing soft about him. Looks like he can do a little sumptin' sumptin'. And any man who can handle himself will never get kicked out of my bed. That is, *if* I ever let him in my bed. Apparently he runs things up there at the radio station and knows it. But you know...."

"Seems like there were times during the interview when you caught him off-guard, Allegra."

"And I'll never understand that, Luisa. Big, bad men like Thunder Poole ruling the world, claim to be speaking truth to power and running up every skirt from the Bronx to Long Island. But when little ole me wants to discuss something as natural as fuckin', these same brothers get tight-jawed."

"There you go, Allegra, rattling the cages again." Luisa chuckled. "Thunder Poole. Wow! Whenever there's a major controversy in the community, everyone looks to him to lead them out of the wilderness!"

"Calm down, Luisa. He's a *man*, Luisa. Just a man. You're always left starry-eyed by a little testosterone."

Allegra and Luisa had been sister-friends since meeting during undergrad at Columbia University. The two women deepened their bond while pledging Tau Omega Sorority and later earning their respective master's degrees. Allegra's degree was in anthropology and Luisa focused on broadcast journalism. Fortunately for Allegra, American Airlines' liberal employee education policy subsidized her tuition, while Luisa held a full-time gig at a Washington Heights nonprofit domestic violence shelter to make ends meet.

"You gotta man, Allegra?" Thunder asked one night, after she finally returned his telephone call, secretly wanting to be told an improvised erotic bedtime story.

"A woman always has a man, Thunder."

"What I mean is, one brother, who takes care of you, provides for you," Thunder explained. "I come from a stock of men who believe the purpose for our existence is to provide and protect women. Even though my pops and even his father were rolling stones, both of them made sure that none of their ladies were ever wanting for nothin'. Made sure the women knew each other and that their children—my half-brothers and sisters—knew each other, too. Maybe that's why there are a thousand people with my last name out in Brooklyn and Long Island. If you ever run into somebody named Poole, more than likely we're related."

"Even though there are also rolling stones in my family, I don't think my father left any children around," Allegra responded.

"You never know, what you never know. The reason why so many black folks look alike ain't no accident." Thunder chuckled. "Still and all, my pops made sure that he kept a close connection with his grandkids. That's my road dog, even to this day. We're more like brothers than grandfather and grandson."

Thunder was adopted by his grandfather soon after the New York State Family Court decided that his crack-addicted parents were unfit to raise him, discovering him one night foraging for food in a neighbor's garbage can. Thunder "Pops" Poole I, still touring with the Rhythm Quartet, bundled six-year-old Thunder, taking him wherever the group was scheduled to perform. When most children were tucked in bed by eight o'clock, young Thunder was transfixed, sitting on stage near his grandfather, watching the band's performance. As he grew older, Thunder assisted the musicians by polishing their instruments, arranging playlists, running errands. Thunder also witnessed the ugly side of the music industry: promoters who cheated his grandfather; band members struggling with alcohol issues, often failing to appear for gigs. Thunder, sleeping on a small cot, would witness his grandfather's sex orgies with streams of willing, jazz-loving damsels. Thunder boasted of his endearing relationship with his grandfather. Pops, though older, willingly became a single father, an accomplished artist, and was later awarded for his body of work. Thunder proudly accompanied Pops to his induction into the American Jazz Hall of Fame.

Allegra shifted in her bed, exhaled a quiet yawn, during Thunder's long yarn about his family tree. Though she was attracted to the deep bass in his masculine voice, Thunder could sense her retreat and returned to his original question. "So like I asked you earlier, you got a man? A real man to take care of you. This is a cold world to be out here by yourself."

"I know what a real man does for a woman, Mr. Poole."

"Well, tell me this, then. Do you need a man? I hear so many sisters out here today always talking about the fact that they don't need a man. Is that you?"

"You'll never hear me say that. I will always need a man, sometimes more than one. My sexual urges are just too powerful to deny the satisfaction I get from being in the arms of a man."

"Hmmm, that's pretty deep. Never heard a woman put it down like that."

"Well, I have a well-earned reputation for walking the road less traveled. Now enough about our family trees, and what man is protecting me from the cruel world. Tell me a bedtime story. That'll scratch my itch, and take care of me. For now."

"For now, huh? What about the future, Allegra? Do you ever think about your future?"

"I live in the power of now, Mr. Poole," Allegra replied, rubbing her breasts, around her erect nipples.

"Oh, so it's like that, huh? I don't remember the last time I told a bedtime story. Maybe to my Goddaughter, when she was two years old."

"Yes. It's like that. All day and all night. So tell me, Mr. Poole. Tell me a story so I can fall asleep."

"Wouldn't it be better for me to come over and tell you in person?"

"Soon come," Allegra answered softly.

"We been spending all of this time on the telephone, but still you won't let me come over? Shoot, I'm ready to give you a key to my crib, Sister. I'm feeling you just that hard," Thunder explained.

"You talk a lot."

"Say what?"

"Soon come. Now tell me that story again...the how-you-would-do-me story...once upon a time," Allegra replied, drowsily coaching Thunder from her bed, with her lace panties pulled down around her arse. Remnants of her dissertation and poster boards were scattered on the hardwood floor, and a dimly lit lamp on her nightstand cast a warm glow. Allegra squeezed a pillow together to form a ridge. She straddled it, pressed her vagina tightly against it, and began a slow, easy grind.

Lying in his own bed, nursing an erect cock, in his Jersey City state of the art condo, overlooking the Hudson River, Thunder cleared his throat and began: "Once Upon A Time, a beautiful, alluring sister named Allegra knocked on my door. I couldn't believe my fortune to see such a queen, as lovely as her, on my doorstep. She stepped into my embrace and I held her hand, poking her with my hard, thick and long dick. I led her over to sit on my leather sofa, where romantic candles, Miles Davis music, and wine lovingly chilled, awaited her visit. She crossed her legs so that her honey-colored calves perfectly accentuated her raised skirt, making me delirious, like the first day I met her at the radio station. Licking her lips, she stared at my pants, and moved her hand tenderly up and down my leg, until finally she reached to squeeze my manhood, as I massaged her shoulders. We kissed deeply, our tongues doing the tango, while she unzipped my pants and firmly stroked my cock. I squeezed her nipples and licked them hard. She moaned as I reached between her legs, fingering her clit until she was extremely wet. Instinctively, I knelt and placed her legs over my shoulders and buried my lips into her pussy until she moaned uncontrollably. I lifted her up and held her tight against the wall, gazing into her brown eyes and slid her onto all of my eight inches. My dear Allegra enjoyed every inch until she sank all of the way to the bottom, rolling her eyes, as she trembled, calling my name, 'Thunder.' For many hours, over and over, Allegra screamed for mercy and joy. Long after the mood had faded from the night sky, we found ourselves fucking on a chaise longue on my patio. And without giving a shit about waking the neighbors, together we unleashed like a tidal wave. As the sun began to usher in a new day, we laid together in my king-sized bed, wanting more. And the Queen Allegra was happy once again and lived happily ever after, until she needed Thunder again."

Allegra rapidly stroked her clit and climaxed just as Thunder said, "And Queen Allegra lived happily ever after, with King Thunder at her beck and call. The End." Allegra returned the telephone receiver to its cradle, and Thunder was left to get off on his own.

"Allegra, you're going to drive him away! Just watch. You keep teasing him like that," Luisa warned her the next day over lunch at a Greenwich Village outdoor cafe.

"Luisa, I'm not trying to keep Thunder or drive him away. I'm having my fun, like I always do. And if he wants to give me a little telephone bedtime story, what's the problem? On the other hand, you sweat Virgil, 24-7, and he acts like a fool, thinking you're his little show piece. Yet still you sleep with him. He still got you dick-whipped?"

"Oh, now why you gotta go there, Allegra," Luisa said, pouting slightly.

"My point is," Allegra said, leaning closer so that the Asian couple, examining their menus at the next table, could not overhear her. "My point is that I don't fuck a man to *get* him. Fucking is for *my* own pleasure."

Allegra had a policy of establishing boundaries early in her encounters with men. "Men are naturally territorial. They attempt to nest within five minutes of meeting you, whether or not they are serious about you. It's the woman's responsibility to set limits," Allegra advised Luisa during one of their recent vision board breakfasts. Through observation over the years, Allegra observed her loveless and sexless female relatives allowing men to dominate their homes, their bodies and their spirits within hours of them crossing their thresholds. Not soon after, Allegra would eavesdrop on their loud weeping and heartbreak. And she vowed as a child, to never repeat their lonely, self-defeating behaviors.

When her keynote address was confirmed at the conference in Rio de Janerio, rather than travel horny and leave a whimpering Thunder on her doorstep, she decided to do as he begged and let him come over to eat her pussy before she left Harlem for the airport. While Allegra thought that would be a good idea, her schedule was tight and so were her nerves, with last minute preparations. Thunder, being the reliable and creative time organizer, whined, "Come on, Baby! How you gonna leave a brother hangin'? For two whole weeks? Come on now, Allegra! If I didn't hate to fly, I'd roll down there with you." Thunder sounded like a man who was not ready to quit Allegraville cold turkey.

To prepare for their first pussy ritual, Allegra entered the limousine with one suitcase, a laptop case, and wearing nothing but a black leather trench coat and her favorite black five-inch spike heel pumps. En route from Harlem's Striver's Row to John F. Kennedy Airport, the Italian limo driver gawked through his rear-view mirror, as cars furiously honked from behind, demanding that the limousine proceed seconds after the traffic light had turned green.

"Oh, my God!" Thunder shouted his great fortune to no one in particular, as he slowly unbuttoned her trench coat to reveal his prize. Kissing Allegra's entire body, Thunder teased and slurped her nipples with his tongue, while rubbing her toned thighs and supple ass. He gently spread her legs as she rested against the silk pillow in the rear of the limousine. Allegra smiled at the awe on his face, and then closed her eyes in anticipation of her arrival at the door of ecstasy. Crossing the Edward Kennedy-Triborough Bridge, Thunder kissed and licked the outside of her pussy, spreading, and exploring to reveal its beauty.

"Omigod, I've waited so long," Thunder whimpered, his breath quickening, as the limousine sped along the bustling Grand Central Parkway.

Allegra closed her eyes and prayed that Thunder would stop running his mouth. One thing that Allegra didn't tolerate was a talkative man. It was her fault though; she knew before she finally responded to his telephone calls and text messages that Thunder was a professional talker. It had been about sixteen days since they had first met at her radio interview. Allegra set the boundaries, never allowing Thunder to initially phone her, and she returned his calls only rarely, and late at night, wanting him to tell her an erotic bedtime story.

"Has your sexual soul quenched its thirst, Mr. Poole?" Allegra purred over the telephone, as she pleasured herself, one evening.

"Well, I-I-I…" Thunder ran his hand over his head, trying to get his bearings. He never believed that he would meet a woman who knew her own needs, who spoke so directly to him, so passionately and without any inhibitions. Thunder knew sexy, gorgeous women who stood by, waiting to provide him with his earthly needs, yet none had ever spoken to his soul. None knew of the carnal, rhythmical relationship between a man and a woman. This woman, Allegra, knew. Perhaps more than he did. Thunder became obsessed in his wish to share his soul's desires with Allegra.

The traffic on the Van Wyck Expressway had crawled to a stop as an ambulance with flashing lights squeezed past the limousine on the right shoulder. Thunder was oblivious, as he had long craved to place his lips on her most intimate of flesh, to taste and smell her aroma.

"You're such a good eater, Mr. Poole. I thought you would be, so I brought a special treat," Allegra cooed, massaging the back of his neck. Knitting his eyebrows together, Thunder raised his head to see Allegra reach into her carry-on bag, revealing a container of whipped cream. Together, Allegra and Thunder cackled.

"You're *some* woman," Thunder mumbled, layering the whipped cream around her clit, then flattening out his tongue, licking Allegra like an ice cream cone, then smashing his head into her wet vagina, as she trembled and moaned. The limousine continued into the traffic congestion on the Van Wyck Expressway, as Allegra clutched Thunder's head, her thighs writhing uncontrollably, her lungs gasping for breath and body stiffening, unleashing a stream of desire.

"I'm diggin' you, woman. I don't know you like I want to, but I dig you," Thunder confided, resting his head on her abdomen just as the limousine driver knocked on the door window, signaling their arrival at the John F. Kennedy Airport international terminal. Allegra ran her fingers through Thunder's locs, letting his confession hang in the air.

"I'm diggin' you, woman, I said," Thunder repeated, patting his forehead with a handkerchief.

That's not what Allegra wanted to hear coming from a man she had only known for his bedtime stories. She just wanted to get her pussy eaten on the way to Brazil. *Was that too much to ask?* she thought to herself.

"Thunder, don't go falling in love with me and telling me you're pregnant," Allegra said.

Thunder's face froze, then dissolved in laughter, his baritone sound rumbling inside. "I miss you already."

"That's sweet, Mr. Poole. Happy Fourth of July," Allegra replied, pecking him on his sweaty forehead.

Startled by her abruptness, Thunder sulked, watching Allegra button her trench coat, his emotions somersaulting. Showing his disappointment, Thunder's mouth curled upside down, as he was overcome with sadness. He did not want Allegra to board that airplane. On cue, after Allegra tapped on her window, the limo driver gallantly opened her limo door, retrieving her wheeled-suitcase, and handing it to a waiting porter. Without glancing back at the sullen Thunder, Allegra stepped out of the limo, tipped the grinning driver, and strutted toward the international airport terminal to check in for her TAM Airlines flight.

Thunder, looking like a cocker spaniel waiting for his master to return from inside a grocery store, waited forlornly until Allegra had disappeared from his sight. His iPhone vibrated, signally an incoming telephone call. The caller ID screen read "Crystal," to which Thunder clicked "ignore."

By the time Allegra had arrived in Rio de Janeiro, and she was sunbathing on the balcony of her hotel suite, Thunder had already phoned and left messages twice.

That was three days ago. An erotic lifetime.

3

Brazil was beautiful at this time of year. The country had weather patterns slightly opposite those of North America, and therefore was experiencing fall with its warm days and cool, comfortable nights. Allegra leaned seductively over the terrace's wooden railing, inhaling the ocean breeze, and hitched her ruffled skirt up around her shapely hips, revealing her muscular legs. A male waiter served her another flute of champagne as Teofilo peeked out onto the terrace, relieved to have found her. "Here you are, *Senhorita!*" he exclaimed, striding toward her, joining her at the railing.

"Here I am," Allegra whispered, gazing up into his brown eyes.

"I was looking all over for you."

"Were you now? Whatever for?"

Teofilo leaned forward to hear Allegra. "*Como?* What did you say?"

"I said, why were you looking for me?" Allegra still whispered.

Teofilo didn't expect such a direct retort. "Well, I-I-I, I wondered where that beautiful, mysterious woman who had entered my home had gone. Had I imagined an angel?"

Teofilo waited for her to be mesmerized by his compliments, like hundreds of other women had been. Allegra was not and Teofilo noticed, coughing to clear his throat and find his confidence.

"Mr. Governor, do you often fantasize about women whom you do not know?"

Teofilo's chest broadened that this woman knew he was one of the most powerful men in Brazil but was rattled on how to respond...how to be with this woman, who had inexplicably turned the tables and made him feel vulnerable. Allegra swayed her shoulders and hips to the seductive rhythms of Gilberto Gil's latest samba, which was moving the dancing guests from inside the estate.

"You like samba?"

"Very much." Allegra smiled, gently tossing her twists and sipping from her flute. Not waiting for Teofilo to ask her to dance, she closed her eyes and moved like a cobra, extending her arms to the full wolf moon. Teofilo's eyes locked on Allegra's body, his dick pumping against the inside of his pants, as he stood in the middle of the terrace, taking in her supernatural vibration, while she danced around him.

A tall, striking, redheaded woman rushed onto the terrace. Her eyes glared at an oblivious Allegra and then darted back at Teofilo. "Teo! *Tenho estado olhando completamente sobre para você!* (I've been looking all over for you!)" she exclaimed, rushing to his side, possessively squeezing his arm. Teofilo, keeping his eyes on Allegra, answered impatiently, "What is it, Bianca?"

"Come, Teo, Paulo and Julietta are boarding their yacht; come say goodbye," Bianca begged, yanking his arm.

"Still a galley hag, Bianca?" Allegra asked amusedly.

Teofilo glanced between the two women. "You two know each other?"

Bianca raised her chin, summoning up the courage to take on Allegra. "Allegra, what are you doing here? Here in Brazil? You left the airline. You always used to brag about your Harlem. I never thought you would leave it again," Bianca said.

"Look, Bianca. We were never friends. And I never answer questions from people I do not know. I don't need anyone's permission or approval to be wherever I damned want to be," Allegra replied firmly. She had grown weary of Bianca, who saw women like Allegra as adversaries instead of the sister-friends they could have been. Teofilo was uncomfortable with the hostile exchange between the two women.

"You go, Bianca. I will come soon." Teofilo continued to stare at Allegra, who was now humming night dreams at the sky, and quickening her hips to a Sergio Mendes bossa nova, which was now heard from inside the mansion.

"Go!" Teofilo, now sharply ordered Bianca, scolding her like a child, gesturing for her to leave. Lowering her head, she frowned and reluctantly departed, glancing over her shoulder again at Allegra, before disappearing back inside the estate, mumbling out of earshot, *"Americano preto dilma* (black American bitch)." Allegra, still facing away from Teofilo, turned her head, and said, "Governor. Go see about your friends."

"Where did you learn to move like that?" Teofilo asked. Allegra chuckled with the full moon, with whom she shared her soul's secrets.

"Like what, Governor?"

Teofilo smiled, "Like a… Like this," he said, wiggling his hips playfully. Allegra laughed.

"Governor, my hips learned to move in Harlem. Striver's Row, 139th Street and Seventh Avenue and long before that, over four centuries ago…Africa."

"Ahhh, Harlem. I've been there on business many times. I led a team of private investors who are considering building a hotel and shopping mall there."

"There hasn't been a decent hotel in Harlem since Fidel Castro visited Hotel Theresa in the sixties."

"Yes. But I don't recall seeing such a *cativar mulher* (captivating woman) like you when I visited."

"Well, Governor. Beautiful black women are everywhere, but you must know where to look." Allegra was facing Teofilo now. "Uh oh, Governor, my glass is almost empty."

Allegra slowly raised her hand to stroke the hair on his chest; Teofilo's eyes followed her fingers, until he clutched them, drawing her palm to his lips. Just as Teofilo's lips were to meet her palm, Allegra advised, "Governor, don't be rude. See to your guests," recoiling her hand from his grasp.

Teofilo lowered his arms, shifted his feet, glanced inside his estate, searching for an attendant, and looked back into Allegra's brown, still eyes. "Okay; you stay here. I come back. I come back straight away."

Allegra smiled and turned back to staring at the moon.

"I come back," Teofilo repeated from the doorway, darting through the terrace entrance, tripping over the door frame, rattling the Corinthian bell wind chimes.

Allegra, still leaning against the wooden rail, lowered her head and chuckled, and painted an invisible message in the night sky: "My nature calls. My duty is to respond. Must go crazy." Gulping the last drop of champagne, she tossed her flute below, the glass splintering against the slippery rocks. The sounds of couples samba dancing permeated the night. *Brazilian dances are true expressions of love*, she thought, her eyes slowly becoming slits from jet lag, a day of revamping her conference presentation, and the potent champagne rushing to her head.

"Well, helloooo!" a female, alto voice called from the terrace entrance. Allegra, consumed with an impending headache, heard the voice, but had not known that the greeting was meant for her. "Beautiful evening, isn't it?" the voice asked, moving closer to Allegra. Looking over her shoulder, Allegra's eyes narrowed to the owner of the greeting, a striking, light-complexioned black woman, wearing African-styled carved bone earrings. A small, silver ring pierced her right nostril. There was an African print scarf over the shoulder of her long, boatneck, gray dress and a white, crocheted beret gathered her white locs in a large bun on the back of her head. "Lovely evening, isn't it?" the woman continued, standing near Allegra at the railing. She took a marijuana joint from her leather waist pouch, licked it, then squeezed the tip and lit it. Allegra was not in the mood for small talk and continued admiring the beach below, hoping the friendly woman would get the hint and disappear back inside with the partygoers. "I, um, I noticed you when you arrived. You're from the States, aren't you?"

Allegra paused, then nodded and answered, "Yes."

"Me, too. I guess we Americans have the radar for each other. We especially know when there's a sister or a brother from back home in our midst. Black Americans walk with their own energy. I'm Dr. Vivian Henderson. University of Detroit. I'm a professor there," she said, with authority, her voice cueing for Allegra to introduce herself. Allegra managed a tight smile and faced Dr. Henderson, who took another drag on her joint, while eagerly extending her wiry hand.

"Allegra. Allegra Adams, New York University," she said, allowing the professor from Detroit to firmly shake her hand, and stare intently into Allegra's face. For Allegra, her intruder provided more hand-shaking than was required, until she firmly removed her hand from Dr. Henderson's grip. As Allegra turned back to face the view of the ocean, Dr. Henderson asked, "So you're here for the conference, I take it?"

"Yes, I am."

"So am I. I recognize your name. I read with interest the title of your keynote address. I look forward to hearing your speech. Looks like a subject I could get into. Sometimes you come to these conferences and it's the same old subject manner. Same old people. I mean, how many times are people going to talk about reparations, blood diamonds and climate change?"

"Thank you. I look forward to sharing it," Allegra replied, relaxing slightly, pretending to appear gracious to a professional colleague.

"Later on, if you're not doing anything, a few of us are getting together to um…to get together," Dr. Henderson began.

"Are you all going to a nightclub or someone's home?"

"Tonight there'll be a midnight soiree of professionals, some Brazilians and Americans who have repatriated and live in Brazil now."

"Midnight? That's not going to work for me, especially having to conduct a workshop and the keynote tomorrow. Thanks anyway."

Dr. Henderson leaned toward Allegra, placing her hand lightly on her shoulder. "Just so you know, I think you're hot and lovely. And you'd be a perfect addition to our women-who-love-women soiree. I know more than a few of the ladies who'd eat you alive! We're a fun, eclectic group of Brazil's most powerful lesbian women. Actually, we prefer to be called women-who-love; we party by the adage, "What's done in Brazil, stays in Brazil."

Allegra jolted, and stood straight, facing Dr. Henderson. "Dr. Henderson?" Dr. Henderson nodded, with a gleam in her eye. "Thanks, but no thanks. I don't do women."

"Are you sure? I could have sworn…"

"Your radar needs its batteries replaced. You zeroed in on the wrong chick. If that's your thing, I'm happy for you. But with all of the men on this planet, I'll be damned and bored as shit, if I did women. I love men, exclusively," Allegra said calmly.

Dr. Henderson shrugged; pursing her lips, she took another drag on her joint, and rocked on the back of her high heeled brown sandals. "Sister, no offense. But nothing ventured; nothing gained. Let me give you a piece of advice. Never burn a bridge, because you never know when you may need this bridge to cross back over," Dr. Henderson said, extinguishing her marijuana joint in a ceramic ashtray, and tossing the warning over her shoulder with an edge in her voice as she stomped off the terrace. Allegra turned around, let out an exhale and fanned the air, in effect erasing the memory of Dr. Henderson.

Allegra checked her watch. She was no longer interested in socializing—with anyone. Her pillow back at the hotel was calling her name. Deciding not to wait for Teofilo to return, Allegra sauntered to the entrance, then turned and retrieved Dr. Henderson's unlit joint from the ashtray, wrapped it a cloth napkin and stuffed it inside her black, patent leather clutch. Allegra slipped through the living room, dodging the dancing couples and moved to the front door of the lively estate. As Allegra rapidly approached, the attendant welcomed entering guests.

"Sir, I'm ready to leave. Would you please assist me to the boat landing? (*O senhor, eu estou pronto para partir. Você por favor me auxiliaria à aterrissagem de barco?*)"

"Does *Senhor* know that you are leaving? I get him for you! (*Senhor sabe que você parte? Eu o receberei para você!*)" He peered around Allegra, in search of Teofilo, his employer.

"No, no. Please. He knows that I'm leaving. (*Não, número por favor. Ele sabe que eu parto,*)" Allegra lied.

"Yes, Miss. (*Sim, perca.*)"

Teofilo's attendant escorted Allegra to a departing yacht and helped her descend into the vessel. Like a protective friend, the attendant stood on the boat landing until Allegra's vessel had motored away into the dark, choppy sea, leaving behind a bewildered governor, a relieved Bianca and a pissed-off professor from Detroit.

"As a doctoral candidate at New York University, consultant, author and keynote speaker, Allegra Adams has consulted for the most renowned international museums, cultural institutions, and non-profits. She is considered the foremost authority on DNA and sexuality. Ladies and gentlemen, Ms. Allegra Adams!" the silver-haired conference president boomed. The audience clapped its warm applause. Many attendees flipped open their laptops or readied their pens to scribble notes. Although still woozy from the champagne the night before, Allegra commanded the stage from the moment she began her keynote speech. Her breasts jutted subtly under her blue linen blazer and her pencil skirt with a back ruffle, though respectable enough, still accentuated her sexy legs.

Allegra explained, "My detailed analysis of the structure and composition of our organs and cells can only conclude that our DNA creates our sexuality and that every group of people has its own unique DNA/sexuality characteristic. This characteristic expresses itself in one's sexual tastes, inhibitions, and sexual yearning."

During the question and answer session, Allegra skillfully countered any theory challenging her thesis with documented evidence, statistics and current research from respected scientists. Dr. Henderson sat in the center section on the aisle, looking more withdrawn, with strained features, and frown lines framing her tense mouth. Her demeanor and posture indicated that she was irritated and poised for a challenge. Allegra recalled their encounter the night before at Teofilo's estate. She had been approached by lesbians in the past, many with whom she had become platonic friends, but Dr. Henderson was the first lesbian who became aggressive; just like a man who was insulted when he heard "Hell, no," for an answer.

"Ms. Adams, you say your documentation comes from where?" Dr. Henderson asked tersely.

"And your name is?" Allegra said, pretending not to know.

Apparently, Dr. Henderson was not used to being out of control. And this made the second time with Allegra. Her sourpuss expression revealed that she had not expected to be asked a question in response to her first challenge. "Dr. Henderson. University of Detroit," she said, with a huffy tone, which indicated to Allegra, she had not been skillfully fucked, by man or woman, in at least a decade.

"Well, Dr. Henderson, the nucleus of my theory was based upon the research of Dr. Leslie Cooper. You are familiar with him, are you not?" Allegra cooed.

"Well, of course. She is a Professor Emeritus from my university. Her vast historical papers are housed at the research library named after her."

"Actually, Dr. Cooper is very much a *he*."

"Well, of course I meant to say…"

"And you would agree, Dr. Henderson, that Dr. Cooper is the foremost authority on this subject, would you not?"

"Well, I…"

"What issues would you then have with the research of Dr. Cooper and my thesis? The citations are listed in the hand-out you were given. You did review the hand-out, didn't you, Dr. Henderson?"

"Well, I-I…" Dr. Henderson stuttered, clutching the pearls around her wrinkled neck.

"If you have any other questions, I'll be glad to entertain them afterwards. And for everyone else, a copy of my remarks can be downloaded from my website: AllegraAdamsPhd.com."

Dr. Henderson caved back into her seat, crossing her arms, and sought to gain allies from her delegation. Instead, her colleagues either stared at the floor or pretended to remove lint from their clothing. Allegra had experienced this kind of challenge before. From men who camouflaged their attraction to her with hostility over her intellectual brilliance, and from frustrated women, who having gone dickless for decades, sensed her erotic prowess and openly resented her for it.

As Allegra answered the next question from a graduate student from South Africa, two male bodyguards, wearing mirrored sunglasses, swept into the ballroom, followed by Teofilo, who pretended he was being inconspicuous, gesturing for the attendees to return their attention back to Allegra. His bodyguards, once they were sure that the governor's life was not in imminent danger, stood against the wall behind their benefactor, their arms perched behind their muscular backs.

After twenty minutes of questions, Allegra concluded her presentation with, "Thank you for inviting me. I appreciate being here. Enjoy the remainder of the conference. *Obrigada!*"

"Let's give Ms. Adams a round of applause. Ms. Adams will be signing copies of her book, *The DNA Psychology of African People*. Please form a line to the right of the podium. *Obrigado!*"

Ninety minutes later, after the crowd of book-signers had thinned, Teofilo, who had remained seated in the back of the now empty ballroom examining his fresh manicure, rose and playfully tiptoed toward Allegra. Ignoring him, she chatted with another attendee, exchanging business cards, while gathering her lecture notes and briefcase, and then paused to drink from the cup of water that was placed on her podium. Allegra was thirstier than she realized. Conference volunteers dismantled the stage and removed the chairs in the rear of the ballroom. Easing close to her, Teofilo wagged his index finger, with a grin, playfully scolding, "You never said goodbye. You never told me your name. You..."

"Have I been a bad girl, *Senhor* Governor? Will you arrest me? Deport me, perhaps?" Allegra asked in a playful, girlish tease, still not offering Teofilo eye contact, double-checking that she had her belongings. Teofilo's baritone chuckle echoed with amusement. Allegra had known powerful men like Teofilo before. They ruled nations and women. Their greatest desires were at their beck and call, but Allegra refused to be on their wait list. She adhered to her own wish list, and allowed no man to set the pace of any potential dalliance.

"Will you allow me to take you on a private tour, Ms. Adams?" Teofilo asked. "Please allow me to show you my beautiful Rio. An adventure awaits you." A loud silence hung in the air as Allegra returned Teofilo's direct, solid gaze. Teofilo, with his secretly held bravado, gentle nature and athletic physique, intrigued Allegra. Allegra was now intrigued with his chase enough to reciprocate his interest in her.

"Show me," Allegra's lips read, her loins beginning to burn.

4

——Original Message——
From: luisah@aol.com
To: allegraphd@aol.com
Sent: Sunday, January 9, 2011 10:30am
Subject: Checking In

Hola, Allegra,

How's it going down there! I hope you are having a ball. Hmph!
Knowing you, you are probably having more than one ball...lol! Rio
doesn't know what hit it! Virgil said that he and his brothers were
going down to Brazil for Carnival and to check out all of the fine
chicks and yada...yada! I told his cheap ass that there was no way
he was going to tear himself away from his desk, his ambition or an
American dollar. So you, Allegra, have the monopoly on Brazilian
love. Now he wants to know what I'm talking about. I told Virgil that
there has to be some changes in our relationship...if he wants to
continue sleeping in my bed. You would've been proud of me, even
though a bottle of Patrón Platinum helped a lot to fuel my words, and
make me say what's been on my mind all along. And of course crazy
Khadijah added her two cents. Same old Bible-toting Khadijah...
thinking that we should keep our pussies and our bodies locked up
in the house. I still wonder how she has so much advice...but it's all
good. She loves the Lord now...LOL! Thunder drove me out to visit
your Aunt Rachael. Of course, she asked about you. Couldn't under-

stand why you weren't there. I told her you'd see her when you get back. I see how she can be difficult; that's why I admire you for hanging in with her.

Anyway, don't forget about little old me...lol! Text, Tweet, e-mail me, Facebook or pick up the goddamn phone and call. I've been ambushed by my assignment editor with the same old cat-stuck-in-the-tree, New Year's resolutions, bullshit assignments. Help somebody...LOL! Please don't pussywhip those men too bad. On second thought, why not?...LOL!

P.S. My doorman has your mail in the storeroom.

Miss ya! Love Ya!

Luisa

Raised in the New York City neighborhood of Washington Heights by Dominican working-class parents, Luisa was sheltered by them from the real world, yet she witnessed frequent physical and emotional abuse by her father toward her mother. Luisa had a cheerful, gregarious personality, which suited her well as a reporter for the local NBC-TV affiliate, but because of what she witnessed as a child, Luisa often mirrored the effects of the abuse her mother suffered. Luisa had a smoke-complexion, with jet black, loose curls which hung loosely around her face. She had a naïve persona and never was aware of her beauty. Her hair was so distracting that her program director ordered her to wear it in a bun, as the station received calls from numerous men, who were so sexually attracted by her that they could not concentrate on her news reports. Luisa's voluptuous body never accepted its grace or power to attract the love she craved, in spite of being in a long-term relationship.

Virgil Douglas, her longtime boyfriend, was the Harvard-trained federal prosecutor whom crime bosses and corrupt political officials feared. He came from old, family money with a black Haitian mother and Scottish father. His family had been among the power elites since the Harlem Renaissance. Tall, with a skinny frame, reddish hair and light-brown freckles scattered across the bridge of his nose, he possessed the earned reputation of tenacious litigator with a dogged attention to detail, which he often used against unsuspecting defendants, who thought they knew how to escape prosecution before their cases arrived in his office on Court Street in Brooklyn, New York. Since he was sworn in, five years ago, New York City tabloids headlined many of his most sensational trials, from teen trafficking and prostitution rings that operated out of the juvenile correction officer's unit to the federal judge who was convicted of stock market insider trading.

Allegra observed that Virgil, despite his professional accolades and powerful connections, lacked social skills. Virgil was the polar opposite of Luisa's warm and generous, bubbly personality. Luisa appreciated the doors he opened for her, introducing her to his friends and colleagues in the entrenched social circles in Martha's Vineyard and New York's Sag Harbor. Virgil and Luisa appeared in stylish photographs on the society pages of *New York Society* magazine at major charities galas, theater and opera openings. But when it came to spending time with Luisa's friends and enjoying her, he refused to squeeze an appearance into his hectic schedule. Whatever Virgil decided, from their weekend activities to the frequency of their sex life, Luisa was an agreeable puppet. Allegra believed that they made a charismatic couple, but that after two-and-one-half years of dating, Luisa had learned how to mask her sadness behind her signature television reporter plastic grin.

In contrast, Allegra's ability to tame men came early in her life. She observed the true nature of men; witnessing them in mourning, with broken hearts or enraged about disrespect or denial of opportunity. Allegra heard what they feared, desired and loved, and used those early lessons to connect with them—never against them. After her parents' divorce, Allegra was raised by a single father, and, surrounded by adoring male uncles and cousins, she was doted on and protected, and grew to trust, scold, exploit at will every unsuspecting man, who entered her lair. And men loved her for it, as pleasing Allegra became the priority of every man, no matter the length or depth of their relationship, because of how she made them feel in her presence. Allegra was intellectually brilliant, sensually beautiful and critically nonjudgmental, as she never shamed men into silence. She made them feel that they were wholly acceptable, primarily because Allegra accepted herself. Luisa admired Allegra for this, but she was not there yet, and she doubted if she would ever be, confiding "maybe it's because my father left us...I don't know...but I haven't gotten to the place where my relationships with men turn out like yours; and men whom I attract, start off being nice, then turn into the ghost of my father."

Bernadine's, the glamorous restaurant specializing in Cajun cuisine, was the new after-work hangout, which attracted Wall Street professionals, attractive men who dangled their affluence in exchange for sexual treats before legions of women, or as Allegra was known to say—*wasted pussies*—who were desperate to participate in their own manipulation as pawns. During Sunday girlfriend brunches at Luisa's, Allegra instructed her girlfriends on how to unleash the power of their pussies. But they were horrified. They were offended by the topic of conversation, exclaiming a thousand times, "Oh my!" or "I just couldn't" or "that's not how I was raised." Until one day, Allegra challenged them, "When was the last time you even touched your pussies?" The collective group, looking like they had stepped out of a church mural of virginal nuns, fell silent. The four ladies could not raise their eyes from Luisa's hardwood floors. "Do you mean to tell me that ya'll…" Allegra began.

The indignant one, Khadijah, interrupted with her shrill-sounding voice, "Stop using foul words for our body parts; you cuss too much anyway."

One woman, with tinted eyeglasses, supported Khadijah's bullshit. "Dat's right. Da word is vagina." Allegra, aided by her fifth mimosa, laughed until tears fell like raindrops. When she finally gained her composure, she counseled, "My dear, sweet sorors, your pus-say is only a vagina when it doesn't entertain a dick, on a regular basis, and your gynecologists don't count! And Lawd knows, y'all ain't seen dick in so long that you believe that your ed-u-ca-shuns and your boring-ass careers actually can have a man speaking in tongues!? Oh yeah, I can see the brothers now: "Man, every time I read her resume, my dick gets hard.""

Luisa hid behind the palms of her hands as Allegra trampled on her bourgeois chastity. Luisa explained, trying not to sound defensive about the lack of passion in her relationship with Virgil, "Allegra, he's practical, intellectual and budget-oriented. That doesn't make him uninteresting."

"Are you fuckin' your accountant or your boyfriend?"

"Virgil just doesn't like to squander his money, spending it on nonsense. And when you look at the economic times that we live in, Virgil does have a point."

"Do you think that you're actually making sense, Luisa?"

Silence was Luisa's only answer, especially when their dates became intellectual discourses on constitutional law as opposed to expressions of affection and verbal foreplay. In recent months, Luisa had become so love-starved that she had to physically force herself on Virgil. And though Virgil enjoyed their sterile, infrequent sex life, Luisa felt an empty craving for a man who felt passionately toward her, as opposed to Virgil, who considered her only as an afterthought and gorgeous arm-candy.

Luisa had heard a toned-down version of Allegra's spiel before, and so she knew what was coming next. "And another thing, Khadijah, if your pus-say was handling its business, you wouldn't be hounding my cousin Max; it would be the other way around. Trust me on that one!" Luisa led Allegra's tipsy ass out of the dining room, into the guest bedroom, and made her dear friend sleep off the champagne, before she suffered a serious beat down with a Bible. But Luisa could not blame Allegra's wisdom on the mimosa; the alcohol only fueled how soon she launched into her tirade. Allegra lived as she believed.

When it was clear that Virgil was going to acknowledge Luisa's thirty-third birthday with a jive-ass, three-dollar musical birthday card, after all of the home-cooked meals, massages and blow jobs she had doled out, Allegra came up with an idea to salvage what was left of her friend's self-esteem.

"Pack your bikini and stilettos, Luisa. I'm taking you to South Beach for your birthday. We're checking into the Canyon Ranch so we both can get a weekend of well-deserved pampering," Allegra announced during a pre-birthday girlfriend's brunch with Luisa and Khadijah at Serafina's, which was to be followed by a performance of *Fela* on Broadway.

"It's way too hot right now in Miami, Luisa," Khadijah interjected, even though Allegra had not invited her. Khadijah was really Luisa's friend, and as far as Allegra was concerned, she was dead weight; a walking rain cloud. Whatever the topic of conversation, Khadijah managed to turn it into doom and gloom. Always wearing one head wrap or another, Khadijah believed the more

African styled garb she wore and the muskier she smelled, the more authentic a black woman she was. In Allegra's view, the more tightly Khadijah wore her wraps, the more she stifled any potential personality she may have had lurking in her soul. And the more Khadijah prayed, tithed and fasted, the more Allegra was stumped as to why the girl never expressed a dewdrop of joy, especially when it came to Luisa. Anytime Luisa experienced any kind of success, Khadijah turned hostile. However, when Luisa got her heart broken or experienced life's hardest obstacles, Khadijah was flying high.

Blinded by loyalty and love, Luisa believed that relationships were meant to last a lifetime, even if she was the only one rowing the boat. Allegra, being the polar opposite, believed that a relationship lasts as long as it lasts, and should never require urging or force. After Khadijah's legal entanglement with Allegra's cousin, Allegra decided that she would only allow herself to be around Khadijah in short spurts, especially when she noticed that migraine headaches followed soon after.

Khadijah continued blabbering, "Plus, ain't nobody got no money to go to South Beach now with people losing their jobs, losing their homes. And there ain't nothing to do down there anyway; nothing but a bunch of beaches, bars and Cubans, and who wants to deal with all of that? And there's no culture, no museums or art galleries to think of."

"Have you ever been to Miami, Khadijah?" Allegra asked sharply. "Or even out of this state? And New Jersey or Connecticut don't count!"

Khadijah paused, then answered, "No, but this lady I used to work with had a cousin who lived there. The only thing she talked about was all of the shooting that happened to tourists. And don't rent a car, 'cause gang members will follow you from the airport and shoot you dead."

Steam silently pulsated out of Allegra's ears. Because she did not want to cause a scene right there in Serafina's, in the midst of a crowd of innocent theatergoers, Allegra glared at Khadijah with a "nobody-invited-you-anywhere-in-the-first-place" look and punctuated her response with tight lips, abruptly silencing Khadijah in mid-sentence. Because of her infamous history with Allegra, Khadijah should have been happy to just be sitting at their table, as she had zero social capital to offer her opinion about anything.

Allegra then turned, placing her hand on Luisa's forearm, "Luisa, I already bought our airline tickets, and made spa and hotel reservations. Our flight leaves at eight a.m. from LaGuardia. Now. Are you coming or what?"

Luisa nodded affirmatively. Khadijah sucked her teeth.

Over the weekend, Allegra held Luisa's BlackBerry hostage, as she was forbidden to accept any communication from Virgil, who insisted on summoning her to tend to his needs. "If he were a real man, Luisa, he'd be proud to take an interest in your life, and treat you like the queen that you are. But you know what, until you accept your own self-worth, you're going to continue accepting his sorry bullshit.

When Luisa met Virgil, she thought that her history with selfish men was changing for the better. Luisa deeply needed a change for the better from the soap opera her love life had become. She no longer wanted to watch Allegra listen patiently as she swooned over what little shreds of attention her fly-by-night man would dole out. And then Allegra repeatedly would tell her that she deserved more. Allegra would probe, wanting to know more about the men in Luisa's life: occupations, where they lived, any sort of history. Luisa would deflect the conversation, giving the appearance of defending the indefensible. Allegra never understood why Luisa refused to claim her rightful place in the world.

Secretly, Luisa feared having the relationship she knew she deserved, and, Luisa would hang on to Virgil Douglas, the man with the proper societal credentials and family connections until something better came along. Without believing that she deserved a mutually satisfying relationship, Luisa, in her attempt to prove her worth to a man that she just met would pamper, listen and solve their endless financial problems and allow herself to be fucked, without ever having the benefit of being on the receiving end. Her relationships with men would never include being escorted out on a legitimate date. Instead, Luisa allowed them to watch a bootleg version of some ghetto flick on her brand-new sofa, with her hand down their pants holding their shriveled dicks.

When it came to a man's bullshit, Allegra witnessed enough troubled relationships of women in her family and around her Clinton Hill neighborhood to last her infinite lifetimes. Like many children her age, Allegra had developed a sense of fairness. She was frequently saddened when the women she loved accepted the short end of a relationship. Adult women would dissolve into puddles of defeat at the hands of the men they believed to love. Then these women would seek the consolation of Allegra, or anyone who would listen to the details of their latest heartbreak. Allegra could not fathom why women tolerated the low-down behaviors of serial, no-name, bitch-ass, trifling, cheap lovers, who revealed who they were soon after meeting them. With each insult, these men grew worse, seeing that no standards were required of them, and that the woman was willing to serve their desires without demanding the same in return. Allegra would be almost invisible, sitting at the kitchen table, listening to adult women, who came together to vent and then console one another. Each gathering would end with the promise, "Y'all are right. I don't need no man. I can do better by myself." The older woman making that declaration would be strong in the company of her sister-friends, until the next time.

There is something about mother-daughter relationships; either the mother imparts empowering, healthy lessons to her daughter on how to deal with men, or the girl-child may be left to negotiate the world of men on her own. Allegra never lost her virginity; nor was it stolen. At age eighteen, she seduced her college track coach in the boys' shower before the homeroom bell. Her coach became the sexual slave of a nymph, book worm. And Allegra never had to run laps around the track again.

Allegra's mother, Vonetta Adams, worshipped the ground any man walked on. The beautiful, statuesque Vonetta spent her life in a perpetual search for the next big catch. Growing up in Thomasville, Georgia, Vonetta dreaded the one-horse country town. Nothing worthwhile ever happened in Thomasville; instead, after years of porch-sitting and mind-numbing traditions, Thomasville happened to you. Vonetta knew from television that there was a world out there waiting for her, and that if she didn't escape her birthplace, she would shrivel up and die from boredom. Thomasville men were good enough for making out in the back seats of rundown cars, but none had the ambition that would sate Vonetta's longing.

Vonetta decided that she would be damned if she would marry some man who wanted her to drop a truckload of babies and be piss poor her entire life. The gods were listening and word got out that a neighbor's nephew, who had recently graduated from the Naval Academy, had just arrived for a visit before his first deployment on the USS Gettysburg. Nine months later, Allegra was born to Vonetta and Petty Officer First Class Calvin Adams. For the next twenty years, the married couple fought and blamed one another for denying their life dreams. Vonetta was happy to be rid of Thomasville, but dreaded being with Calvin. Calvin loved his daughter Allegra, but despised being burdened with a new family which appeared after a night of passionate lovemaking in the back seat of the old Monte Carlo he had borrowed. Determined to find happiness anywhere she could find it, Vonetta launched her search for the next big catch, and began having a string of affairs with married naval officers.

Allegra despised her mother for the embarrassment she brought to her family. As a young girl, Allegra protected her mother by lying to the angry wives of those married naval officers, who often came looking for Vonetta. "Heifer, where is your hoeish mammy?"

"Stop talking about my momma like that!" Allegra replied defensively, knowing Vonetta was hiding in a closet, leaving her young daughter to fight a grown woman's battle. The angry wife would haul off and backhand Allegra across her tiny, tear-stained face.

"Now where is she, I said?! Look at-cha; you'll probably grow up to be no good just like that bitch."

"My momma ain't here!" Allegra would scream.

"Well, you tell her to stay away from my husband, you hear me, gal?"

"Yes, ma'am," little Allegra would say, with tears flowing.

Upon seeing Allegra take the retaliation for her affairs, Vonetta would remark, "Go dry your eyes, Allegra!" before driving off into the night and returning after midnight with the taint of alcohol and good times on her breath.

Following each episode, Allegra shielded her ears with her hands while trying to block out her parents' torrential fights. Furniture was broken; a pistol was waved; and profanity-laced threats continued throughout the night, often with the military police arriving to intervene. Vonetta's torrid affairs continued long after Allegra entered high school and until Calvin accepted permanent deployment aboard USNS Bowditch, which was one of the Navy's few ships without a home port.

On the last Friday before her high school graduation, Allegra skipped and ran home, anxious to show her father her cap and gown. But beloved Calvin Adams was gone; and he was gone for good. Vonetta again advised, "Go dry your eyes, Allegra," before making her announcement. "Now you know Simon, your Aunt Rachael's former husband. Well, we're going to be together. We're going to be a family. Go hug Mr. Simon. He's your new dad."

Allegra prayed that her parents would reconcile in spite of the violence she had witnessed. She continued to pray as her mother's parade of lovers continued to frequent the house. And she would be introduced to new Mister so-and-so, to her chagrin, because in Vonetta's absence, her lovers would frequently focus their attention on Allegra.

"Give me kiss before your momma gets back, little girl?"

"Let me teach you how to treat a man, little girl."

"Those are some pretty little panties, little girl."

"Give me a hug; let me make you feel good, little girl."

Allegra internalized the transgressions of predatory and clueless adults, observing how they would behave toward children, not caring how their adult sexual games would be a series of life lessons for the young girl whom they claimed they loved.

It took three and one-half martinis, a full stomach of marinated grilled breast of chicken, pineapple, cantaloupes, oranges and mangos tossed with a guava mojo over field greens, and a warm, full moon over Miami Beach, for Luisa to find herself on an arm-in-arm night stroll with Delroy, an architect at a local, commercial real estate development firm. While Allegra dozed during the flight to Miami, Delroy, who sat on the aisle seat across from Luisa, chatted her up, until they parted with his business card in her hand at the baggage claim carousel.

"Nothing wrong with calling the man; you didn't give him a way to contact you," Allegra declared, urging Luisa to get her flirt on, and to put all memory of Virgil on ice for the weekend. "I'm not saying you have to fuck 'em, necessarily, but it's nobody's business if you do."

On the morning of her birthday, and after receiving a cactus from Virgil, Luisa nervously dialed Delroy's telephone number. Delroy answered on the first ring, with Caribbean music playing in the background, "Delroy Alleyne speaking."

"Hello, Delroy; it's Luisa Hamilton. We met on the plane yest…"

Delroy's dimpled smile flowed through the telephone before he spoke his first word. "There's no need, Luisa, to introduce yourself. How can I forget you? I'm so happy that you called," Delroy said with a Jamaican accent. Luisa grinned sheepishly, feeling warm inside. "I just returned home, ya know. Had to take my mom to the airport for her flight home to Jamaica. So now I'm here cookin' and cleanin'. Ya know, tidying up me house. Get things back to normal, as they say."

"This is your home telephone number?" Luisa asked, remembering that it was three months before Virgil relinquished his precious home telephone number, citing issues with a security clearance.

"Yes, this is my home; but I want to make sure you have my cell number handy. Happy Birthday, Luisa. Today is your special day. What plans do you have to celebrate?" Eager to immediately see Luisa, Delroy was happy to learn that other than a day of pampering, she had arranged no special evening plans to celebrate.

"You must allow me to create a celebration for you this evening," Delroy said, with serious intent. "There is no way I would allow a woman as beautiful as you to spend another hour in Miami, without the proper festivities. Please honor me with that."

"What about your cooking and cleaning and tidying up?" Luisa teased, adding her fake West Indian accent.

"I would rather live in squalor if I could see you."

"Maybe I should run back up to the hotel room and call Virgil, to check in. Let him know that I'm okay," Luisa shared aloud, arriving in the hotel lobby to meet Delroy at the pre-arranged time.

"If you get near that phone or anything with a dial tone, I swear, I'll break your fingers," Allegra snapped, remembering that she had locked their BlackBerries in the hotel room safe. "Just meet the man, dammit. Enjoy yourself, and let him celebrate you."

Delroy strode across the hotel terrace like a king entering his coronation, wearing a champagne-colored, tunic-length, button-down shirt and matching drawstring pants. Chocolate brown, with a warm smile behind his large brown eyes, he moved with an easy Caribbean stroll, as if the sway of reggae music moved through his soul. When Delroy's eyes laid eyes on Luisa, his left knee buckled, as he struggled to regain his composure. Reminding him of a Spanish porcelain doll, Luisa was even more angelic than when he'd first met her on the airplane. She had spent the afternoon with a manicure and pedicure deep oil treatment, followed by shining her skin with Allegra's birthday gift, Jane Carter Solution's Nourish and Shine. Luisa's silky, black hair purred with the Curl Defining Crème. Her lips shimmered with MAC's Lipglass casting the highlights from her strapless, floral tulip dress which she wore with turquoise Louboutin heels.

"Allegra, you are welcome to join us," Delroy generously offered, knowing he preferred to be alone with Luisa.

"Um, no thanks. I've never been a third wheel. I'll be fine. You two enjoy," Allegra replied, before scurrying off for her second deep tissue massage on the beach, executed with erotic precision by the brother with muscular hands and knowing eyes.

Nervous, Luisa called to Allegra, "If you need me, we'll be at the restaurant on the roof."

"Yes, if you need to make a police report," Delroy joked. "The restaurant is called Imagine. I was the chief architect on the project." Allegra rolled her eyes at an embarrassed Luisa, and finger-waved her goodbye. Luisa, now thirty-three years old, felt like the virginal maiden she was not. Being in Delroy's company, she found herself relaxing in his protective aura. Delroy did not insist on ordering her dinner, challenging her ideas or diminishing her dreams. He was eager to share the details of his life with her, with a focus on what he thought important: family, spirit, community.

"I wasn't always this way. I'm an ongoing project," Delroy said, signing for their dinner bill, and pondering how he could extend the evening with Luisa. Later, standing on the desolate boardwalk, admiring the star-lit, dark sky, Delroy angled his elbow, inviting Luisa to drape her arm over his and saunter out onto the beach with him. "It took one bankruptcy, two divorces, three adult children and a year of just being alone for me to regain my sea legs."

"I think that's what I'm lacking, solitude. My job, my life, is all about what's on the outside. What's hot; what's not. Sometimes I would love to shut out the world, for a year, like you did." Two middle-aged joggers enjoying an evening run on the beach passed Delroy and Luisa, as they descended down the wooden staircase onto the warm sand. "Wait," Delroy said. "Let me help you unbuckle your shoes. So you can enjoy the beach; the feel of the sand. You don't want to soil your shoes." Luisa froze. Delroy noticed. The warm, salty breeze fluttered through her hair. Delroy extended his hand, waited for her to slowly accept his invitation. Thinking that she was behaving like a silly girl, Luisa grabbed Delroy's hand, balancing herself while unhooking her shoes, one at a time. When Luisa had removed both shoes and was able to stand on her own, Delroy continued to maintain his grasp. Luisa tightened, and then melted into the fleshiness of his hand; a sizzle traveled the length of her spine, causing her to swallow. Still wanting to appear nonchalant, Luisa admired the incoming waves and the cloud silhouette crossing the face of the crescent moon.

"This is the most peaceful part of Miami, where I come to relax. As a young boy, growing up in Jamaica, me and my *brudders* spent so much time in the water, we should have grown gills."

Luisa laughed. "Are you sure you didn't?" Delroy smiled.

"In New York, it's not a real beach unless there are cigarette butts, beer cans, broken glass and the occasional dead body or two," Luisa continued.

Delroy raised his eyebrows, "Are you serious? How can people defile the earth like that?"

"You'd be surprised."

Delroy looked at Luisa fondly, inhaled the night air, and shouted over the crashing waves, "Allow me to take your photo! So I can always have memories of you," Delroy said.

"So I can end up on your Facebook wall?" Luisa replied, with a smile.

"Facebook is ruled by Satan. You won't catch me near that devil incarnate," Delroy joked.

"You mean you don't want to share your second-by-second thoughts with the world?"

"No, my angel, only with you," Delroy said gently, caressing her hand. "Just a few photos on your special day. I'll email you copies. Promise."

Luisa's eyes darted from the ocean, the desolate beach and back into Delroy's solemn eyes, then answered, "Where do you want me to stand?" Delroy smiled.

"You're perfect where you are. Just relax," Delroy said. The warm breeze blew through Luisa's hair and roused the ruffles on her feminine dress. Delroy peered through the lens and made sure that the flash was ready. "Okay, smile, Luisa. Relax."

Luisa allowed a half-grin, appearing as if she was posing for a Girl Scout photo. "Luisa, pretend you are the August cover girl for *Vogue* magazine, the Caribbean edition. You hear the melodies of Beres Hammond making love to your ears, causing your body to dance; that's it. Close your eyes, Luisa and move with the melody." Luisa had closed her eyes, but in her head, she was listening to Marc Anthony, not Beres Hammond, moving with a slow cha-cha-cha and a little samba. "Perfect, Luisa!" Delroy shouted. "Just a few more—some close ups. Perfect. Omigod, that was so sexy. Give Delroy your sweet sexy smile. Let's do that one again. I think you blinked." Luisa flaunted her hair, gazing over the right side of the camera, puckering her lips. "Move your feet about six inches apart. Okay, now just lean toward the camera and smile. Purr-fect, Luisa!" Delroy exclaimed, scrolling through the photos on his view-finder.

"I wanna see, too," Luisa said, skipping toward Delroy, to see the photos.

"These are beautiful. See how the flash makes it seem as though it's daylight, and see there in the background? There's an amazing silhouette."

"Not bad. I rarely like photos of myself."

"I don't know why. You're the perfect model. Happy Birthday, Luisa Hamilton!" His announcement was quickly gobbled up by the sound of the waves. "To the stars, the moon, the sun, the heavens above and to all of the gods of the universe, I pronounce that this is the moment that the angel Luisa Hamilton emerged from the heavens and blessed us with her presence."

Luisa wanted to throw her arms around Delroy and tongue-kiss him with wicked abandon. She did not remember the last time Virgil had complimented her with such warmth, tenderness and humor. *What would it matter*, Luisa thought, *to have sex with Delroy right here?* The night joggers had long since disappeared. Delroy hummed a Jamaican tune about pretty women breaking his heart, lifting her arms and twirling her like a ballerina. As Luisa swiveled to face him, a sneaky wave flooded them both to their knees. Luisa shrieked and ran along the beach, with Delroy following close behind her, filling the night with raucous laughter. When Delroy caught up with Luisa, grabbing her at her waist, he drew her close to him, feeling her body tighten with apprehension.

"Don't be afraid, Luisa," Delroy said, trying to calm her trembling, stroking the side of her arms. Luisa took Delroy's handsome face into her gaze, and bit her lower lip. Delroy tilted his head, appreciating this maiden. Luisa knew that she wanted him to kiss her, but she was haunted by her loyalty to Virgil, whose cactus sat on her dresser in the hotel room. Luisa's sadness over Virgil's refusal to appreciate her with affection made her relax toward the warmth of Delroy.

Love the one you're with, Luisa thought, knowing that her thighs were white hot with a warm flash pulsating in her pussy. Delroy pulled her hips forward to meet his, while massaging her lower back and stepping closer, kissing her passionately. Luisa's lips parted, then relaxed, responding, allowing Delroy to thrust his thick tongue deep inside her mouth. Delroy's fingers glided down inbetween her legs, tenderly massaging her swollen pussy. Luisa exhaled, her eyelids slightly parted, as she stared over Delroy's shoulder. Delroy guided her hand down, untying the drawstring on his pants, urging her to rub his pulsing cock. Still kissing, Delroy lowered Luisa to the glowing sand, stretching her out comfortably on the wet sand. Luisa rested on her elbows, waiting for Delroy to remove his pants, unveiling his muscular athletic legs.

"Spread your legs," Delroy said, lying on top of her. Kissing her, his hips began their rhythmical dance. "Let me see you." Luisa wanted Delroy, needed Delroy. For her, his appearance in her life, on her birthday was what she desperately needed to feel whole again. Yet Luisa froze, grasping her surroundings, her emotions, and ignoring the spasms between her thighs.

"Wait," Luisa said.

"What?" Delroy replied, his mouth parting in surprise.

"I can't do this. With you." Delroy fell back on his heels, lowering his head, contemplating that this evening of passion would be aborted by Luisa. Tightening his lips, he looked around at the beach, listened to the incoming waves, and then back at Luisa.

"Who do you love?" Delroy asked.

"What do you mean?" Luisa asked dejectedly.

"Simple question, Luisa. Who do you love?"

Luisa paused, soul searching, then answered, "Virgil."

"He's here with you in Miami Beach?" Delroy began, his eyelids dropping sadly.

"No," Luisa said quietly. "He's back in New York. Working, he said."

"No, he's here with you. He's right here in your heart," said Delroy, placing her hand on her left breast.

Luisa winced and then nodded. She felt like a schoolgirl who enjoyed heavy petting with boys she had no intention of ever fucking. Delroy rose, stepping into, and then retying his drawstring pants. Reaching for Luisa's hand, helping her to stand, Delroy said, "Come, birthday girl. It's time to go." And he dusted sand off the back of her dress.

Luisa never saw Delroy again, and later phoned Virgil, apologizing for abandoning him for the weekend.

5

As the sun set, Teofilo proudly shared the history of Rio de Janeiro with Allegra. For generations, his family had been wealthy diamond merchants from the exclusive Leblon district. With his bodyguards keeping a discreet distance, Allegra and Teofilo strolled on Av. Vieria Souto along Ipanema Beach toward Dois Irmãos, the two mountains at the western end of the city. Semi-nude Brazilian women gathered up their belongings after a day under the hot sun. Men wearing tiny *sungas* (Speedos) played beach volleyball, pausing to acknowledge Teofilo. Lovers playfully squealed on a rainbow-colored beach towel. The woman, wearing only a bikini bottom, ran away from her boyfriend into the crashing waves.

"Come! I have a surprise for you, Allegra!" Teofilo said, suddenly grabbing her hand, leading her to an elegant-looking cabana on the beach. One of the bodyguards rushed over to hold open the door, and gestured for Allegra to enter. Inside, on a long banquet table, was a generous spread of tropical fruits, cheeses and a variety of champagne and beverages. In the rear of the cabana, an assortment of colorful thongs, bikinis and cover-ups were hung on wooden hangers, arranged like the swim and travel section of a department store.

"*Senhorita*, you cannot leave Rio without allowing the ocean to pleasure you. I hope you like?"

Allegra, wearing a burnt orange halter dress and high heels, remembered that she had not felt the ocean since the previous summer, when she and Luisa had played hooky and driven to the beach in Sandy Hook, New Jersey. Allegra was long overdue for a refreshing dip.

Teofilo changed into his white Speedo in the adjoining cabana and waited for Allegra as she changed into a lime green thong and bikini top. When she stepped outside of the cabana, Teofilo removed his dark sunglasses and let his eyes bulge out of his head, as a bright smile spread across his face. His bodyguards tried to conceal their delight, furtively glancing from Allegra to the sun-bleached sand.

Allegra played along the beach, examining shells in the water, feeling the gentle tug of the undertow. The twilight quickly cast her as a bronze sun goddess. Teofilo squatted in the sand, enjoying the view of Allegra's playfulness. "Tall and tan and young and lovely, the girl from Harlem goes walking..." Allegra sang. Teofilo chuckled at her parody, while fantasizing about her curvy legs around his waist.

"*Bela*, Allegra!" Teofilo said tenderly, applauding.

"*Bela*, Allegra!" she mocked, laughing and poking him in his stomach, before turning to run, splashing into the clear blue-green water, with the governor in hot pursuit. Allegra adjusted her bikini top, took a quick dunk under the water, and came back up, flipping her drenched locs out of her eyes, the warm water pouring down her body. The ocean water tasted slightly salty, but was warm and inviting. Allegra swam out fifty feet, combining the freestyle with the breast stroke, loving the gentle waves and peacefulness of ocean swimming, with the skyline of Ipanema becoming distant in the background.

Coming up for air, Allegra treaded water and waved at Teofilo, who stood knee deep at the water's edge, surrounded by his bodyguards, who were urging him to join her. Tossing his sunglasses to one of his bodyguards, Teofilo dived in and quickly swam to Allegra, where she greeted him with a warm smile and sensuous French kiss, wrapping her legs around his waist, as he peppered her neck with playful kisses. Allegra squealed with delight. While Allegra and Teofilo hugged and kissed each other, a medium-sized wave lifted them, plunging them underwater, and then back to the surface, where they gasped for air.

"Come, Governor," Allegra advised, without waiting for a reply and swimming for shore. Teofilo licked his bottom lip, tucked his dick back into his Speedos and followed her.

"Come, Allegra! I have more to show you," Teofilo said, when they both reached the shore. He was holding up an oversized beach towel for her. Allowing Teofilo to wrap her in the towel, she murmured, "That was just what I needed," taking his hand and using her tongue to trace his palm and then suck his thumb.

"Ugh, I so sorry. Um, my hands are so calloused. So ugly."

"They're beautiful," Allegra said tenderly, looking into Teofilo's eyes, as he slowly dried her with the beach towel.

"My father insisted that I understood the importance of hard work, but he left me with ugly hands," Teofilo said, turning the palms of his hands upwards in front of Allegra, pointing out the calluses on his long, dark fingers. "You see, I worked many years building new homes for the people who were living in the *favelas*."

"The *favelas*. Those slums that are perched on the hills overlooking Rio?"

"Yes. My grandparents lived in those *favelas*. Those are my people," Teofilo said quietly.

Allegra listened, patiently waiting for him to gather his words.

"Of course, there's so much more work to be done. It took generations to create the *favelas*, but I'm working very hard for it not to take generations to change. The elite would prefer that the poor rot and live miserable lives. But when I was elected, I decided that I would try to help my people."

"This life you have, Governor..."

"*Por favor*, please call me Teo." Teofilo stared intently into Allegra's calm eyes, as a seagull flew above in search of food.

"As you wish, um... Teo," she replied, tossing her damp locs around her shoulders. "This life you have, is it what you have been given or what you have chosen?"

Drivers, recognizing the smitten governor, honked their horns attempting to get his attention. Sun worshippers raised their heads from the beach blankets, trying to find out the source of the commotion. The governor's bodyguards prevented autograph seekers from getting within twenty feet of Allegra and Teofilo as they re-entered the cabana to change back into their street clothes. They sipped on *caipirinhas* and munched on fruit and cheese before resuming their stroll. Teofilo and Allegra ignored the paparazzi who stalked them from across the street, as they indulged in their intense flirtation along the Ipanema Beach boardwalk.

"No one has ever asked that of me," Teofilo replied. "Nor have I asked that of myself."

"And your answer, Teo?" For the first time that afternoon, Teofilo hid his eyes, as he searched his soul for his answer.

"Allegra, my life is not my own. I live in a bubble day and night. People love me not for who I am, but what I can do for them. And I often dream of leaving."

"Leaving office?"

"Leaving Rio, at least for a time. To live in a place where no one knows me, where I'm just Teo. My life is so confusing. My wife and I have been estranged for years and now I'm being urged to run for reelection...to continue with a life I'm not sure I ever wanted. I still want to help my people, but I believe I now have enough clout to do it, without living in this bubble."

"Never live with regret, Teo," Allegra said.

"Have you, Allegra? Have you lived with regret?"

Teofilo caught Allegra off guard with such a direct question. But now, on this beautiful beach, walking hand in hand with this fine, chocolate Brazilian man, Allegra lowered her guard and decided to share. "Regret, for me is the most frightening word in the dictionary. In Harlem, I am surrounded by people who have had their spirits broken and who are drowning in lives of regret. That shall never be Allegra Adams. Every desire that I have, I will pursue. I will never say, 'I woulda coulda shoulda,' not as long as I have breath."

Reaching the heliport at the end of Ipanema Beach, Teofilo reached for Allegra's hand, squeezing it gently and kissing her palm, as she listened to Sabiá birds sing while flying overhead. "You are so lovely," Teofilo said, staring at her solemnly, and then lifting her inside of the waiting S-70 Black Hawk helicopter. He dismissed the bodyguards for the evening. "You're so different. I don't know any women like you...with your beauty and, and..."

"And what?"

"There's a knowing way, a freedom about you as if you have a direct line to the gods. Here you are. Not in your country. Far from America, and it's as if Brazil is where you should be. But I think you would be comfortable anywhere. Am I correct?"

Allegra nodded, glancing out the window of the helicopter as the rotor blades started whirring. "A cherished life blessing is to own the earth underneath my feet, no matter where that might be and where adventures in my life might take me."

"Allegra," Teofilo murmured, glancing out of the window at

the breathtaking horizon, then back at her, rolling his eyes over her. The whirring sound of the helicopter provided their cocoon.

"Hmmm?"

"I just wanted to speak the name of the woman who has brought me such peace."

"Peace must be the destination for all of us, Teo, but it's an inside job," Allegra whispered. Teofilo moaned as Allegra smiled, unzipping his pants, gently rubbing his curled, smooth cock. Rolling toward her, he slipped his hand under her dress and inside her black thong panties, while nuzzling his face in between her plump breasts, untying her halter top and ravishing her nipples. When her clit was properly wet, Allegra mounted Teofilo's lap, as the helicopter angled a sharp turn. She gripped her brown thighs around his waist. Quickly, the governor pushed his erect cock inside her, gently at first, then thrusting deeper. Allegra gripped Teofilo's head, whispering, "Fuck me! Fuck me" in his ear. A thin film of sweat appeared on his forehead; his eyes rolled back in his head. Their hips rocked furiously as the aerial tour swept over the Maracaná Stadium, Copacabana beach, Sugar Loaf Mountain and finally the Christ the Redeemer Statue crowning Corcovado Mountain, just as Allegra and Teofilo climaxed, with him trembling and then exploding inside her.

"*O, meu deus! O, meu deus!*" Teofilo cried. Allegra gasped, trying to catch her breath, brushing her locs out of her eyes, as the helicopter landed on the helipad, sounding as though the universe was being torn asunder.

Teofilo and Allegra held one another until the blades of the helicopter were silent. "Allegra," Teofilo simply said, as they stumbled breathlessly out of the helicopter, giggling like teenage lovers. Another set of muscular bodyguards appeared, as the two lovers walked past the last trickle of tourists boarding the Estrada de

Ferro Corcovado train to return down the twenty-four-hundred-foot mountain.

"*O governador, amável vê-lo*! (Governor! Nice to see you, sir!),*" the aging security guard called out, while leaning out of the window of his blue wooden guardhouse. Locals recognizing Teofilo ran to him, greeting him. Though polite, exchanging brief hugs and kissing infants, Teofilo was eager to be alone with Allegra. He continued to wave, lacing Allegra's arm under his, as they climbed inside a waiting black stretch limousine to transport them up the steep hill to the statue of *Cristo Redentor Corcovado* above. An evening fog was starting to roll in.

Teofilo explained, "Christ the Redeemer was named one of the Seven Wonders of the World! And you are the eighth, *meu amor* Allegra!"

"*Obrigada* (thank you)," Allegra softly replied, resting her head on his shoulder.

Once Teofilo and Allegra had reached the towering one hundred and fifty foot soapstone statute, she sat against the cool stone with her legs spread. Teofilo dropped his tour guide persona and glided to her; his wicked fingers gripped her bare, ample, sepia breasts under her halter top, sucking them like a hungry infant as they fucked against the base of the Christ the Redeemer statute, her knees cradling his torso as the sun set over Rio.

"I have another surprise for you, Allegra." Teofilo smiled.

"I'll bet you do," Allegra replied, giggling.

"Take my hand and follow me," Teofilo teased. Teofilo eagerly escorted Allegra down the steep steps and into the limousine. "To the *aeroporto*," Teofilo instructed the driver, as he poured champagne into their respective flutes.

"The airport? Where are we going?" Allegra asked, as the limousine sped down the winding, dark road away from Christ the

Redeemer, and then north on Linha Vermelha expressway, for the thirty-minute drive to the governor's private airstrip.

Settling into the eighteen-seat Gulfstream 550 aircraft, Teofilo said, "I'm going to take you to *Salvador de Bahia* otherwise known as the land of the drum."

"But do I need to change into something more formal?"

"You are perfect and beautiful as you are. But if you want to change, there are many styles of clothes waiting in the master suite of the airplane. I'm positive there is something that will fit you, if you would like. And by the time you're ready, we will be landing. But nothing fancy or formal; just be comfortable, Allegra."

Ninety minutes later, Teofilo and Allegra landed in Salvador de Bahia and were transported to Pelourinho, the historic center of Salvador, the capital of Bahia. Followed by four bodyguards, Teofilo and Allegra strolled, holding hands, along the cobblestone streets, lined with multicolored three-story buildings, tightly wedged between hundreds of small churches. The streets were jam-packed with people dining, drinking and dancing together or walking alone. Children, wearing soiled clothing, ran alongside Teofilo and Allegra begging them to buy necklaces and souvenirs. The couple generously purchased something from each child vendor, which attracted more excited child vendors and street children. The bodyguards, worried that the governor and Allegra would soon be trampled, whisked them off the main thorough-fare, into a brightly lit old church, and upstairs to a small balcony, with a French wrought iron balcony overlooking the chaos of bodies meandering through the large, open Praça Tereza Batista courtyard.

"Teofilo, why are all of these people on the street like this? It's Tuesday night," Allegra asked.

"Tuesday night is a festive time in Bahia, similar to your Fridays in America. And because this area is the headquarters for Olodum, the most famous Afro-Brazilian drumming band in the world, people from around the world come to hear their powerful drums. Listen," Teofilo urged, placing his index finger over his lips.

In the distance, an army of drums approached, marching down the cobblestone street toward where Teofilo and Allegra stood on their balcony next door to the Nossa Senhora do Rosário dos Pretos church. Allegra took out her BlackBerry to film the spectacle. A church staff member allowed a child vendor to climb the stairs to bring the couple two plastic cups of *caipirinhas*. The brown-haired young boy's jaw fell open when Teofilo placed one hundred *reais* in his hand. "*Muito Obrigado, Senhor!*" the young boy yelled over his tiny shoulders, scampering down the stairs to share his good fortune with his cohorts.

Allegra and Teofilo sipped their *caipirinhas* on the balcony while dancing to the drums of Olodum. Later that evening, Teofilo and Allegra's erotic gyrations weaved both salsa and samba on the Clubo do Tango dance floor. Matronly women, with freeze-dried sex lives, looked on in disgust and envy, and normally macho men suddenly questioned their manhood, while some joyful dancing couples exchanged bright smiles with Teofilo and Allegra. Spectators yearned to taste her energy, knowing all too well that just one episode would never quench their thirst, and they would be addicted forever. Once the spectators overcame being captivated by Teofilo and Allegra, they joined the sexy couple on the dance floor, mixing it up with the crowd, and taking turns dancing with everyone. Still, because of the sheer joy on their faces, it was difficult to take their eyes off of Allegra and Teofilo. Teofilo twirled Allegra, drawing her close to him, winding their bodies like a hypnotized cobra. Together their sensual salsa dancing caused a heightened adrenaline rush, resulting in a natural, euphoric high amongst the dancers. Spectators cheered, clapping their hands enthusiastically, while dancing with no one in particular, allowed the music to move them, and soothe their unrequited hearts. When the music ended, the partygoers applauded one another, happy that they had unleashed their pains, frustrations and renewal on the dance floor.

"You must live here in Rio, Allegra. I can provide a wonderful life for you here. My mansion in Lebron can be yours. There will be servants for you and a chauffeur. You would have nothing to be concerned about. I will take care of everything," Teofilo explained, as Allegra dozed in his arms on the flight back to Rio de Janeiro.

Teofilo became creative in repeating his offer. He would send flowers with an emotional pleading on the note card; Teofilo's pilot would blatantly state, "Senhor Branco, Ms. Adams must be the next First Lady, no?" Teo's chief of staff would suggest that Allegra would have a better life in Brazil; one of his bodyguards gave Allegra a thumbs-up, his way of urging her to seriously consider Teofilo's offer.

For Allegra, her time with Teofilo was an isolated moment in time. She had no intention of being a factor in his pending divorce or in the upcoming vicious fight of his political life. And Teofilo knew, if he was honest, that Allegra would never completely love him; that she would haunt his dreams for his entire his life.

Allegra chewed on an olive stem from her empty martini glass, as a baby cooed with his mother in the middle section of the plane, recalling repeating the reality of their affair to the deaf Teofilo.

"Life is a series of sensuous memories, none that need to last forever. And Teofilo will have no choice but to accept that. His life is in Brazil, and mine is in the Big Apple."

Time to move on to new possibilities, Allegra thought, standing in the galley, flirting with Marcelo, the pilot of the TAM Airlines jumbo aircraft, with her red silk lace panties stuffed in her leather carryon bag, secured under her seat.

6

The seat belt sign illuminated. "Ladies and gentlemen, the captain has turned on the 'fasten seat belt' sign. We are now crossing a zone of turbulence. Please return to your seats and keep your seat belts fastened. *Obrigado*. Thank you."

Allegra could feel the oncoming turbulence threatening the otherwise smooth flight home. Her mind returned to her playful task at hand, now that she found herself in rare, close proximity with the gorgeous, yet globe-trotting, Marcelo.

"When I saw you last, Allegra, we both had flights leaving at the same time. Remember?"

"Yes. I was headed to Rome. Would you keep this souvenir in the freezer for me? I don't want it to thaw."

"Sure," Marcelo said, tossing it into the small freezer behind him. "And I was returning to Paris," Marcelo added, pausing to admire Allegra's bronzed tan. "I never thought I would have a chance to know you or see you again, especially when Bianca said that you had left the airline."

"I'll bet Bianca was thrilled," Allegra said dryly.

"If anyone should leave the airline, it's Bianca. She never thinks about her job or helping the passengers. Her only thought is trapping a rich, powerful man into marriage."

"Still the same, huh?"

"Yes, Bianca will always be the same. So are you enjoying your work at your university?"

"Very much. I'm fortunate to study subjects that interest me, sexuality, psychology, DNA, etcetera, and from time to time, I can still come to visit with my friends here in Brazil. And make new ones." Allegra chuckled.

"It's wonderful to see you, Allegra. I never believe in coincidences. I guess we were meant to bump into each other. When I met you at my brother's restaurant, I must tell you I was impressed with your knowledge of our foods and gourmet preparation."

"My American friends love my Brazilian dinner parties. The richness of flavors, textures, colors and history of the foods are to die for. My most requested dish is the *Moqueca de Camarao* (shrimp stew). I thank your brother for sharing his recipe." Allegra smiled, resting her hand on her waist.

"My brother would have given you anything that you would have wished; as would I." Marcelo winked.

"Out of all of the flights we could have flown, we happened to be on the same flight. I was actually supposed to leave tomorrow. Yet here we are." Allegra smiled, now fingering his belt.

"Governor Branco appeared upset that you were leaving. He gave me a dirty look when I said hello."

"Teo…"

"Teo now? The governor must be a very close friend." Marcelo chuckled.

"Yes, he has become a new friend," Allegra replied.

As the ten-person flight crew busied itself assisting nervous passengers, the jumbo jet shuddered and slightly lurched, tossing Allegra into a welcoming Marcelo.

"So anyway, you were saying earlier? About your toes," Marcelo asked, grinning flirtatiously. Allegra waited to respond until a flight attendant prepared a rum and Coke and left the galley to serve a first class passenger. Coaxing Marcelo to lean over, Allegra whispered in his ear, "My toes curl when I'm aroused, especially when I'm not wearing panties. Like now."

"*Masturbação*? You...want...me to...you?" Marcelo asked in halting English.

Allegra smiled and nodded her head, like an obedient child, her auburn locs jiggling seductively. Marcelo knitted his eyebrows, his internal brain scrambled to solve his dilemma. Drawing the shutters close to the galley, Allegra solved his puzzlement by unzipping his pants and placing her delicate, but strong, hand inside to greet his now erect dick. Allegra was always the choreographer while male mortals were the willing dancers. Men never satisfied her horniness by allowing them to *do* anything to her.

Marcelo exhaled a gust of air as Allegra rhythmically recreated hand rhythms that had him dreaming of wild orgies before the coronation of King Momo at the Rio Carnaval. Only this carnal rapture was better, as Marcelo knew he had everything to lose. The first and second officers slept, satisfied from a five-course meal, as the jumbo jet auto-piloted its way high above international waters. If caught by one of those officers or a flight attendant, Marcelo would lose his career and his prestigious status in the class-oriented Brazilian society. Allegra purposely selected men who had everything to lose. Power. Wealth. Prestige. The greater the stakes, the more turned on she became, as she believed that life had no meaning unless she was fucking men who had the power to make significant change occur. Fully realized women do not fuck boys...even boys lurking in the body of a man.

Allegra reached maturity in male-dominated circles and had learned not to seek permission or make apologies for anything, including her sexual appetite. She distanced herself from women, no matter what their age, who deliberately cast their femininity to the side and who thought being a sexual martyr was appealing.

Allegra ignored the so-called professional career women who donned the masculine trappings of power but could not cross the bridge back to their own eroticism. Not Allegra. Her determined soul had decided on a different path, long before it was born into this world.

Allegra pointed toward the metal-framed door to the cockpit, with the boldly labeled sign: Flight Crew Only. Marcelo tried to thrust his aggressive tongue inside her mouth, but her index finger met his advance. She again pointed her finger toward the cockpit door, a well-named environment to be the stage to unveil one of her long-held fantasies.

Marcelo had to choose. Lose everything or satisfy his bursting carnal craving to meet the approval of this goddess standing before him. Allegra was the same goddess whom he had desired since first laying eyes on her in his brother's restaurant. Marcelo knew that Allegra was different. While other women threw themselves at him, begging to treat him like a god, he was drawn to Allegra's reserve. She treated him like the mere mortal that he knew he was.

Standing at the erotic fork in the road, Marcelo chose the latter and turned on his heels, bursting through the cockpit door, rousing his sleeping subordinates, pushing them out the metal cockpit door, while Allegra pursed her lips and leaned against the cool, steel wall of the galley, waiting for their passage. Rubbing sleep out of their eyes, the first and second officers wearily passed Allegra, doing a double-take once they realized what they thought was about to occur. Marcelo stood away from the narrow cockpit doorway with his right arm extended as if he were a maître d' at a five-star restaurant. Allegra stepped into the cockpit as if she was surveying a new Harlem condominium.

Despite the thunderous roar of the engines, the small area was eerily quiet. While gazing out of the cockpit window, searching for other jumbo jets in the night sky, Allegra leaned over the flashing electronic controls, admiring the intricate panel, while Marcelo admired her, overwhelmed with temptation. Allegra's warm eyes floated to him, as she hoisted her skirt and arched her ass in the air. Marcelo came to her, wrapping his arms around her body, swaying her in his lean arms, kissing and tonguing the side of her neck. Lowering the zipper on his pants, Marcelo heaved his throbbing dick deep inside her waiting anus.

"Ahhhh," Allegra gasped, exhaling. Marcelo rubbed her breasts from under her V-neck blouse, flicking his tongue along the side and back of her neck. Allegra gyrated her derriere in concert with his dick, as his thick tongue gently suckled inside her ear lobes; Marcelo huffed as if hooked onto a faulty ventilator. The electronic flight instrument system's blue, red and green lights indicated that there were one-and-one-half hours until landing at John F. Kennedy International Airport. Estimated time of arrival: 6:45 a.m. Flight position: north by northwest at five hundred-and-fifty air miles per hour.

With each increasing thrust of the plane's engine, Allegra angled her pussy so that Marcelo could compress his dick to the point of no return. Allegra gripped Marcelo's muscular arms sympathetically as he whimpered on the verge of delirium.

"Flight 782. Flight 782. This is JFK air traffic control. You are approved for initial approach. Copy?"

Allegra and Marcelo abruptly separated, turning their focus to the voice emanating from the console. "Flight 782. Initial approach. Copy?"

Marcelo, coming to his senses, hearing air traffic control, tapped his temple on the side of his head, and then summoned a burst of strength. When he had gathered his wits, Marcelo stepped over Allegra, jerking the microphone out of its holder. "Yes, this is Flight 782. Copy?"

"Everything in order, 782?"

"Everything is good. Perfecto. *É muito bela.* (She is very beautiful.)"

"Come again, 782?"

"Everything is okay. R-r-r-r-oger. Out," Marcelo replied, rolling his "r."

Marcelo ran his hand through his thick, kinky hair and stood, gazing out of the cockpit window, then collapsed next to Allegra, entwining himself around her, kissing her tenderly.

Marcelo then began, "I must…" Allegra reclined away from him on the side bench, stroking herself, distracting Marcelo from his need to return to manually fly the airplane. Resting one arm behind her head, like a Greek statute, Allegra used her other hand to stroke the inside of her pussy. Marcelo was mesmerized.

"*Senhorita*, I will help you," Marcelo said, as if he was trying to help a child lace her roller skates.

"No, *obrigada. No*, thank you. I know how to make my own toes curl," Allegra said softly, experiencing a quiet burst of an orgasm and curling her toes. "See?"

Later, after Allegra had returned to her seat and the flight had landed and was taxiing toward the international terminal, the purser made the final landing announcement thanking the passengers for flying TAM airlines. "*Senhorita* Adams, Captain Marcelo asked me to return this container to you," the purser said. Allegra thanked him, sliding it into her handbag.

After the airplane reached the terminal, the first class crew crowded the door of the airplane, saying their goodbyes to four hundred and twenty-six weary passengers.

"Our flight crew is staying at the airport Marriott but I can come into Manhattan to take you out for dinner. There is a great

Brazilian restaurant on West Forty-Sixth Street," Marcelo began, almost blocking Allegra's path to exit the plane. An airport concierge helped an elderly woman into her wheelchair, as other passengers dragged their luggage around Marcelo and Allegra to leave the plane.

"No, I'm going to be swamped playing catch-up, with piles of students' work waiting for me. And I need to get my lips around some biscuits, southern fried chicken, collard greens and sweet potato pie. But it was great finally connecting with you."

"Well, may I add my telephone numbers to your BlackBerry so that you can reach me before I fly back to Brazil tomorrow night?" Becoming more frantic, Marcelo tried desperately to coerce Allegra into going to dinner, scribbling his written telephone numbers, including his mother's, and the private number of air traffic control in Rio de Janeiro. But she would not have any of it.

"Marcelo, I don't want to mislead you. Unless it's in a cockpit, over international waters, we won't be seeing each other again. Everything has its place and so do we," Allegra patiently explained.

"Allegra, how can you be so heartless?" Marcelo asked, seeing a glimmer of hope as Allegra accepted a red rose he had stolen from one of the first-class dinner carts. She smiled, exiting the plane, as Marcelo whispered, struggling to find the right words, "Thank you for coming, *Senhorita*."

"No. Thank you, *Senhor*," Allegra said, strutting down the ramp. She tossed Marcelo's business card in the next trash receptacle after she cleared customs, along with the *Essence Magazine* article entitled, "Brazil! A Black Man's Paradise!"

Facebook Status Update:
October 4, 2011; 3:16pm
"Essence magazine doesn't know what the hell they're talking about!"

7

Allegra's spiked black boots clicked against the sidewalk, slick from a freakish ice storm, adjacent to the Department of Anthropology building on Waverly Place in New York City's Greenwich Village. Students and various faculty members nodded and murmured greetings in her direction. Others asked about the conference in Brazil. Since her return and her thesis being published in the *Modern Anthropology Journal*, Allegra had become a media darling. Yesterday, her appearance on *Charlie Rose* was finally aired, after being bumped by a PBS series on the brain. Allegra blogged: "Very much respect for Mr. Rose. When I told him that I preferred to answer my own questions, he laughed and declared me 'irresistibly charming.'"

"I TiVo'd the show. I probably have everything you said memorized," Thunder said, picking her up for a weekend excursion to Bear Mountain Friday afternoon. Allegra was reluctant to wear the matching orange and black motorcycle jackets which Thunder had purchased. He insisted that Allegra needed to take a break from working on her dissertation. Over the next month, Thunder often planned motorcycle day trips up to Bear Mountain; or if over a three-day holiday weekend, the two would motor up to the Catskills.

Earlier that summer, Thunder had purchased an elegant turn-of-the-century farmhouse, complete with a huge porch, wide plank floors and open floorplan kitchen. Though Thunder and Allegra fucked in every inch of the farmhouse, she got more kicks sexing in unique locations, such as at the radio station or on the back of his motorcycle. Allegra gave new meaning to Thunder, when she would spontaneously text him: *the mike is hot.* Their secret code meant that he needed to drop whatever he was doing, shove personnel out of the studio, and meet Allegra for an intimate rendezvous.

Squeezed tightly against Thunder, with her arms wrapped tightly around his wide, muscular back, Allegra was mesmerized by the vibration of the motorcycle's engine against her vagina, tickling her to the edge of an orgasm, then retreating.

"You're gonna strangle me," Thunder joked one afternoon, as he steered the motorcycle around a sweeping curve, with steep mountainous vistas serving as their backdrop.

"At least you'd die happy." Allegra laughed loudly over the percolating sound of the motor. After they had waved at a passing cyclist, paid the toll to cross the Hudson River Bridge, and were on an open, two-lane highway, Allegra reached around and unzipped Thunder's pants, removed his rod and began firmly stroking it.

"Woman, you're gonna make me run both of us off this road," Thunder joked, his hands gripping the handlebars, until his fingertips had turned pink.

Later that afternoon, Allegra and Thunder strolled hand in hand through the Village of Nyack on the west bank of the Hudson River, on their return trip, stopping in to have lunch at an outdoor cafe, next to an antique shop. "God, I'm hungry," Allegra said, looking over the cluttered menu hanging in the window. "What don't they serve here?"

"At least there are a lot of people inside. That must mean that the food is pretty good. If not and you don't like it, we can go somewhere else."

Entering the cafe, the aroma of fresh bread was a welcomed fragrance, which only encouraged Allegra's pangs of hunger to howl loudly. Red and white checkerboard tablecloths covered the round tables. Thunder pulled Allegra's chair out for her, gently releasing her kissed fingers when he was certain that she was comfortable.

The waiter greeted the couple with ice water and a basket of warm, fresh-baked rolls. "How you folks doing today? I'll give you a couple of minutes to decide," the cheerful waiter said.

"Oh no, I'm ready to order."

"Yes, we're ready to order now. She's hungry. You may want to bring another basket of rolls," Thunder said with a smile, watching Allegra devour the bread, after buttering each thick slice.

"Show me a woman who can eat and I'll show you a woman…" Thunder said, as Allegra kicked him on his shin under the table, causing Thunder to fake being injured, the two laughing together tenderly.

"I love this," Thunder said.

"Love what?" Allegra asked, dabbing the cloth napkin on the sides of her lips.

"I love being out of that crazy city with you. There's something different about you when we're out of the craziness that goes on back there. I'll bet you're just as beautiful when you're in Brazil. Man, I would have loved to be with you there."

Allegra paused, wondering how Thunder would fit into her Brazilian paradise. Other than local trips to upstate New York, Thunder was not a world traveler. "I don't feel comfortable with my feet leaving the ground on no airplane," he had often said.

"The stress level leaves me, as soon as we reach the New York Thruway. That's why I love to travel. Seems like life. A quality life exists only outside of moneymaking Manhattan. When I travel, I can feel when the plane has entered American air space. I can feel the tension in the airspace," Allegra said, with Thunder nodding in agreement, both sharing the loud silence of this quaint village. Thunder reached for Allegra's hand, and lifted it to his lips, kissing it tenderly, and then holding it until their pancakes, turkey bacon, scrambled eggs and cheese arrived on an overloaded brown platter. Allegra loved these moments with Thunder just as much as he did, until he attempted to escalate their relationship.

"So when you were down in Rio, did you date anybody? See anyone?" Thunder meekly asked. Allegra's stomach leapt. Why did he want to get into this? He knows damned well he can't handle the truth. Placing her teacup back on the saucer, Allegra swallowed, thinking how she was not going to puncture their perfect afternoon.

"Thunder, we have to promise that we won't talk about what we do when we're not together. I love being with you, and you turn me on. You please me, except when you want to talk about men who are not sitting at the table. Because we don't have any commitment, I won't ever delve into who you may or may not be seeing, because other women aren't important to me, only the moments we share. And if we lose sight of these moments, we'll lose all that matters." Thunder pretended to accept Allegra's response outwardly, but inside, he was hounded by his imagination.

Now strutting along West Third Street adjacent to Washington Square Park, Allegra masked her eyes behind dark, reflective sunglasses. Her mind drifted to the mounds of term papers which needed grading and to the research she had to resume for her own dissertation. Brazil, for now, had to be another golden memory. Her BlackBerry vibrated impatiently, signaling that her voicemail was tired of speaking for her. Allegra scrolled through her assorted text and email messages.

"Hey, Baby! Need to hear your voice. Call me." Thunder

and

From: Cyril.winchester@nyu.edu
To: allegraadamsphd@aol.com
Sent: September 19, 2011
Dear Ms. Adams,

I am pleased to inform you that the Committee has evaluated the final draft of your dissertation. You will be notified when your oral defense will be scheduled. Excellent scholarship.

Sincere Regards,

Cyril Winchester, Ph.D.

Dean, School of Anthropology and Sexuality

New York University.

and

From: luisareporter@aol.com
To: allegraadamsphd@aol.com
Sent: Sunday, January 23, 2011
Hey Allegra,

Must have been mercury in retrograde? Your e-mail was hiding out in my spam folder:

Resending the following:

From: allegraadamsphd@aol.com
To: luisareporter@aol.com
Sent: Tuesday, January 11, 2011 2:32 am
Subject: Reply/Checking In
Hey Luisa,

Virtuous Virgil, huh? Funny and tragic! If you didn't set rules from day one, it's a little late to put that train back into the station. I meant to e-mail you sooner but...let's just say I was distracted....lol! Ran into Rolando Barbosa. You know, the forward for the Los Angeles Lakers? He's down here visiting his family and producing a documentary about Brazilian basketball players in the NBA. We'll catch up when I get back on Saturday...and tell you all about my beautiful Rio.

TTYL! Love ya!

Allegra

Sent: Tuesday, January 25, 2011 2:32 am
Subject: Reply/Checking In
To: luisareporter@aol.com
From: allegraadamsphd@aol.com
Check your calendar. I'm stuck editing specials for May sweeps, but let's plan a get-together.

Allegra tried to identify the unfamiliar telephone number that had sent the text message:

"Allegra, I was hoping to see you again before you left Rio. Can't stop thinking about you. The team will be playing the Knicks soon. Gotta see you again. Ciao, Bela. Rolando." 8:05am

Allegra sighed, tapping the edge of her BlackBerry, squeezing her lower lip. Rolando Barbosa definitely was in the unfinished business folder, except she had not decided what else, if anything, she wanted to do with him.

Allegra and Rolando had a random encounter at the cigar bar inside the Pestana Rio Atlântica hotel located in an upscale neighborhood of Rio de Janeiro. Allegra rested her head against the back of her chair recalling their dalliance.

Restless from a day of demanding workshops, and unable to

sleep, Allegra had taken the elevator down to the dimly lit cigar bar, resembling a plush living room, decorated with inviting red leather sofas and armchairs. The candlelit space, with soaring ceilings, possessed an edgy sophistication. Local Brazilians, cuddling couples and corporate types crowded the mahogany bar. With closed eyes and sweet phrasing, a young male guitarist crooned a bossa nova melody on the tiny stage in the far corner.

Allegra sauntered in, sitting on a bar stool near Rolando, who stood at the mahogany bar, chatting with the aging bartender. Rolando glanced sideways, angling his body toward her, as his eyes did an elevator roll over her body. Allegra was oblivious to his intense gaze, which called out for her to recognize him. Allegra refused. The lustful bartender raised his eyebrows, and exchanged a pleased grin with Rolando, in response to her allure.

"May I take your order, Senhorita?" the balding bartender asked, leaning toward her with a smile, carefully placing a napkin and a plate of empanadas before her.

"*Um martini sujo, por favor.* (A dirty martini, please.)"

Rolando possessed a dark, olive complexion, shiny black hair with tight curls and wore a diamond chain, a fitted white tee shirt and black, creased trousers. He drew his hand through his curls, as he expected her to recognize him, meet his gaze and seek his autograph, as three groupies had just done, squealing as they strode away, relishing their acquisition of a piece of him. The banter in Portuguese mixed with English slang between Rolando and the bartender continued, becoming louder and more animated. Allegra's ears perked up at hearing a brother speak impeccable Portuguese and English. She didn't recognize Rolando for the basketball star that he was. To her, Rolando was only a familiar, comforting sight, a brother with bowlegs, and a slight street edge, she surmised.

Allegra recognized the tone in the voices of the two men. Though they verbally sparred and joked with one another, the prize that they sought was to gain her attention, pausing for a millisecond, hoping she would give them this gift, her awareness that they existed. Instead, Allegra waited, continuing to nurse her dirty martini until she had swallowed the last drop; then raising her index finger, she signaled she wanted a refill.

"Senhor Rolando, you surprise me. You no come to Rio for two years?" asked the aging bartender.

"Man, the NBA season gets longer every year. By the time, we compete for the championship, which usually happens in June, I can only come home for two weeks, at most, before training camp starts all over again." The bartender examined a crystal rock glass high in the air, before generously pouring Macallan 1851 Inspiration, and then placing it in front of Rolando.

"Since you left the Brazilian league and signed with the Lakers, the team hasn't been the same. Don't forget, Rio will always be your home," the bartender chided.

Rolando's long, slender fingers held up his glass, then swirled the Scotch around in the glass, coating the sides completely. After smelling the powerful liquid and wrinkling his nose, Rolando slowly sipped, savoring, rolling it around his mouth.

Allegra imagined, if given a chance, what magic Rolando's lips could perform, as he smiled, approvingly, at the taste of the Scotch. "*Este álcool é magnificient.* This is the shit, *meu amigo*," he said, pursing his lips around the Cohiba Sublime LE 2004 cigar. The bartender beamed proudly that he had pleased his sports superstar friend.

Allegra narrowed her eyes and deliberately caught Rolando's gaze in the gold-plated mirror over the bar in front of them. Her directness startled Rolando; he swallowed, taken aback by her brazenness, devoid of the coyness he was used to experiencing. Not a word was spoken, but a charged, loud tension hung between them, so loud and sudden that it caused Rolando to slump next to Allegra on the red velvet barstool.

Wiping the top of the bar, the ignored bartender continued to make small talk, envisioning a threesome with Allegra and Rolando. "You know, Rolando, I've been thinking a lot. I know you and Kobe are the leading scorers on the Lakers, but I think I can take you on—me and you—one on one. I have been practicing very hard, *meu amigo*," the bartender joked.

The bartender's challenge fell on deaf ears, as Rolando's eyes remained locked with Allegra's, his heart beating loudly. He nodded at her through the mirror, continuing to sip. She replied with her wicked half-smile.

"May I refresh your drink, Senhorita?" the bartender volunteered.

"*Sim, por favor, cachaça*," Allegra answered.

"I don't see American sisters here in Rio that often, unless they're old enough to be my mother, bookworms or freaking out because they followed their American boyfriend down here and saw something they didn't like." Allegra raised her eyebrows and smiled.

"And I don't see many brothers who speak fluent Portuguese."

"I'm Brazilian. Originally from Sao Paulo, but I live in Los Angeles now. Rolando Barbosa," he said, extending his hand.

"Allegra," she said, barely touching his fingers, taking another sip of her *cachaça*, acknowledging the lilt of his accent and his ample tongue.

"What brings you to Rio, Allegra?"

"Love and random sex. Why else would one come?" Rolando chuckled louder than her comment merited.

Allegra turned her face back toward the mirror, where her and

Rolando's eyes first met, then lightly slid her hand in between Rolando's open, tree trunk legs, and over his cock. Rolando's head dipped, startled to see her hand now resting between his legs. Allegra's confident eyes provided confirmation to him through the mirror that she had made no mistake; that her hand was not accidentally removing his cock from his pants and tenderly stroking him. The oblivious bartender returned with her refill of *cachaça*.

"Senhor Rolando? Would you like…" the bartender asked.

"No, I'm good. Real good." Rolando gulped, steadying himself by holding the edge of the bar, wondering how he had gotten so fucking lucky. Allegra squeezed her pelvis at the thought of his ample dick inside of her. She lowered her eyes, smiled, all the while stroking the tip of his snake-like dick. Under the bar, Allegra slid Rolando's hand between her legs and inserted his fingers inside her wet pussy. Needing no cue, Rolando fingered her as if he was directing traffic inside of her pussy. "Harder," she whispered, shutting her eyes to enjoy the moment. Rolando obliged.

"Senhor Rolando," the bartender interjected, "I have always wanted to come to America." Soft applause showered the vocalist as he crooned a crowd favorite.

"Um later, man. Later," Rolando answered through tight lips, appealing to the ceiling for assistance, tapping his fist on top of the bar. "Man, let me get with you later."

Puzzled, the bartender retreated to the opposite end of the bar, to take drink orders from an arriving group of British businessmen. Like conducting a dual erotic symphony, Rolando moved his fingers in and out of Allegra's pussy, while teasing her clit; she simultaneously stroked and tamed his wild cock. Rolando whimpered, his spine straightening, as he continued to stare at Allegra through the mirror. Allegra crossed her right leg on top of his fingers so he could tightly finger fuck her. A smile curled at the corners of her lip. Their chests heaved together, still facing forward toward the mirror.

"Hmm, taste me," Allegra leaned over to whisper in his ear.

"Hmm?" Rolando replied.

"Taste me," she repeated.

"I want to kiss you."

"And I want you, need you, to taste me." Rolando unlocked their eyes in the mirror, and faced her to gauge her seriousness. Mischievousness danced behind her eyes, as she continued to stroke his erect cock, urging him to appease her. The bartender appeared at their end of the cigar bar to retrieve a bottle of cognac, and then disappeared in the kitchen behind the bar. Rolando smiled sheepishly.

Allegra joined him, erupting in laughter, and then became still again, tossing her locs from her eyes, as she watched Rolando lick her succulent juices from his fingers, still continuing to tease her clit until she quietly climaxed. Rolando joined her, emitting quiet gasps of air.

"You staying in this hotel?" he asked, again looking intently into her face.

"Yes," a satisfied Allegra answered, pushing her twists out of her eyes, pulling down her wrinkled skirt.

"Let's go up to my suite."

"Not tonight. Early morning appointments," she answered, placing her business card, listing only her name and cell phone number in the palm of his large hand.

"You're gonna leave me like this?" Rolando asked smilingly, his cock regaining its strength, resting outside of his still unzipped pants. "Look, I'm leaving to return to L.A. on Sunday. Here's the key to my suite. Feel free to join me anytime." Rolando slid his electronic hotel key card over to her.

"Um....um, where's the ladies' room?"

Overhearing her question, the bartender pointed before Rolando could respond. Allegra rose, smoothed her skirt and, tipsy from her orgasm and the dirty martini, she balanced her strut on her stiletto heels. Rolando lifted his pelvis to zip his pants, staring at Allegra's ass as she moved across the room. Before rounding the corner into the ladies' room, Allegra glanced back over her shoulder. Rolando had been swallowed up by another group of adoring fans. The bartender rejoined Rolando, waiting his turn to pitch his desire to come to America. Without being noticed, Allegra slipped out of the cigar bar front entrance, leaving Rolando's electronic key alone on the bar.

8

The New York University faculty office building was still covered with scaffolding, caused by delays in construction. Inside, small, unkempt faculty offices lined the long, wide corridor inside the stark, cavernous building. Each office competed for the prize of the highest pile of old, yellow legal pads. Allegra's office was decorated in sharp contrast to those of her tenured colleagues. Her neatly framed professional honors and awards were hung and placed with precision around the cheerful, almond-colored office. Sifting through her red alligator briefcase, she carefully placed it on her oak desk, flipping open the gold buckles. In order of importance, she removed her pink vibrator, a wrapped statute of bare-chested *capoeira* dancers, and an alternate cell phone, the number of which she offered to her lovers as their personal hotline. Her suitors never asked if they shared minutes, or any other thing related to Allegra, as her admonitions and subsequent demeanor taught them that interrogation was something that she would never tolerate. To Allegra, answering questions relating to her thoughts, her time and her emotions was a defensive posture that she would not tolerate.

Allegra went through her office mail until she opened and examined an invoice from Sunrise and Garden Living Center. Without hesitation, she used her keys to unlock the desk drawer, retrieved her checkbook, and scribbled a check payable to the

Center in the amount of eleven-hundred and seventy-five dollars. On the memo line, Allegra printed on the check: *August invoice. On behalf of Rachael Sullivan*; then she sealed the self-addressed, stamped envelope.

As soon as Allegra activated her pink cellphone, it rang, startling her. Checking the caller ID, she smiled softly, ran her tongue over her lower lip and pressed the receive symbol. As she cleared her throat, and answered with a cool "Hello," an irritated female voice on the other end did not wait for her greeting.

"Allegra! Girl, do you always answer your phone like Idris Elba was on the other end? Why haven't you called me back?"

It was Luisa. Allegra let her arm fall against the top of her desk and rolled her eyes, pretending to be annoyed. "I called you back, Heifer. Left a message with your dingbat assignment editor."

"Oh, I haven't been at the station and I forgot to recharge my phone. I was out on Staten Island covering the Borough President race that's boring the hell out of the voting public right now. But I was calling to make sure that you're coming with me to the Town Hall meeting tonight, and dinner afterwards?"

"Ugh. Do I have to, Luisa? I would rather get a root canal without Novocain. Can you arrange that procedure instead of me listening to a bunch of deranged revolutionaries?"

"Allegra, I gotta go up to Harlem and ambush Hannibal Morgan's chief of staff, who wants to flirt whenever I get him on the telephone, but when I ask for his response to all of the rumors about an ongoing criminal investigation of the Panthers by the Attorney General's office, then all of sudden, he says he has to call me back, which he never does. None of the other Panthers return my telephone calls, so I've gotta bust in the place. And tonight, they're having their monthly rally, the best time to do it."

"So what do I look like? Your bodyguard? If I break a nail, your ass is mine, Luisa!" Allegra teased.

Three hours later, Allegra met Luisa at the Urban Panther Watch Movement Town Hall Meeting on Lenox Avenue, near One-Hundred and Twenty-Fifth Street, in a non-descript, ramshackle building, which had been previously used as a community theater. By the time Allegra arrived, Luisa was pacing in front of the elevator, ending her conversation on her BlackBerry.

Until the station's assignment editor informed her that she was assigned to report on Hannibal's infamous Urban Panther Watch Movement, Luisa was not familiar with the organization's legendary street cred. Luisa was normally assigned to traditional civil rights organizations such as the NAACP and the Urban League. The Panthers was new territory, and its members were outside of her educational and professional circle.

Her gray-haired assignment editor advised, when she met with him in his office, "We're hearing that Hannibal Morgan wants to upset the political applecart in Harlem. His supporters were able to get fifty-four thousand people to sign a petition for him to establish the newly formed Panther Political Party. If this party gains some traction, this could affect Harlem politics for some time to come, especially with all of the local and state level seats that will be up for election, due to term limits, and criminal indictments. So find out what you can about Morgan. The research department just comes up with long rants, that he calls speeches, random appearances here and there with hip hop artists, his marches and crap like that, but I'm trying to find out more about his background and more importantly, how his organization is funded. He hasn't responded to requests for interviews....except from black-owned newspapers, that always float him softball questions. Apparently, he doesn't care much for Caucasians. Bernstein and Flanagan went up there and one of Morgan's henchmen threatened them with bodily harm when they tried to enter the building. I figure if he won't talk to two of our most seasoned, trusted reporters, he's bound to talk to you. He'd see you as less threatening and beautiful, if you don't mind me saying; but more importantly, he'll see you as one of *his* people," the editor added, pulling up one of his sagging, brown socks.

"Why is Hannibal Morgan all of a sudden on your radar? You usually keep our coverage pretty mainstream."

"'Cause of those anti-Semitic articles that he published in the Panther newsletter last week. Just call it an old, rusty, Italian journalist's gut feeling; I didn't get these gray hairs on my head from covering the Macy's Thanksgiving Day parade, I'll tell you that much. Since Hannibal wants to be the town crier for Harlem, I say let's shine a spotlight on him. I'm curious, like I said, about where he gets his funding, how he earns his income, crap like that. The research department is checking on their IRS status... see if they have filed their taxes. I just think that where there's smoke, there's certainly fire."

"So many non-profits haven't filed taxes, especially if they have low revenues, so is that cause for a story? I mean, how deep do you want me to go with this?" Luisa asked, adjusting her navy blue blazer.

"The *New York Post* has assigned a reporter to shadow them. We can't let the *Post* beat us on breaking a story, can we?"

"Have any other media outlets been up there?" Luisa asked, twirling her hair.

"Nope, we are the first television station that's interested. My friends over at ABC News dismiss the Panthers as 'irrelevant crackpots,' because they have violent ex-felons in their membership."

"Well, they may be right."

"Maybe and maybe not...see what you can find out; see if there's anything worth covering; any improprieties. And a word to the wise, if you pull this off, that senior investigative reporter/weekend anchor desk could be on your horizon." The assignment editor winked, as he stirred his hot instant Thai chicken soup. The aroma reminded Luisa that her stomach needed more than the black coffee and buttered croissant she had gobbled earlier that morning en route to the electrical outage story in lower Manhattan.

A Yoruba priest, wearing an all-white flowing garment flailed his arms, spreading burning incense through the air, and offered a sacred prayer to protect the Panther organization from spies, infidels and Uncle Toms. Panther supporters bowed their heads in prayer, extending their arms toward the ceiling, swaying back and forth. Luisa and Allegra sat with folded arms, in two metal fold-up chairs on the aisle in the front row, twisting their heads watching the supporters chant "*Ashe* (thank you)," before taking their seats.

The crowd consisted of salt-and-pepper-haired, kufi-wearing, leftover revolutionaries from the sixties, upstarts from the eighties, and youth, with dead eyes, wearing military uniforms and sun-glasses, reminiscent of the music group, Public Enemy. Women in their late forties, wearing neat Afros, dutifully arranged slices of carrot cake, fruit salad and lemonade on the refreshment table in the rear of the sparse, plain basement. While other women, with masculine demeanors, and wearing black berets and military jackets in the ninety-degree heat, stood like soldiers, ready for battle.

A passionate young black man in similar military garb stood behind the podium, announcing the agenda, which signaled to Allegra that she was in for an unplanned, painfully long evening. The next speaker, another black man, slightly older with a strag-gly beard, was introduced as the organization's general counsel.

He gave the audience an update on the lawsuits the organization had filed against New York City on behalf of disenfranchised black men and recently released ex-felons. The supporters were also instructed to place badly needed cash in the baskets that were being passed from row to row by Panther members, wearing black liberation arm bands. When a collection basket arrived on Allegra and Luisa's row, they politely passed it to the young woman sitting next to them, with two black, male children clutching her tightly. Sweet, reluctant children stepped onto the stage singing an obviously unrehearsed revolutionary song. When the children were done croaking, they were met with a standing ovation and waves of "Ashes" from the audience.

"Brothers and Sisters! Welcome! The leader of our movement, Brother Imhotep Hannibal Morgan!" bellowed the general counsel for the Panthers. Panther members leapt from their seats, applauding enthusiastically, as the charismatic Hannibal Morgan strode to the stage, wearing a red, black and green kufi, pumping his fists in the air, encouraging more applause. He was followed by two bodyguard-type men, both wearing mirrored sunglasses.

Allegra and Luisa remained seated during the ovation, appearing like two children hiding in a field of corn stalks. Luisa scribbled notes, detailing who was in attendance and exactly what was being said during this meeting, including the announcement that there would be weekly town hall meetings, given the state of a tense relationship between some Harlem residents and the New York City Police Department.

Hannibal had a formidable physique; his arms bulged under his gray turtleneck. The muscles in his neck sat like a tree trunk under his jaw line. After adjusting the squeaking noise in the microphone, Hannibal began his speech in a low, measured tone which demanded that everyone lean forward to hear his words.

"Good evening, devoted brothers and sisters. Tonight, I come before you as your humble servant with a mission to save black people. Even the ones who don't want to be saved. I come before you as the leader of the Urban Panther Watch Movement and the Panther Movement political party. We did it! You collected over fifty thousand signatures to form our own party, to advocate for your own people; because none of those boot-licking Negroes in either party is going to fight for us. We see that! Like my late momma always said, 'Son, if you want something done, you got to do it your damned self!'"

Panther members jumped to their feet, shouting and applauding, as if participating in a revival meeting. After a two minute ovation, Hannibal urged his followers to sit down so that he could continue his speech. He possessed an impressive command of language, able to use monosyllabic words at one moment and then drop a string of Ebonics the next. If he had ordered that audience to burn down a children's orphanage, they would have been more than happy to comply. He had the physical carriage of a martial arts champion, poised to strike or to bring peace.

"Every night, I get a telephone call from a weeping black mother who has just suffered the loss of her son. Every night, somewhere in this city, a black child is murdered or assaulted by the thugs of the New York City Police Department. Some have said that we need to wait for the murders to stop. We should wait for employment to return to our community. We should wait for our children to be educated. We should wait for the drugs to stop being sold on our corners. We should wait. And I say, wait for what?"

"Wait for what?" the young woman next to Allegra repeated; others in the audience echoed the same question. Hannibal held the audience in rapt attention in the palm of his hand. "These racist crackers understand only one thing—you kill one of ours, we kill one of yours—point blank! How long will black blood run in the streets?"

The energetic audience answered in unison, "Not long!"

"How long?!" Hannibal bellowed with his raised clenched fist. "How long?"

"Not long!"

Hannibal continued, "We must organize, organize, organize, if our people are to survive. Any people who do not organize, will not thrive, and definitely will not rise. If you don't wanna join this organization, it's critical that you start your own. Just do something, damn it!"

The enthralled audience responded in unison, "Do something! Do something!"

"Speak! Speak! Brother!" a heavy-set Puerto Rican man, standing behind Hannibal, wearing a gun belt and *Free Mumia* and *Free Assata Shakur* buttons, interjected. A black woman, wearing a black tee shirt and jeans with a beige apron, tiptoed to the corner of the stage to serve Hannibal a glass of ice water.

"Give thanks... Thank you, sister—," Hannibal said, interrupting his tirade to sip the water from the glass.

"Is the Hudson Grill still open? I'm starving," Allegra asked Luisa, shifting in her chair, crossing and uncrossing her curvaceous legs, as Hannibal's long-ass speech continued for another thirty-five minutes.

"Hush," the man with a disheveled gray beard ordered. Luisa nudged Allegra with her elbow, before returning her attention to Hannibal Morgan.

"We're no longer gonna be ignored by either political party; both are the same wings on the same damn bird," Hannibal continued, as Allegra continued to fidget, whipping out her Black-Berry to respond to her student e-mails.

Hannibal moved like a caged lion, stalking the stage with his bow legs, pouncing on words he wanted to emphasize, engaging his loyalists, attacking his enemies, ranting as though if they were in the room, he would rip off their heads. Danger, intensity and dominance lurked behind Hannibal's eyes, and Allegra found that combination very potent. Still, Allegra sensed that he was emotionally vulnerable. *A man who is that passionate subliminally exposes the many ways in which he can be conquered: cerebrally, physically, soulfully and in his dreams*, Allegra thought. Hannibal, stroking his goatee, noticed Allegra's unblinking gaze.

"Your Stepin-Fetchit Negro preachers and politicians, whose ass you kiss and re-elect, are all being paid off by this billionaire mayor…and like brother Malcolm said, 'You been took, hoodwinked, bamboozled, led astray, run amok!'"

"Nooooo!" a woman in the audience yelled, while others yelled, "Preach! Tell it!"

Hannibal surveyed the audience, his eyes floating back to Allegra's legs.

"Yes, my brotha. Yes. Your Negro politicians and pimp preachers are content to sit back like fat cats, selling their souls and lining their pockets, while our community is dying all around us. And you sit by silently and do and say nothing. You must like your condition, huh? You must like the fact that your children are poorly educated, poorly trained, got no jobs; high crime done run amok because of decades of sloppy, Negro leadership! You must love your condition!" Hannibal paused, pointing at no one in particular. "Nobody in here, hear me! Look at you! You must really love your condition!"

"Noooo! We hear ya! Nooo! Go on, brother…we're fired up!" various voices shouted from the middle section. An elderly man, squeezing a crumpled hat half-stood, pumped his fist in the air, before collapsing back into his chair.

"If any of you were really serious, brothers and sisters, none of this bullshit would still be going down! Like our dear ancestor Harriet Tubman once said, 'I freed a thousand slaves and I would have freed a thousand more only if they knew they were slaves.' So, brothers and sisters, I'm willing to give my life for you. Now what are you willing to do for the Panthers?"

Allegra pressed the send button after replying to a student e-mail, granting an extension to turn in a term paper late. She glanced around the room, looking for a straight path for her to get the hell out of Dodge, without being conspicuous. But since she and Luisa were in the first row, an inconspicuous departure was impossible.

"Luisa, I need to go home and give myself an emergency root canal."

"Shush," the elderly man behind them repeated.

"Shush, yourself," Allegra replied defiantly.

"You're crazy, Allegra. Hannibal will be done as soon as he gets to the part about, liberation now and…" Luisa whispered.

"You've heard this bullshit before?" asked Allegra, crossing her legs again in a huff, pretending she was annoyed.

"I caught him doing the same speech on *YouTube.com*."

Before the annoyed man behind them could shush them again, a note was routed from the contingent of comrades positioned behind Hannibal, to a refreshment woman, who cowered as she walked up the aisle, handing Allegra the handwritten, folded missive. It read: "*Hotep*, beautiful Sista. With all due respect, would you please refrain from crossing your legs? Brother Hannibal no doubt finds your actions distracting from the business of liberation at hand. Hotep and Peace. Brother Dante Salaam."

Allegra revealed the note to Luisa, whose jaw fell and tried to close twice before falling open again. Allegra searched the podium and found the note's author hiding his stony facial expression behind his aviator sunglasses. Dante nodded, and then resumed searching the audience for other leg-crossing transgressors.

"Liberation now. Not tomorrow. Liberation now! Peace, Brothers and Sisters," Hannibal declared with his fist pumping in the air. His loyal followers expressed their allegiance with a lengthy, standing ovation. Luisa leapt to her feet applauding, with Allegra reluctantly joining her, as an excuse to stretch and regain the feeling in her ass muscle.

"Ain't that a damn blip, Luisa? He has a lot of balls to send me that note. Who does he think he is?"

In response, Luisa continued to applaud with the audience, and leaned over to whisper to Allegra, "That's Dante Salaam, the one with whom I've been trying to schedule an interview with Hannibal."

"Dante, who?" a clueless Allegra asked.

"Hannibal's Chief of Staff."

Slinging her brown hobo handbag over her shoulder, Allegra prepared to leave, saying her goodbyes to Luisa, as male and female groupies crowded around Hannibal like a rock star. Allegra returned Luisa's goodbye hug. Before ending their embrace, Luisa, blinking her long eyelashes, asked, "So what do you think of Dante?"

"Luisa, this isn't the time or place to tell you what I think, but that bullshit he wrote in that note about what I do with my legs; humph, to call him a snake would insult reptiles everywhere. Let's scratch dinner; I have an early class tomorrow. Let's talk in the afternoon. Love ya; smooches," Allegra said, turning down the crowded aisle.

"Hold up! I'm leaving, too. Let me talk with him a second," Luisa decided, turning to walk toward Dante, who acknowledged Luisa with a distracted nod. Dante guided Hannibal towards an attractive, middle-aged woman, with long braids, who dabbed her eyes with a handkerchief. Allegra took her seat and crossed her legs, as Luisa waited, standing a few feet away, for Hannibal and Dante to acknowledge her presence. Hannibal rubbed the shoulder of the emotional mother. "Brother Hannibal, you're my last hope for justice. My son wasn't no angel, but he didn't deserve the beat down he got from those white cops. He was standing on the corner minding his own business, when all of these cops rolled up and arrested everybody. Took them two days before they told me that they had my son."

"Excuse me, Mr. Salaam," Luisa ventured. Dante pointed his index finger in the air. "Gimme a second, Sista," he responded nonchalantly, dividing his attention between Allegra's crossed legs and elbowing Hannibal. Hannibal followed the direction of Dante's nod toward Allegra's sultry posture, as she continued to work her BlackBerry. Hannibal's eyes absorbed the shape of her ankles and curvature of her waist, which supported her jiggling apple bottom. Feeling their eyes, Allegra rose, signaling to Luisa, mouthing, "I'll meet you at the elevator." Luisa gestured that she understood.

Parting the aisle of chatting revolutionaries like the Red Sea, Allegra, assumed her queen-like carriage and stalled conversations about the oppressive white man, emergency boycotts and police brutality and strolled down the aisle to the foyer near the elevators. Abruptly making excuses to the tearful mother, Hannibal trotted down the aisle, following Allegra. Dante and Luisa trailed behind out through the double doors to the elevator bank.

"Hotep, my sister," Hannibal said, greeting Allegra, making sure his voice had a baritone resonance, while staring into her gleaming eyes and bursting cleavage. "And Hotep, my sister," Hannibal tossed to Luisa without looking at her. Luisa knew that she was not on Hannibal's radar, but she replied using his vernacular, "Hotep, Brother Morgan. Hotep Dante Salaam."

Dante glumly responded, "Hotep, Sista," as if his voicemail was not filled with her messages. Seeing the focus of Hannibal's affection, his bodyguards, licked their lips, as they checked out Allegra. To Hannibal, Dante and the bodyguards, Allegra was fresh meat deserving of inspection and eventual domination.

Like a storefront preacher working his routine, Hannibal extended his hand to Allegra, repeating. "Hotep, my sister."

Allegra let Hannibal's hand dangle in the air like a LeBron James jump shot and lowered her gaze, announcing, "Luisa, you do want to get what you came for so you get back to the station, don't you?!"

"Luisa Hamilton? WNBC-TV? You didn't inform us that you were coming; reporters got to get my clearance to attend our functions. Anything you heard must be kept off record," Dante said, with attitude.

"Yes, but after we spoke, I didn't get a return call to confirm, so I came anyway, hoping we could arrange something now, in person," Luisa responded.

Allegra noticed the aloofness Dante displayed toward Luisa, and her willingness to accept his disdain, gazing at him like he was a cinema idol. Allegra wondered why Luisa stood applauding for Hannibal. Instead of reporting and observing, Luisa allowed herself to become emotionally involved in Hannibal's performance. Her responsibility as a reporter was to observe the story and not become a part of the story. By standing and applauding for Hannibal, Luisa violated a journalist's holy tenet.

"Are you with the evil media, Sista Allegra?" Hannibal asked, with a smile.

"Not if this is the kind of crap you have to tolerate...Luisa," Allegra said, pressing the call button on the elevator and glaring at Luisa, ordering her friend to snap out of the trance that was consuming her.

"Yes, um, yes I do...lots of work to do! I'll give you a call tomorrow, Mr. Salaam," Luisa answered, the glaze melting from over her eyes as she buttoned her jacket. "Okay, tomorrow then. Mr. Salaam. Mister, um Brother Morgan."

Allegra stepped into the waiting elevator, followed by Luisa and boarded by Panther activists. Hannibal called after Allegra, as she disappeared with Luisa behind the closing elevator doors. Hannibal stared after the memory of Allegra with a wry smile, shaking his head with Dante, before rejoining the tearful mother.

"Brother Dante, find out about that sister."

"The reporter chick... Luisa Hamilton?"

"No, you got *that*. Sista Allegra, the one who floated out of here like she was running shit." Dante and Hannibal grinned, bumping their fists, and reaffirmed their brotherhood.

9

"I never thought that the revolutionary re-mix tour would be over. I thought Hannibal was going to pull Huey Newton out of his hat," Allegra quipped.

"At least Dante and Hannibal are trying to be part of the solution, instead of the problem."

"Whateva...How's Virgil?" Allegra shrugged, as she drove Luisa, in a rental car, down a steep slope into the World Financial Center underground parking garage, braking as a maroon-colored valet, with shoulder-length locs, and bow legs, sauntered, like he was listening to a Bob Marley remix, and in his own rhythm opened their respective car doors, blatantly displaying his attraction for Allegra.

"Me tink me seent angels," the valet murmured under his breath out of earshot of both women, as they walked away. A black 2011 Hummer H2 SUV, with tinted windows, drove into the garage. The phantom driver shifted the truck into park and lowered the driver's side window, spying on Allegra and Luisa.

"Oh, he stayed over last night. Would you believe he fell asleep on top of me?"

"Luisa, you are shitting me...I know you aren't still letting Virgil fuck you missionary style." The valet did a double-take, grinning at the jiggling asses of Allegra and Luisa as they strolled away.

"But it hurts when I'm on top."

"That's so seventeenth century, girl! Flip Virgil's ass over and ride his dick like you're the first black chick to drive NASCAR."

"I tried doin' that and was walkin' like a cowboy for a week!"

"Luisa, you gotta believe that you deserve sexual satisfaction. You've gotta learn to let go and believe that you deserve to enjoy yourself; instead of just lying there and being done to."

"I didn't realize that was what I was doing," Luisa said, frowning.

"Straight up, you're terrified of being alone, and that's your problem. And that's why you keep accepting mediocre sex."

"Allegra, you make living seem so easy. I give all my power away to men. I know I do."

"Change the dick; change your life...hmmm, sounds like the title for my next book." Allegra giggled. Luisa hesitated, and then added her own laughter, tossing her black, shoulder-length curls.

The elevator opened onto a vast, candlelit space. A jazz trio of black men, who could have been Allegra's great-uncles, crooned songs from a hit parade songbook. Patrons spoke in low tones with an occasional hearty guffaw at some corny shit that probably was some ass-kisser reaching for the next highest corporate rung.

"This is really not my scene, socializing with co-workers, but it's university politics. As soon as I've made nice to everyone who chipped in to be here, I'm out," Allegra said to Luisa, before being whisked away by the claw-nailed British department head Dr. Winchester, with Luisa scurrying behind them. Sitting at the circular table were the usual suspects, the dashiki-wearing Dr. Porter, who was always "just back from the motherland;" and Indian teaching assistant Yuni Senthil, who constantly peppered Allegra with questions about the genitals of black men.

"Yes, Yuni, what you heard in India is absolutely true. Black men have dicks ranging from four to ten feet in length, especially the ones from Bedford-Stuyvesant, Brooklyn. What you read on the Internet is absolutely correct! What you should do is hang out in Bed-Stuy on a Saturday night and you'll see that what I'm saying is true. And if you're still unconvinced, why do you think they walk with a slight limp? It's to prevent their dick from throwing them off balance. Every weekend they have dick contests; you have to score an invitation, as the events are always sold out way in advance. Case in point, since from the look on your face, you need concrete proof. When Kobe saw that Shaq's dick was longer *and* wider, Kobe demanded that Shaq be traded. I saw that on CNN. That's how deep this gets, Yuni."

Rounding out the trio of dull people was Dr. Winchester's *hausfrau*, who had emigrated from Germany to the United States in 1971, but refused to speak a word of English. Luisa and Allegra danced in the aisle trying to force each other into sitting next to the most boring person in the world. Luisa lost, sitting between Winchester and Yuni. Allegra sat on the end of the booth, across from Dr. Porter and next to Dr. Winchester, so she could easily escape.

"The thesis committee has granted its approval for your dissertation to move to the next round, Ms. Adams. Truly impressive," Dr. Winchester said, raising his flute of champagne for a toast.

"You were my lead prosecutor, Doctor," Allegra retorted.

"Well, my dear. I had to demonstrate that I wasn't entirely partial to your scholarship."

"Oh, I forgive you, since it was you who told me about the curator position at the Modern Museum of Africa in Harlem. I appreciate that."

"Should you receive the appointment, it will be entirely on your own merit," Dr. Winchester continued, secretly reaching under their table, shielded by the white tablecloth and resting his hand on her thigh, while popping a shrimp-stuffed mushroom into his mouth. Allegra peered under the table to verify that it was indeed, Dr. Winchester's hand on her thigh, while his *hausfrau* chewed on an olive stem, staring into her own wretched daydream. Allegra attempted to wiggle her leg away from her department head's firm hand, to no avail.

New York Art magazine and other anthropology magazines featured Allegra as their September cover story. Tonight's gathering was the third celebration in her honor in the last year. As excited as she was, Allegra looked forward more to bringing African art from the continent into the hearts of Harlem children through monthly interactive, hands-on workshops. If she received the appointment, Allegra was determined to increase the funding for the Modern Museum of Africa to enable them to complete the construction of the three-hundred-seat theater, the children's art school, and terrace sculpture garden with a tranquil view of the East River. She also was excited that the collections reflected the diversity and spirituality of Africans throughout the Diaspora. Dr. Winchester, as chairperson for their board of directors, had the final vote as to who would assume the coveted role as curator. Allegra was angry. As her fellow colleagues cheerfully chatted about the urgency of high school art education, Allegra tactfully tried to remove Dr. Winchester's hand, still with no success.

Winchester leaned over to whisper into his wife's ear, as he re-located Allegra's thigh again under their table, then turned to praise Luisa for her work at the television station. Though, at that moment Allegra hated Luisa, it was great to see Luisa laugh with a man other than Virgil. *Perhaps she will learn to ride Winchester's shriveled-up joystick, so he'll stop sweating me*, Allegra thought. Finally, Allegra raised her fork, angling it from her waist from under the table. Then with the propulsion of a rocket, her wrist arched and she stabbed Winchester's fleshy hand with the four pointy prongs, causing him to yelp like a wronged mongrel.

The sudden agonizing outburst silenced other conversations. Though the jazz musicians continued to play instruments, they turned their heads toward the whimpering Dr. Winchester. With an angelic glow, Allegra stared at Dr. Winchester, who vigorously rubbed his hand, trying to extinguish the pain.

"What on earth is the matter, Winchester?" Dr. Porter asked.

"Oh! Just my arthritis flaring up," Dr. Winchester answered, stealing glances at Allegra, wondering if she had taken leave of her senses. Allegra excused herself, seeking fresh air and swift refuge in the plush ladies' room. Lowering her head, taking deep breaths, she felt suffocated, leaning her palms against the white, porcelain sink.

"You okay, Miss?" a caring female voice asked. Allegra turned and looked into the face of a motherly-looking, black bathroom attendant who appeared as if desire had been slowly drained from a lifetime of disappointments. Allegra felt a chill travel her spine, as this attendant had the knowing spirit of her female ancestors, the great-aunts who knew if Allegra was lying about returning from a night of preplanned debauchery, before she even turned the key in the lock.

"All right, sugar, you take this here towel," the attendant told Allegra, standing just inside the bathroom doorway, wiping her brow with her black-and-white uniform sleeve. "You've got two ladies in front of you; when they clear out you can go on in," she said, in a weary, pleasant manner.

"Oh no, miss. I was just taking a break," Allegra responded, refreshing her Mac makeup. Then, addressing the collection of women inside at the sinks, the bathroom attendant reminded them all. "Make sure, ladies, you don't leave nothing behind. 'Cause there be thieves everywhere. Take every*thang* with you. And have a nice night, you hear?"

The attendant turned her attention back to Allegra. "Don't make no sense, puttin' on makeup in here. 'Cause there ain't no air conditioning. And that bastard supervisor of mine ain't tryin' to fix it no time soon. So be thankful you're out there, sugar, and not in here with me. Just like life, enjoy all the air conditioning while you can." The bathroom attendant wiped her brow again, and checked on the status of the ladies in the inside line. "They moving fast; don't worry," she reported back.

"How did you find yourself here?" Allegra asked. The woman smiled, and used her shoulder to wipe a solitary stream of sweat from the side of her face.

"Oh, child, in this recession, though I thank it's a depression, I *am* blessed, 'cause I can pay my bills, sometimes late, but eventually I get around to payin' 'em." The attendant collected the white towels from a group of chatty white girlfriends. "And this job keeps my kids with a roof over their heads, my man outta jail, and my Bible next to my bed. I'm blessed to be here, 'cause I could be nowhere at all," she philosophosized, wiping the sweat from the side of her neck, beckoning Allegra. "Okay, sugar, you sure you don't have to go?" And addressing the ladies at the sinks, "Remember, ya'll, take every*thang* with you."

Allegra changed her mind and entered a stall without air conditioning. Anger boiled inside of her, anger at what Dr. Winchester had attempted, rage at the life of this bathroom attendant, who was content with living a thankless life. The stall was out of toilet paper. And Allegra was out of reasons why any woman, including her, had to ignore her own self-satisfaction. And indulge predatory men who saw women as nothing more than receptacles for their lust.

In the face of the bathroom attendant, Allegra saw the reason that she provided for Aunt Rachael's room and board at the Sunrise and Garden Living Center. Aunt Rachael insisted on having a man in her bed, even if it meant that he loved his wife more, and hated Rachael for never standing up for herself and being complicit in his dastardly behavior. Each indulgence that Aunt Rachael had for her lovers, the more they conveyed their apathy for her by daybreak. Rachael's simplest requests were denied, from inquiring about her health after a surgical procedure to taking her out on the town for a romantic date. Once Aunt Rachael made it clear that she had zero self-esteem, her lovers made it clear that she was never to be seen with them in public. And Allegra, as a witness, determined that she would never live a life like her Aunt Rachael, and be life's doormat.

Women like Aunt Rachael would have been thrilled that the good Dr. Winchester had tried to stroke her, but Allegra didn't play those workplace games. Succeeding based upon her own intellect, she refused to trade sex for career advancement. "As much as I have an insatiable sex drive," Allegra often told Luisa, "I'm not that chick who's going to lie on my back to get ahead. Not me. Not now. Not ever."

Upon exiting the humid stall, Allegra washed her hands and made sure she had all of her valuables; her time meditating in a makeshift sauna was nearly complete. On her way toward the door, Allegra considered mentioning that the toilet paper in the fifth stall on the left had run out. But the bathroom attendant had a line to direct, a counter to wipe, children to feed and a no-good man to support. Someone else would trouble her, the kind of trouble which she had come to expect in her life, without joy. Saying a silent prayer, Allegra thought, *Please, God, please don't let that ever be me.*

Allegra slipped the surprised bathroom attendant a twenty-dollar bill and rushed to find the maitre d'. Touching the small of his back, she whispered in his ear, and nodded toward Luisa, who was laughing with Dr. Winchester. The maitre d' smiled broadly as she pressed a five-dollar tip in the palm of his hand and sailed out the front entrance with a determined look.

Downstairs in the parking garage, angry, well-heeled patrons tapped their feet impatiently. Idling drivers honked their horns hoping to summon the missing valet.

Parked on Level Six, Allegra's legs were hoisted over her back seat, as if she was in her favorite gynecologist's chair. Her Jimmy Choo high-heels had been tossed into the front seat. Allegra pleasured herself as the missing valet peeped nearby. When Allegra whimpered as she climaxed, the driver of the 2011 Hummer H2 SUV raised his windows, shifted gears and slowly drove away.

10

Several nude black women, members of the Panther organization, carried basins of water and towels from Hannibal's bedside, where he examined his freshly washed feet. One woman remained, rubbing oil on his massive shoulders. Another tidied around his bed, fluffing his king-sized pillows, covering him with a white comforter. Hannibal repositioned his pillow, ignoring the dutiful women around him, and lay in bed with his eyes wide open. He fixated on Allegra, before slowly drifting off to sleep and stirring his vivid dreams.

In the dark of night, Hannibal tossed and turned through his wet dreams. A galloping thunderous herd of black stallions were behind him, chasing him. No matter where he ran, the stallions were always there, causing him to frantically run through the cold night searching for the illusive Allegra. He knew that the only way the stallions would grant him peace would be when he found Allegra, his elusive black goddess whom he worshipped and feared.

As Allegra soaked in her copper Jacuzzi bathtub late one evening, surrounded by sensual, nutmeg-scented candles, with Miles Davis's Birth of the Cool *in the background, the telephone rang. Allegra waited to hear a message being left on the answering machine, but heard only a slow hang-up. Then the telephone rang again. And again.*

When the telephone rang a fourth time, Allegra allowed her curiosity to consume her, and reached for the copper-colored matching extension hanging near her claw-footed tub.

"*Yes?*"

"*Hotep! Sorry to call so late. May I um...may I speak to Allegra?*"

"*Yes,*" she whispered.

"*Allegra?*"

"*Yes.*"

"*Hannibal Morgan.*"

"*Yes.*"

"*Hannibal.*"

"*Yes. You said that.*"

Completely thrown off balance, Hannibal began explaining himself. "*Luisa gave me your number...and I thought maybe you would want to...um...I thought...well, I did not know...how to get in touch...I been real busy—been on TV a lot—you probably saw me.*"

"*No,*" Allegra answered.

"*No?*" Hannibal lost whatever game he normally worked with. Any other female, especially those down for the struggle, would have given their last bean pie to have the Hannibal Morgan on the other end of their telephone receiver. Dawn, dusk, day or night. "*Well, there was this situation that I was called on to investigate...you see the Urban Panther Watch Movement is about nation building, my sister. For far too long, we, as black people, have taken our resources out of the community and reinvested them elsewhere. So what I am about is letting the powers that be know that we are about doing for ourselves and developing progr...*"

"*Look. Do you wanna fuck?*" Allegra whispered, as Miles's "Miles Runs the Voodoo Down" played in the background.

"*Wha-What?*" Hannibal stumbled to ask.

"*Do-You-Want-To-Fuck?*" she whispered again.

"*Wow. That's deep. Do you?*"

"*One more time. Do you wanna fuck or read me the Encyclopedia of Black Nationalism?*" Allegra repeated, growing irritated.

Silence. "*I—I guess I could come through.*"

Allegra waited.

"What's the address?" Hannibal asked when it was clear Allegra would speak no more.

Standing in the nude, Allegra listened from the top of her staircase, as Dante parked his 2000 Ford Bronco. Outside, Hannibal turned off the ignition to his Bronco, and surveyed the block; Striver's Row, the upscale row of brownstones was silent, except for the twinkle of lights behind closed shutters. Hannibal's fingers still gripped the steering wheel, questioning if he was ready to enter this woman's domain. In the beginning, he felt cocky, not intimidated, but now it was dawning on Hannibal that Allegra was clearly not the accommodating type of woman that he was used to manipulating. Crossing 139th Street to Allegra's brownstone, Hannibal wondered what he was getting himself into. He felt off-balance, similar to when police detectives would suddenly appear at Panther headquarters.

Hannibal rang Allegra's doorbell three times before the buzzer sounded, opening the mahogany door. Stepping inside the vestibule and leaving the door slightly ajar, Hannibal immediately began removing his black scarf and his red, black and green kufi. He peered around the darkened foyer and into the dimly lit living room until he sensed Allegra's silhouette at the top of the staircase.

"Hotep," Hannibal said.

"Remove your boots."

"Huh?"

"Your boots...take them off. No boots or shoes allowed upstairs."

Hannibal closed the heavy front door and sat down, removing his Italia, camel-colored boots.

"When your boots are removed, you may join me upstairs," Allegra advised. Hannibal scratched his head, loving the temptation and tiptoed up the wooden stairs. When he entered her suite, Allegra was standing nude, admiring herself in a three-sided, gold-trimmed mirror. His eyes traveled her body like a slow elevator, relishing every floor.

"Sista. Exquisite."

"I'm not your sista," Allegra whispered, opening a glass bottle of kama sutra oil, and rubbing it across her breasts and soft abdomen.

"Come again?" Hannibal asked, straining to hear her.

"I'm not your sista," she repeated, causing his heart to leap, when she whirled around to face him.

"That's just a term of…"

"We don't have the same parents," Allegra continued, massaging each word, moving toward him like a leopard preparing to strike. "There has been no fuckin' between our family trees."

Hannibal chuckled, his head tilting backward, and then returned to drink her in with his eyes.

"I am woman. You are man. Simple, right?" Allegra asked slowly walking toward him.

"That's how I like things to be," Hannibal replied, not knowing what the hell she was talking about.

"Nice and easy, right?" Allegra asked, arriving directly under his chin, and reaching up and yanking him down to sit on the edge of her king-sized, four-poster bed. Allegra sat on Hannibal's lap, rubbing her ass against his crotch, her back arched as her hair tumbled in his face. Hannibal peppered the back of her neck with kisses, as his hard dick grew inside his pants. Allegra turned to face Hannibal, lifting his tee shirt with the Panther logo, revealing his hairy chest. They kissed; their tongues danced like anxious mating squids. Allegra interrupted their tongue-locking, resting her forehead on his, batting her long eyelashes, staring into Hannibal's eyes.

"Some ground rules. I like to fuck. And I want to fuck you. And I want you to fuck me. Tonight. Now. And that does not translate into you're my man; and I'm your woman. You do not have permission to drop by without an invitation or to otherwise insinuate yourself, without my approval, into my life. Nor will I do so into yours." Hannibal's mouth hung ajar like a broken screen door.

"*Now can you handle that, you fine black warrior?*" *Hannibal swallowed and nodded, lifting his hips so that Allegra could remove his pants.*

"*Good boy,*" *Allegra said, lowering her head to his crotch, circling his stiff penis with her tongue. "Now tell Allegra about nation building." Hannibal groaned in ecstasy, resting his hand on the nape of her neck, as his head fell backward. Hannibal tightened his mouth, fearful that he would come at that very moment.*

Allegra rose, lifting Hannibal's arms, holding them above his head, and laid her body, softly, firmly on top of his. Opening her mouth, she received his kiss. Hannibal's tongue played inside her warm, wet mouth, exploring her luscious lower lip. He breathed her, her spirit, her baby powder and rose-ginger scents; her memory. With his other hand, Hannibal grabbed her hair, and gently pulled until her neck arched back, guiding his wet lips across her chin, down her neck, to her ear. He whispered, "So good...so good." Allegra lightly swished her tongue around his ear, breathing slowly into it. Hannibal released her hair, lightly brushed her shoulders, and sucked her hard nipples. He was delirious with dark anticipation, about to burst into flames. Lying on her back, Allegra opened her legs, gesturing for Hannibal to take her. She draped her legs over his shoulders, and Hannibal entered Allegra, heaving his dick deeper into her pussy, as she shrieked with pleasure, moaning, "Omigod! Right there! Omigod!"

Later Allegra still wanted more, pushing Hannibal onto his back. "Now spread your legs and let Allegra ride you. Not like those subservient sisters you have at your beck and call, but how you have desired since before your soul arrived on this planet," she said to Hannibal in a controlled, soft voice. He was already in position before the words spilled out of her mouth.

"*I'm all yours,*" *Hannibal replied with a shiver, while she rubbed his body with vanilla crème/tangerine kama sutra oil, as if she were his original sculptor. Then she wrapped a long black scarf around his eyes. Instinctively, Hannibal gripped Allegra's hips as she began bouncing*

*and writhing on his dick, like she was competing on a trampoline,
grinding against the base of his cock. Hannibal heard Allegra's moans,
quickening with joy. Hannibal loved being denied his sense of sight. It
made his experience and anticipation all the more intense. Hannibal
and Allegra's hips danced together, as she gripped her fingers deep into
his hairy chest, her wet pussy pushing him over the edge to merge their
primal sounds into a euphoric orgasm.*

"Oh Sheeet!"

Hannibal, dripping with sweat, sat up suddenly in his bed,
breathing heavily, which stirred his lover, a petite, nude, Asian
woman, with blonde streaks in her black, braided hair. Through
the floor-to-ceiling windows of his high-rise condominium on
Central Park North, overlooking Central Park, Hannibal could
see the glow of the full moon. His assistant from the Urban
Panther Watch Movement headquarters, placed her fragile hands
on his shoulder and asked, "What's the matter, Baby?"

"Nothin'; go back to sleep, April," he replied briskly, swinging
his legs over the edge of the bed. Hannibal dialed a telephone
number on his BlackBerry, waited a few seconds, and then ordered
in a graveled voice, "Yo, Dante, what you got on Allegra, the
sista that was with yo girl? Yeah, I told you I want her. Get on it.
And don't fuck this up!"

Hannibal then clicked off of the telephone, tossing it on the
nightstand and fell against his pillow, wrapping the silk sheets
around him. The young Asian woman attempted to soothe
Hannibal, laid her head on his six-pack stomach. When she
attempted to give him a blow job, Hannibal forcibly pushed her
off of him, sprawling her onto the other side of the bed.

"What's wrong, Brother? Have I displeased you?" she asked.

11

Hannibal was impatient and irritable. Snapping at those he perceived as underlings, he was frustrated with his inability to control his obsession for Allegra. He hounded Dante to arrange another encounter with her. He wanted to know everything about her: how long she and Luisa had known each other, a telephone number, an e-mail, where she worked, whom she was seeing, her politics and when she breathed. Dante's inability to produce any results had Hannibal irrationally questioning Dante's competence, his loyalty.

After conducting their nightly street patrol, Dante chauffeured Hannibal, in the Panther-owned Hummer H2 SUV, to Hannibal's 110th Street condominium, silently aware of the evil glances being thrown his way. Dante shifted the gears into park, waiting for Hannibal to exit the vehicle. Two young black males wearing gray hoodies waved at Hannibal, before bopping around the corner onto Lenox Avenue. Hannibal sat in the passenger's seat, staring straight ahead, fuming.

"Wassup, Brother Hannibal?" Dante asked, as the Hummer engine idled.

Hannibal replied, through clenched teeth, emphasizing each word, "If I find out you're blocking me, you'll live to regret it."

Dante explained, "Brother, it ain't that easy. It'd be different if she hung out in our circle, but she and her girl Luisa are some different type of chicks, on some different type of shit. The other night they were down at the World Financial Center. Your girl came back to her car later and was getting herself off."

"Say what?"

"I tell you no lie, Brother. Right there is the parking garage," Dante said, holding his hand taking a Boy Scout pledge. Hannibal snatched Dante around the neck, strangling him, "What the fuck you talking about? You sat there and watched?"

"You told me to watch her, Brother. That's what I done," Dante said, through clenched teeth, barely able to breathe. "Don't trip. I-I-I got this. I just been doin' what you told me to do. Have I ever betrayed you?"

In addition to his responsibilities as chief of staff, spokesperson and confidant, Dante was skilled at walking a delicate balance between fulfilling Hannibal's orders and making sure that he gained something out of the deal. If history was any indicator, Dante Salaam always made sure his needs, as fleeting and lowdown as they were, were met. Dante and Hannibal had been co-conspirators in female sex gamesmanship before. For these two men, women were to be dominated, and ruled for their own pleasure, especially the so-called movement sisters, who pledged that they were down for Hannibal's revolution, though he kept changing the date. Panther females were quickly schooled that they were there to work for the liberation of African people, and for the sexual enjoyment of Hannibal and Dante.

Dante and Hannibal relished dominating those mainstream sisters who thought they were above committing themselves to grass roots community work. Hannibal dangled the emotional carrot in pursuing a woman, telling her whatever bullshit she wanted to hear, allowing her to prove her worth by accepting expensive gifts as trinkets of her love, and then fucking her until she demanded to be ruled by him; then he'd toss her away in favor of his next female conquest. Except for the matriarch of the Panther organization, Hannibal and Dante had fucked and tossed every Panther woman, who placed their hearts on stand-by, until Dante or Hannibal summoned them in the dead of night.

Dante resented that he always got Hannibal's female scraps, women he didn't at that time desire, yet Dante accepted his number two position in the Panther pecking order; that he was to get clear orders from Hannibal, before approaching any female. Early in their alliance, Dante and Hannibal had almost fractured their brotherhood over chasing the same pussy. Hannibal and Dante discussed their distorted version of black history and pledged to never allow their lust for any woman to drive a wedge between them. Their mutual oath was to toy with the hearts and emotions of women, to use them as pawns, and to assure that their own needs, physical, emotional and financial, were met.

Both men recognized that they needed each other for the success of the Panther organization. Hannibal knew that Dante was his most trusted aide, who knew where his skeletons were located. In mapping out his strategy to carry out Hannibal's orders, Dante knew that he and Luisa both possessed the prize the other needed. Luisa needed an interview with Hannibal. And Dante wanted access to Allegra for Hannibal.

Parking the Hummer in the 125th Street parking garage, Dante boarded the IRT Lexington Avenue train to his apartment in the North Bronx. On the rickety, crowded subway, Dante decided he was going to be Luisa's new best friend, enticing her with invitations to Panther upcoming Town Hall meetings. Hannibal shared with Luisa via email that this was a privilege, reserved only for the inner circle of the organization and trusted friends.

"Thank you, Mr. Salaam," Luisa replied, thinking that her

assignment was going to be easier than her editor had predicted. Dante promised Luisa that Hannibal would agree to a sit-down interview soon, as their year-end report was ready to be published. Luisa received press releases for their upcoming community efforts before it was faxed to the Associated Press and black-owned newspapers. Dante explained, "Brother Hannibal just needs to make sure that you're down with us. I told 'em that you're okay, but he just wants me to make sure before he's interviewed. You can't blame him, the way white media treats black leaders."

"My journalistic ethics are impeccable," Luisa replied, giving her assignment editor the thumbs-up, when he lumbered past her cubicle during her conversation with Dante.

"So how is your friend? Sista Allegra?" Dante ventured slyly. "I caught her on CNN the other night. That was a real good look."

"Allegra's great. She's swamped working on her dissertation and all, but she's good," Luisa replied, not revealing that Allegra was, at that moment, in Washington, D.C. consulting with several renowned think-tanks. This morning, Thunder had driven to the nation's capital to be with her, while she was waving goodbye to Rolando Barbosa. After the Lakers versus Washington Wizards basketball game, Allegra had a late candlelit dinner with Rolando Barbosa before the Lakers' private jet departed from Ronald Reagan International Airport. Then she heard from Teofilo, who planned to visit the State Department, as he was under consideration to become Brazil's ambassador to the United States. Teofilo shared his disappointment that Allegra would not delay her departure from Washington forty-eight hours to have a dalliance in his hotel. *"Teo, I have to get back to my students. We'll Skype soon. Ciao,"* Allegra texted.

"The reason I'm asking is because Brother Hannibal would like to see her again. Would you make that happen for me, Sista?"

Dante continued, staring without her knowledge at her official eight-by-ten photograph on the television station's website.

Allegra and Luisa had a strong bond, woven with unbending loyalty, and sisterly love as well, which did not include divulging either of their confidences to anyone other than themselves. Luisa was unmoved, as she would not involve Allegra in any situation that she did not sanction in advance. "Well, I can't speak for Allegra," Luisa said conclusively.

"Would you do me this solid, Sista? At least, let her know that Brother Hannibal is asking about her. You wouldn't want to be accused of cock-blocking, now wouldja, Sista? Hannibal digs you. And we both thought that you'd wouldn't mind hooking this thang up."

"I beg your pardon? I don't use my friendships as bargaining chips," Luisa answered.

"You do this solid for me, and I do a solid for you. Point blank," Dante said firmly, hiding his anger that she was making him work so hard.

Over the following week, Luisa continued to phone and email Dante attempting to inch closer to confirming an interview with Hannibal. Production had already begun for November sweeps. Luisa had filed two other specials for eleven o'clock broadcast, but her assignment editor wanted updates about Hannibal Morgan. No matter how Luisa attempted to steer the conversation, focusing on the outbreak of bed bugs, social media etiquette and promotions for a television special, her assignment editor would veer right back to Hannibal Morgan. Luisa wanted to appear that she had his assignment under control; that she was not daunted by the delay tactics Dante was putting her through. Luisa believed that if she were to ask for assistance, that she would appear to be weak. And Luisa would rather die than to let that occur. An appearance of weakness could derail her professional career. Luisa was one of the few journalists who began their professional television careers in New York City, the top market in the country and the city of her birth. The majority of journalists needed to launch their careers in a small town in the mid-west, before breaking into the media capital.

During follow-up telephone calls, after Luisa stated her business, Dante would counter with an inquiry about Allegra. When Luisa expressed a reluctance to involve Allegra, she would receive Dante's cold shoulder, until ultimately, he refused to respond at all. Hannibal knew Dante was strumming this situation, biding his time, so that his needs and those of Dante's and the organization were ultimately met. Dante was ensuring that he was not going to just be Hannibal's flunky matchmaker, and that he would get something out of this dalliance, as per their history.

"Would you have a baby for me?" was the first question Dante hurled at Luisa after she arrived without an appointment at Panther headquarters around noon a week later. "My seed and your seed could bring a beautiful new soldier into this world," he continued, gazing at her long, voluptuous frame. Dante undressed Luisa with his eyes, with a new lustful awareness, appreciating her beauty for the first time; slowly gazing at her long curls, her dark, soft skin and the innocence reflected in her coffee brown eyes. Like so many of the innocent women he had encountered, Dante knew that he now wanted her, could have her, and kicked himself from almost letting her slip away from him. His black turtleneck hugged his athletic frame. Dante had to decide on his approach to obey Hannibal's order to conquer Luisa. Dante knew women who believed that their pussy could be traded on the

NASDAQ stock exchange and were accustomed to men falling at their feet, showering them with trinkets and tender words. Dante was and never would be that dude.

Dante surmised that Luisa's media contacts could be beneficial to the Panthers and he wanted a reporter under the control of the Panthers, so they could garner favorable mainstream media coverage. At the same time, Dante placed a higher priority in having her legs wrapped around his waist. He wanted to feel Luisa shiver beneath him as his stiff cock invaded her pussy with her exploding in ecstasy and weeping as she moaned his name. Dante loved hearing his name being moaned by chicks under his control, and new chicks and his thoughts of their new pussy, turned him on.

"Mr. Salaam, you're way out of line. I'm here to request an appointment with Mr. Morgan. Not to be your next baby mama!" Luisa said, revealing her annoyance, her small nostrils flaring. She thought, *How busy could Hannibal be?*

Dante's temple pulsed on the right side of his forehead. He did not tolerate women speaking to him with a haughty tone. *"Who da fuck does this TV bitch think she is?"* Dante asked himself.

He rested his hands on his eyes, then rose, sitting on the edge of his gray, steel desk, purposely hovering over Luisa, so close she could see his chest expand with each breath. Luisa could also see a dark coloration on the side of his face. "Let me explain how it works around here, Luisa Hamilton. The press doesn't just walk in off the street and demand an interview, nowhatumsayin'?"

"I didn't demand; you and I were talking, weeks ago."

"The media in this city, especially your network, has proven that it cannot be trusted. You already had your story, didn't you? When you walked in here demanding..."

"I didn't demand."

"...demanding your story. You knew, or must have been told in advance, about your station's position on the Panthers and other black community organizations. But the only thing you want to do is rush in here, get a sound byte and build your bullshit around it and what-not; to fill in your European bias; that's how it's always done, isn't it, Luisa?" Dante sneered.

"I dunno what you mean."

"What I mean is, and it's actually kinda brilliant, when you think about it. The white man sends a Dominican sister in here to carry his racist, white supremacy water."

"I beg your..."

"Yes, you should beg. You and your damn network, and others like you, should beg for our forgiveness! For the constant stream of bullshit you choose to report about the black and Latino community, your own people."

"Look, Mr. Salaam, I haven't reported anything derogatory about black people, unless you want to count the black cat that got stuck up the tree in Flushing Meadows Corona Park. Other than that, I think I've been objective in my reporting."

"Dante. Call me Dante, Luisa," he said with a warm smile, abruptly toning down their exchange, as if they had just met at a company retirement cocktail party.

"Mr. Salaam...Dante, I-I-I have an excellent record as a journalist in this city. My credentials are impeccable," she said, nervously buttoning the top button of her pink ruffled blouse, as he continued to lean toward her.

"Before anyone gets access to Brother Hannibal, I must know who they are, nowhatumsayin'? And since you and I will be making a baby, I must first know who you are," Dante stated in a low tone, leaning toward her, with a hint of mischievousness. Luisa was furious and felt disrespected, yet she was totally turned on by

Dante's uninhibited, uncouth nature. Telephones rang in the outer office as she inhaled his musty aroma. His intensity was so carnal that in her head a whisper warned: "Danger." Still, in his presence, Luisa wanted to be like Allegra and relinquish her life-long, lady-like, prim and proper indoctrination. Until this moment, no man had ever stepped up to the plate to serve as the ambassador to her desire for sexual abandon. Luisa's devilish side urged her to run toward, instead of away, from Dante.

When she compared Dante with Virgil, Luisa could not remember the last time Virgil had made her toes curl. Luisa was tired of soothing Virgil's ego, listening to his endless apologies for coming too fast, not being able to get hard, or the familiar, "Sorry, Luisa, my headache is killing me. Can we try again this weekend? I should be better then. And I don't want you to think this has anything to do with you. It's me. I'm just stressed out with the trial and all."

Luisa needed to be dominated, handled by the man in her life. Virgil, with his Ivy League education, proper articulation, Sag Harbor summer home, and Metropolitan Opera box seats had become oh-so-dull over one year ago. Luisa was influenced by how impressed Khadijah and her co-workers were with Virgil's latest courtroom victories.

"Luisa," Khadijah would say, when Luisa sought support in ending the relationship. "Virgil is the best thing that ever happened to you and the best thing to enter New York's Eastern District Office this decade. Look at all of the drug cartels and terrorists he's busted. Elliot Ness ain't got nothing on Virgil Douglas. You are so lucky to have a man like that. Don't you know how many women would want a chance with a man and a future with a man like Virgil Douglas?"

"Virgil is a genius litigator, but…" Luisa's voice would trail off.

"But what?"

"I don't know. There's something missing. Passion? An excitement."

"Don't tell me you're trying to compete with Allegra? Having nasty sex all up in some cockpit...all out in public. She ain't nobody you need to be comparing yourself with, Luisa. All those men be chasing after Allegra, flying in from all over the world, taking her out on the town, buying all of those expensive gifts. What kind of life is that for a woman who's supposed to have some respect about herself? Allegra can afford to be doing what she be doing because she just ain't the marrying kind. You, Luisa, on the other hand, can't. So you need to stop tryin' to keep up with Allegra. 'Cause she ain't nobody to be keepin' up with."

"Khadijah, when was the last time you had a relationship?"

"I'm saving myself for the Lord. I decided to reclaim my virginity. No fornication for me. Been there. Done that. Got my heart broken, so this time, I've decided to wait on the Lord."

Dante interrupted Luisa's defensive rant, rising to answer the knock at the door of his office. His assistant, Anita Wilson, who stared suspiciously at Luisa, handed Dante the poster board and black markers he had requested. Dante then closed the door in the assistant's face, leaving his raised arm against the closed door.

"Mr. Salaam, I'm here to do my job and I won't be disrespected." Dante's tone, his obstinate manner had pulled Luisa into his sphere, just where he wanted her, making her feel there was an unrequited heat waiting to satisfy her longing.

"How is wantin' you to have my seed disrespectful, Sista? How is the black nation to flourish without black babies?"

Luisa's jaw flew open. Her dueling good and bad girl personas were in a full-fledged argument, as Luisa gathered the courage to return Dante's gaze. There was a tsunami behind his eyes and Luisa was electrified by the impending storm. She refused to run for emotional cover.

"Here's my business card, Mr. Salaam. Call me when I can get on Mr. Morgan's schedule. If don't hear from you, I'll follow up. I would prefer to give Mr. Morgan the opportunity to record his own statements, rather than writing…" Luisa threatened.

When Dante ignored her extended business card, Luisa firmly placed it on his desk in front of him, next to his muscular thigh. Her cheeks were burning. Luisa did not mean to play hardball, as it was paramount to establish mutual trust. Her professional experience taught her that some people needed to learn that having the media as your enemy was never in their best interest. And Dante needed to know that his attempt to get familiar with her would not deter Luisa Hamilton from getting the story, especially when she had the opportunity to be promoted from general reporter to a weekend anchor position.

Being the dutiful journalist, Luisa continued to phone Hannibal, leaving countless messages and following up with e-mail. The Panther organization administrative assistant was not impressed by Luisa's interview request and required that Luisa reintroduce herself each time she phoned.

"Luisa Hamilton, WNBC-TV. How are you today? Ms. Wilson?" *Silence.*

"Yes, I'm calling to see when I can get on Mr. Morgan's calendar for an interview."

"He ain't in. And all interview requests gotta go through Brother Salaam," she snapped, smacking on her chewing gum into the telephone receiver.

"Would you please take a message?"

"Leave whatever you got to say on his voicemail."

Though Luisa loved hearing his husky, sexy voice on his voice mail, she was upset that Dante never returned her telephone calls. His aloofness ignited a perfect storm of desire and fury, as Luisa was not accustomed to being dismissed. Although Luisa may have had difficulty attracting men who satisfied her, she was not used to being ignored, professionally or personally. Dante crept into her day and night dreams. At the television station, her mind would drift as she stared at her computer screen instead of writing a script for a story that was already behind deadline. And at night, awakening from a deep sleep, Luisa would punch her pillow, and toss and turn, trying to erase her thoughts of Dante riding her, fucking her brains out. Luisa was disappointed when she awoke, drenched in sweat, and realized where she was, in her own bed, with a distracted Virgil, her perfect, upwardly mobile boyfriend, soundly snoring next to her.

Luisa searched for photographs of Dante and Hannibal on the Internet. Their website was down for maintenance. The few photographs which existed of Dante were at public rallies and marches. He was always standing behind the right shoulder of Hannibal Morgan, wearing a black leather kufi, a long black leather coat and black sunglasses.

"What's wrong?" Virgil asked Luisa over dinner at LaGeorges, a French restaurant on Manhattan's East Side.

Allegra often said that the "what's wrong?" stage of a relationship was when a man and woman were hurtling toward a boring and uneventful end. "When two grown-ass people can't be frank about what ain't goin' on...what is the fuckin' point of wasting time?" To Luisa, Allegra was more brazen than any female friend she had ever known. Allegra never tolerated being bored or not being satisfied. "Everything don't have to last forever, Luisa. Life ain't like a soap opera. If you're unhappy with Virgil, then end the relationship. That way, he can never accuse you of lying to him."

Virgil insisted on ordering drinks, appetizers and dinner for both of them, arguing that he was more familiar with the recently installed gourmet chef. "*New York Magazine* raved about him in their food review, voted him Chef of New York. But back to what I asked, what's wrong, Luisa?" The gallant waiter had already accepted their menus and returned to the kitchen with an eager gait.

"Nothing, Virgil. Just tired. Tracking down some stories, that's all," Luisa answered, dabbing the side of her mouth. The brunette waitress served their creamed cauliflower with smoked salmon caviar appetizers.

"What you working on?" Virgil asked, loudly smacking on the caviar. The last thing Luisa wanted to talk about in a romantic, upscale restaurant with a man who bored her, was her job. Since there was a growing divide of interesting conversation, Luisa held onto the one subject the two conversed about.

"You know anything about the Urban Panther Watch Movement?" Luisa asked, not expecting a substantive answer. Virgil thought *those people* uptown were beneath his Ivy League pedigree and supervisory capacity in the white-collar crime division.

"Those idiots who run around in army boots? Yeah, I heard of 'em," Virgil said, adjusting the rims on his wire-framed glasses, his reddish freckles dotting across his nose. Luisa never noticed how aggravatingly restrained Virgil was until that moment. He wore a sensible beige, double-breasted suit and brown monk strap shoes. "A few years back, a couple of their members were indicted for weapons charges. Home-grown idiots, I tell you. That's all

they are. Always beefing about the big, bad, white man." Virgil
was in his element. He became more confident when he was looking down his pointy nose at other people; especially other lower
economic class, black people. In his mind, everyone was an idiot
except for him.

"Really?" Luisa asked, shocked that Virgil knew anything.

"Don't tell me, you're assigned to cover those characters,"
Virgil said, rolling his eyes.

"Actually I am. What's wrong with that?"

"Nothing's wrong. I just don't think you should be consorting
with those types of people. I mean, I know this is part of your job,
but they are not on your level. And by the way, what happened
to the story you were working on regarding the puppy mill on
Long Island? The one with all of those health code violations?
Hey, do you want me to put a call into the general manager at
your station? He owes me a professional favor...didn't make his
screw-up brother-in-law take a perp walk in front of television
cameras after his arraignment," Virgil boasted, talking a blue
streak. Luisa's knife struck the corner of her plate, causing a
clanging sound, as her cheeks turned red. This was one of those
frequent, glaring moments, when Virgil proved that he just did
not understand her. And he was not interested in seeing her for
more than the notable reporter, arm-piece, sexually obedient and
undemanding girlfriend that she was. Luisa and Virgil were a
perfect image of a perfect couple existing only to impress the
world, no matter how miserable one of them truly was.

"What's wrong, Luisa?"

"Nothing. I'm tired of you asking me that question. Look, I
want to go home." Virgil stared at her, and then searched the
faces of other diners. Seeing that she was serious in her intent, he
snapped his fingers, signaling the waiter's attention, another habit

Luisa detested. "Virgil, forgive me, but I just have to get out of here. I can't catch my breath." The waitress arrived at their table with their entrées of duck foie gras, which Virgil insisted that she try.

"Virgil, did you hear anything that I just said?" Luisa snapped. The waitress searched Virgil's face as to what she should do with their entrees. Virgil waved the waitress away, forcing her to retreat back into the kitchen.

"Alright," Virgil said slowly, checking again to see if other diners were now aware that Luisa was ending their dinner. A blonde, middle-aged couple stared, and then shook their heads in disgust.

"I'll have the valet bring the car around," Virgil offered.

"There are taxis waiting outside. I'll hop in a cab."

"I don't understand, Luisa. Tell me what's wrong!"

Luisa exhaled. "All I can tell you is that I have got to get out of here—now. I can't breathe." Luisa reached for her white clutch. Virgil placed his thin fingers over hers, hoping to restrain her from leaving.

"Look, Luisa," Virgil said. Luisa lowered her eyes, avoiding his eyes. "You can't just walk out of here. How would that look? If you think I'm going to let you walk out of here, you're sadly mistaken," Virgil whispered, his tone turning from begging to serious. Luisa kept her eyes lowered and waited as Virgil snapped his fingers again, signed for the bill. Holding Luisa's elbow and guiding her like a miniature sailboat, past curious onlookers and a perplexed, tuxedo-wearing maitre d'. Virgil pressed a crisp fifty-dollar bill in the palm of the maitre d' and followed Luisa to the valet station outside.

Hours later, with *Nightline* broadcasting in the background, Virgil lay on his side of the bed, staring up at the ceiling. Luisa was lying as close to the opposite side of the bed as she could manage, her back facing him. "I'm sorry, Luisa. I don't know what's going on with me. It must be my caseload. Stress at the office. Just give me some time, and things will return back to the way they were in the beginning."

Luisa slowly closed her eyelids, trying to recall when Virgil had ever worked his mojo and their sex life had ever been satisfactory. She felt that Virgil needed a roadmap to get to her G-spot; that she was a traffic cop directing him to her orgasm. Then, Virgil gyrated on full tilt for two minutes; poking out his chest as if he had performed a sexual marathon. As time went on, Virgil's deficiencies mounted, matching his cold personality, until Luisa was lucky if Virgil gave her thirty-seconds of action. Initially, Luisa ignored Virgil's limp dick, because she was optimistic when he would have a burst of hardness for thirty seconds at least, believing that their relationship was leaving a bad cycle; only to have her disappointment to reoccur soon thereafter.

12

Allegra could not understand what she was saying inbetween sobs, when Luisa phoned her after midnight. Allegra was in the middle of masturbating via Skype with Teofilo in Rio de Janiero. Luisa texted and phoned all three of Allegra's telephone numbers, all of which bounced to voice mail.

Wearing a red negligee, Allegra had her legs perched on each side of the Mac book, so that a nude Teofilo could have an up close view of her exposed breasts and pussy. Atlantic shells made into candleholders were lit around Allegra's home office.

"You're torturing me, beautiful Allegra," Teofilo said, jerking himself. "How can I concentrate on the merits of your dissertation when your nude body makes me want to rush to the airport right now?"

"Yes, Teofilo, but you are forbidden to leave Brazil until your trial is over. That's why Skype is a beautiful thing. No?"

"I must hold you in my arms again. Don't you love Rio? Why don't you come to Rio for Carnaval? It's going to be very exciting. All of Brazil will be celebrating."

"I love me some Rio, Teo," Allegra answered while stimulating her G-spot with the vibrator Teofilo had sent her via international express courier. "But there's no way I can afford to get caught up in your corruption trial. Me being there would only make your political troubles worse. Your paparazzi would love for me to come back so that they could stalk me twenty-four-seven from Catete to Leblon to your estate in Praia do Forte. I value my privacy."

"Brazil adores Allegra!" Teofilo exclaimed, laughing loudly. "But not as much as I do."

"So you decided to go forward with the trial, even though you admitted knowing that your campaign manager took bribes in exchange for business contracts?"

"Yes, what the hell does everybody know? Brazil loves Teofilo Branco and I am sure that I will get re-elected, because the people know that I love them."

"So, do you think turning down the Ambassador post was the best decision?"

"It was a difficult decision. I would've had more opportunity to visit America and to see my Allegra, but I think my re-election looks favorable."

"I'm happy for you, Teofilo. Really, I am," Allegra confided.

"Does Allegra love Teofilo?"

"I will always adore you, Teo, as long as we understand the pleasure we bring to each other."

"I love watching you pleasure yourself, *Bela*. Would you teach Bianca how to pleasure herself? She honestly seems unable to do so. That must be the reason she is so miserable." Allegra burst out laughing, with Teofilo joining her, until they both became quiet as Allegra returned to being occupied with her own self-pleasure. Teofilo rubbed the corners of his eyes and leaned forward, closer to his laptop computer screen to gawk at his sensual goddess explore her beautiful brown body with closed eyes. Allegra rubbed her firm breasts, her plump abdomen and smooth thighs, slipping her fingers on top of her vulva, pressing her clit, gently jiggling her fingers. Teofilo was transfixed as he increased the intensity of his strokes on his hard cock. Allegra continued massaging herself, outside of her vulva and returning her fingers to both sides of her clit. Teofilo and Allegra pleasured themselves, breathing together in sync. Allegra rocked her pelvis, knowing just when to extend her pleasure, not wanting to climax too soon. Sitting in his luxurious black office chair in the private office of the Governor's Mansion, Teofilo gripped the left upholstered arm as he got off, his breath becoming shallow and quick.

A beeping sound emanated from Allegra's Mac book, the Skype icon signaling that someone was trying to connect with her. With her eyes still closed, her hand reached for her glossy red mouse, intending to click: *Ignore.* Her hand played hide and seek, in search of the mouse, as it was not on the mouse pad. Allegra lifted her right eyelid to peer at the bottom of her computer screen. *Luisa calling,* the icon read, at 1:16 a.m. "Oh Gawd!" Allegra exclaimed, turning off the vibrator and swinging her legs from off the top of her desk, while wrapping her nightgown around her body.

"*Como?* What is it?!" Teofilo exclaimed, not believing Allegra was going to leave him at the doorstep of ecstasy.

"Teo, I gotta run, sweetheart. A friend is on the other line."

"But Allegra?!?" Allegra did not give Teofilo a millisecond to launch into his usual tantrum of whining and begging. Clicking *End Call,* she clicked over to answer Luisa on Skype. When it came to her sister-friend, Allegra knew that the lateness of the hour meant emergency.

"What's up, Luisa?" Allegra asked, tossing her vibrator in the right desk drawer and tying her negligee around her waist. There on the computer screen, Allegra had the answer to her question. Luisa had been crying for hours. Her eyes were swollen into slits. She wept and squeezed her nostrils into a used tissue. Her hair was strewn all over her head.

"What happened, Luisa?" Allegra asked again, concerned, her eyebrows knitting together.

"I feel like I'm gonna die. When I'm with Virgil, I feel like I'm dead." Allegra fell back against her chair. In her wildest dreams, Allegra had not expected that response.

"Okay, slowly tell me what happened. It's okay to cry, but I can barely understand what you're saying. What? You feel dead, Luisa? And what does Virgil have to do with this?"

Luisa nodded, blowing her nose. "I feel invisible. Like I don't matter. No matter what I want, somebody wants me to do something else."

"I'll ask again...what happened?"

"Virgil and I had dinner at LaGeorges earlier this evening... and there I was with this man who everyone says that I'm so goddamn lucky to be with, who is being drafted to run for mayor of New York City, and all of that other bullshit."

"Really? When did that happen?"

"Yesterday. Some hedge fund people connected with the Democratic Party and asked him to run, so he took me out for dinner afterwards to LaGeorges to celebrate. But the longer I sat there with him listening to how excited he was about running for mayor, and how wonderful our life would be together, the angrier I got. And I'm thinking, 'Motherfucker, you haven't even proposed to me; you haven't even gotten hard long enough to even make me smile...talking about life together.' And here's the kicker! Virgil tells me that I'm going to have to leave my job at the station if I won't focus on certain kinds of stories. He thought that it would be in my best interest to request a transfer to consumer or entertainment reporting, or he would pay for me to learn how to be a traffic reporter! A goddamned traffic reporter. Virgil said that the station's FCC license could be jeopardized if it appeared that there was bias in its reporting. And I wouldn't want that, Virgil said." Luisa wasn't crying any longer. Her voice had regained its composure and turned to anger.

"You never said you wanted to marry Virgil. You want to marry him?"

"Hell no! I used to, but I sure as hell don't want to now. When I mentioned the assignments that I was working on, he immediately had a problem with the kinds of stories I was doing, like I have a fuckin' choice! Virgil went on to say that I needed to make better professional choices about what I report on, as if I had a damn choice!"

"Girl, does he fuck you the same way...like he's giving an annual job review?" Allegra was perturbed now. She hated seeing Luisa squandering her life with controlling-ass Virgil, but she was not one to tell anyone whom they should be with, because she didn't tolerate anyone dipping into her relationships.

Luisa paused for a moment, as she felt overwhelmed with shame. Tears reappeared in the corners of her eyes. "I-I guess he does. Now that I think about it, whatever shit we do has to be done or not done, in order to please him. And when I say, 'Hey, I need whatever,' Virgil convinces me that I really don't, that my desires are just a figment of my imagination." Allegra was so stunned that she almost laughed, but quickly became serious again when Luisa's tears fell like raindrops changing into hail.

Allegra's pink cell phone beeped. Thunder text messaged her: *"Can I come over? I need to see you."* She did not reply.

"Luisa, you know I love you. You're my sister, my best friend forever, my play cousin. But Virgil was pulling that shit five minutes after you met him!"

"What? What, do you mean?"

"Remember when we were in New Orleans at the Essence Music

Festival? Opening night, there was a private dinner at the mayor's home? And Virgil introduced himself to you, chatted you up. You both were checkin' for each other, but when you said you were cold, Mr. Know-It-All convinced you that you weren't. Didn't he say something about 'How can you be cold in the Big Easy?' And you let that shit go. Then when you and I were ready to leave, Egghead Virgil said, 'You couldn't possibly be ready to leave; the night is young!' And you ended up staying for hours, while I soloed my ass back to the Four Seasons."

"So you're saying my relationship with Virgil is all my fault?" Luisa asked, growing defensive.

"Hell, yeah! That's exactly what I'm saying, Luisa! You've got to check men within five minutes of meeting them. Teach them how to treat you. If you don't set your boundaries early, you're gonna spend the rest of your life chasing happiness, behaving as if you exist solely to please them. And I'll be damned if I allow any man to control what I want and what I need. Some men are interested in making sure that only their needs are taken care of. And if you don't put your foot down from Jump Street, you're gonna be carrying his proverbial water for the rest of your life."

Luisa stared at Allegra through the computer screen, then exhaled, nodding her head. Thunder texted Allegra again: "You Up? I hate talkin' to your voicemail." Allegra sucked her teeth and turned off her cell phone, tossing it into her briefcase.

"You okay, Luisa?"

Luisa nodded. "And you know, the worst thing about tonight, Allegra?"

"No, what?"

"I absolutely detest French food."

Allegra and Luisa paused, and then giggled together.

Allegra raised her eyebrows and ended the Skype call with Luisa when she heard knocking at the door. It was Thunder. When she opened the door, Thunder did not wait for Allegra to greet him or invite him inside. His face was sullen, withdrawn. His blood-shot eyes were creased into narrow slits. Allegra stepped aside, closing the door, asking, "What's wrong, Thunder?" He shoved his fists into his jeans' pockets, and slumped his shoulders. The confident Thunder that Allegra knew was not standing before her. Something had occurred that had taken the spirit out of him.

"He's gone. My pops passed early this evening." Allegra opened her arms and floated to Thunder, holding him tightly. She could feel his tears trickle on her shoulder.

"I'm sorry, Baby. He knew you loved him so much. Come. Sit over here," Allegra said, leading Thunder to the loveseat.

"Of course, I knew his days weren't long, but still, when it happens, it's like knocking the wind out of you."

"Honey, I'm glad you're here. Whatever you need, I'm here for you." Thunder responded by resting his hand on her knee as he relaxed against the sofa. "Who do you need me to call? What do you need me to do?"

Thunder used the back of his hand to wipe his face, before continuing, "Pops always made sure that his affairs were in order. He planned his going home ceremony down the last detail, so there's not much to do other than make it happen."

"Just a second," Allegra said, rushing to the kitchen to retrieve a glass of seltzer water, with a lime wedge for Thunder. "Here, Thunder. Drink something. You hungry? Did you eat today?" Thunder shook his head and sipped the water.

"Just relax, baby," Allegra said. "Let me cook you a turkey omelet, grits and cheese and toast. How's that?"

"If I wasn't hungry before, I sure as hell am now," Thunder said lightly, before his sadness quickly returned.

"Come upstairs, Thunder. You're exhausted," Allegra said, coaxing him to stand on his feet. Leading him to the bottom of the staircase, Allegra removed his shoes, placing them on the shoe rack. She then held his hand as they climbed the stairs. In her bedroom, Allegra undressed Thunder, and forced him to lie down, folding the sheet and the comforter over him. Allegra smoothed his clothes and hung them in her closet. She returned to Thunder's bedside, sitting next to him, kissing him tenderly on the forehead.

"Just relax, Thunder. I'll be back shortly with your food," Allegra said, disconnecting her laptop from Skype.

Thunder nodded, though he stared into space. Allegra rose to leave. When she reached the doorway, she turned, "Thunder, your pops loved you as much as you loved him. When you first introduced me to him at the radio station and during the time we spent with him upstate at the house this summer, I could tell by the way he looked at you that you made him very proud. His stories of raising you, being a grandparent, a mother and a father, were laced with love, friendship and struggle. Right now, I feel your heart is breaking; you already miss him. But I want you to know that when, not if, when you need to cry, shout, weep, stomp, scream or whatever it is you need to do or feel, I'm here for you. You can do it right here. Okay, Baby?" Allegra dimmed the lights in the bedroom, as Thunder used his hands to cover his face, shielding the tears that were streaming. Allegra's heart reached out for Thunder as she crossed the room, wrapping her arms around him, holding him tightly. Feeling emotional safety in Allegra's arms, Thunder let out a low wail that sounded like a wounded animal, and burst into tears anew.

Thunder asked for Allegra's university intern to design and have the program printed, which she gladly consented to, providing the program and the content. Two days later, on Saturday, Allegra accompanied Thunder to the funeral of his grandfather, Thunder Poole I, the only family member who had shaped Thunder into the man he was. Thunder's copious tears fell at his grandfather's gravesite in Mount Vernon cemetery, as Allegra held him around his waist, draping her arms around him supportively. Allegra fed his spirit with silence as he mourned his loss, over the following weeks, during his leave of absence from the radio station. Her presence, her unwavering support during this crisis, for Thunder, was a blessing behind a dark cloud. His tragic loss served to strengthen their relationship and to reveal shades of their personalities the two had not yet experienced.

Forty-eight hours passed before Luisa's assignment editor asked, "So how's it going with the story on Hannibal Morgan?"

"Um, pretty good. I need to follow up with his chief of staff. They're reluctant, sort of suspicious about the press, but I think they're beginning to trust me. I believe I'm making some inroads."

"We want to be the first outlet to do an exposé on him...be the first to gain access to his organization. There's got to be some dirt somewhere. With these loud-mouth, grassroots type of groups, there usually is."

"I should be able to file something in time for their tenth anniversary," Luisa lied, knowing she had only developed a rapport with Dante instead of the man himself.

At an Upper West Side five-alarm, burning a stretch of commercial buildings along Amsterdam Avenue, Luisa tried to remain focused as she interviewed witnesses and the fire chief. Her mind fluctuated from her own hollow loneliness to thoughts of Dante and the feelings of attraction that she had toward him; as well as the interview request with Hannibal Morgan.

Luisa was embarrassed by the lust-filled thoughts she was having about him. In fact, that was the reason Luisa purposely stayed away from Panther headquarters, because her dreams were too haunting and too precise. Luisa felt ashamed by the small details that she remembered about him: his natural aroma; his white, square-shaped teeth; his New Orleans drawl. She relished her recurring naughty daydream—often thinking that his military pants and black belt with the gold buckle were hanging down around his wide hips with his cock buried deep inside of her pussy. Luisa and Dante would grind rhythmically on the desk in his locked office at the Urban Panther Watch Movement. Luisa fantasized her screaming "No's," as Dante ripped off her silk panties and sucked on her small tits, as she circled her tongue inside of his ears. Her pussy became wet as she thought of Dante smacking her ass, demanding that she come again, knowing she would have no choice but to abide, as he fucked her faster, ignoring the administrative assistant tapping on his office door. Luisa blacked out in her fantasy of Dante throwing her legs on his shoulders and lifting her ass to his desk's edge, commanding his cock to unleash inside of her pulsating pussy.

She heard nothing.

"Luisa? Luisa!" Her cameraman raised his voice, trying to get her attention, dragging her out of her fertile imagination, as the two rode back to the television station.

"What?" she answered, irritated.

"Boy, you really got something or somebody on your mind, don't you?" He chuckled. "What is it? You and Virgil okay?"

"I'm good. We're okay." Luisa shrugged her shoulders.

"I'm going to drop off the footage in editing, so we can get this on the eleven o'clock broadcast. And by the way, you and Virgil are invited to our housewarming. I'll e-mail you the invitation," the cameraman said, parking in the station's reserved parking space in the garage on Sixty-Seventh Street. The sunset cast an orange red glow through the skyscrapers, as the cameraman waited for Luisa's answer. Luisa rummaged through her carry-all bag, examining its contents.

Checking her Dolce & Gabanna watch, she answered, "Thanks; that sounds good. I'll have to check Virgil's schedule. It's hard to know these days when he's available."

"Okey-dokey, Luisa. You should get the e-vite in the next day or so," the cameraman replied, unloading the heavy equipment from the rear of the van. Luisa could not hear him. She was already immersed back in the comfort of her erotic daydream, where Dante knew what she needed, and without hesitation, gave it to her. Luisa checked her watch, searched for her Metrocard and decided she was going to the Urban Panther Watch Movement that very evening.

13

"The Lakers are playing the Knicks and the Jersey Nets tonight. We're stayin' at the W Towers on Avenue of the Americas tomorrow, from the 21st to the 22nd. *Espero ver você pronto, bela.* Rolando (Hope to see you soon, beautiful. Rolando)"

Allegra fondly remembered their tryst in Rio de Janiero and their platonic dinner in Washington D.C. She remembered his olive complexion, his shiny black curls and thick cock, and how they lost their minds together in that cigar bar in Rio. Rolando was hard to ignore. His shenanigans were splashed all over the nightly news and ESPN, especially since he had signed a guaranteed $150 million dollar-per-year contract, ending speculation and the bidding war he created when he delayed the public announcement of whether he was going to remain with the Lakers or be traded to the Knicks. Rolando also signed a deal to create his own brand of men's shoes, distributed by an Italian company.

Allegra headed to her *bikram* yoga class near Washington Square Park and New York University. The ninety minutes of contorting and stretching her body in the challenging positions in the one hundred degree heated studio, along with the deep breathing, helped her to restore balance in her life. Juggling her teaching schedule, grading the mounting term papers, perfecting her dissertation and attempts by Thunder to turn up the commitment factor in their strictly sexual relationship often made Allegra forget that her yoga practice was the restorative center of her life.

Allegra unfurled her body on the floor of the yoga studio and practiced deep breathing with closed eyes until she achieved a meditative state. Her fellow exhausted yogis and yoginis slowly dragged their limp bodies out to the dressing room to blissfully return to their lives as NYU students, mothers, or Wall Street professionals. Allegra showered and changed from her sweaty, indigo-colored tank top and shorts to her brown tweed blazer and skirt. Since it was donation day at a local charity, Allegra dropped cash in the glass jar on the reception desk as she departed.

The crisp fall air smacked her in the face as she stepped out onto the sidewalk. Allegra loved New York City when the seasons changed, with the tree leaves showing golden and other brilliant shades. She looked forward to change, in all of its forms, and refused to remain stagnant, always obeying her own restlessness. Being stagnant and confined terrified Allegra, so she closely monitored her life, never wanting to have a life of regret. Allegra's BlackBerry vibrated, signaling an incoming text message from Thunder. "Been thinking about us. Need to talk."

Allegra sighed and rolled her eyes. The last thing she wanted to do with Thunder was talk, as he had distinguished himself as a skilled lover. Unlike most men, who reluctantly abided by the boundaries which Allegra set, Thunder remained oblivious, wanting to restart conversations about their relationship. Allegra turned off the power on her BlackBerry and continued on her way, nodding to the pretzel vendor, who was a West Fourth Street mainstay.

A black, stretch limousine with tinted windows slowly paced Allegra as she sauntered along East Third Street, adjacent to Washington Square Park, returning to her office. Allegra hoisted her black nylon gym bag and buttoned her jacket around her throat. A chilly breeze whipped brownish leaves around her black boots as the limousine driver lurched ahead of Allegra, suddenly stopping beside her. The electronic window in the rear compartment lowered slowly, making a whirring sound. Allegra continued walking, nearing the entrance to the faculty office building. Graduate students, two young men and a woman puffed on high tar cigarettes and laughed together outside the entrance.

"Excuse me?" a rich male voice said. The graduate students glanced at the limousine, wondering whom the man was speaking to. "Excuse me!" the man yelled again, gesturing for the students to get Allegra's attention, who was oblivious as she reached for the door of the building.

"Professor Adams?!" the female graduate student yelled. Allegra turned to see a smiling Rolando step out of the limousine holding a dozen Casablanca Lilies.

"*Bom Dia*, Allegra Adams," a grinning Rolando said, striding swiftly toward her, as she stood on the entrance steps.

Damn, he looks delicious. I could have him for dessert and still want more, Allegra thought. Rolando wore an open-neck white dress shirt under his single-breasted suit and shiny black, Italian shoes. When he reached the top of the entrance steps, he forcefully wrapped his long muscular arms around her body, leaning over to kiss her on the lips. Allegra stiffened her body and stepped back, as Dr. Winchester, the department head, angled his wide body through the open door. "Professor Adams," Dr. Winchester said, tipping his hat, and glancing up at the mountain of a man, that was Rolando.

"Hello, Dr. Winchester," Allegra replied, while Rolando held open the door, attempting to follow Allegra into the building.

"What are you doing here?" Allegra asked, crossing her arms, while nervously glancing around the courtyard and back at the graduate students, who continued joking with each other.

"I'm here to see you of course," Rolando answered glibly, still smiling, and admiring Allegra. "You're even more beautiful when the sun shines on your eyes."

"How did you find me, Rolando?" Allegra asked, still not impressed by his words. As fine as Rolando was, she never appreciated surprise visits from any man, particularly a man she had only stroked in a dark cigar bar in Rio de Janeiro. "This ain't cool, Rolando. I would have preferred it if you would've called first."

"Oh, my bad. I was thinking from our e-mails that...I thought it would've... Look, my bad. I just wanted to see you; said so when I e-mailed you saying that the team was coming here this morning. How ya doing?"

Rolando tried to explain, his dark mouth frowning slightly as he shifted his feet. He was not the type of man who was accustomed to explaining himself. Rolando had swooning women, lying in wait at the airport of every NBA city. Rolando and his Los Angeles Lakers teammates had thirty-five women waiting in the lobby when they arrived after midnight at the Hilton and often more when they traveled to other NBA cities. Hotel security had to be called when three women bribed a housekeeper to let them into a rookie's hotel room. When the three women jumped out of the closet, buck-naked, the rookie, naive to the NBA life, almost fainted, until he realized the benefits of welcoming his excited guests. Rolando discarded the flowers, panties and telephone messages, which were held by the hotel concierge, instructing him to put a do-not-disturb on the telephone in his suite. Media requests for interviews were directed to the Lakers' press office.

"Didn't you receive my e-mail?"

"I did."

"And then I e-mailed you again wanting to see you tonight after the game. My teammates chartered a couple of helicopters to fly down to Atlantic City to gamble and party, but I wanted to stay and spend some time with you." Rolando could not believe that Allegra was not overjoyed to see him. She had not chased, phoned him or dropped hints to visit him in Los Angeles. Allegra eventually gave Rolando her cell phone number, but never returned his telephone calls, and only replied intermittently to him via e-mail or text. Allegra compartmentalized her relationship with Rolando, which made her a man whisperer, and a rare kind of woman.

"Yes, I got your e-mails," Allegra said, letting the entrance door slowly close as she stepped outside, clearing a pathway so that a professor carrying a computer monitor could enter. Students turned to gawk at Rolando with a know-him-from-somewhere look on their faces. "I wish you had given me a chance to get back to you."

"I e-mailed you two days ago, Allegra. And then again last night."

Rolando had e-mailed Allegra relentlessly since they met, their exchanges quickly becoming sexually heated. Following his ESPN, after-the-game interview, she requested via e-mail:

——Original Message——

To: allegraphd@aol.com

From: rolandohoops@gmail.com

"Tell me what turns you on, Rolando." August 15, 2011 10:23 pm EST

"Allegra, my sexual fantasy is you. I have to admit you've gotten in my head. Coach has been on me a lot lately...he says that I been daydreaming, and he's right. My thoughts of you are hard to shake, even though we just met." August 15, 2011 10:31 pm EST

"Your fantasy, please? Turn me on." August 15, 2011 11:03 pm EST

"You want me to tell you in English or Portuguese?" August 15, 2011 11:05 pm EST

"I would rather tell you over the telephone...or better yet, in person. I could fly you to Chicago. We play the Bulls tomorrow night."

"LOL...English, *por favor. Pronto!*" August 16, 2011 12:23 am EST

"Okay. Well, I dream of the soft touch of your lips against mine and your warm hands passing all over my body and the feel of your sweet, wet pussy around my cock. How your muscles hold me inside makes me want to stay in your arms forever. Man, you haunt me!" August 16, 2011 12:25 am EST

"Here's the deal, Rolando. I prefer to keep my personal and professional life separate; I wouldn't show up to see you at the Staples Center out of the blue," Allegra replied, lowering her gym bag between them, running her hand across the smooth nylon.

"I wouldn't have minded that at all," Rolando replied, gazing up at the historical building covered with climbing ivy. His limousine idled at the curb. The dapperly dressed driver stood at the ready for the return of his superstar passenger.

"Hey look, I'm sorry I came at you like this. With a shoot-a-round today and the game tonight, we leave first thing in the morning. And I wanted to make sure that I saw you." Nothing turned Allegra on more than a pleading man, and this one was holding a dozen Casablanca Lilies.

"Those for me?" Allegra said softly. Rolando looked at the bouquet and to Allegra as if he had momentarily forgotten his gift for her.

"Yeah. Yes, they are. Here," Rolando answered sheepishly.

Allegra glanced around the courtyard for any witnesses and eased closer to Rolando. The graduate students said their mutual good-byes, then separated, walking in opposite directions. Allegra sniffed the aroma of the lilies, closing her eyes, and smiled for the first time since Rolando had arrived.

"They're beautiful, Rolando." Relieved that he had pleased her, Rolando relaxed his shoulders, as she rested her index fingers in between his belt buckle and his stomach; above his crotch.

"You must have been in Europe," said Allegra.

"H-how did you know that?" Rolando asked, his eyebrows knitting together.

"Because you can only get Casablanca Lilies in Europe this time of the year. I would say, you were probably in Holland."

Rolando chuckled. "Actually, the team was in the United Kingdom, on an NBA ambassador trip. The hotel concierge knew of a flower show in Holland where I could order and have them shipped here."

Allegra kissed Rolando lightly on his cheek, sliding her hand down the front of his chest. Just as at the Rio cigar bar, Rolando could not believe his good fortune as Allegra's thumb softly brushed the outside of his cock behind her nylon bag. Rolando's eyes grew dark, his throat becoming dry. He edged closer to her, in the middle of the courtyard, in broad daylight, outside her office building. Rolando's dreams had been haunted by the fantasy of having a full blowjob from Allegra. He had fucked many women, having them swing from chandeliers in hotel room across the United States. He'd held a ménage à trois in a cabana off the coast of California on Catalina Island, and in the therapy center of the Aspen rehabilitation center after his knee surgery. Groupies sucked his dick under his box seats at the NBA All-Star game. But his yearning for Allegra dwarfed those episodes.

Rolando did not remember the names of those women, or the husbands who wanted to watch. Rolando never forgot the name of Allegra Adams. His memory of her stalked his soul.

"Meet me tonight after the game? Outside the locker room?" Rolando asked, watching her thumb tickle his hard cock, as she continued inhaling the intoxicating fragrance of her Casablanca Lilies. Dr. Winchester returned again, gawking at Rolando, nodding at Allegra, and then continued on into the building.

"I don't do groupie, crazed fan scenes," Allegra said, gazing into Rolando's eyes.

"It won't be like that," Rolando lied. Allegra's lips curled into a smirk, to which Rolando chuckled. "Okay, as soon as I finish my interviews at the Garden and the one in the hotel lobby, I'm out. I'm done. I'm all yours."

"I have a better idea," Allegra suggested. Rolando raised his eyebrows. "Leave a copy of the electronic key to your suite with the concierge, and I'll meet you there." A wide smile erupted across Rolando's face, as he realized that he now had experienced a sudden reversal of fortune.

Allegra touched his cheek softly then turned, gliding away. "Oh, Rolando?"

"Yes?"

Glancing over her shoulder, before hurrying into the faculty building, Allegra slyly said with a wink, "Just so you know, I can't stand losers, so if you whoop the Knicks' ass, I've got something special for you."

"Alright, that's a bet," Rolando replied, maintaining his frozen half-grin, as Allegra strolled away. When the door to the building closed behind her and a group of graduate students, Rolando loped back to the open door of his waiting stretch limousine, pumping his fist in the air.

14

The Urban Panther Watch Movement offices were empty when Luisa arrived. Used coffee cups, fast-food leftovers, loose-leaf notebooks and half-painted poster boards were strewn across various worktables. The temperatures in New York City had rebounded and the metropolis was experiencing an Indian summer. City dwellers were seen playing Frisbee in the park, wearing everything from flip flops and shorts to boarding the Staten Island Ferry wearing fur-lined parkas and boots.

With Macbook in hand, Luisa tentatively knocked on Hannibal's slightly ajar office door. His sullen, apathetic administrative assistant was nowhere in sight. Hearing only a militant radio show broadcasting from inside Dante's empty office, Luisa peeked through the slightly open door to see an old boom box, with an attached wire hanger. Luisa surveyed the dusty air conditioner, and a cluttered desk piled with folders and an open briefcase, with a half-eaten banana lying inside. A stainless steel spring water cooler stood in the corner next to an abandoned coat rack and the ubiquitous metal folding chairs. On Dante's beige office walls were photos of himself with prominent activists and athletes, a former black mayor, and a longtime congresswoman. Dante posed with Hannibal Morgan in a variety of photographs and memorabilia that spanned two decades. There were photographs of Hannibal and Dante as teenagers showing their bravado, posing while making a jump shot in a basketball game. In the photographs of Hannibal and Dante as men, the smiles were far less frequent, staring back at Luisa with mean, defiant faces. Luisa inched back out of Dante's office and strolled into a large conference room, with newspapers strewn across the table. In search of the ladies' room, Luisa stumbled upon a makeshift, unisex lavatory.

Staring into the mirror, Luisa reapplied her MAC frost lipstick, freshened her powder and sprayed on her favorite Carol's Daughter perfume. "What the hell are you doing?" Luisa scolded to her reflection in the mirror, after she fluffed her curly hair, sprayed cologne and smoothed the bottom of her pleated dress. "You're here to get a damn story...not to go out on a date!"

"Man, the rally is on for Saturday afternoon. Get the word out to your people, and your people's people...yeah, we got somebody dedicated to promoting on all of the social media sites. We're going to need to double our turnout numbers from January's march." Luisa stopped primping and leaned out of the entrance to the lavatory.

"Hello?" she said, to which there was no response. Luisa knew she wasn't hearing voices. She waited a few more seconds, and then heard, "Yeah, the police permits were already secured. Of course, the son-of-bitch police commissioner tried to pull the license, but after our people bombarded his punk ass with emails and telephone calls, he backed off. Dumb muthafucka."

Luisa quickly fingered the bangs around her face, hurriedly gathered her belongings and dashed out of the lavatory only to find the meeting room still empty. She waited until the male voice returned, then followed it across the room and across to the rear circular staircase and slowly climbed the steps to the exquisite view on the roof. Once Luisa's eyes adjusted to the darkness, she scanned the area, in search of the voice that she had heard. Luisa appreciated the famous New York City skyline in midtown, as well as to the north, and the sparkling lights from a night game at Yankee Stadium.

"Yeah, we ain't gonna give these racist pigs an excuse, so bring bats and whatever you got. If one of those bitch cops steps outta line, it's on! Nowhatumsayin'—" Engrossed in his conversation, Dante yelled into his BlackBerry, casually leaning against the opposite burgundy-painted edge of the roof, oblivious to Luisa's timid entrance.

"Man, I ain't gotta worry about no goddamn investigation. Here's our strategy. And this ain't supposed to be released until Brother Hannibal gives the word. Now, we're gonna leak…"

"Er…ummm." Luisa cleared her throat. Dante whirled around, focusing his eyes on his intruder, wondering who had the audacity to compromise the organization's inner sanctum.

"Lemme hit you back," Dante said to the person on the call, clicking off the BlackBerry.

"Mr. Salaam, thought you'd get rid of me, huh?" Dante stared at her blankly.

"Um, I don't know who was supposed to call back whom, but I left you several messages." Dante stared, as Luisa stumbled to invent words to fill the loud, uncomfortable silence.

"I've phoned you several times requesting that interview with Mr. Morgan." Dante stared, his eyes raking over her body. "Well, I was in the area on another story, a fire on the West Side; and I thought since I was nearby that I would see if I could get on Mr. Morgan's calendar." Dante stared. "Mr. Salaam, you do remember me, don't you?"

"How could I not remember you, Sista? And your girl, what's her name?"

"Allegra," Luisa answered quietly. Dante clapped his hands, as if Luisa had won a door prize and he was the host of a game show. Dante still remembered the Allegra-Luisa game plan; he had just been occupied with executing other pussy playbooks.

Dante broke off his gaze, placing his BlackBerry on a patio table nearby, walked slowly to the entrance of the roof and glanced down the stairway, then closed the door quietly behind him. "No way could I forget you, Sista. Luisa Hamilton has been with WNBC-TV since 2004. Graduate of Columbia University. Attended private school at Dalton. Boarding school in Massachusetts, Voted one of the top journalists in the country under forty years old. But still your news director hasn't given you the respect and the promotions you deserve. In the last year, you've been passed over by three white girls with half your intellect, half your talent, and one-third of your looks. Luisa Hamilton covered the visit of the Iranian president and the gentrification of Harlem, before everybody else jumped on it. Single, but seen around town with a federal prosecutor. Old dude works in the white-collar crime division. Luisa lives on the East Side. Had a poodle until about a year ago. Frequent theatergoer who volunteers with a domestic violence organization in Washington Heights. You helmed a panel on the so-called endangered black media at the Congressional Black Caucus Foundation weekend in September."

"How did you… Who told?" Luisa tried to conceal her blush and terror, but loved that Dante had researched her background.

Dante smiled, but became serious again, his huge arms crossing his chest. "My duty to the Panthers is to check out everybody in our midst. Make sure they're really who they say they are; so many people frontin' these days. I always make it my business to find out what's goin' on. Make sure everybody is keepin' it real, nowhatumsayin'?"

"Really? What have you found? What's up...as you say, about

me?" Luisa didn't mean to reveal that she really cared what Dante thought about her; even though she cared more than she wanted to admit, even to herself.

"The streets, and that's what I listen to, say you're a good sista. Our movement can always use another good sista like you. You kinda bridge that black-Latino coalition that everybody is always talking about. In Nawlins, where I'm from, people don't think twice about passin', especially if they can get away with it. You could pass for Spanish, easy." For the first time, Dante took a step toward Luisa.

Uneasy for reasons unknown to her, she stepped backward and then stood her ground as Dante took another step toward her. Luisa managed to return his steady gaze, roaming his wide-open face, dark brown complexion, shoulder-length locs, and the tip of his pink tongue that hung in the corner of his mouth. Dante tilted his head, as he continued scanning her entire being.

"Um, I want to schedule an interview with Hannibal Morgan. I've been leaving messages for you, and I feel that I'm on a merry-go-round." The dizziness she felt had nothing to do with an interview request.

"There'll be time for all that," Dante said, dismissing her request, yet still moving toward her, shoving his hands his pockets, masking his desire to grab her.

"But I'm on a deadline, a hard line-in-the-sand deadline. I need to give my assignment editor an update; by letting him know whether or not this is going to happen." Luisa said, swallowing. *Lord, why does my voice sound like the plea of a little girl*, Luisa thought to herself.

"That's funny because I'm on a deadline, too. But I still know that everything is everything," Dante said. "You see, I don't believe that that's why you came here tonight…to schedule an interview with Brother Morgan, as you put it. You could've done that shit over the telephone...nowhatumsayin'?"

"Well, of course I could have, but you never returned my telephone calls. Seemed like everything got dropped."

"I'm fixin' to have a beer. You want something to drank? Wahrter? A beer?"

"Um, no thanks; actually, water would be great." Luisa removed a tissue from her purse and patted under her neck.

Dante smiled. "Then, water it is for the fine television lady," he said, as he strode confidently to the old white refrigerator near the bar in the middle of the roof. A yellow light shone on Dante's face as he leaned into the refrigerator to snatch two Coors and a bottle of water. Dante was finer, more rugged, than how he appeared in Luisa's lurid fantasies. His red tee and green military fatigues provided a perfect silhouette for his muscular frame. Luisa never before noticed that his bottom lip was more ample than the top and that he had an old scar that traveled from the middle of his cheek to the bottom of his left earlobe. To her, Dante was different from every man who had ever accompanied her to galas at the Waldorf and outings with Allegra on jaunts to the Hampton; or on double-dates to church with Khadijah. Dante was not the type of man who had been seen with her at entrepreneur conferences, the countless Caribbean cruises, art gallery openings, and fundraisers for the non-profit organizations she supported. Dante was not that type of man; still, she could not deny that he was the type of man she had long craved. "Have a seat," Dante stated firmly, holding her bottle of water until she nervously sat across from where he stood. "Don't worry. The chair is clean."

"So what does your organization use this space for?" Luisa asked.

"Meetings. Fundraisers, when the weather is good. I come up here when I need to clear my head, when nobody is around," Dante answered. "Over there, I teach kids martial arts and how to box." Luisa followed his eyes to three leather punching bags hanging in a makeshift boxing ring.

"When I was back home in the ninth ward, we handled our business with our bare hands. Today, young bucks comin' up hide like little punks behind the barrel of a gun or their mammy's dresses. They need something positive to do, to work off their negative energy and learn how to protect themselves, nowhat-umsayin'?" Luisa noticed Dante's large, bruised, calloused hands, with the stub remaining on his left hand's pinky finger.

"What style of martial arts do you teach the kids? Bruce Lee?" Luisa smiled, trying to make a joke. Dante didn't see the humor. "Aikido. But boxing is what kept me off the streets, made me a little money. I was the sparring partner for a lot of famous boxers in the heavyweight division."

"Did you ever go professional?" Luisa asked. Her knee trembled, then relaxed. She wanted to appear nonchalant, as though Dante's masculine fineness was not turning her on.

"Got as far as the Olympic Trials in H-Town. But that ended when I killed one of my opponents in the ring." Dante said "killed a man" as casually as if he had just ordered a flat screen television.

"Jimmy Brown, from St. Bernard's Parish, down in Louisiana. In the second round, the brother took my best left hook, looked like he was going to jab. I was ready for him; then he fell, and never got up. I never understood that, with all of shit he talked at the weigh in and before we got into the ring. I thought we'd get in at least eight, maybe ten rounds," Dante continued, rubbing his knuckles, reliving that moment in his head. When his family asked that the docs take him off the respirator and he died an hour later...that shit fucked with my head for a while, nowhat-umsayin'?"

"My goodness."

"When me and my boys ran these streets, we, I should say I, went out looking forward to that moment in battle when a sucker was begging for his fuckin' life. There was always something about that glassy look in their eyes that I became addicted to. But when my hands were trained on how to dish out lethal doses of pain by the best trainers in Louisiana, it never ever crossed my mind that I would kill a dude in a place where violence is sanctioned...in the boxing ring. There's something magical about seeing a dude take his final breath." Luisa felt moved to touch his bruised hands, massage them, kiss them; but she restrained herself. Dante took a swig of his beer, using his index finger to stroke the curves of his bottle, and then set it down on the cement floor under his chair.

"Wow. Painful time in your life?" Luisa asked, inhaling his intoxicating musk scent. Dante nodded, staring away into the night.

"I wouldn't say painful. That's one of those thangs television shrinks say all of the time."

"Well, I mean," Luisa said, beginning to protest.

"It is what it is, nowhatumsayin'?" Dante answered, snapping himself from his memories and clearing his throat, before returning his gaze to Luisa. "There's somethin' sexy about bringing somebody to the bridge of death, that makes me hard every time I think about it, nowhatumsayin'?"

"You mean, erotic strangulation?" Luisa asked, with knitted eyebrows.

Dante smiled. "Oh, you know about that? You wit' it?"

"No, but last year I reported on an actor who died doing it."

"That's too bad," Dante concluded. "But the earth battle continues, nowhatumsayin'? Everywhere there's something to fight against. If our people are going to be truly liberated, so much needs to be done, and there aren't enough urban soldiers to get it done. Seem like everyone wants you to do their dirty work, while they sit on the sidelines, chilling."

"How long have you been with the Panthers?"

Dante started to answer, then took another swig of his beer, gulping the liquid, until the bottle was empty. "Off the record, Luisa Hamilton?"

Risking everything, and to prove that their conversation was off the record, Luisa slid her Mac book in her carry-all bag and rested it against her chair, nonchalantly sipping on her water. Dante's drawl was turning her on, so gentle, but with a hard edge, reminding Luisa of some down home gritty lovemaking. Luisa was finding it difficult to maintain her professional demeanor. She felt that her attraction to Dante was obvious, at least to herself. As it was, she was perspiring; the back of her neck was moist, along with her vagina. Her eyes dipped down to Dante's crotch, as he rubbed together his sweaty palms.

"When I was in the joint, on some bogus charge," Dante began.

"For what?" Luisa asked, jolted by the notion that Dante had been so blunt.

"Huh?"

"Why were you in prison?"

"On some bogus assault charge. They accused...said I beat up some dude when I was a minor...I don't remember doing it; I don't even remember the dude. I mean that coulda been so many dudes. But when I started to get on my feet, all of sudden they want to resurrect some bullshit."

"How much time did you do?"

"Three years and change; it wasn't nothing. Whatever the dispute was, that's how we do things; handle them ourselves without bringin' cops. But, um... Hannibal, who I knew from when I used come up here from the Big Easy with some rap groups that I was bodyguarding for, Hannibal, he used to come to the joint to see me. He'd tell me about his vision to build a grassroots organization which would directly serve our people...provide them with services that the current leadership didn't want or refused to provide. He asked me was I down wit it, nowhatumsayin'? And because the brother had always been loyal to me, when nobody else was, my answer was 'absolutely.' That was fifteen years ago and he and I have been rollin' together ever since. Knowing Hannibal the way I do, I don't know that the Panther organization would be what it is, with all of its successes, without me."

"You and Hannibal seem close."

"Oh, Hannibal; dat's my brother, my ace boon, my road dog. But usually in every relationship, someone is stronger; leads the way. And I'm just glad that I've been there for Hannibal to make him into the champion for our people that he has become."

Luisa admired the closeness of Dante and Hannibal's relationship. Rare that two men set aside competition and sacrificed themselves for the needs of black people. Luisa believed that their story needed to be told, that other community activists needed to use their commitment as a blueprint.

Dante continued, "The bad thing about it, is that the same shit we were dealing with ten years are the same problems we dealing with today." Luisa heard a tinge of anguish and loneliness in Dante's voice. He spoke as though he had been in an echo chamber his entire life.

"It's a lonely, unappreciated life, Mr. Salaam. Dante?" Luisa asked, feeling moist inbetween her legs.

"It sure as hell is," Dante said gently, knitting his eyebrows, devising a secret strategy on how he was going to seduce Luisa. "Through all of the work I do to empower our people, nothing is worth living this life without a black queen, a strong black woman by my side; a black queen whom I can love and protect; children to nurture and offer to the African gods. I want a black queen who can stand with me against the world; and love me without hesitation; be my friend and my lover throughout this lifetime; and be my helpmate in maintaining peace within our home. I need a black woman to be strong when I am weak and to be weak when I'm strong. Nowhatumsayin', Luisa Hamilton?"

"Why do you insist on saying my full name?" Luisa asked, loving to hear Dante speak tenderly about his need for a black queen and children. Virgil never told Luisa that he needed her for anything, except to retrieve his clothes from the dry cleaners, Luisa remembered sadly.

Dante remained serious as a police siren sounded nearby. He waited until street sounds from Lenox Avenue below drowned out the siren. Luisa continued to play it cool, though she was desperate to be touched by him, and believed that her dream of his arms around her would never be fulfilled.

"I say your full name, Luisa Hamilton, because you deserve to have your full name said; that's why. What kinda shit you done seen, Luisa Hamilton?" Dante asked, in such an unpolished way that Luisa blinked. No man had ever asked her that question before. Here in this moment, Luisa was at a professional crossroads: allow the person who could provide access to Hannibal, and who was in her erotic dreams, to take control; throw up her defenses; or get the hell out of there. Luisa could not channel the talents of an Oscar winning actress and fake wanting to leave. Luisa was content and afraid. In Dante's intimidating presence, there was no other place that she wanted or needed to be. Anchoring her hair behind her left ear, Luisa cleared her throat, glanced up at the night sky, as she prepared to share her soul experience with this street soldier...this man.

"My father had a death wish."

"Oh, yeah? How's that?" Dante asked, still drinking his beer.

"He must have, with all of the drama he caused at home; it was as if he wanted the police to come and take him out. One time, when I had come home early from school, he was having sex with the hoochie from Apt. 6G, who was obviously not my mother. In my parents' bed. With the window blinds wide open and Luther Vandross's 'A House Is Not A Home' blaring."

A smile curled at the edge of Dante's lips. "Like a good girl, I went straight to my bedroom and tried to focus on my biology homework and what would happen if my mother, Isabella, would come home and catch him."

Intrigued, Dante asked, "Your father didn't know that you were at the crib?"

"Oh, he knew. But somehow he had suckered me into being his keeper of secrets and he knew I didn't want to hurt my mother by telling her what she already knew; that my father was a dog who got off by bringing his shit...um, his whores into our home."

"I like it when you say that word." Dante smiled for the first time, his face appearing so gentle and loving, masking the clouds behind his eyes.

"Whores?"

"No. I like it when Luisa Hamilton says shit," Dante said. "I covered my ears trying to drown out the screams emanating from my parents' bedroom."

"Emanating?" Dante smiled again, his lips mouthing that word.

"Are you making fun of me?" Luisa asked, pretending to scold him. Dante chuckled, his head rearing back.

"Would you rather I say that my father and his trick were knockin' boots?" Luisa teased, her eyes twinkling. Dante feigned innocence, placing his hands over his heart.

"Not if that's not how you roll, and it's not. I would say knockin' boots, gettin' busy, fuckin'. You would say...what was the word... *emanating.*" Luisa waved her hand at him, proud that she had made Dante, who had just confessed that he had killed someone, to now, in this moment with her, be happy and at ease. His laughter became her intoxicating aphrodisiac. If Luisa were completely candid, she would have shared with Dante the abusive nature of her parents' relationship. Her father's alcoholism and mother's frequent rages, where Luisa, an only child, would watch her parents destroy their Washington Heights apartment; and then see them physically attack one another, leaving her mother with frequent black eyes and her father with bruises and scars.

Luisa felt it was her duty to play referee for two adults, who should have known better than to plead their cases to their nine-year-old child. No matter what her parents were arguing about: their mutual infidelities, his drinking, her rages, they would create a temporary peace with noisy, passionate lovemaking during the same time that Luisa was in her bedroom with her childhood friends trying to work on their science projects. Luisa's parents were determined to fight, to love and to never end their volatile marriage.

"So what happened?" Dante asked, suddenly reaching down and slowly removing her black high-heels, placing them perfectly under her chair.

Luisa stopped breathing. "What happened with what?" she asked, staring at her stocking feet with her brain in a traffic jam.

"With your pops and his trick," Dante answered, moving like the conductor of an orchestra, placing her right foot on his pulsating dick.

"I can't remember," Luisa replied, not knowing whether to relax or remove her foot.

"Try."

"Some things I don't want to remember."

"The things that matter, you can't ever forget." Luisa felt her foot relax, knowing she was enjoying Dante's slow foot massage.

"Relax, Luisa Hamilton. Just relax. Dante got you." Continuing to stroke her feet, softening muscles that she did not know that she had, Luisa audibly let Dante know that he was pleasing her, until he let her other foot rest between his legs on his waiting cock. Needing no coaxing to return the favor, Luisa massaged his balls and cock like a butterfly, applying pressure to elicit his groan. Grabbing both of her feet, he ran his tongue around her feet and sucked each of her red-painted toes like lollipops, as Luisa shivered.

Dante squatted in front of her, yanking off her blazer, then lifting up her dress to around her torso as he guided his wet lips across her belly, up her chest and nibbled on her alert tits. Grabbing her long hair, Dante yanked hard on her neck, forcing her open mouth toward his waiting tongue, where they deeply kissed, refusing to come up for a breath. Luisa was relieved that she was finally in his strong arms, and he was no longer the subject of her lust-filled fantasies. Dante abruptly pulled away and unzipped Luisa's yellow spaghetti-string dress, tossing it in the darkness behind him. Luisa returned the favor, forcibly removing Dante's military pants. Kneeling, she stroked his erect cock with her firm lips, weakening his knees. Dante grunted, rhythmically guiding her head as she gave him a most satisfying blowjob. When he had almost climaxed and could barely continue to stand, Dante carried Luisa to the nearby sofa, throwing miscellaneous papers, and sunglasses, which remained from that day's series of meetings, on the ground, and tossed her on the soft seat cushions. Luisa loved it when he grabbed her feet, tossing her legs over his shoulders.

"You need to be taken, don't you, Luisa Hamilton?" Dante growled.

Luisa had never been asked that question, but she knew that she did. "Yes," she answered quietly. Dante let Luisa's beauty sink in. "Shit, bitch, your hard titties are talking to me."

Luisa moaned, "Take me." Dante pushed open her thighs, and then leaned in to smell her swollen, pink, soaking wet lips.

"Your pussy smells so good. You seen me staring at your pussy all damn night, haven't you, bitch? Why you keep me waitin', bitch?" Luisa moaned in agreement as Dante glided three fingers slowly and deeply into her pussy, tickling her clit while still nibbling on her breasts. Then he added his long, thrusting cock. Dante whispered, "You feel so damn good, bitch." He wriggled his tongue around her ear, breathing slowly into it, as her hips circled to meet his thrusts. Like two starved lovers, they received each other's kiss as tears escaped down Luisa's cheek. Instinctually, Dante flipped Luisa over to straddle him, and knowing exactly how to seize the opportunity, Luisa rode him like a cowgirl. Dante, like a professional baseball player, scored a home run as he continued to hit her G-spot. "Ride my shit, Bitch," Dante instructed, in his husky, New Orleans drawl.

Luisa was in complete rapture, tossing her hair, with eyes closed. Jumping on top, Luisa teased the tip of his dick with her already wet pussy, and then slowly slid down, looking Dante in the eyes, as she slowly rode him, digging her nails into his chest. "Goddamn. Goddamn," Dante grunted, like an exhausted thoroughbred, taking Luisa in until he busted, his cum spilling between them. Luisa shivered from the evening temperature taking an unexpected dip. Dante wrapped a plaid-colored blanket from the back of the sofa around her thin shoulders as she jacked him off and cleaned him up with her tongue.

"Hmmm," Dante said appreciatively. "Like I said, the movement needs another good sister." Luisa giggled, and tossed her liberated hair in the billowing breeze, as Dante leaned over and playfully bit her left breast.

"The Most High has blessed us. We are now one," Dante said.

15

D r. Winchester, the department chairperson, sat in the leather brown chair across from Allegra's desk, impatiently chewing on his unlit cigar. He wore his customary gray sweater, sagging socks, and wrinkled gray pants that were four inches too short, exposing his hairy calves. The aroma of cigar smoke seeped through his pores. Allegra was startled to see him in her office.

"Dr. Winchester?"

"Good Day, Ms. Adams."

"Did you not receive the curriculum for next semester that I forwarded to your secretary yesterday?" Allegra continued, reviewing incoming mail on her desk, and making sure that she had not left her pink vibrator on top of the paper-burdened desk.

"I did. But that's not why I'm here," Dr. Winchester replied, scratching the nape of his neck, near the red blotches.

"Oh?" replied Allegra, still standing.

"Have a seat, Ms. Adams," Dr. Winchester firmly said, rising to close Allegra's office door. Obediently, she sat down, on the edge of her chair, waiting for her department head to reveal whatever he had on his mind. Allegra prayed that he did not want to revisit the incident when she stabbed him with a fork for secretly feeling on her thigh. In her mind, four prongs stuck in the top of your hand should have been discussion enough.

Dr. Winchester cleared his throat, with a hacking cough. "I shouldn't be telling you this...need to maintain my objectivity and all, where you are concerned, but there might be some opposition with one of the professors on the panel for your oral argument."

"Opposition. How's that?" Allegra's mind was reeling. Her cheeks were warm. She had spent four years working toward her Ph.D. in anthropology, racking up nearly all A's, winning a prestigious teaching assistantship, and earning a 3.90 grade-point average. All that remained were her final exam and oral presentation, each to be scored by a panel of professors chosen by Dr. Winchester.

"Well, Dr. Rosenthal has had to take a leave of absence. Health issues, I'm afraid."

"Sorry to hear that. Who do you have in mind to replace her? Dr. Porter? They're both familiar with my work."

"It's not that simple, Ms. Adams. Dr. Rosenthal has recommended that her friend and colleague, Dr. Henderson, who has just joined the NYU faculty from the University of Detroit. The Dean appointed her as Dean Faculty Representative, and thought this would be an excellent opportunity to begin her tenure here at NYU. Since she has guided several dissertations back at the University of Detroit, she was the obvious choice." Allegra froze, blood draining from her face. In Rio de Janeiro, Dr. Henderson had made it a point to openly challenge Allegra during the question and answer session after her keynote speech.

Dr. Winchester cleared his throat once again. "I gather you know Dr. Henderson."

"We've met. When I attended the conference in Rio, she was one of the attendees who had a few questions regarding my thesis."

"How do you know that?"

"Well, she raised her hand and said as much. To keep her from disrupting the question and answer session, I had to cut her off."

"It appears that Dr. Henderson has a fly in her bonnet about you for some reason. And frankly, I smell an ambush. I wrestled with bringing this situation to your attention, knowing that you could handle any opposition, but because I respect your scholarship and work ethic, I decided to be that proverbial little birdie," Dr. Winchester said, squeezing his nostrils.

"Are you serious? I'm not going to let four years of work go down the drain, Dr. Winchester. Who told you about Dr. Henderson?"

"I've said too much already. There's no doubt in my mind that you'll be prepared, but Dr. Henderson may try to make it ugly. I've seen this kind of thing before with ex-husbands, ex-wives, etcetera," Dr. Winchester said, standing up and walking to the office door, placing his hand on the doorknob. "I just wanted you to know that I'll try to handle things on my end. But in the meantime, make sure that your material is original, no secondary sources, that your conclusions are specific...nothing vague, is all I'm trying to say to you." Dr. Winchester waddled out of her office, leaving Allegra pacing behind him out into the hallway.

After Dr. Winchester had disappeared down the hall, Allegra mumbled, "I'll be damned if I let somebody come here and derail everything I have poured my life into. Fuck that!" Walking back into her office, Allegra threw a reference book against the far wall, just as Yuni, the research assistant peeked in her office door.

"Everything okay, Ms. Adams?" he asked with a heavy accent.

"No! But it will be," Allegra barked, slamming her office door in Yuni's bewildered face.

When Allegra's car service arrived at seven o'clock outside of her brownstone, she was dabbing Mac powder on her high cheekbones while listening to Luisa defend Khadijah on the telephone.

"Allegra, Khadijah has a good heart, but she just has issues, like we all do." When the two friends finally decided on a date for their girls' night out, Luisa begged Allegra to allow Khadijah to tag along that evening.

"And she's anal," Allegra interjected.

"Okay, I'll give you that. But I can't reach her now. She's already left work and is probably on the subway headed to Morocco's," Luisa explained during their quick telephone call to reconfirm.

"Tonight is not the night I need to be dealing with Khadijah. Plus I was hoping that you and I could play catch up, Ms. Missing-In-Action."

"Look who's talking! It'll be all good. See you in a few, Girl."

"Be there on time, Luisa, so I don't have to be with Khadijah alone. And I gotta make a run afterwards."

"Do you now?" Luisa teased. It had been about a week since since their Skype chat. Allegra recognized Luisa's *modus operandi* years ago. She had the habit of becoming clandestine when a new man was the source of her distraction.

Morocco's did not garner its name from the excellent reputation of its menu selection. The West Side, upscale restaurant was named after its former infamous, now convicted, owner who currently was serving prison time for cocaine distribution. Luisa knew the lurid details of Morocco's conviction because Virgil Douglas was the lead prosecutor. Despite the establishment's criminal history, it still attracted the well-heeled crowd from Wall Street to A-List stars to infamous reality television stars. The beautiful decor and floor to ceiling windows overlooking Central Park made it the perfect place for an evening of great food and plentiful, potent drinks. Light jazz music flowed through the sound system.

The Lakers/Knicks game had just ended the first quarter, with the Knicks leading by seven points, when Allegra arrived at Morocco's. Out of a spirit of congratulations, Allegra remembered her promise to break off Rolando if the Lakers won the game. The other day, the man was too delicious-looking to resist. But now, her meeting with Dr. Winchester had put her in a contemplative, ornery mood. Allegra had to fight for every accomplishment in her professional life. She went into an emotional zone, saddened that another woman would knowingly attempt to derail her progress.

As Allegra reluctantly entered the dining area in Morocco's, Khadijah was already seated in a center booth in the middle of the elegant, lemon-colored dining room. Noticing Allegra, Khadijah nonchalantly paused her crocheting and finger-waved. Khadijah was always in possession of her metal crocheting needle and a stream of acrylic green yarn wrapped around her thumbs, no matter what the environment. Tensing her mouth, Allegra glanced around the dining room noticing that Luisa was nowhere in sight. Wearing a fuzzy, braided up-do, tweed jacket with lint balls, a black knee-length skirt, and bleached white sneakers and socks over her dark pantyhose, Khadijah was the perfect chick to hold your purse while you're grinding it out on the dance floor with an investment banking brother from Park Slope. Khadijah was the perfect chick to cock block when you welcomed the advances of the muscular brother with the pillow lips, who owned the Harlem supper club and was gathering his courage to approach. Khadijah was that chick with the grinding, shrill voice who reminded you of that blackboard screeching noise. Khadijah was also the perfect chick to arrive thirty minutes early to everywhere. And the one to greet you with a bucket of gloom to douse your happiness because you are not your anally early self.

"Allegra," Khadijah said with attitude, glancing up momentarily over her cat-shaped eyeglasses, which had slid down to the end of her narrow nose, and perched like a window frame around her erect round nostrils, appearing like entrances to the Holland Tunnel.

"Khadijah," Allegra replied, scooting into the booth. "Luisa not here yet?"

Khadijah rolled her eyes, ignoring Allegra's question, while opening a pouch to replenish her supply of yarn, and then sliding the package of yarn back into her black handbag and zipping it closed. "Whose idea was it to come here?" she asked. There it was. Khadijah had thrown her first sullen bomb, as she pulled two loops on her crochet hook.

"Did Luisa say she would be running late?" Allegra tried asking again.

"I don't know why we came here tonight. There are plenty of black owned restaurants that we should patronize. These people don't want us in here. Look how they looking at us." Just in case Khadijah happened to be right, after three years of being wrong, Allegra glanced around the cavernous restaurant at the other, mostly white, diners who were immersed in their own conversations. Their pleasant waiter replenished their table with Perrier water, fresh butter and hot, steamy rolls, then handed Allegra a menu. Khadijah took out tiny scissors and cut the end of her piece, which apparently was a hat.

"This is a surprise gift for Luisa," Khadijah announced, unaware how frumpy she appeared, with the bargain basement hemmed yarn, trying to pass itself off as a hat on her head. Joy, sparkling conversation and positive energy emanated with other diners, who delighted in chatting and laughing amongst themselves. But a dark cloud hung over Allegra and Khadijah's table. Allegra checked her BlackBerry for messages from Luisa, then the scores from the Lakers-Knicks game at Madison Square Garden. Halftime was over now. The Lakers were up by ten points. The Knicks center was in danger of fouling out. Allegra felt suffocated. She couldn't breathe in the presence of Khadijah. Never could.

Luisa is going to be surprised alright, Allegra thought, as Khadijah carefully folded her new creation and stuffed it inside her cluttered handbag.

"Luisa said that you're almost done with your thesis," Khadijah said apathetically.

"Are you ladies ready to order?" the waiter reappeared and asked.

"We're still waiting for a friend," Khadijah answered. The waiter slightly nodded his head and sauntered over to another table of two arriving young couples, one of which was the star of a morning coffee chat television show. Khadijah, struck with a sudden itch, scratched her scalp. In Allegra's imagination, the clock on her BlackBerry was playing tricks on her and refused to move this evening along. Khadijah buttered her bread, smacking her lips. The clock read: 7:50 p.m. Allegra gripped her clutch and rose to leave the booth.

"You need to come to church with me, Allegra," Khadijah said with authority.

"Oh, really. Why's that?" Allegra said, sitting down again.

"Because my sense of you has been that you could use salvation."

If tension were a killer, Khadijah would be dead by now, and Allegra would have been arraigned and charged with first-degree murder. Allegra swallowed, clenching her fist, and spoke in a measured, controlled tone.

"And my sense of you, Khadijah, is that your brains could benefit from being fucked out."

Khadijah gasped, attempting to grasp her non-existent pearls, and regain her composure; her lips trembled. "See, that's exactly what I'm talking about!"

"Oh, really?" Allegra asked, resting her chin in the palm of her hand. "What the hell are you talking about?"

"Well, now that you ask, ever since Luisa started hanging around you, I've seen a change in her. And Luisa tries to keep up and be you."

"Excuse you!" Allegra's eyes narrowed, as she tapped her fingers on the tablecloth. "First of all, Luisa and I have known each other for over fifteen years, long before you came on the scene."

"Yeah, but Luisa used to be satisfied being herself, was comfortable with being alone. In the last year, all she talks about is how great you are...and if she could only be like you, having men throwing themselves at her feet, then her life would be different; happier." Allegra stared through Khadijah as though she had four heads. Allegra didn't know whether she should curse out Khadijah or throw holy water on her. The waiter reappeared, but quickly turned on his heels when Allegra waved him away.

"Luisa does not need my permission to be herself. And she has never had problems with men," Allegra lied. "Is all of this concern really about Luisa or is it really about your issue with me? Or is it the fact that you have old lint up your pussy from non-usage? If your pussy was a building, the city would declare it abandoned property!"

"Make yourself feel better with all of that nasty talk, Allegra. But God don't like ugly."

Allegra glanced again at her BlackBerry; still no e-mails or texts from Luisa. Steam slowly evaporated from her ears, as she lost her patience with Khadijah. Luisa usually played the referee between the two women, but now without her intervention, a full frontal assault was taking place. Allegra crossed her arms, resting her hands on her elbows on the table. She was hungry, but instead of enjoying delicious food and conversation, Allegra was engaged in a moral battle with a sexual recluse and hypocrite named Khadijah Bennett.

"Have you ever been finger fucked, Khadijah? By anybody besides yourself and your cellmate?"

"I'm gonna ask God to forgive you for that, Allegra."

"Oh, you want to bring God into this conversation?"

"God is everywhere. He's sitting right here at this table. 'Cause I'm always covered by the blood of Jesus."

"Where was God in your life when you and my cousin Max got caught cashing Social Security checks from a woman you had a sworn duty to take care of? My Aunt Rachael!" Khadijah swallowed. Though she had tried to put her past felonies behind her, clearly there were others on the planet who were more than willing to hang them out for the world to see.

"And where was God in your life when you stole…"

"Borrowed."

"Stole money from Luisa for some bullshit, multi-level, colon cleansing business, but you used it for a cruise vacation and never paid her back. A judge had to order the marshal to seize your bank account in order to pay her. Luisa is down for all of that forgiveness bullshit; but that ain't my shtick. I would've beaten your ass in Times Square, right in front of the studios of *Good Morning America* and called it a damn day." Allegra was now incensed; her cheeks had a rosy tint to them. Nearby patrons stared at Allegra and halted their conversations, holding their forks, heavy with food, in mid-air. Then when Allegra returned their stares, patrons sheepishly pretended to return their attentions to their meals and expensive checks. Khadijah was backed into a corner, and she could no longer chew her buttered roll, refusing to look at the fury in Allegra's eyes.

"I am a grown-ass woman. I stopped explaining or apologizing for my fucking lifestyle a long time ago, especially to bullshit, small-time con artists like you," Allegra said, jabbing her index finger toward Khadijah.

"You obviously forgave your cousin," Khadijah became bold enough to accuse. "You have him working in your house." Allegra rifled through her clutch bag for her coat check ticket, and then rose to leave, deciding first to hover close to Khadijah's startled face. "The difference between you and my cousin is blood. I will always be loyal to blood. You got me? You're nothing more than some dumb-ass Luisa decided to introduce to her circle of friends out of sympathy; because your ass didn't have any." Allegra leaned still closer, her lips nearly touching Khadijah's left earlobe. "Now, I'm going to leave you with this. Blood is thicker than water. And I would suggest that you get that broomstick out of your ass and replace it with a dick before your pussy dries the fuck up. *Capiche*?"

Los Angeles beat the New York Knicks in overtime by a foul shot, made by Rolando. Allegra turned heads as she quickly exited Morocco's, hitting redial on Luisa's telephone number, while the valet hailed a waiting taxi to drive under the canopy as raindrops began to drizzle. Allegra left a message on Luisa's voice-mail. "Luisa, I don't know where you are, but I hope you're okay...and if you're okay, then I'm really going to kill you."

16

Sports fans wearing their favorite Knicks or Lakers jerseys, and carrying Madison Square Garden paraphernalia, trickled through the lobby, replaying the court action with their cohorts, boisterously arguing over who was the best player in the NBA. "If Rolando hadn't made that foul shot, the Knicks would have lost. At the end of the day, the Lakers won that fuckin' game on the foul line," a short bearded man retorted. "The Lakers ain't shit. They ain't nothing but a bunch of overpaid pussies!" yelled another man, wandering through the lobby carrying an open beer can.

An airport van parked in the hotel's four-lane circular enclosed driveway, disembarked passengers and their luggage. Front desk clerks assisted hotel guests checking out of the hotel. The bellman carried their luggage on a red-carpeted, gold-plated luggage rack through the revolving glass door.

A wiry-looking concierge handed Allegra an envelope containing the electronic key to Rolando's luxurious penthouse suite. "Mr. Barbosa has given me specific instructions that you be immediately escorted upstairs. Right now, he's being interviewed here at the hotel," the concierge advised. Allegra raised her eyebrows, not expecting that Rolando would have returned to the hotel this soon, particularly with the media interviews he was required by the NBA to participate in after every game. "Ms.

Adams, Edgar, the head bellman, will escort you to the private elevators, which are straight ahead and on your left. Do you have any luggage?" Allegra shook her head.

"Very well, Ms. Adams. Front!" A petite man, with the posture of a sentry, introduced himself as Edgar.

"Welcome to the W Towers and Suites. Right this way, Madame."

Another stream of noisy fans entered the hotel lobby followed by Kevin, Thunder's coke-bottle eyeglass-wearing producer, carrying a manila folder and a Samson studio condenser microphone. Immediately impressed by the lobby, the producer looked around as if he had never been in such an opulent setting before. Allegra followed Edgar's brisk steps toward the private elevator, as the producer sauntered over to the front desk.

"Yo, I'm here to meet Thunder Poole. He's interviewing Rolando Barbosa." The front desk clerk eagerly leaned in the direction in which Allegra had traveled. "Just keep straight, right past the private elevators; there is conference room to your left. Messrs. Barbosa and Poole are already there. The technical arrangements were made to your specifications, Sir. Everything is all set up."

"Thanks, Man! Appreciate it!" the producer replied, trying to give the clerk a black man's handshake, which the clerk politely waved off. Turning in the direction he was given, the producer froze as he recognized a familiar sight, sashaying ahead of him. The producer opened his mouth to yell, but stopped, as he knew it was futile to get her attention. Recognizing her as Allegra Adams, Thunder's lover, the producer raised his eyebrows, just as she turned to face forward as the private elevator door closed.

After the elevator door closed, Edgar inserted his key into the console, and entered a password, then pressed a "proceed" button. The glass elevator whirred and sped vertically to the upper floors. Manhattan's midtown skyline provided a breathtaking backdrop en route to the penthouse. Edgar keyed in another password when the elevator reached its destination. When the doors flew open, Edgar extended his arm, gesturing Allegra to proceed on into the ivory-colored, candlelit suite, with the soft sounds of Kem making pleas of love through tiny Bose speakers. It was apparent that a man had been expecting a woman, though he omitted the detail of his open gym bag tucked under the newspapers strewn on top of the walnut end table next to the coffee-colored, suede, oversized recliner.

"'Night, Miss," Edgar said, tapping his shiny, red and black leather cap, after Allegra rewarded him with a handsome tip. A weary Allegra stood in the foyer, taking in the two-story, two-bedroom suite. *Whoa*, she thought to herself. Allegra had grown accustomed to fancy digs, but she loved it when another architect's design took her by surprise. Allegra kicked off her suede stilettos and provided her own self-guided tour in the superstar's suite. The bamboo marble foyer, soaring nine-foot ceiling, spacious sitting area, the fireplace in the sunken living room, the fifty-two-inch, wall-mounted LCD flat-screen television were strategically placed to inspire. Allegra sauntered through both bedrooms which featured king-sized canopy beds, running her palm across the pillow top mattresses, down duvets and feather pillows. An ambient glow from the reflective mirrors framed and lit from behind the white, crocodile-skin headboard.

Allegra stood in front of the translucent glass window appreciating the meditative view. The windows made it appear as though heaven, Rockefeller Center and the trees in Central Park were reachable with the tip of her fingers. Allegra found the wine bar and inspected the impressive display of red wines. She selected a Chateau Lafleur to erase the melancholy feeling which was trying to strangle her. Taking multiple sips, Allegra sauntered over to the newspapers on the walnut end table, surveying the headlines of the various newspapers. Rolando had separated the sports sections. He obviously had an interest in what sports' reporters were writing about him. Allegra gathered the *New York Daily News* and plopped down on the plush, animal skin rug in front of the sparkling fireplace. One sports columnist had devoted six hundred words to Rolando's community service and the 'obscene' fortune he would have earned if he had signed with the New York Knicks.

"Rolando Barbosa blew a major professional and financial opportunity. He lost the respect of every New Yorker. But to be fair, blame must be placed squarely in the hands of Knick management. This was not the first time that management has let the signing of a marquee game-changing player slip through their fingers. Now we can expect the Knickerbockers to have another lackluster season," the columnist opined.

Framing the article were photos of Rolando with a bevy of beauties, varying in ethnicities, on his arm at different Los Angeles parties and charity events. Allegra's eyebrow raised, amused that Rolando got around. She expected as much, as she never let grass grow for long under her feet. Curling up, Allegra rested her head on her elbow, as the fire warmed her like a heavenly bear hug. Surrounded by the newspapers, Allegra relaxed, letting her thoughts drift, her eyes becoming heavy, until she fell asleep.

"Ms. Adams, you have failed your dissertation. Your Ph.D. will not be granted. And you'll need to repay the $114,000 that was awarded to you based upon your successful defense. But that has not happened, has it? Too many secondary sources. We suspect that the work is not your own. Not your own. Not your own. You are dismissed from NYU.

Dismissed. Dr. Henderson was right about you. She was right. No university will ever hire you. Community college is where you need to be. That's where Allegra Adams needs to be. You need salvation. Khadijah was right."

"Hey. Hey. Hey, *Bela*," Rolando whispered, kneeling next to Allegra, watching her sleep. The glow from the fireplace cast an orange shadow against her warm brown complexion. "Hey, Beautiful," Rolando whispered in her ear, kissing her lobes. Allegra began to awaken, her eyes blinking slightly, like young butterflies. Not recognizing Rolando's voice, she lurched, sitting up suddenly, coming within inches of his gorgeous face.

"I fell asleep," Allegra said, rubbing her eyes.

"You look so beautiful lying there. And at war."

"What do you mean?" Allegra asked through a yawn on the back of her hand.

"You were sleeping, with a little snore."

"Get out of here!" Allegra laughed, slapping Rolando on his muscular thigh. "I don't snore."

"Oh no? Well, what is this?" Rolando teased, mocking the whizzing sound Allegra had made. Allegra giggled softly, her eyes marveling at the man she had been e-mailing for the past few months, who was frequently featured on ESPN.

"How were your interviews?"

"The usual. Different dudes asking the same questions, but I gotta do it. The league requires it. We get fined if we don't. This last brother, he was pretty cool. We talked about what's goin' on here in the black community. Seem like no matter what city we play in, I hear about the same issues, and don't seem like local community groups have the resources that they need to make things better. People mean well, yet it's like the work that they do is like a pebble dropped in the ocean." In the short time Rolando had taken to answer to her question, Allegra began to daydream, staring at the dying embers in the fireplace.

"Hey, what's bothering you, Beautiful? Don't I get a hug? I haven't seen you since we hooked up in D.C.; at least let me look at you. Let me see you."

Allegra felt strangely close to Rolando, though they had only communicated via telephone or e-mail. She felt as though they had seen each other yesterday. Rolando had that kind of familiar persona. Rolando took her hand, assisting her to a standing position, and then slowly twirled her around. With wrinkled skirt, tossed locs, removed diamond earrings and all, Rolando murmured, "You're still beautiful." Allegra lowered her gaze, not looking at anything in particular on the floor.

"You okay?" Rolando asked.

Allegra paused. Not sure if she knew the answer, but as a result of the meeting with Dr. Winchester, she was unusually troubled. Rolando quietly slipped into the suite without her knowledge. His surprise arrival took her off guard, and she was finding it difficult to find get her bearings again. "A lot's going on. No point in rehashing it again. I just need a break," Allegra answered rubbing the temples on her forehead.

"You sure? You sure it's not these photos of me in the newspaper?" Rolando asked, holding up the photos of him out on the town in the newspaper. Allegra's eyes darted from the newspapers back to Roland. When she realized the seriousness of his questions, Allegra chuckled. "Honey, I'm not that chick."

"What do you mean?" Rolando asked, not getting the reaction he was most accustomed to.

Rubbing the side of her nose, Allegra replied, "I'm not that chick who becomes jealous over a man who she is not committed to, that's all."

"Most women would be upset."

"I'm not most women, Rolando." Allegra was growing annoyed. She despised having conversations about a non-subject. Rolando was not her man. And Allegra was not his woman.

"Obviously. I thought that something was wrong," Rolando tried again, feeling that the mood he desired was slowly evaporating.

"Frankly, I need a break."

"That's easy. Where do you want to go? I'll take care of it."

"I wish it was that easy, Rolando. Though my students are brilliant and starving for knowledge, the more I give, the more they need. This is the third week that I have had to extend office hours, and it's still not enough. My house is in renovation hell; and I have to defend my dissertation in two weeks."

"That's a good thing, right?"

"Normally, it would be, but one of the professors is determined to deny my Ph.D., and one of my closest friends is going through a rough time."

"A man? Other than me, Allegra? Are you saying that I'm no longer the love of your life, *Bela*?" Rolando joked, clutching his heart.

"And I'm not the love of *your* life, Mr. 2011 Sexiest Sports Superstar," Allegra replied, joining in the fun, holding up the recent issue of *ESPN Off-Court Magazine*. Rolando attempted to grab the magazine, as Allegra slyly hid it behind her back.

"Okay, you got me, *Bela!* I confess. I'm the sexiest superstar in the world. Don't you agree?"

Allegra's mouth wedged at the corner. "Humph, you're alright." Rolando pretended he was removing a sword from his waistband and plunged it into his heart, faking his death, collapsing next to Allegra.

"You really need to get your mental condition evaluated, Rolando," Allegra said, still teasing.

"Allegra, you can't keep giving all of the time. Pretty soon, there is going to be nothing left of you. You need a superstar like me to be with you."

"Oh, do I?" Allegra replied sarcastically, tossing her locs from her eyes, amused by how much shit men like to talk.

"Yeah, you do. You've got it altogether. You're confident, fine as hell, educated, world-traveled, speak my native language, but I wonder with all of that, what else do you need?" Allegra raised her eyelids and looked into Rolando's caring eyes. His enticing lips beckoned to her. "Did you eat yet?"

"Did I what?" Allegra answered, snapping to attention.

"Eat. You know food? *Comida*?"

Allegra reminisced back to the episode with Khadijah that had erased her need for food, but her body was competing with an appetite for food and for Rolando. "I ordered a fruit and cheese tray. Champagne. And we have a private butler on call twenty-four hours," Rolando continued, loosening his Hermes silk tie, unfastening the buttons of his shirt, leaving it hanging open.

"No, I'm okay."

"You sure?" Rolando asked, gently touching her cheek, kissing the palm of her hand, making a circle with his tongue. Allegra nodded.

"I never thought I would get out of there. Just when I finished one interview, here comes another guy asking the same dumb questions."

"That's the way of the world, huh?" Allegra offered.

"I guess it is. Coach always makes us wear these business suits on the road. I wish we could wear what we wanted," Rolando said, using his humongous hands to neatly fold his neck tie, then taking off his size sixteen, handmade leather shoes.

"If your coach didn't, I'll bet somebody on your team would show up looking crazy."

Rolando thought for a few seconds, and then chuckled. "You know, you gotta point. Our center would show up looking like he had joined the circus in the seventies or something."

Yawning, Allegra said, "Wow, I needed that nap."

"I'm so glad to see you, *Bela*. Come," he continued, not waiting for a response, "Let me take care of you," and with that, he lifted her in his strong arms. Standing at six feet eight inches, Allegra had forgotten how tall he was and prayed that he didn't drop her.

"Whoa! I'm gonna get a nose bleed up here." Allegra laughed, as Rolando carried her into the sanctuary of the master bathroom, placing her on the circular, gold-plated designer chair, which was built like a throne. Rolando lit scented lavender candles and dimmed the lights.

He glanced back at Allegra, and then leaned over the shower Jacuzzi, with marble floor and ivory handles, to turn on the faucets. Hot steam filled the bathroom, slowly fogging the mirrors, which were on every wall, including the ceiling. Rolando peeled off his yellow, fitted tee shirt, baring his broad, oak tree chest, and then sliding out of his black pants. Standing before Allegra, in his bright yellow Speedos, Rolando was bigger and better than she remembered. He was reminiscent of a humble god. His cock sat perched behind his Speedos like a giant boa constrictor. For the first time, Allegra noticed the tattoos of mermaids and the two devils, which decorated his long, muscular arms. Rolando leaned over the Jacuzzi again, adjusting the water flow from the faucets, testing with his fingers to find the perfect water temperature. Warm water, creating bubbles, shot out of the water jets, as Allegra and Rolando kissed with a frenetic intensity, surprising them both. Rolando nibbled her neck then returned, to plunge his tongue back down her hungry throat, her tongue waiting desperately to greet him.

"*Deixe-me cuidar dele, Bela* (Let me take care of you, Beautiful),"

Rolando murmured, pausing to gauge her reaction, staring sincerely into her eyes. Allegra puckered her lips, kissing Rolando tenderly, squeezing his bottom lip. Abruptly, Rolando lifted her to a standing position, carefully unbuttoning her blouse, unfastening her bra strap, and then placing each item on a padded hanger in the bathroom closet. Allegra shivered.

"You're cold. Let me hold you, Allegra," Rolando said, wrapping his arms around her. Allegra felt like mother god was nurturing her in a warm cocoon, protecting her from the world. Rolando knelt down in front of her, unbuttoning her skirt, gently pulling down her black bikinis. Nothing remained on Allegra except her toe ring. "Let me take care of you." Rolando lifted Allegra, placing her in the Jacuzzi, adjusting a bath pillow behind her neck. Stripping out of his Speedo, Rolando carefully lathered a body sponge and lifted her legs above the water, scrubbing her legs, sucking her toes. Allegra closed her eyes. Anything that was troubling her, was, at least for now, forgotten. She relished the sensation of her tingling skin. Rolando, like a kind caregiver, worked his magic down the back of her thighs, her calves, up and across her shoulders, pausing to kiss in between her shoulder blades, sucking her erect nipples. Allegra thought Rolando looked adorable and wretched at the same time, his face consumed with desire. She tempered her need to possess him, and allowed Rolando to cause shivers to go up her spine, his face convulsing with focused delirium.

The water temperature continued to climb, as Rolando lifted the murmuring Allegra to rest on the edge of the Jacuzzi, spreading open her thighs, determined that they remain ajar, forever. Hanging onto her waist, he allowed his tongue to travel from her abdomen down to her crotch and greeted her clit, squeezing gently, causing Allegra to moan. Her thighs tried to close, yet

Rolando firmly held them open, so as not to interfere with his dessert. The intense steam from the water amplified her pleasure, until Allegra lost control, her hips gyrating uncontrollably. Rolando lifted Allegra, holding her against the tiles, her legs wrapping around his waist, as he grinded his magnificent shaft deep inside of her, splitting apart her need to possess him and her need to be possessed. Her sharp fingernails dug deep into his muscular back, leaving dark purple half-moons, causing Rolando a mixture of pain and delight. Turning on the shower nozzle, the water streamed down over their intertwined bodies, when Allegra climaxed first. The veins on Rolando's shaft pulsated, clearly wanting to explode, yet Rolando waited, or tried to, with a severe look on his face, until he jerked a couple of times, splashing his cum outside of her, across her abdomen.

Lying limply, Allegra rested against Rolando's chest; a long sigh exhaled from her mouth. "Grapes?" Rolando asked, reaching from the fruit and cheese tray sitting on the vanity. Allegra nodded, accepting the fruit Rolando placed between her lips.

"*Eu sou sempre aqui para você, Bela.* (I'm always here for you, Beautiful)," Rolando said tenderly.

Allegra exhaled again. "Yes, you are," she replied, with a wink.

17

The sudden frigid temperatures surprised most New Yorkers. When the chiseled-featured, blond-haired meteorologist announced that a cold front would take up residence for the next three days, people were thrown off guard. Many people did not know whether they should retrieve their winter clothes out of storage or hold onto their fantasies of a long gone summer for another week by wearing flip-flops outside in the chilly temperatures.

Allegra had taken out a home equity loan, consulted with an architect and the Harlem Land Preservation Board to meticulously plan to have her renovations completed in her dining room by Thanksgiving at the earliest, mid-December at the latest. Although her home was in an uproar as her home office was cluttered with her students' term papers, she fought to find some solace and to hibernate in the four-story brownstone she had invested in ten years ago. Her evening with Rolando was consoling. Allegra appreciated that he was intent on nurturing her, and at least temporarily, shaking her blues. In her quiet moments, the warning from Dr. Winchester would echo inside of her head, like an obsessive, stalking shadow. And as much as she immersed herself in her robust teaching schedule, her renovations and life itself, Allegra remained haunted by the possibility that Dr. Henderson would attempt to derail her from receiving her coveted Ph.D.

Sipping from a white ceramic cup of piping hot ginger and green tea, Allegra chatted with Rolando on her BlackBerry as the Laker team's MGM jet landed, five hundred miles away, and was taxiing down an airstrip to a private airport terminal southeast of Cleveland. "I wish you would let me fly you out here."

"To Cleveland? No way."

"Cleveland ain't that bad. There are a lot of good people in Cleveland."

"I don't doubt that; but have you checked out how cold it is? Cold enough to freeze the balls off of a brass monkey! I'm hiding from the cold here. Call me when you play Tahiti," Allegra said with a smile, listening to Rolando laugh his ass off on the other end of the telephone.

"You are so crazy, *Bela*! I think that's why I really dig you. But you won't have to ever worry; I'll keep you warm," Rolando said.

"I know that's right." The pounding sound of hammering from the floor below abruptly interrupted their interlude. "We'll talk soon, Honey. I've got to get downstairs and stop this racket."

"Cool. Check me out on ESPN tonight, okay?"

"You got it."

Allegra clicked off her BlackBerry, quickly wrapped her nude body in her white terry-cloth robe, and stretched her arms toward the ceiling, grunting softly. Drinking the remainder of the ginger tea, she walked in her bare feet, down the wooden staircase, carrying the tea cup, along the hallway into the dining room, where a crew of five soiled men, wearing dust masks, banged, chipping away at the scarred walls. "Never hire a cousin no matter how much construction experience he says he has," Allegra mumbled, shaking her head. Looking around at the rubble, she doubted the work would be completed by Christmas.

"Max, I thought we agreed that there wouldn't be any hammering before seven o'clock," Allegra said. Max wore earplugs to block out his own hammering noise and more importantly, any of Allegra's pending complaints. Max didn't notice or hear Allegra standing behind him. Max was on parole after being released from an eight-year stint on a robbery conviction.

Lifting up the dusty facemask after Allegra tapped him on his shoulder, Max asked, "Yo, Cuz. Wassup?"

"Until this racket started, not me, that's for sure."

"Watch it. You shouldn't be down here with no shoes on," Max replied, deflecting her annoyance, wiping his nose on the back of his forearm.

"I didn't plan to wake up to all of this noise. Not this early," Allegra replied, her eyes darting, inspecting the old sheet rock chips falling around her. Max and his crew collected paint chips in a large trash bag. On Tuesdays and Thursdays, the crew would drag the trash bags out to the sidewalk for sanitation to retrieve.

"Exactly when is this wall going to be done, Max? The furniture store has been on me to deliver the dining room furniture for the past two weeks."

"Yeah I know, but at the last minute, I had one man out sick and the other one didn't show up…didn't call. Nothing."

"I don't want to hear your problems, Max. Got plenty of my own. Let me explain this to you in terms that you'll understand. If this renovation isn't done by December 15th, you can forget about getting paid. And don't go runnin' to Rachael, because I mean what I say. *Capiche?*" Allegra threatened, whirling around to enter her state-of-the-art kitchen, just as her house telephone was ringing. Shaking his head, Max wiped his dirty hands on his dirty pants and continued hammering. Max understood that there was only so much he could say, as Allegra had been more than generous to him, before and after, his parole. Allegra sighed and walked into her kitchen, rinsing her teacup and placing it in the dishwasher underneath the counter, as she grabbed the black telephone receiver from the wall.

"Hey, Luisa. I thought you would've been in church by now," Allegra said, by way of a greeting. "Morning, Girl. I decided not to go this morning, because I didn't get home from the station until about two o'clock."

"Two in the morning? What are you working on? I thought your reports for November sweeps were already in the can."

"They are, except that interview with Hannibal."

"Still giving you the runaround?"

"Well, Dante has been helping me out," Luisa purred.

"I'll bet he has. How *big* has his *help* been, may I ask?" Allegra giggled.

Silence.

Allegra felt Luisa recoil into a hurt silence on the other end of the telephone. She had hit a nerve. "You are giving him some aren't you, Luisa?" Allegra ventured.

"How did you know?" Luisa countered defensively. Allegra's hand flew to the side of her hip as she whirled around to face the opposite counter, on which was poised a bouquet of fresh cut yellow and burgundy Grand Cru Cymbidium orchids, showing off their gorgeous blossoms. Closing her eyes, Allegra sniffed a petal, appreciating the mild scent, and began searching through the tissue paper for a note card.

"Allegra?" Luisa asked again.

"Hmmm?"

"How did you know that Dante and I were sleeping together?" Lulled out of her delight with the beautiful orchids, Allegra folded her arms across her chest, bewildered by the question from her best friend.

"Luisa girl, in all of the years I've known you, I probably know you better than you know yourself. When you get quiet like you have been over the past week or so, I know it's because of a man. It couldn't be Virgil, because I and the rest of the world know how you already feel about him...which is nothing, *nada*, zip."

"Yeah, but how did you know it was Dante?"

"Because who else have you repeatedly said that you hate? You always go after men you hate. What bothers me, girlfriend, is that I had to draw my own conclusions instead of you keeping me in the loop," Allegra playfully scolded, carrying the bouquet back into what was previously known as her dining room.

"Luisa, hold on a second," Allegra said, raising her voice above the hammering. "Max!"

Max continued to hammer at the chips on the wall. Instead of tapping him on the shoulder again, Allegra kicked him behind his kneecap.

"Yo! Wassup, Cuz?"

"When did these arrive?"

"Oh, they came this morning. When I got here, the flower dude was on the doorstep so I took 'em for you and brought them on inside."

"Where's the card? There wasn't a card?"

"Oh, yeah. There was," Max answered, letting his hammer fall to the floor with a thud, and then digging into the pockets of his overalls. "Here it is." Max placed the white, now soiled card between her fingers, and then returned to his work. Allegra carried the bouquet up the staircase to the second floor, using her foot to slam the door to her bedroom suite.

"Your cousin still trying to destroy your house?" Luisa asked, sounding more cheerful. Allegra glanced around her bedroom for the ideal location for the orchids, ultimately deciding on the armoire in the center of the bedroom. Smiling appreciatively, Allegra sat on the edge of her king sized bed, and lip read aloud the sentiments written on the card: "Like orchids, I hope our relationship will take years of careful tending. Amor, Rolando."

"Rolando!? Rolando Barbosa was in town?" Luisa asked with a high shrill in her voice, adding a Spanish accent when she pronounced Rolando's surname.

"Luisa, how do you work at a television station and not know when tall, fine-ass, black men, and ten of his not hard-on-the-eyes teammates, are in town. Tell your news director to hire me so I can provide your audience with man alerts."

"Yep, we'll call you the man whisperer!" Luisa said with a hearty laugh. Allegra added her laughter, collapsing backward across her bed.

"Luisa, that's a good one. *Man Whisperer* would be must-see television and broadcast in prime time."

"Allegra, your life has too much reality for any network. The Federal Communications Commission would ban your reality before the first episode even aired."

"But really, is everything okay, Luisa? Everything all right with you?"

"Yeah, it's all good. Dante scratches my itch. I don't have any illusions about him anymore. But the thing is, is that nobody can know that I'm involved with him, because he's a source. If my big bosses hear about Dante and me, they won't assign me to the big stories; and they'll question everything I do. Right now, I'm angling to be assigned to the sex scandal surrounding Governor Moreland."

"You're a big girl, Luisa. But Dante and those uptown brothers rule by the brutal code of the streets. Just make sure that he doesn't throw you under the bus. Alright? And by the way, what did Virgil say when you ended it with him?"

Luisa clamped her mouth closed. Allegra was not sure if her friend had heard her question. Allegra believed Dante was using Luisa and told her so, a month before. "Luisa, right now your assignment editor is probably looking at you like you're crazy. Don't you think this is all going to come out? Don't you think you're jeopardizing everything you've worked for?" Allegra heard from her friend's voice, that her warnings had fallen on deaf ears.

"I haven't," Luisa confessed, like a small child.

"You haven't what?"

"Broken up with Virgil."

"Luisa, what the hell are you doing? You're not built for this."

"Allegra, I'm not exactly sure what I'm doing. I'm in new territory, involved with two men at the same time."

"I'm not suggesting that you be a saint. But what I'm saying is that above anything else, you should be honest, with both men," Allegra advised.

"I need to ask you a favor," Luisa said, breaking the silence.

"Sure. What is it?"

"Hannibal won't agree to an interview with me, unless he can talk to you again. I know it sounds weird and everything, but…"

Allegra sat up on the edge of her bed. "Huh? What the hell do I have to do with him?"

Luisa went on to sing her praises about Dante, then Hannibal. Allegra remained unimpressed as she listened intently to her friend justify Dante's bitch-ass rationale to use a meeting with her as a bargaining chip. He should've hooked her up just on general principle. More so, Allegra did not recognize this Luisa who was sleeping with two men, when she never was very adept at handling one, and was previously always satisfied with being the eternal doormat.

Allegra was mildly intrigued with Hannibal. She was curious to see if all of that bravado translated into some serious fucking.

Allegra recalled that she hadn't dealt with an activist type of man since her freshman year of college. Though New York City was teeming with revolutionary brothers, she never believed in extra men hanging around just to take up space. For her, men needed to serve a specific function—to serve her needs. Though there was bound to be an opening at any time, Allegra was satisfied with her current committee of lovers.

Her eyes randomly landed on the face of the clock on the nightstand. Allegra double-checked the time on the clock, which read ten forty-five in the morning. Startled, she flew off of the bed, letting her terry-cloth bathrobe fall to the floor as she dashed to the bathroom and turned on the shower.

"Luisa, can we talk about this later this afternoon? I have to drive out to Garden City to see Aunt Rachael."

"Oh sure," Luisa replied, not sounding very cheerful. "Allegra, before you jump off, I really need you to do me this favor. I've never asked you to get involved with my job. But this time, it's really different. Hannibal is on Dante to get you two together."

The roar of the water flowing from the double shower head sounded in the background. Allegra yanked back the teal-colored shower curtain. "Can I think about this, Luisa? I'm always here for you, girl, but let me think this through. Because frankly there's more at stake here than your interview."

"Allegra, for God's sake, can't you do me this one favor, without the damn analysis? I never ask you for anything!" Luisa shrilled.

Allegra froze. The blood drained from her face. Luisa and she had never spoken to each other in that tone.

"Luisa, if it's that important to you, then give him my telephone number." Luisa exhaled a sigh of relief on the other end of the telephone.

"Sorry, I yelled, Allegra," Luisa said quietly, before hanging up. Allegra stared at her receiver, her eyes expressing concern.

18

A thick plume of cigarette smoke hung in the air in the assisted living apartment at the Sunrise and Garden Living Center in Garden City, Long Island. Allegra rented an automobile to make her dreaded, bi-monthly sojourn to visit her mother's sister, Rachael, an octogenarian, who furiously defied the center's policy against smoking. In fact, she defied all policies which did not suit her temperamental mood swings. Allegra attributed Rachael's ornery personality not to her age, but because of who she was. She was determined to never live like Rachael—friendless and bitter. Allegra made this two hour trek, depending on traffic, out of a sense of obligation and karma. On her drive to Long Island, she had listened to Thunder's interview with the current Mayor of New York City. The Mayor was obviously unhappy with Thunder's line of pointed questioning.

Allegra felt obligated to visit Aunt Rachael as a reminder of a karmic obligation to pay her respects to her last known living relative, despite the fractured nature of their relationship. Arriving on the campus, Allegra had gone to the accounts receivable desk, to make a payment on Aunt Rachael's account. The Filipino clerk behind the glass window, scrolled through the patient database, searching for current invoice.

"Hmmm," the clerk said.

"Is there a problem?" Allegra asked, removing her dark sunglasses.

"Your aunt's bill was paid up through next year. Nothing is owed on her account."

"Who paid her account? I just paid last month's bill."

"Let me check on that," the clerk replied, scrolling. "Okay, looks like a Thunder Poole paid off her account."

Allegra gasped, knowing that the yearly amount would total over ten thousand dollars.

Transfixed on the flat-screen television which broadcast a court reality show, Rachael took another drag of her high tar cigarette, stubbornly holding onto the smoke, before releasing, the smoke cascading against the windows, which overlooked the facility's newly expanded recreational park. The so-called plaintiff and defendant were at war over a disputed unpaid loan. Rachael was engrossed in the drama as if her life depended upon the outcome of the television mock trial.

Allegra sat across from Rachael wearing a navy blue, pant suit and black, pointy high-heeled boots. Rachael still held a grudge against Allegra's mother for having a torrid affair with her husband. Because her sister and husband suddenly died together in a tragic car accident, Rachael was never able to heal from her pain. Her attending physician strongly recommended that she seek therapy, consult with a minister, meditate, but Rachael wore her rage like a badge of honor. Allegra's physical appearance did not help Rachael to forget the tragedy in her past, primarily because Allegra was the mirror image of her mother, the woman who had betrayed Rachael. Rachael's life had come to a screeching halt the moment her husband and her sister were side-swiped by a truck on the Garden State Expressway. A police investigation concluded that Rachael's husband may have fallen asleep behind the wheel, as they returned from a weekend rendezvous in a Poconos motel.

With each passing birthday, Rachael became more rigid in holding on to that tragic memory. In her soul, that betrayal was the only thing that kept alive her connection with her deceased husband. During one visit, Rachael admitted as much when Allegra unadvisedly suggested that she just let it go.

Screaming so loud nurses and ward attendants from down the hallway burst into her apartment to restrain her, tying her flailing wrists, one by one, with plastic restraints. "Don't you tell me what to do, you bitch. I don't have to let it go, you fuckin' slut!" Rachael yelled, spewing her venom, her eyes bulging from her head. When Rachael telephoned Allegra days later, begging her niece to visit the following weekend, she donned an angelic persona, behaving as though she had no memory of her recent outburst.

The television judge dismissed the plaintiff's case, citing lack of evidence. "He was a damn fool for suing his brother in the first place," Rachael complained as the credits rolled. "Aunt Rachael, Max is almost done renovating my brownstone," Allegra lied, hoping that positive news about her son would lighten her aunt's mood.

Rachael sipped from her now cold cup of coffee and crossed her leg away from Allegra, letting her pink, fuzzy house slipper dangle from her foot.

"I hope you're paying him, and not cheating him out of his pay. 'Cause if you're anything like your no-good mammy, you'll just wanna take and never pay nobody like you said you would."

Allegra's nostrils flared, before she answered. It was pointless explaining to Rachael that Max was a complete failure at everything, including as her son, and that any day, he would do something stupid and swing at his third strike with the criminal justice system.

"Max promised that the work will be done before Christmas. Perhaps you can come join me and my friends for dinner on Christmas Eve?"

"Your momma never cooked on Christmas or any damn holiday. I was the one who ended up having to do all of the cooking and cleaning. That's why I can't understand what he ever saw in her. Slaving over a stove for him for thirty-five years of my life, raising his only no-good son and I was always commended for keeping a clean house. And then he throws it all back in my face by sleeping with your mother! That's a no-good man for you. And your mommy wasn't nothin' but a damn slut, no matter how perfect you thought she was. And I'll tell anybody, 'cause that's exactly what she was." The rage abruptly halted, as it always did on these visits, and was replaced with tears. "Why did they leave me, Niece? All of 'em. My husband, your momma, my son?" Rachael wept like a helpless baby. Then just as suddenly, she angrily flicked the cigarette ashes, smashed the butt into the already filled square glass ashtray, and took another cigarette out of the drawer in her wooden side table. Lighting another cigarette, she hacked loudly, as she puffed on the butt, generating gales of smoke. Allegra cleared her throat, knowing that she needed to get out of this nicotine den, before the odor was absorbed into her clothes. More importantly, she knew that she needed to come to terms with the fact that she and her Aunt Rachael would never be able to conduct a cordial, lucid conversation.

Rachael would crumble if she knew the reality of her son's life, especially if he was incarcerated again. Allegra bailed him out of jail, after his theft and cashing of Rachael's Social Security checks.

Out of obligation, Max repaid Allegra by renovating her dining room. Rachael's salt-and-pepper hair framed her finely lined face, yet still she was a beautiful woman, similar to the black-and-white photos which dotted the room, showing her as a youthful, outgoing and optimistic girl. But now Rachael's internal lights had been dimmed and that is where she was most comfortable. Rather than lock away her pain, Rachael chose to wear it on her sleeve and envelope Allegra in her delusions. She chose to unfurl her lost soul, like an oversized banner, across the human sky.

Driving west in bumper-to-bumper traffic on the Long Island expressway, as sunset neared, Allegra pondered if she would ever tell Rachael the truth, that Max was not the prince of a son that she thought he was; that he and Khadijah had concocted a plan and ripped off Rachael's Social Security checks. The two forged her signature and cashed them for eight months before getting caught. A senior administrator from the Sunrise and Garden Living Center contacted Allegra as a last resort before they were going to suspend her leasing agreement.

"Though we sympathize, Ms. Adams, with your aunt's predicament, and understand that the situation she finds herself in was not created by her, we will need to bring her account current with a full payment of eight-thousand, five-hundred dollars, for her to continue as a resident here at Sunrise; otherwise we will need to move forward with collection proceedings. I'm sure you can understand our position." Allegra was stirred from her daydream by the evening traffic crawl, drivers honking out of frustration, rather than impending danger. Her telephone had been ringing, stopped and then rang again before she heard it. An unrecognizable cell phone area code displayed on her caller id. Normally, Allegra refused to answer to unscreened incoming telephone calls, but her finger pressed "Answer" instead of "Ignore."

The caller heard the headset being untwisted and placed on top of her head, before he heard a voice.

"Yes, hello," Allegra said.

"Well, hello, Ms. Adams." Allegra's mind reeled over who could possibly be calling her on her cell phone from a number she did not recognize.

"Who's calling?" Allegra asked with irritation in her voice. A loud silence followed as the male caller gathered his courage and evaluated if dialing her telephone number was such a good idea.

"Hannibal. Hannibal Morgan, Sista. Luisa said that you would be expecting my telephone call," he said, with a tone that suggested Allegra should be thrilled that he had dialed her number.

"Luisa?" Allegra's mouth fell open like a starving baby goldfish.

"Did I catch you at a bad time? Sounds like you're outside somewhere."

"I'm actually stuck in traffic. What can I do you for, Mr. Morgan?"

"Ah...right to the point, huh? I can dig that, my sister," Hannibal replied, as Allegra rolled her eyes.

"The deal is that you've been on my mind. And I'm curious about that fine as hell woman who came into my organization's town hall meeting and disrupted my train of thought."

Though Allegra rolled her eyes again, she had to laugh. Hannibal replied with his own laughter. "I'm serious as a heart attack, Sista. If you could see me now, my hand is reaching up to God, praying to the Almighty, promising that what I'm saying is true. I been thinking that any man who gets down with that sister must be throwing it down, fo' real." Allegra veered off the Long Island Expressway to the Grand Central Parkway, praying that the traffic on the Queensborough Bridge would not be as heavy, plus she could save nine dollars by avoiding the Queens-Midtown tunnel.

"Okay, but you still haven't answered my question...what can I do you for?"

"May I see you? That's all this brother has been wantin' to do. Just let my eyes feast on you. Do I have to beg, Sista? 'Cause if I do, I'm willing to do that. This brother never ain't too proud to beg," Hannibal added, with a smile.

Allegra's second line beeped. This time her caller id display revealed the caller. It was Luisa.

"Hold on, Hannibal," Allegra said, clicking over to the second line. "Luisa, Hannibal sure didn't waste any time!"

"Omigod, Allegra! Did he already call you?"

"He's on the other line."

"Thank you for speaking with him, Allegra. I just need so badly to get this interview. Please talk to him until I get my interview with him. Then do what you want. Thank you for doing me this favor." Annoyed, Allegra exhaled, not responding to her friend's chatter, then clicking back over to the waiting Dante.

"Hello," Hannibal said. "You there, Sista?"

"I'm here," Allegra answered, making a wide left from Van Dam Avenue onto Queens Boulevard.

"You probably heard that I formed a new political party. For far too long we've been taken advantage of by the Democratic Party and the Republicans don't give a shit about black people. So we've decided to rebuke political representation led by our oppressors. It's time that we do this now."

"Actually, I had not heard. But that's nice," Allegra said, thinking that Hannibal sounded like he was reading from a Huey Newton sixties revolutionary playbook.

"Yeah, no one thought that we could get on the ballot to run for the mayor's office. But we did. Our street team has traveled all over New York State and came back to our headquarters last Thursday with seventy-five thousand verified signatures. Though that Uncle Tom, Chauncey Jones down at the Board of Elections, said he was going to challenge them."

"So you're running for mayor?" Allegra's tone insinuated that she thought he was a crackpot.

"Uh huh; got to. How else are our people going to access contracts and resources to rebuild our communities? The current regime from both parties obviously is gonna keep rewarding their cronies with opportunities, while black men have high percentage rates of unemployment...over 50 percent depending on who you ask; and that's no longer acceptable, Sister. It's time for our community to step up to the plate and get what's ours," Hannibal replied defiantly.

Allegra remembered that Luisa had shared that Virgil had been drafted to mount a campaign."Are you a lawyer or a businessman, Mr. Morgan? Every person who has been elected mayor in this city has had some professional experience in law or business."

"Yeah, that and being incompetent. But hell yeah, Sista, I qualify. When I graduated from Howard Law, Negro sell-outs in my class went to work for corporate America or to Wall Street. I went a different route because I wanted to help our people at the grass roots. So I became a legal aid attorney for a few years, and then went to work for the Innocent Now Project, exonerating wrongfully incarcerated prisoners. Sista, you'd be shocked at how many of our brothers and sisters are locked up only because they could not afford competent legal representation."

"While that may be commendable, that does not answer my question," Allegra replied.

"I've been a community organizer in the black community on a variety of issues since I graduated from law school. So I'm more than prepared to run this city."

The unimpressed look on Allegra's face showed that she was

not persuaded. Still not needing her encouragement, Hannibal continued on rambling about his life, his achievements, and his disappointments regarding the advancement of black people. He also included a rant on the diabolic actions of the devilish white man.

"And not because they got caught robbing some bodega owner in the hood?"

"Naw, it ain't none of that. That's not the kind of cases that I dealt with."

"So, how're our people supposed to know if the lawyer they hired is competent or not?" Allegra asked. "I don't recall seeing the word *competent* on the sign outside of the offices of attorneys that I know."

"You go hard, Sister," Hannibal said, assessing her power.

"Come hard or go home," Allegra said, clucking her tongue. Her double entendre flew over his head.

"No, but that's cool. Excellent observation, Sister," Hannibal praised. "And therein lies the problem. Our brothers and sisters don't know, can't know the difference. That's why the work of the Panther Urban Institute must continue. That's why I decided to build my own full service community organization to fully empower and mobilize our people. I always say, if you don't want to be part of someone else's organization, build your own. But the point is, that we as a people must be organized to address the avalanche of attacks coming our way. Ya dig?"

"So you and your friend Dante created the Panthers?"

"More like I hired him. Made him what he is today. He was one of the cases I worked on at the Innocent Project. Got him cleared off of a murder conviction."

"Murder?" Allegra questioned, alarmed that Luisa had been dick whipped by a murderer.

"Murder one, but he was innocent. Dante's problem was that he had been convicted of manslaughter before, killed a dude in the boxing ring, so Virgil Douglas, the assistant district attorney back in the day, used that against him. I mean, Dante ain't no angel, but he was innocent of killing his landlord."

"You think so?" Allegra asked, hiding her sarcasm.

"I know so. But Dante and I been rolling together ever since. He got a lot of support from his wife. She's a strong, black woman. Found out his wife and I went to high school together, though I don't remember her because we ran with two different crowds. But after he got out, after she stood by him while he was locked up, Dante didn't want to have anything to do with her. But I told him that he wasn't going to find a strong, black woman like that around every corner. Told him that he needed to get back with her and get his life together. If it wasn't for me, Dante and his wife wouldn't be together today."

"I'm sure she's thrilled," Allegra replied dryly.

"Huh?"

"I said, when did he go to prison?"

"Brother Dante wasn't in no prison. The only thing that was in prison was his mind. He suffers from the same post-traumatic slave syndrome that black people suffer, due to the four hundred years of oppression suffered at the hands of white people. There needs to be a whole field of study devoted to this reality. But I guess if I wait for Harvard, Columbia or NYU to do it, I'll just be waiting, huh?"

"Wait a minute. You didn't grow up with Dante? Visit him in prison after he was sentenced because he killed an opponent in the boxing ring?"

"Dante told you that?" Hannibal laughed. "He tends to be secretive about his life, but he's an extremely dedicated brother. Dante is a good brother."

"You need to teach him some manners," Allegra said defiantly.

"What do you mean?"

"When I came to your meeting with Luisa, he sent a note that I needed to uncross my legs. What's that about?"

"We believe, Sista, that it's unhealthy for black women to cross their legs. If you examine the images from ancient Egypt, the Nubians crossed their legs."

Allegra stifled a giggle, thinking, *Hannibal is certifiably nuts*. She sighed, remembering what Dante had told Luisa; conflicted with what she was now hearing. Allegra didn't mean to sigh so loudly, at least so that Hannibal could actually hear the oxygen leaving her lungs. "Oh my bad, I talked your ear off. I kinda get carried away sometimes," Hannibal apologized.

"It's been a long day," Allegra replied, turning left onto 125th Street behind a Metropolitan Transit Authority bus, with a smoky exhaust system. "So, it's been interesting listening to you."

"Oh, wow! Is that what this was? I thought we were having a conversation. I-I mean that's why I called."

"It was more like you called because you want to fuck me. Aren't I right, Hannibal Morgan?" Allegra replied softly. Stunned, Hannibal almost swallowed his cell phone.

"Are you there? Cat got your tongue?" Allegra continued with a wide, devilish grin, turning right onto the bustling Adam Clayton Powell Boulevard.

"Yo, word. Um, well it ain't nothing that I would run from. I'll say that much."

Deciding against traveling north on the FDR Drive, Allegra veered onto First Avenue, wondering what game, if any, was in play here. Luisa had been cagey about discussing her relationship with Dante. Allegra questioned why Dante had not been able to advocate on behalf of Luisa to get the access to Hannibal that she needed. Allegra had known men who would leverage a piece of

ass to get what they wanted. Luisa was not savvy enough to negotiate sexual gamesmanship. For Luisa, sex always came with the
strings of emotion and attachment, instead of the satisfaction of
carnal desire. Allegra was intrigued enough to investigate further
out of protection for Luisa; if need be, protection from Dante.

As Allegra waited for the traffic light to signal green, Hannibal
continued to sing his own praises, making a heroic attempt to
impress Allegra. She remembered Hannibal as the charismatic
man that he was, able to captivate his followers into doing his
bidding. Though Allegra was mildly intrigued by Hannibal, she
was curious to see if all of that bravado translated into some serious fucking.

"So can I see you, Sista?" Hannibal asked again.

"Thursday evening. Ten-ish. Touch base earlier that day. I'll
let you know where."

"Thursday, there's a Panther meeting."

"Looks like you're going to have to cancel it, now doesn't it?"
Hannibal was stunned by the control Allegra was asserting. His
emotions were at the cross-section of dominating her, like he was
used to doing with other women, manipulation and respect.

"Okay, Sister. Awright. Thursday. Ten o'clock?"

"Ten o'clock," Allegra confirmed, clicking off of the BlackBerry,
as, on the other end, Dante entered the Hummer, handing a cup
of coffee to Hannibal in the passenger's seat.

"You get her?" Dante asked. Hannibal angled his head toward
Dante, with a conspiratorial smile, and bumped their fists savoring the anticipation of accomplishing their divine mission.

Back at her home office, Allegra conducted a random search on
her computer for Hannibal. No matter the search result, for

Allegra, it was abundantly clear that controversy was determined to find Hannibal. For the last twelve years, he was shown photographed underneath bold print, sensational headlines almost daily and over the last year, he could be found on numerous political blogs. Hannibal led the investigation eventually exonerating a group of black teens from a murder conviction. *The New York Post* called him, in an editorial, a "criminal" and a "thug," accusing that Hannibal was a threat to a civilized society. "Hannibal Morgan would be clearly happy if the doors of the jail flew open, allowing rapists, murderers and drug dealers to roam, plaguing our vulnerable society," another editorial read. Panther Movement members were seen on the nightly network news leading marches, boycotts and community meetings. *The New York Times* wrote, "The Panthers? Fraud or Movement For Change?"

Hannibal seemed to delight in mocking the insipid nature of the questions posed by aggressive network reporters. "What exactly is it that your group wants, Mr. Morgan?" a reporter asked on an archived YouTube video.

"We want don't want, we demand what all people want. Justice, by any means necessary," Hannibal taunted them, through a bullhorn, as the self-anointed director of New York City's revolutionary political theater.

Allegra was amused by his machinations. She admired that he had the courage to speak on issues, where others held their tongues. Cowards whispered, cowering behind their tightly held beliefs, while Hannibal wore his rage against the "white man" and about the "condition of black people" on his sleeve. If one didn't know his position on a given racial issue, then he just was not paying attention. But in the pit of her stomach, Allegra sensed that there was much about Hannibal which the followers of his movement chose to ignore.

Allegra picked up her telephone and Thunder answered the studio's private line. "Hey, Baby! To what do I owe this honor?" Thunder asked, waving Crystal and his crew out of the studio.

"I just called to say thank you. And—," Allegra trailed with a giggle.

"And what?" Thunder asked eagerly.

"And the mike is hot!"

"The next sound you hear will be of me fainting on the floor." Thunder smiled as bright as a summer solstice.

19

"Ms. Hamilton?"

"Yes, Quincy," Luisa replied through the speaker of the intercom upstairs in her condo.

"As you instructed, I informed Mr. Douglas that you weren't in."

"Did he leave?"

"Not at first. He wanted to know what time you had left. I told him it must have been before I started my shift. Mr. Douglas sat in his car for a while across the street. He looked like he was talking on his cell. Then after about twenty minutes, he drove away."

"Thanks, Quincy," replied a relieved Luisa reading a text from Virgil, "Where are you? Must have just missed you at my office today."

Luisa was unprepared to see Virgil tonight, or perhaps ever. He had done exactly what she asked him not to do; phoned her general manager to get her removed from covering the Panthers. What infuriated Luisa the most was that Virgil didn't have the integrity to tell her. Instead, she was ambushed by the assignment editor as the morning assignment meeting was wrapping, and her fellow reporters dashed to their first assignments of the day.

"Nice to know people in high places, Luisa?" the assignment editor insinuated, sipping hot cocoa.

"It can be, I guess," Luisa replied, assuming that he was making a point, without being direct about it.

"If you wanted off the Panthers, I would have preferred if you had come directly to me, instead of going over my head to the big bosses."

"Excuse me? I did no such thing. What're you talking about?"

"The big boss apparently got a phone call last night from your boyfriend, Virgil."

"He. Did. What?"

"You can imagine how surprised I was, waking me and my wife up at that time of night."

"Wait a minute. What did the general manager say?"

"Oh, he did the right thing. Said he'd talk to me, because he tries to stay out of the day-to-day operations. But frankly, I'm disappointed, Luisa. If this was an assignment that you couldn't handle, or that you were having problems with, you should've called me. And that doesn't make good office politics."

"Wait a minute! I never asked Virgil to call the general manager; I'm not having problems with the story and I've never said that I wanted off of it."

"Well, it seems like to me that you and your boyfriend have a huge case of miscommunication. You might want to look into getting some counseling. It's made a world of difference with me and the wife."

"Thanks. I have to go," Luisa said, shoving past the assignment editor and running down the hallway to the elevator.

"Luisa! When is the story going to be done?!" he yelled.

"I'll email you this afternoon!" Luisa yelled back before the elevator door closed.

The No. 2 IRT express train could not have rumbled into Times Square station soon enough for Luisa. The subway was the fastest mode of transportation for her to achieve her objective; to find Virgil. Murderous thoughts drowned Luisa as she plotted how to destroy the man who treated her as if she was invisible.

Who the fuck does he think he is? Every fucking thing I do or say, goes in one ear and out the other. He wants me dead. He wants to make sure that I know that I don't matter. I will destroy him. I'm gonna tell everyone in his office how much of a bullshit artist he is. I'll embarrass him in front of everybody and destroy his office. I'm gonna show him who calls the shots. I should have listened to Allegra; should have dumped his ass as soon as I saw that he couldn't fuck. He wants me dead. He wants me to feel dead.

Her BlackBerry persistently vibrated with emails from the assignment editor demanding how soon she would turn in not only tape on Hannibal but two other stories she had volunteered for to prove her abilities.

Luisa flew up the staircase into the United States Attorney's office in Brooklyn's Cadman Plaza and flashed her press badge to the security officers, one of whom recognized her. "Long time. Go right on in, Ms. Hamilton."

"Is Virgil in his office?" Luisa asked, rushing through the metal detector.

"Mr. Douglas just returned from the grand jury. He's probably on his way to his office now."

Built in 1871, the building could be mistaken for an urban monastery whose stark corridors still harbored the odor of finality and tradition. Federal workers spoke in hushed tones or buried their heads in reams of papers and stuffed red wells. Luisa's breathing had slowed to a measured rhythm, when she realized that she might appear to be a frazzled lunatic. *Office of Virgil Douglas, United States Attorney* was carved on his office door. Luisa turned

the doorknob, pushing open the door onto a small waiting room,
with one law clerk and a receptionist, Barbara and Tanya, sitting
behind the large wooden desks, glued to their computer screens.
Glancing up to see Luisa, both women squealed and rushed to
greet her with open arms. "Luisa, it's so good to see you. Where
have you been? We watch you on television all of the time. My
husband has been asking for his autographed photo. How are
you? Have a seat? Cold out, isn't it? Do you want something to
drink?" Barbara and Tanya's questions cascaded over one another. Overwhelmed by their kind innocence, Luisa was touched by
their pure happiness and by the fact that they were oblivious to
the reality that their boss was a son-of-a-bitch.

"No, thanks, I just had lunch," Luisa lied. "Is Virgil around?"

Imagining that Luisa was the love struck girlfriend of their
wonderful boss, Barbara and Tanya instantly tried to play cupid
and his cheerleader. "He must be around here somewhere. He
got the indictment this morning for that terrorist who tried to
blow up the school bus filled with children. And I've got to tell
you that when my husband came down with prostate cancer,
Virgil gave me an all-paid family leave, until my husband was
back on his feet. Yep, Virgil is a real hero, Luisa. You're lucky to
have him in your life. But you already know that, don't you?"
Barbara and Tanya babbled. "Do you want to have a seat in his
office until he comes back? He should be here any second."

"Um, no. Thank you. I'm going to step out into the hallway
and return some phone calls," Luisa replied, retreating.

"Well, Virgil won't be able to miss you out there, Luisa. Just
come on back in where you're done, and you're welcome to wait
for him in his office, Hon." Luisa never returned.

Luisa massaged her right temple. She slowly walked to the vanity in her bedroom, catching her weary image in the gold-plated mirror, and plopped down. Reading Allegra's text message again, Luisa prayed that her eyes needed an examination. "Bitch Alert! Dante is married. Yes, you read it right. The bitch is married. I'm here to help you sort this out," her eyes reconfirmed, before she hurled her BlackBerry across the room.

Holding a drop blue quartz earring, and fingering the other in her free hand, Luisa wore a black, sequined mini-dress and black stilettos. Her last conversation with Allegra didn't end well. The more Allegra criticized Dante, the more Luisa was determined to defend him. *Allegra was dead wrong. Dante was not married. If he was married, where was he keeping his wife? At the Schomberg library?* Luisa asked herself. Allegra thought that she was a relationship expert about every man, never taking into consideration that sometimes she could be wrong. To Luisa's chagrin, every conversation with Allegra lately had turned into her defending Dante. Allegra never admitted that she only knew Dante from what Luisa shared with her and opinion.

When Luisa dropped by Allegra's brownstone the next evening they got into a heated discussion about her fascination with the Panthers. "Why not? The station keeps whitewashing their programming. People need to know what's really going on in the black and Latino community and it's my job to bring the work of grass roots organization to viewers' attention instead of what's happening to some drug addicted, no-talent actress."

"Of course. But there are other community groups needing the same kind of exposure. You just need to check yourself and make sure you haven't completely lost your objectivity. And the fact that you insist on fuckin' Dante-the-bitch's ass just might put your career in jeopardy, if word got out. Just check yourself is all I'm sayin'."

Luisa's loyalty was her most endearing and self-defeating quality. She possessed a bleeding heart for a stray kitten and beret-wearing conspiracy theorists. Allegra hurt Luisa's feelings when she criticized Dante. Allegra knew it, especially when Luisa hid her hurt by tossing her curly black hair and blinking back her tears. Allegra often forgot how sensitive Luisa was, but sometimes, she surmised, her sister-friend needed tough love. Allegra refused to let Luisa walk into a threatening tsunami without lifting a hand or a prayer to try to protect her. And deep down, Luisa knew that Allegra was the mother she never had, the sister she always wanted and the friend everyone deserved.

Experience was a powerful teacher, yet Luisa seemed determined to get her heart stomped on by every man in her life. Men dissed her, kissed her, fucked her, stole from her and viewed her as arm candy, consistently serving her bullshit like: "I thought you were a real sista. Thought you were gonna be with me through thick and thin. I guess I was wrong." Or, "Is all you ever think about sex? There's more to life, you know." Then another cycle would begin. Luisa's heart would melt, believing she was not patient or supportive enough and she would try her best to prove to the no good motherfucker that she was worthy of his bullshit.

"Hell, no! No way, Luisa! You don't deserve that shit! As gorgeous as you are, you need to open your eyes and recognize that good men are dying to be with you. You can't see them because you don't believe you deserve the love of a good man. You let men commandeer your shit instead of the other way around," Allegra often told her. Luisa would nod obediently as if she understood. Then as soon as a stiff dick attached to a brainless meathead would express any interest her way, she would be eager to throw her self-dignity to the wind.

Luisa abandoned her annoyance with Allegra. She planned to join Allegra and Khadijah for dinner at Morocco's followed by salsa dancing at Puente's, a Dominican nightclub in her old Washington Heights neighborhood. Due to the flu bug sweeping the newsroom, Luisa had had a tense, demanding, ten-hour shift and she needed to unwind on the dance floor. Instead, Luisa kicked off one of her stilettos and listened to Dante talk his way back in between her legs, after a two week absence. He boasted on the telephone about the Panthers' latest clandestine operation.

"Can we talk about it when I get there, huh? Can we work this out when I see you?" Dante asked, in one of his let-me-come-through telephone calls.

"Um, I don't know," Luisa answered, shaking her head, hearing an instant replay of Allegra's warnings about Hannibal. "Allegra and Khadijah are waiting for me. We're supposed to have dinner tonight."

Any man who won't acknowledge you in public ain't shit. And the more you tolerate his bullshit, the less you're going to feel about yourself in the long run.

"I know I should've called, but my days been getting away from me. Me and Hannibal had to make a run out to East New York. A kid was holding his whole family hostage."

"Really? I didn't hear anything about that on the police scanner!" Luisa exclaimed.

"By the time Hannibal had the kid comin' out of his house, the cops were just gettin' there."

"No one phoned the police?"

"In the hood, in situations like that, the last thing you wanna have are some white pigs, with one lone Uncle Tom riding shot gun, rollin' up to the spot, with guns drawn, shooting up innocent bystanders."

"What happened to the hostage taker?"

"You mean the kid?"

"He was holding hostages, right? That is what you said."

"He was a knucklehead. He wasn't even carrying no real gun."

"So what happened to him, when the police arrived?"

"We told 'em it was a false alarm. One of our female lieutenants pretended that she was the kid's aunt."

"Lied to the police?"

"Pigs lie all of the damn time. What's a little lie to the enemy? Look, that's not why I called. I'm comin' through. You miss me?" Luisa rolled her eyes. How could she cancel on Allegra and Khadijah at the last minute, yet in her heart she knew that she missed Dante and needed to feel his arms around her, no matter how angry she was with him.

"Hello?"

"Yeah, I'm here. Uh huh," Luisa said, melting.

"Tell your punk doorman and your dude that I'm coming through, so I don't have to stop and show that muthafucka no ID. And put on that tiger print thong of yours, wouldja? Be ready for me," Dante said, in his lusty tone, adding with a knowing chuckle, "You know how we like to get down."

"Okay," Luisa answered, barely audible, in conflict between needing to be with Dante and knowing that she wanted to cast revenge on Virgil. Inside, Luisa desperately wanted to turn what she already knew was true—Allegra's admonitions into a lie. Her stomach cringed in shame, as Luisa could not find the words to explain to herself that she was about to cancel the car service which was within ten minutes from her scheduled pick-up time. Yet her heart skipped a beat, and her emotions shifted toward optimism as she sprayed perfume behind her ear lobes and between her breasts. "This is what grown-ass women do. We sometimes have to juggle shit."

"I'll be through in a minute."

Luisa cancelled her car service, while removing her quartz earrings, tossing them into the walnut jewelry chest. She then retrieved peppermint-flavored condoms from her nightstand drawer and settled on the loveseat to wait for Dante.

Three hours later.

Luisa replied to Allegra's heated voice mail with a text message to avoid hearing her disappointment and anger. Luisa texted while the credits streamed for *The Monique Show on* her flat screen television: "I'm okay. On call at the station; plus nausea is doggin' me."

Past midnight, Dante strolled into Luisa's condo, just as she posted a status update on her Facebook page: *"I'm no longer accepting friend requests here (we're maxed out!) Please join my Like page instead. Thanks!"*

Annoyed, Luisa sat on the edge of her bed, wearing the tiger print thong Dante had requested and a short nightgown tied at her waist. Dante sat across from her, on her newly upholstered, beige chair, yawning, and untying his boots. "I said I was sorry. Brother Hannibal called a meeting with the police commissioner just when I gettin' ready to split and it ran longer than I thought."

"You could've called."

"You should know by now that the type of life I have…it's not my own, nowhatumsayin'? My life ain't neat and nice where everything wraps up at five o'clock. When some shit jumps off, Brother Hannibal and me got to be there, no matter what time it is and who it's inconveniencing. That's what my life is about. And Hannibal and me pledged together to do everything in our power to stand up against all of the negativity that's going down. But when the day is over, what I do need is some damn peace, nowhatumsayin'? I thought you were going to provide that for me. And that you'd be down for being that woman who would bring me peace. Humph, maybe I was wrong about you."

"You could have called, Dante," Luisa whined, unable to restrain herself.

"You're killin' my mood, Babe," Dante said, his arms folding across his chest. "I've always been here for you, and I need the same thing in return."

"I know that's what you want, but I don't know if I'm that brother that's gonna be able to give you that—when you want, on the drop of a dime. The Panther Movement ain't no nine-to five job; sometimes I'm gonna be able to call, sometimes I'm not; and then there's gonna be days when you ain't gonna hear from me at all. Sistas who are really down with the struggle, they know that. They know what it takes to stand by a brother. Now, my question is, 'do you?' 'Cause this nigga don't do no check-ins wit nobody, nowhatumsayin'? You gotta lotta fuckin' nerve, tryin' to tell me that I'm supposed to be at your call and you still dealing with old boy." Luisa was dumbstruck. She was at loss for words in how to answer Hannibal.

"Maybe it was a mistake coming over here," Dante said, abruptly standing up, grabbing his military jacket.

"Wait! Wait," Luisa said, holding his arms, pressuring him to return to a seated position. "Don't go. I'm sorry. It's just been a long day." Dante offered a triumphant grin, as he fingered her negligee.

"Come here. Let me hold you," Dante said, as Luisa folded herself into his arms.

Luisa loved Dante. Despite what Allegra said about him, she decided not to spoil this moment with him. Luisa knelt down in front of Dante, removing his other boot, then his socks, and massaged his feet. "Be right back," Luisa said, rushing into the bathroom, turning on the faucets to fill up the bathtub with lavender and soapy hot water. Luisa returned to Hannibal, reaching for his hand, "Come with me. Let's take a bath together," she said.

"Take care of me first?" Dante asked, gazing up at her, stroking her thighs. Luisa knelt down in front of Dante, pushing him back against the chair and removing her nightgown, she danced around him, bare-chested, still wearing her tiger print thong. Slowly, she hung up his military jacket, and then undressed Dante, removing his tee shirt, his boxer shorts and jock strap.

"Damn," was all that Dante said appreciatively, rubbing her body against his, stroking his broad chest down to his pelvic area, then turning her back toward him and performing an erotic lap dance. He smiled with his eyes half-closed as Luisa licked and sucked his fingers, moaning with pleasure at the taste of his fingers in her mouth. Slowly handling his cock, Luisa placed it in her mouth, exploring it with her tongue, delighted that it was growing stiff in her mouth. With her tongue, Luisa explored its texture as if this was not a replay of their many previous encounters. Dante squirmed with joy as Luisa sucked his balls tenderly, while gazing into his eyes, then running her tongue up his shaft and circling his head, moving it rapidly in and out of her mouth. Dante stiffened his torso as if attempting to bear his imminent explosion. Luisa gripped his cock, continued to suck on its head, watching Dante attempt to kiss her, as he gripped the arms of the chair, writhing with pleasure until he climaxed. Laying her head on his crotch, Luisa found joy in pleasing Dante, as he rested his head against the wall, muttering, "Humph, Humph, Humph," rubbing his hands through her long black hair.

Luisa rose and lit a lavender scented candle, grabbed a condom, and stretched across the bed. "Now it's your turn. You come here," Luisa said demurely. With an alluring smile, she threw him a kiss. Dante leaned forward, watching her with hungry anticipation, his dick becoming stiff again. Luisa used her teeth to open the condom wrapper and held it out for Dante to use.

With raised eyebrows, Dante asked in a hurt tone, "Whatchu doin'? What's that?"

"It's a rubber, Silly," Luisa said, thinking that Dante was making a joke.

"A rubber? Since when do we use a goddamned rubber?" Dante asked, harshly. Luisa's eyes darkened and searched Dante's face for a glint of humor. There was none in sight. "You still fuckin' that other nigga?" Dante continued. His question felt like a punch in her stomach. Luisa was still sleeping with Virgil but on an infrequent basis. However, her unsatisfying relationship with Virgil had nothing to do with her decision to use a condom with Dante.

"No, but I think this is something we should've done from the beginning, don't you?"

"I don't do rubbers. Never have and never will. And frankly, I'm insulted that you would bring me this dumb shit."

"I don't think wearing a condom is dumb at all."

"If I'm the only one you deal with, why do we need to do this?" Luisa's ears perked up and replayed Dante's words, "if I'm the only one you deal with." This was the first time that Dante had hinted toward dealing with Luisa exclusively. Now she was hearing what she had always wanted to hear from him.

Sounds of splattering water jarred Luisa out of her delirium. "Oh shit, shit, shit!" she exclaimed, jumping from the bed, running into the bathroom, and tiptoeing through an inch of warm, sudsy water. Water streamed over the edge of the pink bathtub, leaving islands of white suds scattered across the floor. Luisa stepped carefully, assuring that she did not fall, until she reached the water faucet.

In the bedroom, Dante shook his head, then checked his watch, grabbed his pants and shirt and quickly got dressed. Around the corner, Luisa continued cursing and mopping the bathroom floor. Dante stood, zipping up his military pants, and pulled his tee shirt over his head. He spied around Luisa's feminine, lacey styled bedroom, glancing at the perfectly made bed, her high heels.

Once he had laced his work boots and folded his military jacket over his left arm, Dante announced, "Hey, I gotta bounce."

"What?" she answered, from inside the bathroom, removing a mop and bucket from the utility closet.

"Yeah, we're rollin' up to Councilmember Wilkins' house in a few hours, so I gotta bounce and catch some shuteye so I can pick up Brother Hannibal."

"You mean you're gonna leave me like this? You're not going to help?!" Luisa yelled, tiptoeing to the doorway of the bathroom, standing nearly nude, with her hand on her hip, the mop in her hand and without a Dante generated reciprocal orgasm.

"Um, sorry, Hon. But I gotta bounce. I'll get witchu later, nowhatumsayin'?" Dante said, putting on his military jacket.

Luisa angrily threw her designer towels on the marble floor to absorb the water. Tears crowded the corner of her eyes as she surveyed her beautiful bathroom flooded with water and bubble bath—the water and bubble bath that she was preparing for Dante and her to enjoy.

"So you not gonna give me no sugar before I go?" Dante asked, standing at the entrance to the bathroom. Luisa pouted in response and continued mopping the soaked floor. Dante backed away from the doorway, then peered back around the corner to make sure his movement was hidden from Luisa. Spying Luisa's Louis Vuitton wallet, he secreted it under his military jacket. Dante removed and counted the cash, then returned a lone twenty-dollar bill and pocketed the remainder in his pants pocket.

"Okay, I'm out," Dante tossed through the bathroom doorway. "I'll catch up witchu later. I'm gonna grab a beer on my way out."

Luisa refused to even look at Dante as she continued mopping, shielding her hurt pride from him. When she heard Dante return from the kitchen and then the front door slam behind Dante, Luisa dropped the mop to the floor, and sobbed a torrential rain.

20

Allegra rode Thunder's joystick until they both collapsed from exhaustion, falling fast asleep. Thunder stirred first, going downstairs and checking on Max's progress on the renovations. Allegra awoke, after feeling the empty space next to her, realizing that Thunder was no longer in bed with her. The BlackBerry sounded that a text was waiting for her. The author was Hannibal: "Hey, you! Check me out this morning on Face New York. I'll be on the last half of the show."

Allegra clicked on her plasma flat screen television, wrapped the lavender-scented silk sheets around her body just as the show's theme song was beginning its return from a commercial break. Hannibal's brown skin glistened under the television studio spotlights. The two Caucasian hosts hurled their biased questions, while Hannibal remained defiant and calculating, clearly relishing the debate. Hannibal chastised them for daring to ask someone with his standing such ignorant questions. He went on to sarcastically challenge what he termed *bourgeois* black folks for failing to get involved with the community that they abandoned in the seventies.

"You can't abandon a neighborhood, take your resources, your money, your mindset; and then expect for it to flourish. And then be shaking your Negro head at those people. Our future is in our hands! We don't need the help of no white cracker!" Hannibal exclaimed.

Thunder returned from downstairs, "Max wants to know if you want that table near the kitchen door?"

"Hmmm, tell Max if anything disappears from my house, I will personally break his hands," Allegra responded with her eyes glued to the television screen.

"Hannibal on TV again?" Thunder asked.

"Hush!" Allegra responded. Startled by being silenced, Thunder stormed back downstairs.

Allegra dialed Luisa, leaving a message on her voicemail, "Hey, Diva, Hannibal is on Channel 7. We're way overdue for some sister talk. Call me. And yes, he and I spoke. Call me."

Allegra used the remote to click off the television after the host thanked his guests for appearing on the program. After soaking in the Jacuzzi, Allegra stepped into her newly installed sauna, hoping the steam would wash away the expectations of the world, especially those that men had of her. Her main priority in her life was to successfully defend her thesis and no man and no dick was going to interfere with that. Because after all was said and done, Allegra believed that the life she made was up to her. Emerging out of the sauna, Allegra shifted her meditation to love and whether she would ever feel that emotion. "Whether it is with Teofilo, Rolando or Thunder, I adore them all, but I refuse to lose myself in some romantic novel. My happily ever after is making sure my next orgasm is better than the last." Allegra chuckled to herself, exiting the sauna and showering.

Thunder returned from downstairs with a troubled look on his face. He stared at Allegra, gauging her emotional temperature before he spoke. "Allegra, don't you think we have a good thing going here? 'Cause sometimes I feel like I keep repeating myself.

I keep saying that I want you to be *my* woman. But you act like you don't be hearing me." Thunder lay down, spooning Allegra, caressing her breasts and gently massaging her abdomen, loving her natural aroma.

"Thunder, I've made it plain with you from the beginning that I'm not ready to be owned by anyone."

"I'm not trying to own you, woman. I just want us to be clear about what we're doing."

"I'm very clear," Allegra interjected.

"You know what I mean. I'm sayin'...okay, I'll admit. I'm the one who is confused. When we're not together, I don't know what you're doing...who you're with. I mean, I know you got your dissertation and teaching thang goin' on, but outside of that, and hanging out with your girl Luisa, I don't know what you're doing, or who you are," Thunder said, playing with one of her locs, kissing her shoulder tenderly. He could feel Allegra's body becoming tense.

"You've got something on your mind, Thunder?" Allegra asked, recoiling, then suddenly sitting up, swinging her legs over the edge of the bed, her feet landing flat on the floor.

"How long do you *expect* me to wait, Allegra?"

"I don't expect you to wait. I don't expect more than what we have. What we have is what I want or I wouldn't be here," Allegra said, leaning over to blow out the ancient mood incense in the crystal burner on her nightstand.

Thunder was adept at satisfying her sexually, but Allegra felt that their fuck parties were becoming less fucking and more talk-about-the-future. Though she had made it clear from the beginning of their relationship, Thunder still pushed for a commitment from Allegra.

"So I'm the guy who comes here to eat your pussy and fucks

you all night long, and that's it? That's all that it is? I mean, what kind of shit is that? Don't you want more? Don't you know how many women wish I would be with them? Inviting me to meet their families and shit? Don't you want to be the one I dedicate my world to? Why do I only occupy one part of your life? Most women in New York City would love..."

"Thunder, let's end this now!" Allegra sighed, annoyed, sucking her teeth.

"Say what?"

"I'm not going to continue *not* being heard. I'm not going to continue having these 'be-my-woman, don't-you-know-how-many-women-want-me' chats with you. You should know that I'm the last one to be coerced into doing something out of fear of other women. If you're not happy here, with what I have to offer, then we should end this now."

"But I..." Thunder attempted to find his words, using his elbows to prop himself up in the bed.

Turning sharply to face him, Allegra said, "All anyone has is their word. And my word has been clear. From the beginning, I never led you on."

"Don't I satisfy you?"

"Yes, you do, but that doesn't mean that I'm willing to submit myself exclusively to you. And I don't want you hanging around thinking that there'll be a chance that I might change my mind and be Suzy Homemaker to you. So I think it would be better if we ended this now."

"Okay, then, if that's what you want," Thunder said, with a trampled ego, pretending that he was taking her harsh words like a man, with no heart. Shielding the hurt on his face, Thunder rose and sat on the edge of the opposite side of the bed. The white silk sheet hung over his nude lap, like a tablecloth. Allegra rose, and slowly walked around the bed to the window, eyeing her gay next-door neighbors. Bentley and Marvin were searching for their house keys in their pants' pockets, after their routine night out partying in Chelsea. Thunder remained seated, with his head lowered, his hands tightly clasped as if in prayer. "This is not what I meant," Thunder murmured to himself, retrieving his jock strap from the floor, and then sliding it on, followed by his pants. The gravity of the moment hit Thunder hard, causing him to sink down again to the edge of the bed. Allegra held open her sheer curtains and tapped on the window, waving hello to Bentley and Marvin, who both returned her greeting before returning to their dilemma. Just as her sheer curtains closed, Thunder came and stood behind her, hugging her and whispering, "I love you." Allegra did not return his embrace.

Thunder felt the stillness of her breath and her shoulders tighten. Her taut body refused to return his affection. Thunder's eyelashes blinked, trying to make sense of this woman whom he loved, who constantly unfolded a new essence, like an emerging butterfly. Thunder had shared his innermost secrets, his life ambitions, iced relationships with other women, shared his pain from losing Pops, and his imperfections with Allegra. Yet she was still reluctant to commit her heart to him. Allegra moved away from her bay window as Bentley and Marvin drunkenly argued with the arriving locksmith, disputing the cost of his service to replace the lock. She turned and walked around Thunder without meeting his eyes, and entered her walk-in closet to choose her clothes for class. Thunder's eyes followed her, then dejectedly snatched his keys off of her nightstand, and somberly walked toward the bedroom door. Then he stopped, slowly turned and stood at the bathroom door, facing Allegra.

"I need to ask you something, Allegra. And I think we need to put everything out on the table, so I know what the hell to do with my life." Thunder paused, biting his lower lip. Allegra slowly turned to face him. In that moment, his heart fell for her all over again. Allegra held the key to his soul, though she never asked for it. The knowing arch of her eyebrow, her calm brown eyes were where he found peace. Thunder was addicted to her lips. Their soft fullness became the gateway to his liberation. Nowhere but with Allegra had he ever had his desires quenched, even the urges he never knew he had.

"Yes?" Allegra answered, tossing her locs from out of her eyes.

"Is this about Rolando Barbosa?" Thunder said, haltingly, enunciating the basketball superstar's name in an insulting tone. "Is he the reason you won't or can't commit to me?"

In a rare moment, Allegra was taken off guard; she stood straight as a rod. Her brain froze. No thoughts were able to carry words to her vocal chords. Thunder searched her face, not knowing what to make of her stoic silence. Inside, he questioned whether she was guilty by omission. A flash of anger danced behind Allegra's eyes, her arms folded across her chest. "You already have your answer, Thunder. So why don't you say what's on your mind? You obviously have something up your ass!" Allegra's voice trembled with controlled anger.

Thunder stepped back into the bedroom. His worried brow mirrored his internal conflict, as he originally had no intention of confronting Allegra tonight, if at all. He wanted to experience soul healing and tender moments with her. But his emotions conspired to imprison him with his constant nightmare of Allegra being in the arms of another man.

"My man said he saw you up at the Hilton, the night the Lakers were in town," Thunder stated without looking at Allegra.

"I'm not having this conversation with you," Allegra answered, pouring baby oil in the pulsating water.

Thunder was angry now as he always prided himself on his self-respect. As much as he loved Allegra, he was not willing to be the subject of gossips and whispers by his subordinates and other employees who worked for him. "Don't you think you owe me some kind of an explanation?"

"I don't ask permission or explain myself, Thunder. You should know that about me by now."

"How do you think that makes me feel, makes me look? My producer tells me that he sees you getting on the private elevator at the Hilton, while I'm interviewing Barbosa in the lobby. I could feel that somebody else has been inside of you."

Allegra never wanted to hurt Thunder. She knew what she did was shady so it was always her intent to keep her lovers geographically separated so that the drama that she found herself now in would not occur. Allegra could have tried to lie her way out of this situation; saying this must be a case of mistaken identity. She witnessed how constant lies in the lives of her parents often mushroomed into other, more hurtful delusions.

Allegra closed the closet door, as her cell phone rang from deep inside of her purse, somewhere in the brownstone. She let the telephone call transfer to voicemail. Despite her efforts to satisfy her sexual ambitions, it was never her intention to wound the man standing in her bedroom, Thunder Poole. With lowered eyes, Allegra faced Thunder and whispered, "Yeah, it was me."

From the moment she uttered those words, Allegra regretted it. By doing so, she unintentionally inflicted another wound on him. Thunder knew the truth, but the sword of truth pierced and twisted deep inside of his heart, when he heard the words fall from her lips.

"So you fuckin' Barbosa?" Thunder asked bluntly. Allegra turned her head, trying to find something interesting in the golden brown shag carpet. "I'll take that as a 'yes.'"

Thunder rattled his keys and began, "Look, you're right. We never had a commitment. You never lied to me. But out of fuckin' respect, the least you could have done was to keep your legs closed with the dude I had an exclusive interview with. The interview that has been broadcast on media outlets throughout the sports world. The interview that got me quoted by the Associated Press. Man, you know how to fuck, don't you? How do you think this shit makes me feel? All I *expected* was respect, but I guess that was asking for too goddamn much, huh? And through all of this, I never mistreated, lied or threw no shit up in your face. I cancelled all of the other shit I was doing with other women. Silenced all of them. And the very least you could've done was give me the same respect," Thunder chided, then paused before delivering one final blow. "You know, I really thought you were different, but I guess I thought wrong."

"I never meant to hurt you, Thunder. Rolando and I..."

"Oh! So it's you and motherfuckin' Rolando now, huh?"

"It's not like that, Thunder!"

"Oh really, so why don't you tell me how it is then?"

"Rolando and I met only once before I saw him at the Hilton. We're good friends."

"You expect me to believe that shit?"

"There's nothing I can do to stop you from believing what you want to believe. But you know I've never lied to you. As much as you may be hurting right now, and you have every right to be, you have to admit that," Allegra explained, pleading her case. The sound of water dropped slowly from the bathtub faucets, making loud hollow sounds striking the water.

Thunder was not in the mood to admit anything. He was furious with himself for not confronting Allegra once he knew of her connection with Rolando Barbosa; and loving her still more. Yet

Thunder feared a future without her if he said another word, or punched a hole in the wall, like his fists were urging him to.

Allegra continued, stepping closer to him, her arms waving in the air. "Thunder, I never meant to hurt you; never meant to end it in this way. But we should stop before you or I gets hurt any further or says something neither one of us mean." Thunder swayed, his body wavering, then he exhaled, and dejectedly looked at Allegra. He made another attempt at speaking, cast his eyes to the ceiling, then turned on his heels, and pounded down the staircase, slamming the front door behind him, the rattling of its frame echoing throughout the brownstone. Allegra quickly walked to the bay window, to watch Thunder cross 139th Street. He peered up at her from the street, hoping she would motion for him to return. Allegra did not. Thunder boarded his orange and black Harley-Davidson XR1200 and checked that his kill shift was set to run, squeezed the clutch lever. He held the start button until the engine turned over. Then without letting the motorcycle warm up, Thunder sped away. The tires screeched along Striver's Row, interrupting the calm of the otherwise, quiet morning.

"Thunder," Allegra said, "you forgot to wear your helmet."

Ten hours later, after Allegra arrived home from the university, Thunder texted: "I couldn't sleep. I'm outside."

Allegra rose from the newly upholstered sofa in the living room and went to her window, to see Thunder standing on her front porch, holding two-dozen, long-stemmed red roses, with the sweetest puppy dog smile. Happy to see him, Allegra glided to the foyer, wearing a sheer pink baby doll nightgown, just as he rang the doorbell.

"You right. You right. I don't know what I was thinkin'. Just... um, just let me be with you," Thunder said, standing inside the open doorway.

"Thunder, are you sure you can handle this? Handle my terms. Hear what I'm saying?"

"Yes, yes. I just need to be with you. You're all I think about. Not being with you tears me apart."

"You deserve a woman who can give you more."

"One thing, I know for sure, Allegra Adams, is that I don't want no other woman. I want you. And if this is what you can give, then this is what I'll have."

Stepping in and slamming the heavy front door, the sound vibrating throughout her brownstone, Thunder guided Allegra by her waist to face her foyer wall, placing the palms of her hands on opposite ends of her Romare Bearden art collection. Parting her legs, Thunder fell to his knees. He lifted her nightgown, ripped her thong down around her ass, and used his stiff tongue to circle her welcoming anus.

Allegra murmured, "Oh shit, Thunder; eat it."

Obeying her command, Thunder spread her butt cheeks and lowered her ass onto his open mouth, and used his pulsating tongue to make her juices pour over his jaw line. Allegra groaned, holding her erect breasts and frantically gyrated her hips on Thunder's sucking lips while her thighs trembled. Allegra turned around as Thunder rose, removing her nightie over her head, and he licked her breasts, down to her wet pussy. Kneeling again, Thunder held Allegra's abdomen, arching her torso against the foyer wall. Instinctively, Allegra angled her hips, meeting Thunder's anxious lips, which pulled on her clit. Allegra was in ecstasy, pulling Thunder's face deep inside of her vagina. "Oh fuck! Oh fuck!" Allegra shouted, pounding the wall, until she exploded, sliding down the wall with a smile of glee spread across her face. Thunder returned from the bathroom patting his face with a towel, and sat next to her on the floor, soaking her in with his eyes.

"I love to see you like this, right after I've pleased you."

"And you do, Thunder," Allegra whispered, leaning over and kissing him tenderly. "And I hope knowing that, will be enough for you."

Thunder nodded, comforted that Allegra allowed him to remain in her life. "Um, school is tomorrow and I need to get back to my dissertation. My showdown is in forty-two hours. So, um..."

"You ready? How's that going?"

"Good, I just need to double verify more of my sources. I have to be ready for any attacks."

"You're expecting some opposition? The professors on the committee seemed like they've been supportive of your work."

"Yeah, but there's a new one. She just joined New York University. Met her in Rio, when I was down there for a conference. I rebuffed her at a party, so I'm sure she remembers that. But maybe not."

"You're going be great, Baby. If there was a doctorate for how you make me feel, you would get a hundred Ph.D.s, as far as I'm concerned," Thunder said. "They'd be like, 'And now presenting Dr. Allegra Make-Me-Feel-Good.'"

Allegra laughed. "You're crazy. Get outta here so I can get to work, Silly!"

"Why don't I just sleep down here? I could serve you breakfast in bed in the morning. Give you a massage with my special organic pomegranate, macadamia and jojoba seed oil to relax you. I'll suck your toes and even do my famous Denzel Washington imitation."

"You are sooooo crazy, Thunder. You know that you'll be a

distraction," Allegra giggled softly. "With you here, I won't want to do any work. I'll just be thinking about wanting to suck my just arrived royal black honey off of your dick."

"Well now, is that such a bad thing? And why am I just hearing about your royal black honey now? You holding out on me?" Thunder teased, though he knew he was being asked to leave her brownstone at ten o'clock at night, just as she was seducing his mind.

Allegra became serious as she rose and crossed the living room to sit on the velvet loveseat. "Thunder, I have something to ask you."

Thunder studied her carefully and rose, following her to sit next to her on the loveseat. "What is it, Baby?" When it came to women Thunder slept with, he was used to soap opera confessions; where his lover would confess that she thought she was pregnant, needed money, wanted to move into his condo, wanted to marry him or ask if he loved her as much as she loved him. With the exception of requests for money, where Thunder was always more than generous, his answer was always no. Thunder would explain that he had been honest with the women from the beginning; that he cared for them as people, but he was not interested in intensifying their relationship. So if they were willing to be at his beck and call, satisfying his momentary lust, then they could continue. Thunder would place the decision of whether or not they were emotionally willing to continue with their relationships—as they were. But these women were all before Allegra. Since her appearance in his life, his bevy of female lovers had been ignored, terminated, silenced. Thunder knew that there was only one woman for him, and that was Allegra Adams.

"What, Babe?" Thunder asked as he draped his arm behind Allegra on the top of the loveseat.

"What do you know about Hannibal?"

Thunder let out a "whew" sound, and leaned forward toward Allegra asking, "Hannibal Morgan? The question is, what do *you* know about him?"

"At first Luisa was trying to get an interview with him. And now, between me and you, she's gotten involved with his flunky, Dante Salaam, and I don't get good vibes about either one of them. So what do you know?"

Thunder rubbed his eyebrow. "Salaam. Dante Salaam? That's not good. Humph, let's start out by saying trouble."

"What do you mean, Thunder?"

"Before I got in the radio game, I knew of the noise that Hannibal was making up in Harlem. Community organizing. And because I was doing some of the same things, we ran in the same political and social circles. But then, things started to spiral out of control about eight years ago, when word got back to me that Hannibal was running guns, stocking arsenals of AK-47s to handguns, hiding them in storage bins around the city. Hannibal was telling people that he was preparing for an urban Armageddon. Then stories started coming out that sisters were being mistreated, showing up at Panther meetings, suddenly meek and with black eyes. Many of his so-called lieutenants, who stood up against him, ended up as unsolved murder cases. In the last few years, it's become common knowledge that he keeps aluminum foil wrapped cocaine on hand at all times."

"And Dante?"

"Dante is a loose cannon. An ambitious loose cannon though. As much as he pretends that he is loyal to Hannibal, I feel that Dante would let his ambition rule, and he would take Hannibal out in a heartbeat. I stopped letting Hannibal come on my show, because people who knew what he was about began to think that

I was silently endorsing his bullshit. That I would never do. For me, Hannibal Morgan is the most dangerous kind of sell-out, Allegra. And what I'm sayin' ain't no secret."

"What do you mean?"

"Let's just say there ain't no love lost between me and the brother."

"Now you're the one leavin' me hangin'. You're gonna have to explain that." Thunder shifted his feet, pursed his lips, deciding if he wanted to relive his past encounter with Dante. Allegra tapped his shoulder, coaxing him to speak. "You remember, Kevin, my producer, right?"

"How I could I not?"

"Yeah, right. Well, about ten years ago, his sister Eva, was involved with Dante. Lived with him, got pregnant by him and the whole nine. But when she started showing up to family dinners with black eyes and busted lips, Kevin knew he had to do something, especially when she refused to stop talking to Kevin. So after the Million Man March, after all of the speeches were done, Kevin and I ran up on Hannibal and Dante when Hannibal was done making his bullshit speech about unity and building a strong black family. So just as they were coming down the stairs off the podium, Kevin and I tightened their asses up and hauled them beneath the bleachers under the Capitol building."

Allegra was slack jawed listening to Thunder. "You didn't?"

"Who? We pulled a *drop squad* on their asses. The element of surprise was the only way we got away with it. Threw their asses in the chairs we had waiting for them, taped their mouths shut and read them their rights. Well, it was Kevin who did most of the talking—with his fists. By the time Kevin, and then I, got done with them, they were a mess, but understood the message: Both Hannibal and Dante needed to keep their motherfuckin' hands off Eva."

"So that was it? Eva stopped being abused after that?" Allegra asked. "She never knew what you and Kevin did?"

"Everything seemed to be okay between Eva and Dante. Kevin said they told her they were jumped by some dudes and robbed. Eva nursed them back to health; but later, when she was about eight months pregnant, she disappeared."

"Omigod!" Allegra exclaimed, shielding her eyes in disbelief. "Eva was never found?" The grandfather clock in the dining room chimed.

Thunder shook his head. "And both Dante and Hannibal had tight alibis; their passports proved that they were in Cuba at the time."

"But that doesn't mean that they didn't order somebody to do it."

"Precisely. Eva's family believes to this day that Hannibal and/or Dante ordered the hit on her. The problem is that we just can't prove it."

"Omigod. Luisa," Allegra said, imagining the worse.

"Hannibal speaks all of the right words that get black folks, who don't know any better, all riled up, but behind their back, Hannibal is perpetuating deals with people who are enemies to our community; who are responsible for laundering dirty money, distributing drugs, prostitution and gangs into our neighborhoods. With Hannibal, if there is money involved in the situation, then he's down with it, no matter how negative the consequences are. So if Luisa is involved with Hannibal and Dante, I would tell her to step off. It's not a good look, professionally or otherwise."

"Her assignment editor has been dangling an anchor position in front of her if she gets the goods on Hannibal, including an exclusive interview with him. Then Luisa got hooked up with Dante, and now she's too far gone. Hannibal let it slip that Dante was married, an important detail he has never shared with Luisa.

When I couldn't get her on the telephone, I sent her a text message that Dante was married. And she texted back one word."

"What was that?"

"*Lies*. And that was two days later. She's not returning phone calls as quickly as she used to."

Allegra relaxed into Thunder's arms, allowing him to gently console her, kissing her on her temple. Thunder knew that with his revelations Allegra was even more concerned about Luisa.

"If you need anything, anytime or anywhere, you know that I'm here for you, woman. You know that, don't you?" asked Thunder, leaning in for a passionate kiss.

Allegra smirked, giving him a peck on his lips and nodded playfully. "Um, I've got to get to work, Thunder. Morning is not going to wait on me."

"Save some of that black royal honey, wouldja?" Thunder joked, rising and sauntering toward the front door.

"You are soooo bad, Thunder Poole." Allegra smiled, walking behind him, playfully whacking him on his behind. Allegra stood in the open front door until Thunder had sped away on his motorcycle, this time wearing his helmet. Closing the door behind her, she folded her arms across her chest and mumbled, "Omigod."

"Hannibal, boy, don't let me have to go in on you," Thunder said to himself outside, climbing onto his motorcycle, fastening his helmet.

21

Just an hour earlier, journalists assigned to the city hall beat poured into the green carpeted second floor press room, patriotically decorated with the American and State of New York flags, for a scheduled media conference to cover the much talked about announcement of Virgil Douglas's entry into the competitive race for mayor. The incumbent mayor, unable to seek office again due to term limits, offered his official endorsement, which Virgil politely declined. Local political reporters sat in the front row according to an unwritten pecking order: television reporters in front, followed by radio, print reporters, and then political bloggers in the last row. Campaign aides, with close-cropped hair and tense personas, darted throughout the crowd distributing media kits and responding to inquiries. Camera operators tested their microphones and set up their equipment in the rear of the gallery.

Felix, Virgil's wheelchair-bound campaign manager, consulted with Virgil in the side foyer. Luisa held hands with Virgil and provided him with a supportive presence. The *Virgil Douglas For Mayor* campaign intended to make the twelve noon live broadcasts for the local television and radio affiliates. "Virgil. Luisa. It'll be just a minute. I'll signal when we're set to begin," Felix said before steering his wheelchair to chat with campaign aides.

"You seem nervous, Luisa," Virgil said, massaging her shoulders.

"This whole thing will be a piece of cake. And if I haven't said it before, I love you for being here."

"No, I'm fine. You focus on what you have to do." Luisa smiled weakly, adjusting Virgil's power red necktie. His white shirt and navy blue, custom-made suit was chosen by Luisa as the best power statement for the next leader of New York City. "This city needs you. Go get 'em, honey," she encouraged Virgil, as he embraced her, kissing her sweetly on the cheek.

Virgil knelt down in front of Luisa taking hold of her hand, "Luisa, I may not have been the best man for you, but I love you more than life itself. I need you to know that. No other woman has been more beautiful, loyal, faithful and loving than you. I'm a blessed, flawed man. And to find the one woman who has made my life complete, confirms for me that our love is true, and that our future together is bright. Will you honor me by saying yes? Would you be my wife?" Tears welled in Luisa's eyes, as she gasped, cupping her hand over her mouth. Virgil slipped a 3.21 carat Roza2 diamond mounted in 14kt white gold engagement ring on her left ring finger, and then pecked the top of her hand and rose, kissing her on the lips. Swept up in the surprise and the emotional moment, Luisa wrapped her arms around Virgil's neck. "Is that a 'yes'? Did Luisa say 'yes'?" Luisa nodded, letting her tears fall, squeezing Virgil once again.

"Oh, I'm sorry. Did I interrupt something?" Felix asked, his eyes darting between Virgil and Luisa.

Smiling brightly, Virgil turned to Felix, his arm wrapped around Luisa. "Yes, everything is great. Luisa has consented to be my wife."

"Oh, Man, that's spectacular! You lucky devil, you!" Felix shouted, shaking hands with Virgil, and then tugging on Luisa's arm so that he could give her a kiss. Felix regained his focus, checking his watch. "Okay, look Virgil, we're up against the clock here.

I'm going to head out to introduce you. You and Luisa enter and stand behind the podium. There's a small piece of tape on the floor, Luisa. Be sure to not step beyond that mark, because then you will be out of the camera shot. And we want New York City to see your lovely face. Okay, kids, two minutes before we go live," Felix advised. Virgil gave him the thumbs up. Luisa smiled, lifting her eyebrows. Felix returned the same facial expression. The press room buzzed with the sound of camera shutters flashing as Felix wheeled in, carrying his prepared introduction on his lap.

Clearing his throat, Felix began his remarks. "Members of the media, our great city continues to endure perilous economic times; our children's education has been ignored; rising inflation and unemployment as well as the rate of home foreclosures continue to soar. How do we change course in the middle of such a difficult period? With strong, emboldened leadership. For nearly a decade, Virgil Douglas has been the federal prosecutor that crime syndicates and mob bosses have come to hate, but respect. Through vigorous prosecution, Virgil Douglas has eradicated entrenched criminal enterprises, including teen prostitution in East New York; illegal drug and gun running throughout our city. Virgil Douglas led the swift prosecution of Wall Street fat cats. Virgil Douglas is no friend to those want to destroy our city. His work is not yet complete. He is a decorated lieutenant who served with distinction in the war in Afghanistan. Two of his former soldiers are here today to share with you his first-hand unblinking courage and leadership on the battlefield. They are available for interviews after the press conference. I know leadership when I see it. I know courage and vision when I see it. New York City is in crisis mode and cannot afford to be without Virgil Douglas. So without further adieu, I am honored to bring to you the next Mayor of New York City, Virgil Douglas!"

Still holding hands, Luisa, led by Virgil, entered, meeting the applause of eager campaign workers, and the flash of various digital cameras. Virgil and Luisa's entrance was promoted as "Breaking News" on the noon broadcast. Luisa stood behind Virgil wearing a lemon-colored, sleeveless dress and white pearls and earrings. She surveyed the reporters, noting many whom she knew and had worked with. Virgil stood behind the podium adjusting his note cards filled with talking points and flashed his confident, wide-toothed smile.

"Good afternoon. I'd like to thank everyone for joining me on this momentous occasion. Today, I would like to end weeks of speculation. I'm here to officially launch my candidacy for Mayor of the City of New York. Today is in auspicious occasion, not only in my life and in that of my beautiful fiancée, who has just agreed to be my wife by the way, but in the life of our noble city. There is no denying that it's time for new leadership. Time to chart a new course, a new direction.

"While today is ultimately about what lies ahead, it's important as we chart a new course to review the precarious position in which our great city now finds itself. As it's been reported, the City of New York is on the brink of bankruptcy. Our bond rating has declined twice. We have witnessed the reckless spending by the current mayor and we are facing enormous budget deficits. When there was an opportunity to put thousands of our chronically unemployed citizens back to work, our mayor blew the opportunity, refusing to accept billions of federal dollars to rebuild our city's infrastructure. Going forward, I humbly ask for your votes to become the next mayor, so that I can rebuild each borough of this city, brick by brick. My detailed urban agenda is posted on the VirgilForMayor.com website. My vision for a new New York City is that we live up to our full potential.

"Under my leadership, ladies and gentleman, there will be a renaissance in our city; a renaissance of neighborhoods, a renaissance of lives, as together we focus on making New York City a livable, affordable city. For far too long, our citizens have had to leave here, no longer being able to afford the city that they grew up in and love. I will make great strides in cleaning our streets, further reducing crime and reestablishing community policing so police officers can stop the violence that plagues some of our city's hardest hit neighborhoods.

"Finally, my administration will be transparent and accountable. I will require that all city contracts are available for public inspection throughout the process. I know that there will be some detractors to my initiatives. I've come to know that not everyone who says they want change is ready to do the work to bring about that change. Some mean well; others have ill motives. But to the public officials who want to be contrarian for the sole purpose of not serving our citizens, I say, resign now. I will not let those nay- sayers among us compromise our hopes, dreams and aspirations for this city that we call home. I promise you that I never will. Instead, I, with your support, will move New York City to a better, brighter future. Together, we will lift New York City higher. I have the plan. I have the vision. I have the foundation. And with your vote, the future is ours and New York City's time is now. Thank you."

Virgil grabbed Luisa's hand, both raising their arms in victory with bright, cover story smiles. Felix moved his wheelchair close to the podium. "Okay, we'll entertain a few questions." Hands of reporters flew up into the air, as the local television stations returned to their regular broadcasts. Felix called on the reporters he knew by first name, and then a few from the bloggers' table. Virgil's answers on gun control, unemployment, immigration and attracting manufacturing jobs to the city were answered concisely with the occasional satirical joke to lighten the moment. Reporters loved Virgil Douglas, though many already knew of his legacy as a federal prosecutor.

In the rear of the press room, reporters stepped aside as Dante entered wearing sunglasses and his familiar military green camouflage pants, black army boots, and a black tee shirt, with his hands shoved in his pants' pockets. Dante made sure to center himself in the rear of the press room, in direct eyesight of Luisa, who now found the floor more interesting than looking adoringly at Virgil. Dante rocked back and forth on his heels, rubbing his chin.

"So if there aren't any more questions—," Felix began.

"I have a question. Dante Salaam, Chief of Staff from the Urban Panther Watch Movement. You know who I am."

Felix attempted to dismiss Dante, but Virgil motioned to let him ask his question. "Yes, Mr. Salaam, I'm very familiar with your organization."

"Oh, I know you are, Boss. Since your office convicted me and twenty percent of our strongest soldiers during your first year in office."

"Is that what you're here for? To try your case again? Well, I won't allow that. I stand by those convictions. Including yours."

"What's your question, Mr. Salaam?" Felix asked dryly.

"First of all, congratulations on your engagement." Dante smirked, as Luisa's cheeks turned a crimson red. "Um, nowhatumsayin', if you're elected mayor, will you seek our organization's endorsement? And where's your agenda for the black community?"

Reporters stopped scribbling their notes and focused on Virgil. Was this newly declared black mayoral candidate going to align himself with an organization with street credibility in the black community that was considered by his office as a grassroots organization comprised of loud-mouth ex-felons?

Virgil swallowed, then answered, "My office is open to any group of people with viable leadership and who have demonstrated a track record of working with others to improve our great city."

"Okay, that's all. Thank you, folks," Felix interjected. "Thank you for your time." Reporters gathered around Felix; others dashed from the press room, while photographers dismantled their camera equipment.

Dante maintained his position, gloating. Luisa stole glances at him, while smiling and accepting the congratulations of campaign workers. Virgil consulted with Felix nearby. When Luisa noticed Dante walking toward her, she abruptly walked away from a well-wisher and met him in the middle of the aisle.

"Mr. Salaam, what a surprise seeing you here today," Luisa began, licking her dry lips and glancing around to see where Virgil was. "What brings you here? I was going to phone you today to set up that interview with Mr. Morgan." Luisa prayed that Dante did not embarrass her and ruin her life. She prayed that he would just follow her lead.

"You looking good in that dress, Luisa. Humph. Humph. Humph," Dante replied, tugging at the fabric near her dress. "You know that was a great performance you gave right there. I should give the folks at the Academy Awards your telephone number, 'cause you were something to behold. Did you feel my eyes on your pussy? While your fiancé was bullshitting everybody, did you want me to do what we do? Did you want me to bend you over the podium so that your pussy was in full view—wet, exposed and with my name on it? Didja? Huh?" Dante whispered, leaning closer.

"Mr. Salaam, would it be possible for us to arrange that interview tomorrow?" Luisa asked with a raised voice, as Felix motored by.

"Tomorrow? Why don't we do it today? Now?" Dante replied, biting his mouth. Luisa glanced furtively at Virgil who was being interviewed by a *New York Times* reporter. "You know the old saying: "Never put off 'til tomorrow what you can do today."

"Okay, give me about an hour. I'll meet you at Panther head-quarters."

"Uh, I'd rather ride up with you. My car is in the shop and like you, I don't do the subway. That way, we can discuss the topics you want to get into so I can brief Brother Morgan beforehand." Luisa nervously glanced around the room. Virgil met her eyes, sending her a wink, before continuing with his interview.

"I'll meet you on the front steps of City Hall. I'll get somebody to take out picture together, so I can tell all of the deprived Negroes in the hood, that I met Luisa Hamilton. See you outside, Baby."

Dante strolled out of the press room, and Luisa felt as though she was about to dissolve. Virgil remained engrossed in his interview. Luisa scribbled a note for Felix to deliver to Virgil. "Darling, I have to get back to the station. See you tonight. Love, Luisa."

"Virgil won't be much longer, Luisa," Felix advised.

"Duty calls, Felix," Luisa replied, giving him a goodbye peck on his cheek.

"Is that why you've been acting like you got your ass on your shoulders ever since I got in the car? Just 'cause I called you a bitch? You didn't have no problem wid it when I was fuckin' your brains out," Dante argued loudly, riding in the front seat of Luisa's new red Mercedes-Benz C200 sport sedan—the one Virgil gave her that morning as a token of his love before his press conference announcing his run for mayor. "So you gotta problem wid it now, alla sudden?"

Luisa raised her chin to protect the remnants of her pride, shifted gears and veered onto the FDR Drive, and sped north. "I always had a problem with it, Dante. I've told you that that kind of language just isn't necessary."

"Who the fuck are you to tell me when anything is goddamned necessary, huh? What you need to be doing is tellin' me what your boy...your *fiancé*, Virgil, is doin'. That's what you need to do," Dante said surlily, pursing his lips to light a thick blunt.

"And I've asked you before, Dante, not to smoke around me," Luisa added quietly, flipping the turn signal to merge into the middle lane to pass a yellow school bus. Dante inhaled, then took a second breath of air behind the puff, forcing the smoke into his lungs. Defiantly, he held onto the smoke until he was forced to expel it, slowly, exhaling the gray-white smoke directly into Luisa's face. Coughing and waving, trying to deflect the smoke and focus on driving, Luisa yelled, "Stop!"

Dante responded with a maniacal laugh, mocking Luisa in a high pitched voice, "Stop, Dante! You're gonna get the smell of smoke into my brand new Mercedes-Benz that my prosecutor bitch hooked me up with." Returning to his own voice, Dante continued, "And how would that shit look, being that he's running for mayor on the lower taxes, lower crime and keep-the-negroes-locked-up platform? How would it look if people found out that his *fiancée*, is fuckin' me? I don't think you're in a position to tell me what's necessary, Miss Fiancée. Negroes need to stop trying to speak French, the language of our oppressors," Dante continued, cracking up and puffing on what was left of his blunt, as Luisa changed gears and exited onto Harlem River Drive toward the 125th Street off-ramp.

Luisa stepped on the gas pedal, passing drivers who were clocking at least seventy miles per hour. She intended on dropping Dante off at Panther headquarters before anyone recognized her. "Let me ask you a question, Luisa," Dante began, still smoking his blunt, "how did it feel standing next to Virgil 'Sell Out' Douglas looking like Miss-Prim-and-Proper and having me standing there watching your ass? How did it feel when he introduced you to the world as his fiancé, while I'm sitting in the front row watching your ass?"

"Dante, what did you expect me to do? Interrupt the press conference and announce that I'm fuckin' both you and Virgil? Is that what you want to hear? Is that what you expected me to do?"

"Actually, that woulda been kinda cool." Dante thought for a second. "That woulda been kinda fly if you woulda woman'd the fuck up and put your shit on the table. And give old Virgil the choice to roll with it or not. You never know, ya boy might got some freak in him. But see, you didn't give the brother no choice at all. He thinks he's getting ready to marry Miss Dominican New York or some shit, but instead what he got is a straight up Dominican round-the-way girl—which in my mind, is a good thing, but for old Virgil, I don't know." Luisa honked the horn, swerving around a Honda Civic slowly entering the highway from the on ramp at Ninety-Sixth Street. Dante gripped the top of the glove compartment. "You ain't tryin' to get me kilt, is you, girl? Because how would that look, Miss Dominican New York involved in West Side Highway car crash with her lover who is a member of the Panthers. Both parties are being evaluated to determine if drugs or alcohol were in their system. Now how would that look?" Dante was mesmerized by the sound of his own voice. Luisa's BlackBerry beeped; it was Allegra, leaving another text marked *Urgent*.

Removing a piece of tobacco from his tongue, Dante continued, "You know the way I look at it, you like this. You like being dominated. And that's why I know you ain't goin' nowhere even if you do walk down the aisle with that Stepin Fetchit. You can be with Douglas for a hundred years and you still will need me to take control and discipline you. You told me yourself that no man has ever satisfied you, brought out the freak in you that has been dying to emerge. Yeah, you need my dick. That's why you come when I call you. You like feeling helpless, dominated and not in control. Remember when you trembled when I ran up in the parking lot, next to your building. You loved me ripping off your panties and taking you right there on East Seventy-Fifth Street, while the parking dude pretended not to notice. When we were done doing what we do, we continued with part two and three upstairs in your apartment, excuse me, condo. Is that what you gentrified Negroes call it? I live in a condo," Dante said sarcastically.

"Dante, so there's no interview with Hannibal, is there?" Luisa asked, stopped behind a city bus releasing passengers, as she drove west in heavy traffic across 125th Street.

"Why you say that? Where is your optimism?" Dante said innocently.

"What is that you want from me, Dante?"

"Thank you for asking. First, there is that little matter about your girl Allegra."

"I fulfilled my end of the bargain, Dante. Dante and Allegra connected last week."

"Yeah, but they haven't connected like they need to, like you and me have. Look, if nothing else, I'm a man of my word. And when Hannibal gives the word, and lets me know he has gotten what he's wanted, you're good."

"Gives you the word?"

"Here's the other thing, you'll get done. Brother Hannibal will announce that he's running for mayor tomorrow morning." Luisa nearly swerved out of her lane of traffic. "What?!"

"Now we recognize that the Panthers do not have the financial war chest that Virgil does, but here's how old Virgil can help Brother Hannibal to become mayor." Luisa could barely breathe; hives spread across both forearms.

"Wh-what are you talking about?" Luisa managed.

"Virgil will suspend all investigations that his office is conducting into donations we get. Virgil will call off NYPD thugs from trailing me and Brother Hannibal everywhere we fuckin' go." Luisa read the Associated Press report that morning that the Panthers were mired deep in a financial crisis, barely meeting their monthly expenditures. Unnamed sources from the Panther organization alleged that approximately one hundred thousand dollars was stolen in early spring. Since then, finger-pointing has swept the organization with the prime suspect being Hannibal Morgan himself. Morgan allegedly hired an investigator, who was unable to determine what had happened to the funds. Hannibal Morgan's assistant was fired, "not because she stole the money, but because she left the safe open," the report read.

Glancing from the rear view to the side car mirrors, Luisa attempted to see if she was now being trailed by the police. Luisa felt as though she was having an anxiety attack. Tears gathered behind her eyes, as she felt ashamed of allowing herself to consent to this drama; to jeopardize everything she had worked hard to create in her life.

"There's no way Virgil will agree to do this," Luisa blurted.

"Oh, you'll find a way, Luisa. I know how creative you can be, especially if you don't want old Virgil to know about our sacred love," Dante said, touching her ear lobe.

"Where do you want me to drop you off?" Luisa said, jerking her head away from Dante.

"That's a bad-ass engagement ring! Goddamn! Those crackers must be paying old Virgil some major benjamins to cough up that kind of dough. You must be happy. Are you going to be happy, Luisa?" Dante asked sarcastically.

"I'll be fine, Dante," Luisa replied tightly.

"You sure?" Dante said, stroking her hair, though she kept deflecting his hand. "Is that the kind of life you wanna live? A life of being *fine?* I'm getting hard asking you this; but does Virgil recognize that in spite of you being a career sister and all, that you feel locked up in that ivory tower of yours. You're a normal sister, like a lot of them out here; constrained by societies' conventions and frustrated by your inability to realize your innermost fantasies. I saw that on some talk show. That's how y'all run it down, ain't it? See that's what has been good about you and me. I've been able to open you up. Let you live out your fantasies. But I want you to consider something. While you're busy planning this fine life, will old Virgil will ever out-of-nowhere push you down over your sofa, lift your skirt, pull down your moist panties and invade your slippery wetness, stretching you wider than you thought possible and making you feel oh so deliciously smutty, like I have? While you're living your fine life, will he ever spank you when you've been bad and you know how bad you can be, don't you?" Ahead at the traffic light, a city bus allowed its passengers to disembark onto the busy sidewalk before proceeding across 125th Street.

"Look atcha. I know you're getting wet just thinking about it. Now we can work somethin' out of course. We can still deal, nowhatumsayin'? 'Cause the way I look at it, what we have is a once-in-a-lifetime thang. We shouldn't let a little engagement ring stand in the way of our mutual happiness, you dig? I know you're gonna call me. And then I'll have to lecture you, sex you up, no matter when and where I find you. Just make sure that the delicious smell of your aroused pussy rises to meet me. And that you'll feel cool air on your body as I undress you and make you revel in anticipation of how I prepare to do you. I'll make you wait for me by standing you in the middle of the room, with your hands on your head, appreciating your sweetness, while I pace behind you as your clit tingles with excitement. As the time for our union with the Most High draws near, I'll let you feel my fingers probe your beautiful slippery slit. I'll make you gasp with pleasure and ache for me to penetrate you. Baby, you won't know whether to cry or scream with joy. So you're gonna have to decide what kind of life you're going to choose to live."

Driving within three blocks of the Panther building, Luisa swerved onto Lenox Avenue, almost striking two teenagers crossing the street. Luisa, despite her annoyance, anger and frustration with Dante, knew that he had again ignited her passions, beyond what Virgil could ever do. Luisa knew that if she stayed with Dante much longer, the two would end up fucking at her condominium, at some time that evening. Double-parking in front of the Panther building, Luisa shifted the gears into park and waited for Dante to get out of the car.

"Look, Dante, forget about Hannibal. I'm not going to do it. Just forget it!" Luisa said, throwing her hands in the air, before returning them to the steering wheel. Dante's eyebrows lifted into a villainous arch, as he shook his head, amazed over Luisa's naiveté. Dante momentarily felt empathy for Luisa, knowing that she did not have enough clout to make any demands. Changing the subject abruptly, Dante asked, "So why didn't you tell me about your engagement, Baby?"

Luisa's head whirled toward Dante. "Why didn't you tell me

you were married? Married to Joyce Salaam with five daughters and one son? How dare you question and judge me? Who the fuck do you think you are? You think that I'm your little side piece and that you can just play head games and come and go as you please. And I'm not supposed to move on and make a life for myself? Well, that's not who I am, no matter what you think."

Passersby, hearing Luisa shouting, turned to stare, then saw Dante's menacing stare, and continued on with their business. Dante stared straight ahead, letting a roaring furnace percolate. After thirty seconds had passed, and there were no potential eye-witnesses, Dante grabbed Luisa at the back of neck, "Don't you ever speak my wife's name again as long as you live, youknow-whatumsayin', bitch? Don't you ever. Cross me and you'll see your little world crumble," Dante said, shoving her head against the side window and then bolting, slamming the door so hard it caused the car to reverberate. A Panther comrade appeared to open the door to the Panther building for Dante, saluting him as he stormed inside.

Squealing schoolchildren, wearing crisp, blue-plaid uniforms, raced out of the red brick charter school on the corner of 124th Street and around the corner. Lowering her head, Luisa, suddenly battered the steering wheel, bruising her hands. Hearing her commotion, a disheveled man tapped on the passenger side of her car window and asked, "Hey! Are you that TV lady?"

Luisa's face contorted with rage. "Get the hell away from me!" She floored the gas pedal before realizing that the car was still in park. Punching the gear shift, then changing into drive, Luisa cut off an oncoming taxicab and sped south on Lenox Avenue, the screeching of her tires merging with cacophony of bustling traffic.

22

University interns performed a technical check on the podium microphone and video system; they arranged copies of candidate dissertations so that they could be examined by members of the university community. Thunder messengered, the day before, bound duplicates of Allegra's two-hundred-and-fifty page dissertation, entitled: "*DNA and Sexuality: The First Glimpse Into A Woman's Soul.*" Allegra knew that she would be in front of Dr. Winchester, her mentor, and other pioneers in the study of DNA and sexuality, plus the newly added Dr. Henderson, so she dissected every detail, from her appearance and mindset to her presentation.

That morning, Thunder arrived at Allegra's brownstone to haul her visual aids, including video, charts and cue cards listing famous quotations from renowned scholars at New York University, the site where doctoral candidates are thrown to intellectual lions, emerging victorious or mired in defeat.

"Baby, I checked in the auditorium. Don't look like Luisa made it yet," Thunder advised Allegra. "Max tried to convince your Aunt Rachael to get out the car, but judging by the way she's complaining, it's a good thing that he drove her back to Long Island."

Inside the freezing auditorium, supportive friends and family members were seated, waiting to observe their friends defend their dissertations. The Dissertation Committee conferred together waiting for debate to begin. Running late, Dr. Winchester huffed into the building carrying his large, ragged briefcase.

"Dr. Winchester?" Allegra called.

"Yes, Ms. Adams," Dr. Winchester replied, patting the perspiration around his plump neck with a folded handkerchief.

"I received confirmation from the Dissertation Committee that they had received my thesis."

"Very good then; everything is in order," Dr. Winchester replied with a puzzled expression, turning to waddle away.

"That is, except for Dr. Henderson. I emailed her several times, with no response. Even left a telephone message at her office."

"Hmm, peculiar; I'll mention it to her," Dr. Winchester answered, his mouth squeezing into a pucker. "See you inside, Ms. Adams." Thunder hovered behind Allegra listening to the exchange.

"Dr. Henderson never got back to you, huh?"

"No, which tells me one thing; that she's still harboring a grudge because I rejected her at that party in Rio."

Thunder placed a protective hand on Allegra's shoulder. He had worked overnight at the radio station, overseeing the production schedule for commercials for various political candidates. Thunder nursed a cup of hot, black coffee to erase the fatigue he felt. Still handsome, he was freshly shaven and wore a light blue shirt and single-breasted suit. Allegra felt comforted by his support, appreciated his steady, warming presence, and the scent of his spice cologne. Over the past few months, that Allegra and Thunder had been together, he had learned how to sense what she needed and she, in turn, strummed his soul with her soft power. With Allegra, Thunder had come to learn that less was more, especially when all she needed was his strong embrace.

Now in the final moments before her professional debut, Allegra reviewed all that she had risked and sacrificed until this moment; making an abrupt career transition while she was ascending to senior management at the airline; turning her back on the colleagues and constant travel she had grown to love to begin a new career to satisfy her intellectual curiosity. Like a soldier, Allegra had spent the last two years making sure that her arsenal contained a number of defenses for her thesis. She had heard horror stories of doctoral candidates who were arrogant in their preparation. The rejected candidates were required to conduct further research, because their arguments ran counter to leading authorities at the university and the politics which governed funding allocation.

"Now that I think about it, Luisa may have gotten the times confused; maybe she thinks we were going to the radio station first, instead of later on, after we're done here," Allegra said, with a furrowed brow. Thunder tossed his empty coffee cup in a nearby trash receptacle, and then sauntered back over to Allegra.

"Right now, you, my dear, need to focus your attention on defending your dissertation. You've worked all hours of the day and night doing what you had to do, while I sat by holding the remote control and my johnson watching my lady move to the next level. There's no way in hell you won't win today. Just go in there and knock 'em dead. Even though you care about Luisa, and we both do, let's not lose sight of this moment. Your moment. Now, I'll be in the back of the auditorium, fantasizing about our celebration later. Proud of you already." Thunder beamed, kissing her gently. Allegra's eyes glistened at his kindness. No matter what changeable conditions Allegra threw his way, Thunder was completely devoted to her. And more and more, Allegra looked toward Thunder for relief, companionship and support. Allegra knew that Thunder understood her, and never tried to minimize who she was.

Thunder hugged her tightly, and then disappeared through the double metal doors into Schwartzman Hall. Inside, the dissertation committee members checked their watches, while invited guests conversed in murmured tones.

Allegra paced, her red Manolo Blahnik pumps clicking against the shiny marble corridor outside the auditorium, when Dr. Henderson, broke the sterile silence, rushing through the exterior doors, glancing in both directions. Finding her way, Dr. Henderson's eyes targeted Allegra, freezing both women like statutes, causing an uneasy tension. Dr. Henderson's jaw tightened when she saw Allegra, her eyes smoldering into an artic chill. Allegra, in an attempt to be pleasant, formed the corner of her lips into a partial smile, and then immediately forfeited the effort.

Dr. Henderson immediately loathed Allegra, but tried to hide her returning attraction. Allegra accentuated her physique from the cinch-waist red blazer with ruffled neckline and pencil skirt to her sheer, nude nylon stockings. Allegra possessed the feminine mystique, the essence of a woman that Dr. Henderson craved. Dr. Henderson dominated her intimate female relationships, never losing in pursuit of her lust. It was her experience that, if given an opportunity, Dr. Henderson knew how to seduce any woman of her choosing, even those who claimed that they were heterosexual. For Dr. Henderson, Allegra Adams was the woman who got away. And for that solitary act, Dr. Henderson would never forgive Allegra.

Dr. Henderson had aged significantly since meeting her on Teofilo's balcony. She had the essence of a dormitory resident advisor, who was intimidated by the real world, preferring to exist in the claustrophobic world of academia. Still wearing carved-boned earrings, she had added another silver nose ring to her other nostril. Her light complexion was now a gray-yellow, signaling that her spirit was slowly leaving her medium frame. Instinctively, Allegra folded her arms across her chest, and then relaxed. Dr. Henderson, cleared her throat, rolled her eyes over the length of Allegra's body, and then strolled defiantly past her, into the auditorium, without a word, with the doors clanging behind her.

A few moments later, Allegra heard the ringing of a bell, signaling from inside the auditorium that the oral defense had begun. The first candidate, an eighteen-year-old, blond-haired, blue-eyed prodigy was summoned before the committee. Thunder was right. Allegra reminded herself that she was a renowned expert in the emerging scientific field of DNA and sexuality. Inside, she silenced the murmurings of self-doubt, and replaced it with the resolve to have mischievous fun.

After eight candidates had presented, five successful and three defeated, Allegra heard, "Ms. Adams, the committee will see you now." Allegra rose, straightened her pencil skirt and calmly strolled into the auditorium, like a movie star meeting her public on the red carpet at a Hollywood movie premiere. The stark auditorium lighting was in sharp contrast to her bright red apparel. The sound of the clicking of her heels woke Thunder out of his slumber in the rear of the auditorium. In an effort to support Allegra, Thunder wiped the fatigue from his eyes and clapped his hands, then realized his inappropriateness.

The Dissertation Committee sat behind a conference table, resembling an apathetic parole board. "Good Afternoon, Ms. Adams," Dr. Winchester greeted, gesturing for her to sit on the wooden chair before them. Instead, Allegra handed a cassette to a university intern, who inserted it into a DVD player.

"Good Afternoon, committee members and invited guests," Allegra replied, taking command of the room, adjusting her chair directly in front of Dr. Henderson, who continued to seethe her hostility. Allegra, stunningly elegant, was the first candidate to acknowledge the bored audience members, who nodded appreciatively.

"You may begin," Dr. Winchester said, hitting the timer. Dr. Henderson noticed the obvious admiration that Dr. Winchester had for Allegra, and that only heightened the resentment burning inside her belly. Allegra sat and moistened her lips, and crossed her legs, relaxing against the back of the chair, staring into the hostility of Dr. Henderson with a cool, cunning smile.

"Now wait a second," Dr. Henderson interrupted, shaking her head. Everyone except Allegra was stunned by Dr. Henderson's insolence. "In the interest of my precious time and that of the committee's, I think it prudent that we get right down to the matter at hand. Most of us have had ample time to review your thesis. And while my esteemed colleagues are anxious to heap unwarranted praises on you and your research, I, for one, am not willing to be a party to biased scholarship." The hollow sound of shock permeated the auditorium. Thunder leaned forward. His lips read: "Say what?"

Dr. Winchester's cheeks turned a beet red, matching the blotches on his neck. "Now, now, Dr. Henderson," he began, waving his hands. Undaunted, Allegra gloated, as if she had seen nirvana. Allegra re-crossed her legs and leaned toward Dr. Henderson, who glared with her arms across her chest, confident that she had thrown Allegra off of her game.

Allegra rose, held a pregnant pause as she contemplated her remarks, strutting like an attorney arguing her case before a jury. "Dr. Winchester, I can perfectly understand Dr. Henderson's misgivings and she's absolutely correct. Each doctoral candidate should be accessed on their merit and not on the basis of biased scholarship, as Dr. Henderson, so bluntly put it. Which brings me to the title of my thesis, 'DNA and Sexuality: The First Glimpse Into A Woman's Soul.' Dr. Henderson, have you ever examined the soul of your sexuality? Have you ever considered the origins of your lust, who you crave, who you choose to sexually dominate, who you choose to expose to your vulnerabilities and who you punish for rejecting your overtures? My thesis demonstrates that the answers to those questions lie within your DNA, Dr. Henderson. Under a microscope, if I were to conduct a full genome-scan sample of your saliva, for example, Dr. Henderson, I'm quite sure that we would find an excessively greater amount of testosterone than estrogen. I highly suspect that you also might have slightly deformed cells and more highly refined sugar than any board certified nutritionist would recommend." Dr. Winchester tried to hide a snicker behind his swollen hands. Dr. Henderson exhaled her annoyance; her jaw fell open, as she tried to catch the eye of Dr. Winchester, who focused only on Allegra. Dr. Henderson was startled that Allegra used her as the foil for her remarks, to the delight of Thunder who silently cheered her on.

"You see, Dr. Henderson, women and their sexuality have ruled nations and the hearts of men since time immemorial. Cleopatra and other Queens of Africa commanded men, nations and legions of armies, with a whisper or a nod. Cleopatra conquered the hearts and imagination of Julius Caesar and Mark Antony with her womanly manner and sexual prowess."

Allegra returned to the chair, slowly lifting, then on a whim, deciding to leave her brown, strong legs, which shimmered like wet mahogany, slightly ajar. Dr. Henderson's eyes floated down between Allegra's legs. To provide Dr. Henderson with an unobstructed view, Allegra parted her legs further, so that Dr. Henderson could see the fluff of hair on Allegra's vagina.

"The Power Point presentation, please?" Allegra cued the intern, while Dr. Henderson frowned, hunching over her crossed arms, as the auditorium lights dimmed.

"Dr. Henderson, the DNA of women shows that those who are sexually free are not afraid to express their sexual whims and to let others know who they will or will not fuck, um, indulge in sexual relations with. Sexually uninhibited women usually display deformed DNA, often seen like the example on slide one, in a round shape. Notice? Cleopatra and Dorothy Dandridge were shown to have round-shaped DNA. Powerful women with round-shaped DNA tend to bring peace in their sensuality, not drama or confrontation. For example, your DNA, Dr. Henderson, would mistake dominance for sexual intimacy, rage for lust, loathing for attraction. DNA, such as the one I possess, enjoys sexual encounters with men, fully, openly, lavishly, without guilt, permission or regret. My genome scan reveals a predilection for the male gender. On the other hand, your DNA, Dr. Henderson seeks to have flings with the same gender, even after your overtures are rebuffed. See slide four, with fragment edges of the cell."

Sputtering, trying to regain control, Dr. Henderson interjected, leafing through Allegra's thesis, "I found issues with your grammar and the punctuation is unacceptable."

Dr. Winchester said, "You're out of line, Dr. Henderson. Your scope of questioning is out of line."

"It is highly inappropriate for any candidate to address a committee member personally," Dr. Henderson replied, grasping for straws to derail Allegra. "Ms. Adams' conduct quite clearly shows that her scholarship is not qualified to be included in our ranks."

"Quite the contrary," Dr. Winchester replied, "The science community must learn to bridge laboratory research with the real world. And by providing personal anecdotes, Ms. Adams has done an admirable job of bringing her science to life, so that our work, and what we do here, is more than an academic exercise. You may continue, Ms. Adams." Thunder pumped his fist.

Allegra smiled at Dr. Henderson, whose face was flustered, as if her blood was boiling and returned to her chair. Giving Dr. Henderson her final glimpse, Allegra opened, and then crossed her legs, resting her hands on her lap, as if listening to the pope's sermon. "Throughout the ages, women have been shamed for embracing their sexuality as opposed to being applauded for it. More than ever, women must stand up for their sexuality and be forceful about it. The soul power lying in our DNA urges us to open the floodgates of our power. Thank you," Allegra added.

Breaking protocol, Dr. Winchester applauded, joined by the remaining committee members. Thunder stood, clapping enthusiastically, as well as the invited guests. Dr. Henderson was alone in her rage, staring at Allegra.

"Ms. Adams, please wait in the hallway, while the committee deliberates." Allegra smiled, turning to climb the stairs to exit the auditorium.

Dr. Henderson slowly rose from her chair, her eyes throwing darts at Allegra's back. "Dr. Winchester, I have already made my decision." Thunder and Allegra froze on the stairs. The eyes of everyone inside the auditorium rested on Dr. Henderson.

"Well, Dr. Henderson. The committee must first discuss our decision privately," Dr. Winchester said sternly.

Ignoring Dr. Winchester, Dr. Henderson continued, "Ms. Adams' entire defense must be rejected. Her research was based upon conjecture, speculation and her opinion. Where I come from, what she presented here today does not rise to receiving a doctorate. And if she is granted a Ph.D., I will need to reconsider teaching at a university, with such a lack of intellectual standards."

Weary now, Dr. Winchester asked, "In what specific area of Ms. Adams' thesis do you have a concern?"

"The entire…"

"Specifics, Dr. Henderson," Dr. Winchester said, losing his patience.

Dr. Henderson smiled brightly at Allegra, knowing that she was about to destroy everything that Allegra had worked for. "On the slides, which Ms. Adams cited as her evidence, where she linked my DNA with my sexuality. This is the speculation that I'm referring to. How would Ms. Adams gain access to my DNA?"

Dr. Winchester knitted his eyebrows; defeat permeated the room, as Allegra swallowed, thinking. "This bitch did it. She came to destroy me, and she succeeded in throwing every obstacle at me, but one."

Allegra slowly descended the stairs and returned to the middle of the auditorium, where she faced Dr. Henderson, defiantly, slowly gathering her words.

"Excellent question, Dr. Henderson," Allegra said, maintaining her poise.

"Committee members, invited guests, Dr. Henderson. DNA can be found in semen, blood, skin and saliva. Dr. Henderson's saliva was found on a marijuana joint that she was smoking at a party in Rio De Janeiro this past summer. After I rejected her overtures, Dr. Henderson extinguished the joint in an ashtray. I took the evidence, later froze it in our chemistry lab, until I was ready to examine it." A loud gasp sounded in the auditorium. Dr. Winchester squeezed his lips to stifle a grin. Dr. Henderson almost fainted; her knees shook. "Curious about her aggressive behavior, I studied her DNA, documented her behavior and included her in a case study. She's identified in my footnotes as

Case #666. In case there are any questions about the DNA being properly stored, Dr. Henderson's marijuana was stored in my hotel refrigerator, then on the airplane's freezer. A pilot friend was kind enough to store it there. So I'll have to respectfully disagree with you, Dr. Henderson. My research is quite thorough and beyond conjecture." Allegra smiled brightly at Dr. Henderson's sheer embarrassment. Thunder led the audience with his applause.

After a five-minute deliberation, as Allegra and Thunder paced outside, Allegra was notified by Dr. Winchester that she had successfully defended her dissertation, receiving a unanimous vote and one glaring abstention. Her Ph.D. was confirmed to be awarded at graduation in May 2012.

"Now you've got to promise to let me serve you breakfast in bed," Thunder said, as they walked hand in hand toward the parking lot.

"Only if you suck warm chocolate off my toes," Allegra flirted.

"I never sucked chocolate off no doctor's toes before," Thunder teased. Allegra laughed, feeling that a burden had finally been lifted from her shoulders. Every facet in her life felt as if she was beginning anew. As Thunder paid the parking lot attendant, and waited for his Mercedes to be retrieved, he asked, "Is there any way we can get out of going to the restaurant?"

"Duty calls. But don't you worry, I'll break you off sumptin' sumptin' before we get there," Allegra promised. Thunder smiled sheepishly, and replied; "Now that's what I'm talkin' about."

"Luisa, where are you? Missed you today. Thunder and I are going to be at the Pegasus around eight. I guess I'll see you tonight,"

Allegra said, leaving a solemn voice message, as she arrived home, after leaving a note with Luisa's doorman. In the years Allegra had known her best friend, they had never missed out on an important occasion, in the other's life. From Luisa's awards dinners, to funerals and birthdays, the two women pledged to support one another. Luisa's glaring absence troubled Allegra, and she prayed that all was well.

"Um, Dr. Adams," Thunder said, sneaking behind Allegra as she hung up the telephone in the kitchen. Allegra whirled around to see Thunder holding four dozen red roses in one hand and a velvet, rectangular box in the other.

"Congratulations, Baby! You did it and I'm so proud of you." Thunder leaned over, kissing Allegra gently on her lips, tasting her, his tongue dancing lightly with hers. "I got you this. Hope you like it."

"Thunder," Allegra said softly, as he handed her the velvet box. Slowly, she opened the lid to see a floating solitaire pendant. "Thunder, baby. It's beautiful."

"Let me put it on for you," Thunder said, as Allegra turned around, gathering her long locs up around the nape of her neck, fingering and admiring the pendant. Thunder wanted Allegra badly, but he restrained himself, watching her beam with happiness. "We have to be at Pegasus in an hour. We really don't need to go," Thunder reminded.

"You're the one who's getting an award," Allegra replied.

"You've seen one awards ceremony, you've seen them all," Thunder said, settling in his chair.

"Don't even try it. You're going, but first I need to fulfill my promise to you."

Thunder raised his eyebrows, slow to remember, then he sent a smile to heaven, as Allegra pushed him against the kitchen counter, unzipping his pants, yanking down his black briefs. Allegra stood admiring Thunder's cock, talking as if his Johnson had been a good little boy. "You're so beautiful and you've been so good to me. I'm gonna treat you like you've treated me." Allegra kissed Thunder on the lips, while unbuttoning his shirt, running her tongue along his jaw, down his neck and around his erect nipples, sending him groaning with ecstasy. Allegra's kisses greeted his searching lips before plunging again to his nipples, while his cock throbbed outside of his briefs, his pants hanging around his feet. Allegra moistened her mouth, and flickered her tongue along the length of his cock. Tenderly, she placed his tip on the edge of her mouth, squeezing it with her lips, slowly guiding his cock inside her mouth, while using her tongue to make rapid circles, taking in more of Thunder, as he moaned her name. Allegra could not suppress her moans of enjoyment, seeing Thunder lose his mind, until his hips lurched and droplets of cum oozed from his cock. With dark intense eyes, Thunder grabbed Allegra, carrying her to the kitchen table, shoving their early breakfast dishes crashing to the floor. Quickly, Thunder and Allegra shared in the task of removing her red blazer and lifting her skirt. With one strong lift, Thunder lifted her onto the kitchen table, threw her legs over his shoulders, and then dived to eat her pussy, shoving his tongue, teasing, around her clit. Allegra grabbed Thunder's head, pulling him deeper inside of her crotch. Thunder grunted, as her hips swiveled in midair, causing cream to pour from his jaw. With his cock regaining its intensity, Thunder lifted Allegra to a sitting position, wrapping his elbows around her open legs, positioning pussy at the edge of the kitchen table. "Fuck me," Allegra moaned, with closed eyes.

Thunder entered her, slowly, and then paused, appreciating Allegra, the woman he loved from the moment he met her.

Allegra smiled as she wiped the sweat that dripped from his face, licking the salty fluid from her fingers. Thunder continued entering Allegra, her tight pussy, expanding to welcome all of him. Pumping, slowly at first, then quickly, Thunder rode Allegra, fucking her, like to lose this moment would cause his sudden death. Allegra tightened her pussy around his cock, refusing to free it, until Thunder's torso stiffened, his face clouded and he finally exploded, collapsing on top of her. Allegra wrapped her arms around Thunder, holding him, as a tear fell.

"I'm glad you're here, Honey," Allegra whispered. Thunder squeezed her, kissing her on her forehead.

23

Thursday, one week before Thanksgiving, hundreds of supporters streamed into the sold-out dinner fund-raiser for the New York State Broadcasters' Association. The seen-and-be-seen annual event attracted Broadway, film and television stars who posed for interviews outside of the swanky ballroom of the Pegasus Hotel on Fifth Avenue on Manhattan's East Side. Black stretch limousines idled in front of the hotel for ten blocks, as uniformed chauffeurs waited until their clients ended their evening of hobnobbing with the political and cultural elite. Adorned in a full-length, form-fitting, lavender gown, with matching stilettos and clutch, Allegra rocked her black mink jacket with flair sleeves and a diamond trim hemline. Thunder wore a bow tie and black tuxedo, with black silk lapels. Together Allegra and Thunder were a charismatic couple, as they arrived on the star-studded red carpet at the conclusion of the serving of cocktail hour. Thunder and Allegra were escorted to their table in the middle of the ballroom, just as a hidden announcer spoke. Already chomping on the first course of Caesar salad, was the owner of Thunder's radio station, Kevin the producer, and hosts of other day programs. Their tablemates greeted Allegra and Thunder warmly.

"Ladies and Gentleman! Welcome to the New York State Broadcasters' Gala. Please welcome your co-hosts for the evening,

WNBC-TV's David Rollins and Luisa Hamilton." Appreciative applause welcomed Luisa and David as they emerged from behind the curtain, looking like an older Ken with a younger, Dominican Barbie doll. Yelps and whoops rose from the WNBC-TV tables, as a cameraman filmed them from the edge of the stage. Allegra noticed Luisa's eyes nervously dart around the audience, as if searching for a familiar face. Allegra smiled and waved, but Luisa did not see her from the stage.

"...so on behalf of WNBC-TV and the New York State Broadcasters' Association, please enjoy your dinner. Luisa and I will return with an exciting program and a full line-up of your favorite stars," David droned. Luisa smiled, dimly, following David off the stage. Unsure on how to respond, the audience applauded as David and Luisa exited.

"Hey, Thunder! How's it going?" Felix, Virgil's chief of staff, asked, wheeling over to their table.

"I'm good. Real good. Meet my lad...meet Allegra, Dr. Adams."

"The pleasure is all mine," Felix said, extending his arm to shake hands with a smiling Allegra. "Say, Thunder, I want to schedule Virgil for your show. You know, talk about his mayoral campaign."

Thunder nodded. "Virgil and I go way back. He always has a seat at my microphone. But I would've appreciated a scoop on his announcement. I'll never understand why you'd want to court the white media then come to black folks for support after the fact. Black media should be the first step, not the last stop."

Felix felt warm, fidgeting with his necktie. "Heh-heh, well, you know how these things go sometimes. As his campaign manager, I advised him to keep things on the low because everybody south of the Tappan Zee Bridge was talkin' about throwing their hats into the ring. Timing it the way we did, lining up endorsements and what not, threw the competition off of their game. By the time certain people, whom I won't name, were ready to declare, we had already sewn up legitimate endorsements from around the state, union bosses, current officeholders. So if you have to blame somebody, blame me."

Thunder noticed Allegra sip on her lobster bisque. Resting his hand on her arm, Thunder replied, "Okay, I'll blame you and Virgil. Call my producer. He'll set you up for Thursday. And the interview will air on Sunday night. Cool?"

"You got it, Thunder," Felix said, rolling away in his wheelchair.

"Luisa should be around here, somewhere. Since she's one of the co-hosts, she had to arrive early," Allegra suggested, buttering a dinner roll.

"Do you wanna check and see if she's backstage?" Thunder asked, pointing in the direction of the door under the exit sign.

Allegra nodded as Thunder rose, helping her from her chair. "Come on, Baby," Thunder said, leading Allegra, teetering on her heels, through the chatty crowd into the shimmering ball-room, pausing to chat with various well-wishers and friends. Thunder accompanied Allegra to the uniformed security guard wearing an earpiece and standing at the stage door. "Hey, Brother, I'm Thunder and this is…"

"Thunder Poole, you don't have to explain who you are. I never miss your show."

"Thanks, man. We're trying to get backstage to see Luisa Hamilton."

"Go on back, Brother. Sister. She's probably in the green room up the stairs, last door on your left." Allegra and Thunder moved through the door, as the security guard mumbled into his micro-phone. "Thunder Poole is coming through. Copy?"

Thunder led Allegra through the plainclothes security detail, protecting a United States Senator, a former U.S. President and the current mayor, who stood in the foyer, laughing and slapping each other on the back, trading insider secrets about the mayoral candidates. Personal bodyguards swarmed around one of the cast-offs from *American Idol*, now performing on Broadway. Thunder and Allegra peered into various open doors, where robust laughter from political bigwigs drifted on the air. The debonair, but aging David Rollins, the anchor of WNBC-TV's Breakfast Club broadcast concluded his interview with a fashionista who handed out barbs on the fashion choices of the celebrities in attendance. Thunder and Allegra continued searching, passing large posters dubbing Luisa and David Rollins as co-hosts for the evening.

"Wait here. I'll check the ladies' room," Allegra said. "Maybe she's in there." Before Allegra moved away, the door of one of the side rooms flew open and Felix wheeled into the hallway, followed by a smiling Virgil and his giddy staffers, dressed in dark tuxedos, carrying manila folders and their requisite BlackBerries. Virgil spied Thunder and Allegra, and immediately strode toward them.

"Thunder, my man! How you doing? And, Allegra, you're more exquisite than ever!"

"I'm good, Virgil. Like I was telling Felix, kind of disappointed that you didn't announce your campaign on my show."

"Bruh, I take complete responsibility for that. Things just got away from me, and it won't happen again. I tell you the support that I've been giving is humbling and I hope I can count on your endorsement."

"Virgil, you and me go way back. But right now, I can't endorse you until I review your platform and see what specific services and resources you're prepared to deliver to the black community.

We don't need no shadow mayor," Thunder said, with his arms crossed across his chest. Virgil blinked his eyes, internalizing Thunder's words, and then he grinned.

"It's like that, huh?"

"Twenty-four-seven."

"Thunder, my man, you haven't changed in the fifteen years I've known you. Always a man of the people," Virgil said, patting Thunder on his shoulder. Virgil knew that he had to initiate the thaw hanging over their relationship. While Thunder and Virgil were never friends, their alliance remained cordial, as they recognized that they were both lions in their respective fields. But Thunder had the power to destroy one's reputation every time he opened his microphone.

"And I trust that you will be, too, Virgil. Frankly, we don't need another politician. People need resources, jobs, small business help, better public education; my listeners tell me that every day."

"I agree completely. In fact, perhaps you will join my transition team."

"That's *if* you win," Thunder countered. Virgil blinked, taken off guard. He never expected that the possibility of defeat would be shoved in his face.

"Virgil, where's Luisa?" Allegra asked, interrupting his attempt to score brownie points with Thunder. Virgil glanced around, remembering that his fiancé hadn't been by his side to stroke his fragile ego.

"Um, you might try the ladies' room." Allegra released Thunder's hand and dashed down to the opposite end of the corridor and around the corner, into the desolate, yet plush ladies' room.

"Luisaaaaa!" Allegra called, the loud murmurs from conversations in the corridor closed behind her. Hearing only her echo, Allegra exhaled her frustration and slowly turned to leave, and then paused. Allegra heard the faint sound of someone crying, her eyes widening in surprise. "Luisa?" Allegra asked softly, looking under the doors for her sister-friend's feet until she arrived at the handicapped stall. Luisa's ankles and feet wearing her favorite tangerine Jimmy Choo high-heels were in full view behind the olive-colored stall door.

"Luisa, open the door," Allegra said patiently, tapping on the door. Luisa's cries grew more audible. Sitting on the closed toilet seat, Luisa hung her head in her lap. She had not planned to burst into tears when she entered the bathroom, where she came to escape Virgil whining that she review his note cards for his speech that evening, retrieve his breath mints, contact Pegasus' concierge to get his shoes shined. Virgil ignored that Luisa had her moment in the sun to prepare for, as co-host of the evening. But after the repeated threats from Dante demanding that she convince Virgil to fall out of the mayoral race under the threat of exposing her, Luisa collapsed from the pressure. "Don't think I'm gonna disappear," Dante hissed, over the telephone before she left home. "Tonight is the night. Brother Hannibal wants Virgil to announce his withdrawal tonight. Now what color panties you gonna be wearing tonight? You know your pussy is all that I think about." In that bathroom stall, Luisa lapsed into a dream. She had the power to turn back the hands of time to the moment she decided to have sex with Dante. A voice was speaking to her from a distance reminding her that she was no different than her mother. That she was doomed to repeat the emotional and sexual abuse suffered by her mother. Her soul's voice chastised her for daring to live an absolutely happy life. "Who in the hell do you think you are?" the voice asked. "You're way out of your lane. You know you love men like Dante because they dominate and demean you. You love men like Virgil because they ignore and objectify you. For you, love is meant to hurt. That's why you wouldn't walk away from Dante. That's why you agreed to suffer from Virgil's benign neglect. 'Cause you like it."

"Open the door, Luisa. Don't make me have to mess up my B Michael couture gown. 'Cause if that happens, I'll really give you something to cry about!" Luisa unlocked the door and stepped out of the stall, becoming aware of the lemon freshener in the bathroom. Sounds from walkie-talkies belonging to security guards could be heard from the corridor. While her hair was perfectly coiffed into shiny ringlets around her oval face and draped over her shoulders, her eyes were swollen. Luisa had also bitten off most of her tangerine lip gloss. The Vera Wang, asymmetrical Japanese print gown that Luisa had saved up for complemented her small waist. Holding a used tissue paper in her hand, Luisa stared through Allegra, defeated.

"I can't go back out there, Allegra. Dante texted that he and Hannibal are on their way here. Virgil's going to find out about me and Dante. He said that he's going to destroy everything if I don't get Virgil to drop out of the race. Like how am I supposed to do that? And my bosses and colleagues from the station bought three tables for tonight's event. They're all out front. What am I going to do, Allegra? There's no way I can go back out there on that stage. I have to get outta here," Luisa said, taking steps toward the door.

Allegra blocked Luisa, placing her arms around Luisa, hugging her tightly, which encouraged more of her tears to fall. Then pushing her away abruptly, Allegra gripped Luisa's shoulders, shaking her, sternly yelling, "Snap out of it, Luisa! You're going to dry your tears and you're going back out on that stage and give the performance of your life. Do you hear me? As long as you're breathing, don't you let any man, or *anything* rule you." Behind Luisa's bulging eyes, she believed Allegra had taken leave of her senses. She was being blackmailed, personally and professionally. Luisa knew she had naively allowed herself to become entangled in sexual politics that threatened her reputation, and that of Virgil, the man she thought she deserved.

"First of all, what do you have to lose, Luisa? You don't want Virgil anyway. And Lord knows what you saw in Dante's army boot ass—," Allegra said, with her hands perched on her hips.

"I'd rather have somebody, Allegra, then nobody at all," Luisa said sadly. "You've never been without a man."

"Seriously? You've got to be kidding me, Girl," Allegra said incredulously. Allegra knew that Luisa was talking out of her head. And that she would never take the kind of shit Luisa had accepted from countless number of trifling men.

"I know that sounds bad, but it's true," Luisa said, with her eyes on the floor.

"Tell it to Dr. Phil. Now's the time for you to fight for yourself. That bitch Dante may have knocked you down, but it's up to you, if you stay down," Allegra sternly said, irritated that Luisa would be reluctant to fight.

"But what am I going to do?" Luisa asked, as if one part of Allegra's orders had gone in one ear and out of the other. Ripping from the towel dispenser, Allegra wet the paper towel and patted Luisa's face, removing her smudged make up, like a caring mother. Opening Luisa's handbag, and retrieving a round sponge, she dabbed Luisa's face with MAC's warm bronze foundation, covering the redness. "Luisa, right now all I want you to think about is going out on that stage. I'll come up with a plan." Luisa searched Allegra's eyes for an injection of confidence that she desperately needed. She needed to believe that perhaps she could have a victorious moment before her world came tumbling down.

"Now let's go; the stage manager was looking for you," Allegra ordered, sounding like an officer in the military.

Allegra pushed Luisa out of the bathroom, down the corridor, where the balding, wiry-framed stage manager waited to hook her back up to the wireless microphone. Thunder and David Rollins, ended their conversation. "Hey, Luisa! You just missed the General Manager. She said that we make a pretty good team. Who knows, maybe they're thinking about a show for us. You never know! Okay, let's get this baby going. I need to be in my bed by ten o'clock. That four o'clock wake-up call always comes too soon."

"Everything alright, Baby?" Thunder asked. David Rollins and Virgil exchanged curious glances, then searched Luisa and Allegra's faces. Allegra faked a smile. "Everything's great. We just needed some girl chat." Thunder angled his head, glancing at Luisa and Allegra, and then back at Allegra.

"Places, everyone! Anyone not on the program, please take your seats in the ballroom!" the stage manager yelled. Celebrities and their guests scurried out of the alcoves and were escorted to their tables in the ballroom. Virgil brushed Luisa with a peck, before rushing out, followed by Felix in his wheelchair. Allegra whispered in Thunder's waiting ear, "I'm going to hang here with Luisa. She needs me. I'll join you in time for dessert, okay?" Thunder knitted his eyebrows, hugged her, and then bow-legged his way back out to the ballroom. Allegra rocked back and forth on her left heel as Luisa conferred with David. She agreed that Luisa had placed the quality of her life in jeopardy, but she was determined to support her friend with a solution. The stage manager waved Luisa and David through the doubled curtain to take their places. Luisa nervously glanced over her shoulder seeking an affirmation from Allegra, who offered a thumbs-up sign. Luisa and David stepped back out onto the stage, received by warm applause, as waiters darted among tables serving the main course.

"David, did I tell you you're looking dapper this evening?"

"Actually, you didn't, Luisa. I wouldn't mind hearing it again." *Luisa had regained her composure*, Allegra thought. *Shine, Luisa. Shine.*

From the corner of her eye, Allegra sensed the remaining backstage guests halt their conversations, and move aside. The previous easygoing energy radically shifted. Allegra turned, to see four, sinister-looking, black men, muscular from prison exercise, wearing long black leather coats, stroll through, suspiciously inspecting the backstage area. A chill cascaded behind Allegra's eyes, observing the taller man of the group signaled his stout cohort, who remained at the entrance, holding court. Wearing a silver tuxedo with a black cape around his shoulders, Hannibal purposely strutted, followed by Dante, with dead eyes, toward Allegra. The stage manager, monitoring Luisa and David onstage rubbernecked, checked out these intruders.

"May I help you?" the stage manager asked, fear sounding in his voice, a chill traveling his spine. Dante, smelling of sweaty leather, held his finger in the air, daring the stage manager to move forward.

"We got this, my man. Go on back to what you were doing while I greet my lovely sister," Hannibal said, with charm, holding his gaze toward Allegra. "Sister, you're drop-dead gorgeous," Hannibal said, spreading his arms, attempting to embrace her. Allegra took a step back, though she caught a whiff of his dark musk fragrance, as he slightly bowed, respecting her autonomy. Onstage, Luisa and David narrated the accomplishments of the former United States President's humanitarian foundation. Though a steely grin was plastered on Hannibal's face, the dark shadows under his eyes housed his war to reflect the aggressive investigation launched against the Panthers.

According to *The New York Times* Sunday edition, "In papers filed in U.S. District Court in Brooklyn, Anita Wilson, 29, claimed that Hannibal Morgan, 39, ordered Dante Salaam to pressure her for sex over several months and that she repeatedly rebuffed him. In September, Salaam showed up at her house without his usual bodyguards, according to the documents, complaining that he had not had sex with his wife for six months. Salaam suddenly grabbed Wilson's breasts while grabbing his erect penis and said, 'I want to make love with you,' the suit charges. Wilson claims she informed Hannibal Morgan about Dante Salaam's harassment, pointing out that they both were married. A few weeks later, Wilson charges, both Dante Salaam and Hannibal Morgan asked her for oral sex and a *ménage à trois*. When she refused, they allegedly told her: 'This is the will of Allah that the three of us be together.' Then the two men 'coerced her into' letting them 'perform oral sex' on her. The lawsuit also charges that after that incident, both Morgan and Salaam often made lewd remarks to Wilson and asked her for sex at Panther headquarters."

"Hannibal," Allegra said coolly, with Dante standing behind Hannibal, scanning her body.

"Ouch, that was cool, my sister. Like an Arctic wind. Don't I get a little more love than that?" Allegra considered unleashing a torrent of profanity toward Hannibal and Dante, his flunky, but raised her eyebrow, considering another strategy.

"Apologies, Hannibal. Greetings, Dante," Allegra said, changing the mood. "It's been one of those long days."

"Thunder around, huh? I was told you two came together. He's your man? I mean, if he's your man, why would he leave you alone. I know I wouldn't." Allegra believed that Hannibal was a blubbering, kufi-wearing fool, who saw her, and all women, as meat to devour.

"Would you like to talk about Thunder? Or you and me," Allegra asked alluringly. Applause framed Hannibal's smile, as onstage, the WNBC-TV General Manager accepted praise for sponsoring the gala, and recounting the station's historical support of the association. Hannibal dismissed Dante with a wave of his hand. Then Hannibal stepped forward, within inches of Allegra, devouring her with his eyes, his tongue resting on the side of his closed mouth.

"That's all I've wanted to do, Sista. Is be with you. But it seem like after all of these months, you never had time for a brother," Hannibal said, in a deep, guttural tone. "Seem like all you got time for is your work, but that's cool. However, I think it's time for us to do the damn thing. You know what I mean, Sista?" Rubbing his palms together, then resting one hand on her forearm, Hannibal's longing for Allegra was ignited. Allegra assessed him from head to toe, as Luisa and David, still onstage, introduced a film tribute to a broadcasting legend who had recently passed away.

"Ahhh, no one's showing you any love, Hannibal?" asked Allegra.

"No one that matters," Hannibal replied flatly, brushing, like butterfly kisses, the side of her bare arms.

"Come," Allegra whispered, drawing him into a small alcove, off the corridor, leaving the door slightly ajar. Allegra had Hannibal right where she wanted him, but she needed to execute her plan and return to the dinner table by the time dessert was served. "You're in turmoil, Hannibal. Your soul is in an internal war. You've dedicated your life to helping the black community, but never have enjoyed any rewards, no appreciation." Hannibal's chocolate brown eyes became clear, listening to Allegra speak to him. Allegra leaned against the back of a zebra print arm chair, her feet slightly apart. She placed her hand on the side of Hannibal's head and pulled it to her, close enough for her lips to brush his ear lobe, then continued, "Everything you've worked for is being jeopardized right now. You trust no one, because everyone who has promised his loyalty has shattered your trust. Yet still, you fight for your people. And no one understands you, but me."

"Thunder," Hannibal mumbled with closed eyes, remembering the ass-whooping he had received from Thunder.

"What about Thunder?" Allegra said, switching earlobes, whispering on the other side, with Hannibal's arm on her waist.

"You and Thunder."

"Do you see Thunder here right now? Relax into this moment. Enjoy our moment together, Hannibal." Hannibal's cock danced behind his zipped pants. His lusty mind wanted to weave his fingers through her hair, while planting passionate kisses along the nape of her neck. Yet, Allegra's soft words, acknowledging his struggles, was what he needed more. His breath quickened at the thought of his cock deep inside of her on the floor of this alcove at the Pegasus hotel. "Doors have slammed in your face. Those who before welcomed you, now turn their heads. Those who you've helped, now don't know your name. Yet through it all, you've continued to be the warrior that you are."

"I want you. Right here. Right now," Hannibal said, pressing his cock against her.

"I know you do. Your cock feels so liberating to me. That if I could only squeeze it…"

"Yes, I want you to squeeze it. I want you to suck it," Hannibal panted, starting to unzip his pants.

Allegra placed her hand on top of his, thinking, *Hannibal has got to be out his freakin' mind.*

"They'll be plenty of time for that."

"For what?" Hannibal said, in his delirium.

"They'll be plenty of time for fucking. That's want you want to do, isn't it?" Hannibal nodded. "But you see, I'm a practical woman, Hannibal. It's got to be just right."

"Where? How?" he said, desperate for answers.

"You've dreamed about me, haven't you?"

"Yes," Hannibal said, a tear of swear inching down his face.

"Don't you want it, better than it was in your dreams?"

"He-he, don't we all?" Hannibal asked, noticing her hard nipples. He wanted to take them in his teeth and delicately toy with each one. His chest filled with air, as he started to reach for her nipples. Allegra grabbed his hands, holding them.

"Dante watches you fuck me. That's my fantasy," Allegra said, with a mischievous grin. Hannibal's eyes bulged, followed by laughter, recognizing that Allegra had spoken into existence what the two men had done for years, before he became serious again.

"I could cum right now," Hannibal said, his knees buckling, as the tip of his cock tingled.

"Tomorrow night, you'll announce your candidacy for mayor on Thunder's show."

"Thunder?" Hannibal asked, shifting his feet. "We have history and it ain't good."

"Where else can you get your candidacy out to the masses? Leave Thunder to me," Allegra admonished, then she returned to a gentle whisper, a smile settling on his lips.

"Then after your interview with Thunder, my fantasy is... and I know this is really wild...my fantasy is that you'll fuck me in one of the dark, locked studios. I'll slip you two building passes to return to the building. Then after the stroke of midnight, I will wait as Dante arrives, entering the dark studio, where he will sit silently in a darkened corner, next to my neatly piled clothes. Fifteen minutes later, you'll arrive. Without any words being spoken, you grab, then kiss me, delivering a kiss of raw passion, wrapping your arms around my nude body. Our lips will part and our tongues shall meet in a Harlem street fight. As I do now, I'll feel your body pressing against mine. From there, I will push you back on to the blanket covered console, and move over you. 'I like to ride cowgirl style. Any objections?' I will ask you. Without waiting for your answer, I'll move into position and with a knee on either side of your hip and my cunt directly over your cock, I will lower myself to engulf the head of your cock. You will see the look of satisfaction in my eyes, as I rise to lean forward to kiss you.

"As you lay under me; with me riding your stiff dick cowgirl style, you won't be thinking about anything other than the pleasure you're feeling. For each thrust that my cock delivers into me, I will respond with a counter thrust that brings us heightened pleasure. You'll see the blaze with the fires of lust behind my eyes and feel my burning desire to have you as my willing lover. You will move in rhythm with my thrusting. Minutes later, I will live out my orgasm gasping, 'I couldn't wait,' as I lower my breasts to you, then kiss you. Meanwhile, Dante will be jerking off in the corner. My fantasy; how does it sound?"

Licking his lips, Hannibal replied, "I'll see you tomorrow night then."

"Yes, you will," Allegra stoically replied.

Hannibal turned, then paused, then turned back to kiss Allegra, which she avoid with a raised index finger. Hannibal smiled, taking long strides out of the alcove. Snapping his finger, he summoned Dante and his cohorts to follow him out the backstage entrance. "But what about our girl, Brother?"

"I said, let's go," Hannibal said angrily.

Allegra stepped into the foyer, as the backstage door slammed and Luisa and David came through the curtain off of the stage. Luisa was smiling, her eyes crinkled up in tiny slits. "Whew! That wasn't as bad as I thought," she said, accepting a glass of water from the stage manager. "So, Allegra, how was I?"

"You were fabulous, Luisa. Just like I knew you would be. Now let's join Thunder for dessert," Allegra said, with a wink.

24

"WBBC-FM news. It's ten p.m. Do you know where your children are?" the female announcer delivered the newscast in adjoining Studio C, smaller than the main Studio A assigned to Thunder. Allegra had some explaining to do when she asked Thunder to interview Hannibal, so he could announce his candidacy for mayor.

"Baby, I wish you hadn't done that. The last time I saw him, Hannibal was eating my knuckle sandwiches," Thunder said, after they arrived at Allegra's brownstone, the night before, after the gala. Loosening his tie, he continued, "Now I'm going to have to make it clear to people that his being on my show, does not mean I'm endorsing him."

"Thunder, you've never wavered from bringing the painful truth to your listeners. They depend on you for that, even if it's about their beloved community leaders, who don't deserve their allegiance. Allowing Hannibal to hang out in the shadows, running his games on people to satisfy his selfish needs has to end. Hannibal's days are numbered; the streets are already buzzing about his investigation. Hannibal coming to the station will confirm for the community what they already know," Allegra said, as Thunder smoothed scented massage oil across her back, after their steam shower together.

That morning, Allegra's new mahogany furniture was delivered.

She was thrilled with Max's restoration of the dining room. Brightening the room in a bold yellow shade, white moldings and widening the triple hung windows cast the previously dark space, in a warm golden glow, day and night. Thunder hung her black-framed Brazilian paintings. Max surprised Allegra with custom frameless doors for the shower, which she and Thunder were happy to test out.

"I love what Max did; but I still won't leave my wallet around him," Allegra joked seriously, as she and Thunder shared a pint of butter almond ice cream.

"You're right. The time is now. I just hate being around slime like him."

"Thunder, I'm not so naive that I'm not aware that you're about to take some heat for doing what's right. But people have to stop propping up con artists in our community."

"Frankly, I could give a damn what other people think. I haven't survived in the radio game this long by playing it safe."

"Luisa is on board, so all you have to do is open the microphone."

"How the hell did you get Hannibal to agree to go to the station?" Thunder said, massaging the oil on the back of her thighs. Allegra raised her head, giving Thunder a side eye, "You should know by now that I have my ways."

"Yes you do, woman. Yes you do. Come here," Thunder said, playfully turning her over and tickling her, as Allegra squealed.

Heavy, chilly rain fell outside of the radio station in midtown Manhattan, as Thunder and Allegra entered through the revolving doors and signed in, after clearing security. Allegra had not been at the station, since first meeting Thunder. Absent ringing telephones, and celebrity guests flowing in and out of the green room, tonight, the mood was dim, quiet, with one blinking light on the console. The overnight mixologist on WBBC-FM's sister station across the hall joked around with his friends, while blasting hip hop. Thunder had scheduled Kevin to work overtime, producing the segment. As they boarded the elevator, Kevin shared with Thunder, "And Virgil is confirmed."

"Virgil?" Thunder replied, exchanging glances with Allegra.

"Yeah, I figure we can kill two birds with one stone. We'll have both in the can, so we can air them anytime we want."

Thunder and Allegra, followed by Kevin, strolled past darkened studios and the engineering room, where two workers, wearing soiled black blue jeans, tinkered with dismantled computer parts. "Yo, Thunder! Wassup?" the workers greeted.

Thunder waved, returning their greeting. Old newspapers and used paper cups were scattered on the abandoned circular reception desk.

"Kevin, wouldja get Tina to clean up this place before she signs out. There's no reason that this place needs to be looking like this."

"No problem, Thunder. I got it." He gathered the garbage, tossing it in the trash can around the corner in the employee break room. Kevin dashed into Studio B, turning on the lights and checking the equipment.

"Relax, Baby," Thunder said gently to Allegra, gesturing to the sofa outside of his Studio A. "Let me check inside, and make sure that everything is ready to go." Allegra relaxed on the sofa, crossing her legs, admiring her vampire red Jimmy Choo heels, as Thunder darted into the studio, the door closing behind him with a muffled sound. Virgil, dressed in his customary beige, three-piece suit and wing tip shoes, emerged out of the men's bathroom, fingering his BlackBerry. Allegra noticed Virgil first. "Hey, Virgil. Luisa with you?"

"Allegra? How are you? Didn't expect to see you here. I haven't been able to reach Luisa. Why?"

"Hmmm, we spoke briefly this morning. I just assumed she might be with you. So how's the campaign going?" Allegra asked, regretting the moment she formed the question. She prayed that Virgil wouldn't launch into a boring diatribe about his favorite topic—himself.

"The campaign contributions are coming in, I'm happy to say. We should have quite a war chest to ward off any challengers. I trust I'll have your vote, Allegra?" His appeal for her vote took Allegra by surprise. She had never before known any political candidate personally. And though she thought Virgil was boring and self-absorbed, Allegra admired his work ethic, commitment to achieving justice, and courtroom successes. "You have my vote, Virgil."

Kevin swung open the studio door, peeking out. "Virgil, we're ready for you now. Allegra, Thunder would like for you to come in, too." Allegra checked her watch. The time was eleven o'clock. Allegra strutted ahead of Virgil into Studio A, where Thunder was positioned behind his console, wearing headphones, adjusting the microphone.

"Hey, Virgil. Wassup, Man?"

"Thunder, still burning the midnight oil, huh?" Allegra sat facing Thunder and behind Virgil, who sat erect, wearing headphones and ready to perform as the media-savvy candidate. Kevin stood next to Thunder adjusting the sound levels.

"Man, we got to get it in, whenever and wherever we can. This studio wasn't available any other time because we syndicate the Legends show in here. But anyway, glad you could do this."

"Can I get a copy of the interview?" Virgil asked.

Kevin interjected, "I got you," holding up a DVD cartridge.

"Kevin will edit, make it sound pretty and then we'll probably air it Sunday night," Thunder said.

"Glad to have the opportunity," Virgil replied, removing his suit jacket, laying it across his lap. "Now, I'd like to talk about...." Thunder's raised hand caused Virgil's jaw to flap open.

"Brother, I don't accept pre-determined talking points. I have questions to ask you, which reflect what my listeners want to, and need to know. So why don't we just roll and see where this goes," Thunder said, with finality.

"Thunder, no problem. Ask me whatever you need to," Virgil replied, raising his hands, surrendering, then returning his note-card back into his suit jacket. Kevin aired Thunder's theme song, then signaled, giving him the countdown. The on-air sign became a neon red. "You're listening to WBBC-FM and the voice of the community. I'm Thunder Poole, the Night Rider. Tonight, in the studio, we have mayoral candidate, and U.S. federal prosecutor, Virgil Douglas. Welcome to the broadcast, Brother." Allegra checked her watch, mindful of the arrival of Hannibal.

"Good being with you, Thunder. Been a long time."

"Okay, let's approach it this way; every election cycle, a slew of political candidates line up to ask for the black vote; but rarely do they make specific pledges that will benefit the black community. What guarantees will you deliver?" Thunder asked.

"The problems of the black community are not foreign to me. Remember, I'm Black, too. Ha! Ha!" Virgil laughed at his failed attempt to make a joke, then covered the loud silence with a cough, clearing his throat. "But seriously, when I become mayor, in the first six months I intend to rid our city of no-bid contracts. Our current mayor has allowed his friends to receive millions of dollars of city contracts. In my administration, black business owners will be able to compete through a transparent process on an even playing field."

Kevin leaned back in his chair as Thunder skillfully made Virgil address the issues he deemed important, as a shadowy figure peered in the glass window, then another black man. Allegra recognized them as Hannibal's bodyguards. The wall clock read: 11:20 p.m. Allegra nodded at Thunder, giving him a knowing look, then rose and tip-toed out of the studio. As the studio door muffled closed behind her, Allegra was stunned by what she saw.

Surrounding Hannibal, with Dante at his shoulder, was a platoon of his so-called revolutionaries standing at attention. All wore military garb, dashikis or black berets and boots. The easy-going mood in this foyer had drastically shifted to one of suspicion and tension. Hannibal stood close to Dante, whispering into his ear, dictating instructions. Noticing Allegra before Hannibal, his henchman tapped him on his shoulder, nodding in her direction. Hannibal still appeared weary; the dark shadows under his eyes were starker under the fluorescent lighting. Seeing Allegra, Hannibal raised his jaw, taking in her image, and then he mustered a smile, striding toward her. Dante followed, until Hannibal stopped him with a glance, freezing him in his steps.

"Sister Allegra," Hannibal quietly greeted, leaning over to kiss her cheek, with bourbon on his breath.

"Hannibal," Allegra responded, with lowered eyes.

"You're trying to kill me, woman."

"Oh? How's that?" Allegra replied.

"You're always more than I imagine in my dreams."

"No harm in that; dreams are the food for life."

"Your words have been haunting me. I'm tellin' you no lie," Hannibal said, rocking toward her, like a cougar examining its fresh kill. Allegra glanced over his shoulder through the rectangular pane of glass into Studio A. Virgil was still being interviewed by Thunder. Kevin sat on a stool listening, periodically checking the audio levels.

"Your words, your deeds have been haunting me, too," Allegra replied. "I'm glad the world will soon hear from Hannibal Morgan himself."

"I like how you say that. So when is Virgil Douglas going to be done?" Hannibal asked disdainfully, stepping around Allegra to see Virgil for himself, and then turning back to her.

"They should be wrapping up shortly."

"There's no way in hell, he should be in this race. He'll just carry the same policies for his master, the white man."

Allegra placed her hand firmly on his forearm. "This race can't be about anybody but you. If you focus on Virgil, you'll lose your focus." Hannibal's eyes followed her hand to his forearm, then back up to her eyes. His lips yearned to kiss her. "Come. Let's go into the other studio," Allegra said, sashaying toward the adjacent Studio B, not waiting for Hannibal. "See that dark studio over there? Studio C?" Allegra whispered, lightly touching his chest. Hannibal nodded. "That's where our fantasy took place."

Hannibal felt like a frisky puppy trailing behind Allegra. As she entered Studio B, Allegra noticed Thunder's body language toward Virgil growing contentious. Hannibal's supporters moved to follow him, then paused, watching him follow Allegra. Studio B contained a circular console and hanging microphones with attached WBBC-FM logos. Hannibal inspected the area, and then turned to glare at an unaware Virgil through the window pane. Hannibal pursed his lips. "Does Thunder know about you and me? About this thing we got going?"

"Thunder knows, but he wasn't happy. I explained that you and I have a connection that I'm not willing to ignore," Allegra said, crossing her legs. Hannibal turned and sat across from her, admiring them, shaking his head. "Should I uncross my legs, Hannibal? Like the Egyptians?"

"No, my sister. Fuck the Egyptians! It's time to focus on the present." He ran his hand down her calves.

"Your present isn't chaotic enough? What're you going to do about the lawsuit filed by your assistant?" Allegra asked, ignoring that she hated his touch.

"That black bitch. She's like a lot of chicks today, who say they want a man in their lives, but can't take it when one steps to them. First thing they do is go running to some cracker, or some black face in a high place who does his slave master's bidding."

"So you *were* involved with her?" Allegra quietly asked, to avoid making him feel defensive. Hannibal weighed whether to answer, assessing Allegra's tone and her seductive body language, and then proceeded.

"Like most sisters who work at the Panthers, they pretend that they are down for the cause, when in reality they want me for themselves. And for a minute I wanted her. Because I'm a grown man, I have the prerogative to fuck, I mean, roll with any sister I want. Black men must rule our communities, our homes, and our…"

"—women. You believe that you must rule women," Allegra said, adjusting the cleavage of her blouse, and then staring deep into his eyes.

"The white man has taught our women that they should disrespect our leadership. And now black women wouldn't recognize a good black man."

"So it's true that you and Dante had a *ménage à trois* with her? I think that is pretty freaky. I don't remember ever having one. Maybe there's a limit to my own freakiness."

Hannibal beamed, licking his lips. "Well, we can get down, Sista. Heh! Heh!"

Allegra replied with a stone face. "Was April Wilson your assistant? Was she down for it?"

"You're asking a lot of questions. You sure you don't want to be on the radio?"

Allegra chuckled. "Radio doesn't interest me. My plate runneth over with a new semester beginning in January. Besides, you know my fantasies. I've revealed myself to you, so…"

Hannibal leaned back in his chair, placing his hand over his mouth. "You know, there's something intoxicating about a sister who's married, or committed to another man. You can spot the unhappy ones. Like in her case, she was really Dante's thang, somebody he had messed with; and then she came to me wanting marriage counseling."

"She was married?" Allegra asked, confirming what she had read in the newspaper.

"Yeah, but what man allows not one, but two brothers to get down with his wife? I mean, who does that? She would show up to my office wearing short skirts, tight-fitting shirts, staying late, arriving early. Rubbing her body against me. She became jealous and petty about the women she knew I dealt with. You know, getting an attitude with other women and all that petty shit. So one night, I was working late. She kept coming into my office asking if I wanted anything; and she wasn't satisfied until I told her that I wanted her. Hell didn't break loose until one of my women came to drive me to a meeting at the Lincoln Projects. The next day, April wanted me to come to her apartment in East New York. Dante drove me out there. And she invited us both in. We talked, but you know there was this heavy vibe in the air. Like April didn't want us to come out there to just talk, like she wanted more. Dante proposed a ménage à trois. She resisted, like most bitches do when they don't want men to believe that they are whores, when they're already doing every brother on the block. But after I told her how beautiful she was and that no one had to know but the three of us, it was on and poppin'. Next thing I know, the bitch files a lawsuit accusing me of stealing money from the organization. How could I steal from what I created? I deserve that money." Hannibal bristled from his belief that he was not the victim.

Allegra rose to check on Thunder's interview. Kevin was chuckling at a comment Thunder had made, then sipped from his water bottle. The mood in Studio A appeared to have lightened. Thunder extended an open hand to Virgil, who retrieved his notecard from his jacket. Hannibal rose and stood close behind Allegra, inhaling her floral fragrance. He felt his hard, curled dick against the round curve of her derrière. Thunder and Virgil were unaware that they were being observed.

"Thunder should be ready for you soon."

"You think Thunder knows that right now I can feel the arch of your back squeezing against my dick?" Allegra sighed, strategizing her next move.

"Hannibal, how does Luisa figure in with you and Dante?"

"Humph," Hannibal said, stuffing his hands in his pockets. "I figured we would get around to talking about your girl." Hannibal hung his head, feigning shame.

"Her name is Luisa."

"You want me to keep it real? You want me to keep it real, don't you?" Allegra asked.

"Luisa Hamilton was a pawn for me to get you; I didn't know no other way; then Dante wanted to satisfy his demons. I don't know what he had going on. I was digging you. I was willing to do anything to get next to you."

"Are you serious? Really?"

"Look, you don't know how much you affect me. You're different. I was willing to do anything to be here with you right now. Luisa was a casualty in this situation, and I'm sorry for that; but the vibe that I feel between the two of us right now was worth it. I could eat you right here, right now. Right here on the floor. That's *my* fantasy," Hannibal said, rubbing his dick still closer against her derriere. Allegra stared at Virgil and Thunder. Hannibal noticed.

"He's the walking dead," Hannibal said, bristling. Allegra whirled around to face him. "What?"

"Virgil Douglas won't be alive long enough to take office." Allegra hid her facial reaction, and moved away from Hannibal returning to sit at the console, biting her lower lip.

"You can't mean that," Allegra said, scheming how to coerce Hannibal into digging a deeper hole for himself.

"Serious as a heart attack. He's been a tool of this white supremacist system to destroy me, so he's no longer necessary to take up space on this planet. He's dead, Sista. True dat," Hannibal said defiantly, his eyes turning stone cold as he stared at Virgil. "One less nigga like him, and no one will miss him."

Allegra's eyes shot up in surprise as the studio door flew open, and Kevin entered. Hannibal relaxed back in his chair, donning an angelic persona. "Hey, Brother Hannibal!" Kevin greeted Hannibal with a complicated black man handshake. "We're ready for you!" Kevin announced.

"Cool, man. Cool," Hannibal replied, smiling at Allegra with a victorious smile. "Oh, let me get that," Hannibal whispered, leaning toward Allegra. She reached into her hobo purse hanging on the side of her chair, retrieving the building pass, sliding it into Hannibal's hand. Allegra stood to glance into the main studio. Thunder and Virgil were no longer there.

Opening Studio B's door, Hannibal stepped out into the reception area into a phalanx of plainclothes and uniformed police officers, standing behind Virgil. The Panther bodyguards were in handcuffs and seated on the floor. While two officers struggled to handcuff Hannibal, the Latino arresting officer announced, "Hannibal Morgan, you're under arrest. You have the right to remain silent and refuse to answer questions. Do you understand?" Hannibal refused to answer, turning his hateful eyes on Allegra.

"Do you understand?!" the officer yelled, tightening his hand-cuffs, causing Hannibal to squirm. "Look, we can be here all night; it's up to you!"

"Yeah, Pig," Hannibal managed. "Get my lawyer."

"Anything you do say may be used against you in a court of law. Do you understand? You have the right to consult an attorney before speaking to the police and to have an attorney present during questioning now or in the future. Do you understand? If you cannot afford an attorney, one will be appointed for you before any questioning if you wish. Do you understand? If you decide to answer questions now without an attorney present, you will still have the right to stop answering at any time until you talk to an attorney. Do you understand?"

Hannibal glared back at Allegra, hurling, "Fuckin' bitch!" Thunder pushed past an officer, and hauled a hard punch against Hannibal's jaw. "Now who's the bitch, Bitch!" Thunder shouted over the sprawled out Hannibal on the floor. Two officers yanked him to his feet and carried him, yelling, down the corridor out of the radio station. Other plainclothes officers followed him, as Virgil stepped forward.

"Allegra. Thunder. Thank you for your help. Our office has been trying to get him on the record, to get enough evidence to garner arrest. Well, now we do." Virgil shook Thunder's hand, kissing Allegra on the cheek.

"Where's Luisa, Virgil?"

"Here I am," a voice said. As the police officers cleared the area, Luisa, smiling, was sitting behind the receptionist desk, with a telephone receiver in her hand.

"Luisa!" Allegra said, rushing to hug her.

"Thunder gave me the heads up that Hannibal was going to spill the beans. Kevin made sure that the studio you were in had hot microphones, so everything you and Hannibal said, we heard."

"Yeah, everything," Thunder said, twisting his mouth. Allegra tapped him on his shoulder playfully.

"I can never repay you for what you did. You saved me," Luisa said.

"You, too, Thunder."

"No problem, Luisa. Allegra and I got your back."

Luisa informed Allegra, "Thunder had Kevin email the recording to my assignment editor."

"He did?" Allegra said, smiling proudly at Thunder.

"Giving Thunder credit, the station is already airing a tease about Hannibal's arrest. Charged with rape, extortion, grand larceny and threatening a federal prosecutor, the station will be Tweeting and Facebooking Hannibal and charging Dante as a co-conspirator, in less than five minutes."

"Good news travels fast," Allegra quipped, wrapping her arms around Thunder and Luisa.

"You okay?" Thunder asked.

Allegra nodded. "Now I am."

SIX WEEKS LATER...

EPILOGUE

Allegra and Thunder lounged nude, wrapped in silk sheets, in their king-sized bed at the luxurious Copacabana Palace well into early afternoon on New Year's Day. In between one of their lovemaking sessions, panting and kissing, rolling around and laughing, Allegra ordered brunch from room service; *farofa* (tapioca grains flavored with spices), salads, rice, chicken and *marajucá mousse* (fruit), a traditional Brazilian feast. As Thunder dozed, Allegra went out onto the balcony overlooking the Atlantic Ocean. She pondered how her life had changed since her last visit to Brazil.

Allegra took a deep breath, appreciating the warmth of the sun and sounds of the ocean. The warm ocean breeze briefly ran through her negligee and caressed her breasts softly. During their lovemaking, Thunder explored her with such tender passion that Allegra gleefully wept in his arms. Never before had any man touched untapped regions of her soul. With the first semester on the horizon, since receiving her Ph.D. and accepting the curator position at the Modern Museum of Africa, Allegra felt more at peace than she had in recent memory. The burning hunger for unrequited passion had been fulfilled, unlike any time before.

On the eve of Teofilo's inauguration as President of Brazil, Allegra declined his VIP party invitation for two in Leblon. Allegra

sent her apologies with a bottle of champagne to Teofilo by mes-
senger with the note card signed, "Teo, congratulations on your
election and your marriage to Bianca! Thunder and I are confident
that with your leadership, Brazil will continue to thrive! *Feliz Ano
Novo!* (Happy New Year!) *Ame e Risada*, (Love and Laughter),
Allegra." Allegra preferred to enjoy the holidays with a special
getaway with Thunder in a country she loved. She wanted to show
the man who accepted her as she was and protected Luisa, the
country which mirrored her love for food, loyalty, music and sex.

Back in New York, over the last six weeks, Luisa confronted
the reality of her anemic relationship with Virgil. She offered to
return the engagement ring, but Virgil, being the publicity con-
scious man that he was, begged Luisa to remain by his side until
after the election. Because of her assignment editor's recommen-
dation, Luisa was promoted to the weekend anchor desk. However,
she wrestled with how she had allowed herself to become a sexual
pawn between the now-indicted Hannibal and Dante, who both
were being held without bail.

At dusk, after the sun melted with the sunset on New Year's
Eve, with stifling humidity, dressed in traditional white clothing,
Allegra, wearing a white halter dress, and Thunder, wearing
rolled-up pants and a buttoned-down shirt, watched a group of
bare-chested, brown-skinned teenagers launch small decorated
wooden boats full of flowers and gifts into the tide, in honor of
the Goddess of the Seas *(Iemanja)*. Locals conducted sacred prayers
of appreciation for past favors and made requests for the year to
come. Flowers, gifts, perfume and rice were placed in rafts, boxes,
pots or whatever the giver could use. Common belief held that if
Iemanja did not return the offering with the tide, the prayer was
granted.

Some two million people crowded Copacabana Beach as Allegra coaxed Thunder to wade into the water after her to make his own wish.

"You know, I'm not into no religious stuff."

"Yeah, and you said that there was no way I was going to get you on a plane, too. And look where you are," Allegra teased. Thunder blushed and appeased her, inching into the powerful sea with a rising tide. "Here's a flower." She handed it to him.

"Um, can I get something more masculine?" Thunder smiled.

"You'd better quit," Allegra said, poking him. "Now close your eyes, make a wish and throw the flower into the sea."

Thunder sighed, then followed her instructions.

"Now, that didn't hurt, did it?" Allegra asked. Thunder reached to hold her hand as a wandering samba band stirred them to dance. "What was your wish, Thunder?"

"Am I supposed to tell?" He moved his hips to the music.

"You don't have a choice," Allegra joked.

"I prayed that you would know the depth of my love for you," Thunder said seriously, as they held hands strolling along the crowded boardwalk, moments before midnight.

"Hmmm," Allegra said.

"Hmmm? What does that mean?" Thunder asked. A group of children carrying lit white candles paraded past them, as Allegra stepped under Thunder's chin, gazing up into his eyes.

"I had the same prayer. That you would know the depth of my love for you," whispered Allegra. Thunder's heart paused, then skipped a beat. At the stroke of midnight, under the colorful fireworks splashing in the cloudless night sky, they shared a warm, passionate kiss.

Thunder and Allegra slept peacefully until morning when he tickled her out of her slumber.

ABOUT THE AUTHOR

In order to increase her readership, Allegra Adams has radio producers on speed dial, and maintains a robust schedule of speaking engagements. She also has a loyal following cultivated from media appearances, a variety of social media such as Facebook, Myspace.com, and 6,300 website subscribers.

Visit Allegra Adams at the following locations:

Myspace.com: http://www.myspace.com/allegraadams
Facebook: http://www.facebook.com/allegraadamsauthor
Twitter: http://twitter.com/allegraadams

IF YOU ENJOYED ALLEGRA'S ADVENTURES IN
"MAN WHISPERER," WAIT 'TIL YOU MEET LENA MACY!

THE I.O.U.

THE ELLE SERIES

By ELLE

AVAILABLE FROM STREBOR BOOKS

CHAPTER ONE

Lena Macy rummaged through her Super Bowl party swag bag in search of the only thing she could think of that would satisfy her urge for sex—chocolate. On any given day, Miami was a hotbed of testosterone, estrogen, alcohol, drugs and hot and horny beautiful people, there to party and have sex. But on a Super Bowl weekend, the place was like an orgy on steroids. The Miami heat was definitely getting to her, in more ways, and in more body parts, than one.

She'd been down in Magic City for two days, losing much needed sleep and reluctantly partaking in the pre-game festivities— all in an attempt to land her man—Rickie Ross. Lena wanted Rickie. She needed him. And she wasn't leaving town without him knowing how much.

She'd been damn near stalking him for months—calling,

emailing, showing up wherever and whenever, trying to make a good impression. But getting next to a famous and hugely popular football hero, a man surrounded by groupies and hangers-on, all trying to get him or give him some, was no simple task. It would be a lot easier if she merely wanted to fuck him, but she didn't. Lena wanted to hire him.

Since being put in charge of Sports Fan Network a year ago, her job was to turn the struggling SFN around and make it a must-see experience for sports-loving viewers. Lena's plan was to shake up the programming by moving away from the traditional talking head analysis, making the network more user-friendly and inviting to women as well as men. Fine-ass, charismatic Rickie Ross was central to that task, but until he finally decided on a new agent, talking business with a man whose main mission in life was to fuck, fraternize and play football, was a non-starter.

Lena bit into a Godiva hazelnut truffle, let the sweet creamy goodness settle on her tongue, closed her eyes and savored the moment. She heard several wordless moans, the kind let loose when THE spot gets hit, escape her lips and settle into the air. She'd read somewhere about a study where fifty-two percent of the women surveyed said they preferred eating chocolate to having sex. Lena couldn't rightly say where she stood in that poll, but at this moment she understood it. Between her demanding work schedule, her last break-up nearly a year ago, and her crazy family issues, the only thing rushing her endorphins these days was chocolate. Usually all she had the energy and desire for was Godiva and Big, her trusty, always on the ready, never argumentative vibrator. But at this moment, after two days spent immersed in the closest thing to a modern-day Sodom and Gomorrah, she wanted more than chocolate. More than Big. She wanted dick. Real. Live. Hard as a rod. All up in her fuzzy stuff, penetrating dick.

Lena moaned again, this time out of frustration, and popped another truffle into her mouth. It was halftime and being upstairs in her suite watching this gridiron face-off alone was depressing. She decided to head down to the bar, grab a bite, down a drink or three, and watch the rest of the game in the company of strangers. Changing into a slim, white, shirt dress with a long string of gray, gold, and white pearls, Lena slipped on her strappy Jimmy Choos, added a spritz of Bellissima by Blumarine, and headed downstairs.

"One Gran Patron Platinum coming up," the bartender said, removing her empty glass and smiling over the anticipated size of his tip. This pretty lady not only had looks, but class, and a wallet to match. He removed the sterling silver stopper from the lead crystal decanter and poured the thirty-dollar-a-shot, premium tequila into a shaker, gently chilling the liquor before pouring it into a shot glass with a twist of orange.

Lena sat, sipped her drink and people watched, uninterested, like most in the room, in the half-time show currently in progress. His cologne, a heady shot of Creed, hit her nostrils and commanded her attention seconds before his words. He smelled delicious. Downright edible.

"Well, it ain't nipplegate, that's for sure," a low voice painted with wit and audacity, spoke to her as the celebratory crowd milled around them.

"Where's Janet when you need her?" Lena responded, making friendly bar talk but keeping her eyes purposely glued to the row of flat-screen televisions lining the lounge walls. "But in the big picture, does it really matter who plays during halftime?"

"Absolutely! Everyone knows that if you wanna hold someone's attention, a little sex, or even the idea of a little sex, will always do the job." He finished his statement and let a devilish grin loose on her.

She heard his tongue-in-cheek delivery, and it made her laugh. *Do I have* horny bitch *flashing across my forehead*, she wondered. Usually, such an obnoxious opening would have been ignored, but the shot of tequila that preceded his arrival was too smooth, and she was too bored to brush his comment aside.

"So you're saying that a two-second glimpse of a naked breast—

fake at that—trumps a world-renowned, internationally revered rock band?"

"Fake but with a pierced nipple. There is a difference," he schooled her, the flirtatious smile in his tone enticing Lena to turn his way.

Not sure if it was the talk of erotic piercings or the chocolate brown face sporting a dazzling combination of pleading brown eyes and a can't-say-no smile that made her nipples stiffen, but he'd proven his theory. He definitely had her attention.

STOP IT, her brain shouted, demanding that the girls ignore his Djimon Hounsou look-alike qualities and simmer down.

"So you're saying all men like body piercings on a woman?" his prize questioned, surprised to find herself willing and wanting to engage in the conversation.

"Nooo. Not all men. And not all body piercings. Take belly button or nipple rings. What men are drawn to is *the idea* that a woman who would do such a thing is sexually free and adventurous. The piercings suggest that she's daring and willing to experiment."

"And down there?" Lena inquired, too polite to say the word *clit*, even though hers was warming up, without permission mind you, to the conversation.

"A clit ring? That's like crazy sexy, and not in a good way. Little too hard-core S & M for my tastes."

"And tongue piercings?"

"Nah. That just screams slut. Too visible. Too obvious. Unless, you know, you're simply looking to get your knob slobbed."

Witnessing the widening smile of this bodacious charmer, one who had the nerve to be talking blowjobs to a perfect stranger, for some odd reason, only made the girls tingle all the more.

"But I thought the idea of you know…getting worked over by a studded tongue…really turned men on."

"Well, yeah, but no man wants *other* people thinking that his woman is a blowjob machine. That just ain't right."

"I don't know…why else would all these young girls be doing it?"

"Cuz they're stupid little girls and not thinking about how ridiculous they're going to look when they're real women," he said, adding a silent but complimentary, *like you* with an appreciative eye caress of her glistening bare legs. "Look, if you don't believe me, let's ask him," he suggested, calling over the bartender. "I'll bet you the next round, that if given the choice, he'd pick nipple ring over tongue ring."

"You're on."

"Dude, could you settle a bet for us?"

"Sure."

"Tongue ring or nipple ring?"

"Depends. Girlfriend or one-nighter?"

The face with the uninhibited grin, sitting below a perfectly bald, domed head, erupted into a deep and rolling laugh that shook the cobwebs from her vagina. Lena joined in, her sing-song chuckle blending nicely with his.

"Bartender, another round please, on me," she requested, taking her loss with grace.

"Sir, what can I bring you?" the bartender asked over the hubbub of fans cheering the second half kick-off and the New York Jets' bullet train return to the New Orleans Saints' forty-yard line.

"Grey Goose, straight, on the rocks with a twist."

"You got it."

The cheers following the Jets' touchdown turned to boos as the snap was bobbled and the extra point drifted wide. Still, New York moved ahead of their rivals 20-7.

Lena raised her glass to his before tipping it to her lips.

No wedding ring. His eyes grabbed hers, electric interest flying between them, before lowering to check out her luscious, peach-stained lips wrapped around the rim of her drink. He exhaled the decidedly devious request for those same lips to be wrapped around his wakening dick, replacing them with a more apropos, stranger-friendly query.

"Jets or Saints?"

"Well, I'm definitely no sinner," she cooed, raising her eyes to meet his, while fingering the edge of her glass. Her looks, actions and words didn't match, leaving him wondering how much of an angel she could possibly be.

"I'll take that to mean that you're rooting for the Saints."

"You are correct."

"So you're a big Kim Kardashian fan?"

"What?" The out-of-left field quality of his question threw her. "Oh please, do explain," she requested with an amused chuckle.

"After she put Reggie Bush on her show, every woman in America became a Saints fan. They love her, so, by association, they love him, too."

"Women love her?"

"Yeah, they relate to her combination of innocent, but smoking hot, sex appeal. It's like she's saying, 'I'm a good girl, but I can be bad when I want to.' Beyoncé is the same way."

It's like he's reading me, Lena thought as she felt the good girl inside of her smile in agreement. Even at 42 years of age, she understood all too well the concept of being good while her bad girl was screaming to get out. But like most women she knew, she'd been taught from birth to be refined, respectful and mindful of her reputation, so she ignored the screams and carried that good girl mind-set in and out of the bedroom.

"No, I'm a Saints fan because I appreciate the skill and drive of Drew Brees. Given his foot agility, his release, his accuracy and the fact that he is smart as hell, he's got a skill set that makes him an amazing athlete and great quarterback.

"And, yeah, Reggie is a cutie, but he also can haul ass," Lena continued. "In just four seasons, he's rushed for nearly four thousand yards and scored twenty-four touchdowns. And let's not forget Garret Hartley. The boy has a leg on him. Deadly accurate inside of forty-five yards. He would have never missed that field goal like Feely did in the first half."

"Hey, it happens. But you're selling the Jets short. Mark Sanchez is just now coming into his own. He's got a strong arm, makes good decisions and is a leader on the field. His first year in the league, he led his team to the playoffs. How many rookie quarterbacks have done that and actually even won the first game?"

"Four," Lena offered, happily showing off her knowledge of sports.

"Really?" he asked, biting his lip and turning up the twinkle in his eye. "Damn, I think I'm looking at the perfect woman—a hottie who knows football."

And basketball, and baseball, and even a little hockey and NASCAR, she wanted to tell him, but didn't. You can't sit at the helm of one of cable broadcasting's first sports networks and not pick up a thing or two.

Lena gave him a wink and a tilted smile before turning her attention back to the Super Bowl. It was an exciting game; one that looked like it might go all the way down to the wire. The two watched as possession of the ball changed hands several times, neither team giving up enough yards for a score. On occasion, Lena could feel the stranger's eyes drifting away from the television and over to her. They never seemed to settle on one spot for long. Instead, his gaze roamed like a player in the backfield, weighing the options in front of him.

They jumped up with the rest of the crowd, brought to their feet by the running prowess of the Saints' Rickie Ross. His dodging and weaving brought New Orleans three yards shy of the Jet's thirty-seven-yard line and a first down.

"What do they say? Poetry in motion."

"Oh, so you're a Rickie Rosster?" he asked, referring to the player's legion of fans while trying to determine if she was just another groupie in town to get laid by a baller.

"He has skills." Lena downed the rest of her tequila, allowing the silky smooth liquid to coat her throat and loosen her tongue. "So skilled that he's about to take the lead. I will bet you another round that the Saints will *penetrate* the Jets' defenses and *score*."

He took in the body language that accompanied her offer—one heavily punctuated with sexual innuendo. She crossed her shimmering bronze legs and drew them closer to her body, all the while allowing one high-heeled sandal to dangle from her well-pedicured foot like a fishing lure. Was she fishing? He certainly hoped so, because between the foot, the flirting, and that woodsy floral scent that kept wafting over to his side of the bar, he was already hooked.

"You're on." He smiled, happily taking the bait.

"Bartender, another round on me," Lena requested with good-humored exasperation after the Jets stopped the Saints at the line of scrimmage with no gain.

"Here comes your boy," he teased. "Care to sweeten the pot?"

Her competitive nature, like the rest of her, was now aroused. Lena threw back her shot of tequila and smiled in response, secretly wondering if his chest was as smooth as his head. "Name your wager."

"If Hartly hits this field goal, dinner is on me. If he misses, it's on you."

There's that smirk again. Goddamn, this boy is good looking, she thought, while quickly visualizing the literal interpretation of his suggestion.

"That makes the assumption that we are having dinner together," she replied, adding a little cat to her mouse.

"But aren't we?" he asked. There was no challenge, just matter-of-factness in his eyes.

"It's on." *Who am I trying to kid?*

"Excellent."

"YES!!" Tequila and competitiveness combined caused Lena to stand up and cheer, and add a corny Cabbage Patch dance to her celebration. Thanks to Hartley's sure foot, Lena had dinner plans and the Jets lead was narrowed to seven points.

"Looks like I owe you. So I assume eating here at the Setai will work for you?" he asked, while in his head running down his room service menu, one that included everything *but* food. "I mean, I'd love to take you anywhere you'd like to go, but considering the fact that this town is crawling with Super Bowl fans, I don't think we're going to have much luck."

"Are you staying here?" Lena asked, not revealing that she was already a guest in one of the suites.

"Yes. I'm here on business. And you?"

"Same." *Though mixing in a little pleasure seems like a real possibility*, she thought, but didn't add. "And, yes, dinner here is fine."

Another round later, the two-minute warning sounded, leaving the Saints with possession of the ball. Lena and her mystery man watched as their quarterback led his team up the field and into scoring position. On the next play, with only twenty-six seconds left on the clock, the New Orleans fullback rushed past the New York defense and into the end zone, making the score 21-20.

"He's got to go for it. They need two points to win," he declared.

Tipsy and feeling flush, Lena leaned in close enough to breathe in his smell and with it, watered the seeds of arousal sprouting like wildflowers in her. "I'll bet you *anything* that they make this conversion."

"Anything?"

"Yep. Winner takes *all*."

"That's a hefty wager to make with a perfect stranger."

"I'm Pocahontas," she said, raising her empty glass to his. "Nice to meet you."

"Pocahontas?" he asked with a chuckle. "No last name?"

"Why be so formal?"

"True, and Disney characters don't tend to have last names anyway."

"Exactly." Lena smiled at him. When she upped the ante, she'd already decided to have sex with this stranger, but she had no intention of being herself while doing it.

"Well, in that case, Pocahontas, I'm Mr. Johnson." He smirked.

Lena giggled to herself, amused by not only his willingness to play her game, but his choice of moniker. She leaned in close to his ear. "As in Mr. *Big* Johnson?" she whispered coyly.

"Oh, I see you've heard of me," he said, shivering slightly from her warm breath tickling his ear.

"I have a *very good* friend with the same name," she continued while lightly brushing his earlobe with the tip of her tongue. Johnson turned his face to meet hers, leaning in, wanting to touch her lips with his own.

Lena gently backed away. "You haven't won yet, Mr. Johnson."

"It appears that I have," he said before devouring her mouth as the room exploded into joyous bedlam. The New York Jets held firm, denying the Saints their two-point conversion, and winning the championship game by one point.

The room melted away under the heat of Johnson's kiss. It was the perfect kiss for the occasion. It was not fueled by quiet discovery or the sweet pretense of sensuous coupling between lovers. This kiss was powered by an overwhelming need to get to know each other on the basest of levels—a lust demanding to be satisfied. This kiss was the prelude to a fuck.

His tongue crossed her lips, at first like a wandering vagabond looking for a place to land, but as Lena greeted it with her own, it stiffened and began to rhythmically move in and out between her lips as a preview of things to come. Lena felt every erogenous zone on her body come to full attention. Through a series of well-choreographed tingles, pulses and throbs, they informed her that the bad girl was making a break and the bitch wanted a full-out, one-night-only, fuck-fest. A sexual romp designed to clear her mind and body from the want and need that had been distracting her for months—hell, years, if she owned up to the truth. Forget her reputation, her mother, her peers and colleagues. Even forget Douglas. Tonight, she wanted hot, heavy, uninhibited, one-night stand, never see your ass again, *stranger* sex.

The party atmosphere reappeared as Lena pulled away and opened her eyes.

"So, you won. Name your prize," she said, her voice rough with desire.

"Do you have to ask?" he said, gently running his finger across her lips. "I want you."

"Looks like everyone's a winner tonight," Lena declared as she gathered her things to follow him upstairs.